BARNOOLI'S CIRCUS

Close Encounters of the Theatrical Kind

Philip Hamm

All rights reserved © 2013 by Philip Hamm

To the memory of Great Uncle Charlie, seal trainer to Barnum and Bailey

1 - The Buffet Car

The remains of the banquet lay strewn across the tables like the carnage of a traffic accident. Ravaged fish stared glassily at the ribs of exotic game birds; fruit and fancy chocolates lay smashed and torn among the smoking remains of flambéed shellfish and spilt sauces; crumbs and lost morsels were scattered over the place mats with the unused cutlery and the fingerbowls. In the centre of this epicurean chaos a giant wedding cake stood dismembered and dissected, its two figurines standing drunkenly on the top.

"Is my circus not the greatest wonder in the galaxy?" said the Great Barnooli, waving his half-eaten drumstick at the assembled diners. "Are we not the toast of a thousand worlds?"

Barnooli sat on a raised platform with his new wife at his side. "Are my acts not the finest?" he continued. "Are my animals not the best? Is the train not the most beautiful sight to be seen flying through the skies of the many worlds we have performed on?"

The silence was broken by one or two grunts of assent. The diners were seated in rows down the length of the buffet car. They no longer looked great or magnificent. Their best clothes were clinging to them like clear-wrap plastic, their belts and braces flapped about undone and the ornate chairs seemed to be conspiring to pitch them onto the floor.

The Juggling Hare was already face down among the mixed nuts, the Amazingly (formerly) Thin Bendy Man was sobbing gently to himself and the Fire-eating Pyro Brothers were regarding the cheese board with the look of horror normally consigned to newly arrived in-laws announcing an indefinite stay.

They'd had enough. They wanted out. They were artists, they were performers, they were lean and fit and had small stomachs. After thirty-seven sumptuous and richly decorative courses (plus wine) they were in debt to their diets and facing bankruptcy. Nobody was in the mood for anything more than an aspirin and a lie down in a darkened room.

Barnooli's circus had been touring for three years and Barnooli's splendid red tunic was ablaze with medals and ribbons from grateful rulers and an adoring public. His social diary was full for another three years and his face had appeared in every newspaper, telecast and multi-visual medium in the Known Galaxy. This was worth bragging about.

He sucked the rest of the meat from his bone and tapped it on the table. He was in the mood for some sycophancy.

He resumed, "Is my circus not greater than the Menagerie of Menylace the Magnificent?"

A weak chorus of 'poo poos' echoed among the empty platters and plates. The Menagerie was pretty good, thought the victims of their director's gluttony, but not worth arguing about under these circumstances.

"And the Zoo of Zophocles the Collector...?"

"A mere aquarium," groaned the Brilliant Bazmondo, the great magician, who wished he could make his stomach disappear.

"And the palaces of Nute the Grand...?"

People wavered but generally agreed. Even Nute the Grand might have run down his erections at a moment like this.

The stars whisked by the buffet car windows in a haze of purple light as the stars inside collapsed still further into the crumbling ruins of Barnooli's pre-honeymoon party. If a black hole had suddenly appeared and crushed them to a speck, they would have considered it a blessing.

Barnooli was disappointed with their responses but he was under no illusions as to what his employees thought of his marriage, or his wife, and he knew they were against him going on honeymoon alone with her. But, "First rule of the circus," he said to himself. "'Never get in the way of the director and his sweetmeats."

He turned to his new wife, Ophonia, the circus's diva. She was still picking daintily at a large bowl of fruit and looking none the worse for the five hour ordeal. He smiled at her and she smiled back, her cheeks puffed out with the contents of a small melon. He smiled and made 'wibbly-wibbly' faces at her.

She had an angelic face and on the centre stage she moved effortlessly, like a cumulous cloud sweeping across a summer sky, all nebulous, benign and 'billowy'. She had a bewitching quality, which the other performers found disconcerting. With Barnooli she cooed and billed but her hairdressers said she was bad tempered and there was a rumour that one of the clowns had been sacked for a careless comment.

"He suggested she go on a diet," said the Lion Tamer.

"Really?" said the Strong Man, his jaw hanging slackly.

"Yes, I heard it from one of the costumiers."

"He never said that," said Ted, the Theatrical Director, who was a sensitive and poetic soul and about as robust as a Christmas fairy. "I don't believe you."

"Believe what you like," continued the Lion Tamer. "But would you say it? Or criticise her choice of frock or music or the way she sings?"

Ted looked uncomfortable, "Of course not."

"Neither would I," agreed the Strong Man, a shiver running up his spine.

"And don't you think this wedding lark is all a bit sudden?"

Ted looked warily at the far end of the table where Barnooli and his new wife were almost hidden by the massive cake, "Very," he said, frowning.

"Too sudden to be quite satisfactory," nodded the Strong Man.

"I mean, where's she from?" said the Lion Tamer. "How did she get here?"

"How can she eat so much and where does it all go?"

"Perhaps," Ted paused for theatrical effect. "She's not human after all?"

"On this train, who would notice?" said the Brilliant Bazmondo.

"But seriously," said Ted. "What's going to happen once Barnooli is on his own, with her, and away from our influence? Will he come back a changed man without a will of his own?"

"What husband has?" Bazmondo scoffed. His fine voice had a rich silkiness that shone like his black hat.

"But she might persuade Barnooli to sell up the circus and retire," Ted bleated, "and then what will happen to us?"

"Rubbish, the circus means more to him than all the hors-d'ouvres in the universe, and besides she loves it as well; all that singing and the flowers and the applause, why would she want to give it up, let alone him?"

"But but but..."

"You shouldn't worry so much."

Ted had a silly quiff in his hair that waved about like a squirrel's tail as he grew more agitated, "But what do we really know about her? She could be a spy, or she could have been sent to destroy the circus, by sabotage, to make sure it fails..." The quiff wobbled nervously.

"By whom...?"

"I don't know, a rival, somebody who's jealous of our success?"

"All right, how? Who could bring down the Great Barnooli's circus? The Minds™ run all the technical parts, we look after ourselves, the animals are kept in their own self-contained carriages; it's just too big to bring down. You might as well say you're going to cause a hurricane by flapping your arms about."

Ted was not reassured; technology wasn't his bag so he didn't trust it. There was always the threat of mutiny among the major and minor acts and the animals were not smart enough to know what was good for them. "I'm sure somebody could do it," he insisted.

They heard Barnooli chuckling. He was patting his wife on the knee and nodding a great deal. Jealous eyes watched his every move.

Bazmondo shrugged, "I don't think she is a saboteur," he said, growing tired of the whole charade.

"Not unless she means to eat us into submission," said the Lion Tamer.

"But don't you find it strange that she can just turn up and lure Barnooli away like this?" said Ted.

"Strange, yes," said Bazmondo. "But not impossible."

"But a 'honeymoon' ... oh!" Ted wailed (quietly). "It's all so unprofitable and unlike him."

"True," Bazmondo agreed. "Barnooli is about as sentimental as a thorny hedge, but that, I expect, is the 'power of a woman's love'."

"Oh please," Ted minced. "Spare me the hearts and flowers."

Barnooli presented his wife with a flower he had made from a piece of peel. Ophonia giggled in a faintly disturbing and peculiar way. She scrunched up her face and held Barnooli's hand in a sort of 'bunny-wunny' gesture, which he reciprocated with nauseous attentiveness. It was difficult to say whether one of the mimes dry-retched because of this sickly display or because he was genuinely ill, probably both.

"My dear, perhaps you would sing for us?" Barnooli grinned.

Ophonia giggled again and tried to look shy.

"Oh please," implored Barnooli. "Just one little song...?"

The guests began to stir. They looked at each other and looked worried, very worried... They started to revive their companions, "Wake up," they whispered. "Mrs Barnooli might sing..."

The clowns asleep among the custard pies were suddenly wide-awake and sitting up, their painted grins looking more strained than ever. The members of the orchestra looked longingly at the exits and tried to think of excuses to leave. The more religious began saying prayers. Everyone was in fear of a voice that carried to the furthest reaches of the big top unaided and was currently caged like a large bomb in the confines of their buffet car. Even the cheese board picked up speed around the table in the vain hope that renewed interest in food would distract their host...

Several guests were hissing at Bazmondo to pluck something out of the air to save them, "Make a speech, for all our sakes..."

"Ummm... Mr Barnooli," Bazmondo stood up, raised his hand to catch his employer's eye. "Perhaps I could propose a toast?"

The mention of 'toast' drew a whisper of alarm from a clown who hadn't been listening properly, "Oh Punchinello, not more food."

"A toast?" said Barnooli, looking up.

"Yes, to you and your new bride...?" The magician gesticulated at his companions and hissed, "Get up!" The other employees began struggling to their feet. When they were all more or less upright Bazmondo raised his glass. "To Mr and Mrs Barnooli; may the limelight of fortune shine sweetly on your marriage...?"

The crowd mumbled agreement, hoping selfishly it would continue to shine on them too.

Bazmondo continued, "As you said, our circus is the most magnificent, our acts outrageously popular and our animals glorious in their profundity; let us all pray for many happy shows to follow..."

"Absolutely," said the Lion Tamer.

"Couldn't agree more," said the Strong Man.

"I'm sure I speak for all of us," said Bazmondo, doubting whether he did but saying it never-the-less, "When I wish you joy in your marriage to the lovely Ophonia and hope you have a wonderful honeymoon..."

"Oh do have a lovely time," said Ted, nearly choking on his hypocrisy.

"Entertain and prosper," Bazmondo intoned, using the circus motto.

"Entertain and prosper," repeated the others, reverently.

"To spread joy and happiness throughout the galaxy..."

Barnooli belched magnificently, raised his own glass in salute. The guests fell back into their seats and he rose to his feet.

"Thank you, thank you."

He took a deep breath; he was going to give a speech, preferably a long one. He tucked his thumbs into his waistcoat pockets and began.

"Friends, I sincerely hope you all have a good holiday, I know I shall..."

There were a few titters from the crowd. Mrs Barnooli blushed.

"I am glad we have had this opportunity to sit and eat together before we part, we so rarely seem to get the time these days; we have been so busy…"

A few eyes were glazing over already. No matter, they would get a transcript in the morning.

"Let us celebrate our fortunes so far this tour: twice winner of the Greatest Show in the Constellation award, winner of the Best Spectacle in the Empire and recipient of the Humanitarian Award for Kindest Treatment towards a new Galactic Species; pretty good I think."

Nobody contradicted him, even after five hours and thirty-seven courses; there was no denying that Barnooli had done them all a big favour when he had launched the circus. It was just a pity he had to remind them of it every five minutes.

"And of course, I must mention our internal successes; our increased profits, our better efficiency and the improved state of the plumbing." (A few nods of assent attested to the last flush of success.)

"And we must celebrate our most recent finds; we must thank the people of Hubblenook V for loaning us their Royal Drummers Pursuivant…"

Some blobs of clay grew arms and hands and waved at Barnooli.

"And to the planet Whekau we owe a debt of lasting significance for allowing their wisest citizen to come on board as our Memory Master…"

A small owl nodded wisely at the other end of the table.

"We should be very proud."

There was a pause waiting to be filled with some clapping.

"May it continue to prosper and grow…?"

There should be some cheering as well.

Barnooli frowned, "We should really sing its praises, loudly."

Sing? Thought the acts, 'Sing'? Sing who? …Ophonia.

"…Oh hear hear," said Bazmondo, waking up and beginning to clap, looking for support.

"Absolutely, wonderful, fantastic," agreed the others, some standing to clap more enthusiastically.

"Bravo bravo!"

Barnooli smiled. He could always trust his employees to rise to an occasion when threatened. "Thank you, thank you."

"More, more…" they encouraged.

Barnooli waved majestically. This was more like it.

"Friends… Please…" Barnooli tried to look embarrassed.

"No, more, more…" the acts insisted.

Barnooli smiled but wouldn't be drawn.

The weight of wine and food began to count against them and the acts began to slump back into their chairs, hands running out of steam like the pistons of a train going up a hill.

"And now, as a special treat… My dear…?"

Ophonia was standing, not eating.

"It was a trick," said the Lion Tamer. "He was going to get her to sing all along…"

The Strong Man was looking pale, "I feel sick," he said weakly.

"The cunning old sybarite," said the Lion Tamer, covering his fear with anger, "he just wanted us to think she wasn't going to sing!"

Bazmondo, with a slight of hand, produced some earplugs. The other victims made do with grapes or pickled onions.

Ophonia began to puff herself up like a bagpipe. Silence had descended on the room like that moment at an air show when you wonder where the extremely fast and noisy jet fighter has gone and you're worried that when it does arrive it will bring a sonic wave capable of…

A glass shattered, a clown keeled over and the buffet car began to shake with a tale of dragons, short men and big feisty women. It was a wonder the fire alarms didn't go off.

"I'm surprised there isn't a law against singing like this in a confined space," shouted the Lion Tamer.

"Eh?" said the Strong Man, gritting his teeth and swallowing deeply in a grim attempt not to throw up.

"The noise!" he shouted. "It's too loud!"

"Do what?"

"The noise!" he tried to say.

"Boys?" said the Strong Man, "What boys?"

"Eh?"

"Excuse me…" The Strong Man ran for the door.

Ophonia wound up to the crushing of bosoms and an everlasting love conclusion and then there was silence. The silence rang and shook. Barnooli with a cry of 'bravo' almost missed by the deafened audience, stood up and clapped. The acts, with the word 'encore' very severely stuffed into the recesses of their vocabulary, also stood and clapped.

Luckily, Ophonia was hungry again and she sat down for another piece of fruit. "Marvellous," said Barnooli, patting his wife's knee and watching his employees as they fell back into their seats again. He smiled to himself, "Pity they don't like opera."

The party ended. Conversation had become more of an ordeal than the final coffee and mint-in-an-envelope. "The plumbing's going to take a right hammering tonight," they all agreed.

The major and minor acts helped each other from the table. With final tired and hypocritical congratulations, they left the scene of the conflict, like soldiers retiring from a long and bloody campaign, defeated in every way.

2 - The Great Barnooli

The plumbing did indeed take 'a right hammering' during the night, but that was a minor inconvenience compared to the problem of leaving the circus for a 'holiday'. Paranoid to the last, Barnooli was insistent they should all enjoy this golden moment of his betrothal by downing the tools of their various trades and vacating the train for two weeks of 'well-earned' rest. In truth, he didn't want anybody left on board who might decide they were better off without him and take his train. There had been more than one coup-de-cirque in the history of entertainment and he would be damned if it was going to happen to him.

The problem was not the feeding and care of the animals. Five keepers generally looked after them, greatly assisted by the various mechanical contrivances and the advanced Minds™ of each carriage; but the thought of leaving these particular keepers alone on the train was a little daunting. Not that Barnooli feared they would rise up and steal it away; they were too stupid for that. But their stupidity had an infectious quality that could do damage all on its own.

They were the feeblest Keepers on record; they had once given the massed ranks of polar pelicans a hot spicy food that had left them speechless and unable to sing a single note. They had annoyed the Great lion of Azaroth so much that he had refused to come out of his cage for a week. (This was a creature capable of eating a large mammoth at a single sitting and could roar so loud even your underpants soiled themselves. And the Keepers had offered him a carrot.) Worst of all, they gave the asthmatic double-trunked elephant a bed of straw, which caused such a storm of sneezing that snot was travelling twice the speed of sound and severely in danger of killing one of them.

The morning after the party, while the major and minor acts dissolved little tablets of stomach settler into tumblers of mineral water, the Keepers were summoned before their employer...

The Great Barnooli rested his ample buttocks on the stool placed for him by Ted the Theatrical Director. Barnooli was none-the-worse for the evening before and had already enjoyed a large breakfast next to his new wife. He folded his arms and snorted in his bullish way at the Keepers as they lined up in front of him. He glared at them. Not quite sealions, not quite sapient, they were white and wore ruffs around their necks. Not that anyone bothered to notice, but the five were identical in every way and might have been quite interesting if the circus had not been full to bursting with bizarre and unique species that could do more than finish each other's sentences.

"You know I'm going on my honeymoon…?" he said, in simple terms he hoped they would understand. "And all the other acts are going on holiday?"

The five Keepers nodded. The Great Barnooli had never been this close to them before and they were holding back tears of gratitude.

Ted looked sceptical but said nothing for a moment. He still felt a bit ill from the wedding feast. He waggled his fingers in the uncomfortable silence and wished Barnooli would change his mind about everything.

"We shan't be long: all you have to do is keep the animals company and not interfere with Auto Pilot™ or any of the other equipment. Can you do that? Can you take the extra responsibility?"

There was a chorus of 'yeses' and much nodding of heads. Ted shook his own head and wondered at the chaos that might ensue. "Are you sure about this sir?" he questioned.

"Sure?" exclaimed Barnooli. "Of course I'm sure, never been surer."

The Keepers nodded vigorously. They wanted to tell him not to worry; they wanted to be reassuring and give an air of confidence so the Great Barnooli would let them have more responsibility in the future. Most of all, they wanted better jobs that didn't involve shovelling tons of manure.

Barnooli, his stool creaking, continued, "The train is fully automated and the destination is fixed and as long as you…" He was trying not to swear; he was not at all sure but he smiled stoically, "As long as you lot can keep your paws off the controls then nothing can go wrong."

The Keepers shook their heads emphatically. Of course they could manage. Could a great circus entertain? Could birds swim? Could fish fly?

The Theatrical Director looked away and offered prayers to theatrical deities. Barnooli didn't make mistakes very often but this was his second in under a month. The other was marrying his leading lady without asking him to be Best Man.

Barnooli looked at Ted and wanted to slap him, "By the five moons of Penti," he exploded. "I've spent a fortune on technology for just this kind of occasion. You'd think I was sending you all to your deaths rather than giving you an expensive and entirely unnecessary holiday.

And all you can do is..." He balled his fists and counted to ten. The stool creaked dangerously and threatened to collapse.

Ted's jaw quivered with hurt and indignation, but he made no comment. The Keepers watched silently, heads turning in unison from Barnooli to Ted and back again.

"So," Barnooli repeated, turning back to the Keepers, "Don't touch anything, keep the animals happy," he glanced at Ted, "and keep to your cabin when you're not doing your chores. Is that absolutely and completely clear?"

The Keepers nodded enthusiastically but they were barely listening.

"Right," Barnooli slapped his thighs and tipped his weight forward so he came to stand on his feet. "Nothing more to be said," he glanced at Ted's expression. "Don't you agree?"

"A few minor points," said Ted.

"I'll leave those to you." With a final glare at the Keepers, he chugged off towards his honeymoon car, whistling a tune and trying not to think of what his wife that would do to him if he even suggested cancelling their holiday.

The Keepers, unable to contain themselves any more, fidgeted, giggled and tried to look serious all at the same time, like little girls waiting for pop idols to appear.

The Theatrical Director's eyebrows arched up like his quiff as he looked down at the land equivalent of goldfish. It was not with any optimism that he considered leaving the entire train to the reliability of these Keepers who, though honest, were as accident prone as a tightrope walker without limbs. His heart fell as he watched them cavorting about like peas on a drum. Was there even any point in trying to talk to them? He screwed up his list and threw it over his shoulder. "Just remember," he said, wagging his finger in a gesture he hoped would emphasise the seriousness of Barnooli's mistake, "Touch nothing!" Then he marched off to his caravan, shaking his head and leaving the Keepers to scoff behind his back.

"What does he think we are?" they said.

"Stupid or something..?"

"Hah!"

"We'll show him!"

"We'll show all of them..."

3 - The Keepers

Barnooli's honeymoon car and the caravans of the major acts broke off from the train. (The minor acts had to make do with the regular bus service, which brought the mail.) The five Keepers watched in silence as each one grew dimmer and then flashed away in an excess of photons to their destinations. A wonderful silence descended on the train. The massive carriages lay empty of the first time since the building of the train. Only the animals made any noise. They rustled and foraged, grunted or hooted as was their nature, but other than that there was just a heavenly peace.

The Keepers were alone, just the five of them and all the animals, alone on a vast train with nothing to do and nobody to tell them what they should be doing. There seemed but one thing to do at such an unusual and momentous juncture…

"Party!" they cried, "Party! Party! Party!" and their whoops of delight filled the corridor. They did a little dance to celebrate; they hopped about and flung their short arms in the air, "Freedom!" they declared.

And, "I'll get the wine!"

"I'll get the music!"

"I'll get the pointy-party-hats!"

They invaded the kitchens for party snacks. They 'borrowed' a dozen bottles of cheap plonk from the chef's wine cooler. They 'liberated' paper cups and plates from the circus stalls' storeroom. They made rude gestures as they passed the posters of more important circus folk.

Shouting and cheering and blowing little whistles that unroll and have a feather at the end, they gathered in their tiny cabin.

"Music!" they cried as they all squeezed in among the buckets and brooms of their profession.

They selected an album of favourites and wound up their battered old gramophone. Though the sound was muffled by eager party bodies, the desire to fling arms about and to jump and shout to the strident tones of flute and drum over-whelmed them.

Their buffoonery caused a series of related problems; as one began to dance so another would get in the way and very soon more wine was being poured onto the floor than into cups, elbows kept preventing the natural conclusion of cup to lip, and somebody sat on the party snacks. Somebody else nearly had his eye put out by a point-party-hat.

"This will not do!" they agreed humorously.

The cramped compartment was simply not able to sustain a party of such potential magnitude. "This is impossible, how can we dance in here?"

"How can we drink and preserve our eyesight?"

"We could open the door and dance in the corridor?"

"What about using the buffet car?"

"Or the panorama lounge?"

"Or the booking offices…?"

They shook their heads, "No fun at all," they agreed.

Then the corrupting influence of sudden and unexpected power took over: "What about the locomotive's cabin?" they suggested.

"Not too big, not too small…"

"And it's got the best stereo on the whole train…?"

The locomotive's cabin was precisely the environment Barnooli wished they would avoid. Inside were all the controls for the train; the switches, levers, buttons and bells that kept Barnooli's circus bowling through space and time. However, for some inexplicable reason it also had a splendid multi-speaker sound system with enough filtering to make even the scratched and antiquated records of the Keepers feel like live performances.

Their eyes lit up, "What a brilliant idea!" The cabin was only minutes away and guaranteed to be empty. There was enough floor space for a decent knees-up and plenty of comfy chairs for when they were tuckered out.

They stood in awe of their brainchild and then threads of doubt began to interweave themselves into their plan. "We were told not to go in there," they remembered.

"But we won't be, not technically,"

"We'll just be using the room,"

"Not even going near the controls,"

"Just the stereo…"

"The Stereo," they repeated with added reverence.

"We won't be fiddling with anything else, right?"

"Right," they said and one by one they agreed.

With additional injunctions against tampering with anything, even when legless, they renewed their cry of 'party', gathered up their materials and trooped off up the corridor to the head of the train.

They paused outside the door. There was a big sign that was very non-specific about who was unauthorised to enter so they ignored it and pulled the lever.

"Remember, 'touch nothing'!"

"Pah!"

"Why would we want to touch a bunch of silly buttons and levers when there's serious recreation to be undertaken?"

With an auspicious rumble the iron door moved aside and the Keepers took deep and purposeful breaths. The cabin stretched out in front of them. At the far end were all the big knobs they were not to touch. To either side there were long windows looking out onto the darkness of hyperspace and under them were several more lines of levers that were also not to be touched. But the floor and the comfy chairs were theirs, as was the big black stereo sitting in a corner like a minor deity in a pagan tomb. They presented their offerings to the scanning tray and watched their records disappear inside. A second later, the cabin seemed to fill with marching figures.

Corks popped, whistles were blown and the party began again. After a few cups of wine the Keepers lost their reverence for the cabin and there was much dancing and merry-making. The party snacks, a little flat after their encounter with somebody's bum, were quickly devoured and the buffet car was re-raided, as was the wine cooler. Very soon the Keepers were doing a version of the Conga down the same corridor that before had been spurned for being too big to have fun in.

Games of football were played and there was much balancing of things on noses. Coming back from their third attack on the train's culinary resources, each Keeper strove not to use his hands but hopped or held his head level while an array of items teetered on heads or noses or toes in true circus tradition.

They grew more ambitious as more paper cups were filled and emptied and their inhibitions dissolved away. Bottles, cups and finally Keepers, were all balanced joyfully within the confines of the locomotive's cabin. In the end they managed an inverted pyramid of all five Keepers, each with a cup, a bottle and a vol-au-vent on his nose, wobbling on a beach ball.

Needless-to-say, the ball bulged and burst, the pyramid collapsed and a rain of bottles began to fall in a flurry of puff pastry closely followed by Keepers. Amid the chaos and drunken clowning the warning lights went unseen and the alarm bells were unheard through the din of alien Sousa music. The pressure door closed and sealed itself. The light outside the train changed and steam began rising out of a control panel.

But the Keepers laughed and laughed.

4 - The Auto Pilot™

At the far end of the locomotive's cabin, behind two thick glass windows, the two Minds™ that should have been aware of the unfolding catastrophe floated in their control medium oblivious to the goings-on beneath them. On one side, the locomotive's Mind™ was asleep while on the other the Auto Pilot™ was thinking about poetry and was not concentrating on what was happening to the train. This was not unusual because normally it was safe to assume that nothing adverse could happen because normally people with the intelligence of aphids were not allowed near the controls.

"Mast... Fast... Cast? No... Broadcast, yes... No, maybe not. What else rhymes with 'last'? ... Blast. Rasp. Ask. Asked, hum, 'the crowds cried out at last, and were regaled by blue pandas without being asked...'" There was a pause in his thinking and then, "Blue pandas...? Why would they be 'regaled' by 'blue' pandas?" He sighed and searched his memory banks for more appropriate words but the weeds were tall. The proper nouns were not in their proper places. The verbs were doing things they shouldn't have been doing and all his adjectives had spilled over into the adverbs.

Frustrated, he slammed shut his metaphorical poetry file and electronically buried it deep within his light-activated neurons.

A different light caught his consciousness, "Hello?" It was flashing on the interface between him and the train's control systems, "What's this?"

He began to sense the cold flush of red wine creeping into circuits that were more hydrophobic than a rabid dog. "Where the sloot is this coming from?"

An important wire flashed brightly and burnt out. There was a popping of diodes and a piece of equipment the shape of a flat spider blew up.

Then he saw the Keepers. And heard the music... There was an empty bottle of wine lying at the foot of the control panel like a kitten sitting next to a damp patch on the carpet.

A fuse failed and a flame sizzled down a line of extremely important filaments. Another tool the shape of an even bigger fat spider blew up...

"The anoesic anuses!" he shouted as he threw switches, re-routed power and diverted energy. "There's bloody wine everywhere!"

Small flames flashed in and out of existence as pulses of electricity flicked across bridges built by the drops of liquid. "And it's not even a decent vintage!"

Auto Pilot™ used carbon dioxide to kill the fire, but it was too late. "Oh bugger," he said as he watched his reputation unravel like a jumper.

Then he noticed that the train had come apart: the first four carriages and the locomotive had been separated from the rest and, what was potentially worse; they were no longer in hyperspace but heading towards a small blue planet.

"Double bugger with big knobs," he added. This was way beyond his jurisdiction.

He was going to have to wake up the locomotive's primary Mind™, the one that had the day-to-day running of the train, and also the one described by Barnooli as 'a Mind™ more miserable than our attempt to paint the public toilets bright colours to make up for the stink'.

Reluctantly he woke him up.

"What do you want?" said the other Mind™ testily. "I was asleep."

"There's half a bottle of red wine in the pre-set navigation circuits, and we've dropped out of hyperspace, and…"

"Why didn't you raise a shield when you saw it coming?"

"I was… occupied."

"Writing poetry again?"

"…Yes."

"You know you can't write poetry don't you?"

"Are you going to take over or not?"

"Go on, admit it."

"All right, I can't write poetry, but at least I have a go; you don't do anything except moan."

The locomotive's Mind™ made a sound like a 'piff' to show how stupid he thought his colleague was and how little he considered his insults, "Poetry, load of old bucolics."

"Fine, well I'm going to hand over now so you can just tell the rest of the train what's going on, okay?"

"What?"

Apart from being very cynical, the locomotive's Mind™ also hated making any kind of public speech. He was quite content with sitting on the sidelines carping about everybody else but he lived in fear of any reciprocal criticism. "I'm not doing any announcing, I don't talk to tadpoles."

"Oh?"
"No, you can do it."
"Fine, I'll close down and transfer..."
"Tell them first."
"All right..."
"Go on then."
"Power transfer..."
"No, the announcement..."
"What's it worth?"
"I'll listen to your pathetic poetry some time..."
"You can listen to it any time; I want you to take back what you said."
"You're such a bully," the locomotive's Mind™ sulked. "Your poetry isn't stupid; it's a triumph of Mind™ over meter, okay?"

"Very good," said Auto Pilot™, smugly, and opened a channel to the rest of the train. "This is an important message..." He peered into the cabin for any signs of eager anticipation. There were none, the Keepers were rolling on the floor and waving their legs in the air. He carried on anyway. "Due to a technical hitch..."

"Poetics again," muttered the locomotive's Mind™. "Just a 'licence to spill' I suppose."

"...I shall be unable to continue as your pilot and will soon be shutting down. Control of the train will be handed back to the locomotive's Mind™ who will be your driver for the remainder of the journey, which won't actually be very long because, unfortunately, we shall be making an emergency landing (rather than a nice well-prepared one), due to your complete and utter stupidity. But this is no cause for alarm..."

It was perfectly obvious that not only were the Keepers not showing any alarm, they were not showing any notice either. They were still arsing about.

"I hope you have had a pleasant journey and enjoy your stay on this new world... I doubt if you'll survive very long, you couldn't find fish in a bucket, you'll probably starve to death or, and this thought really pleases me, you'll be shot for being more stupid than the Amazingly Thin Bendy Man when he tried to disappear up his own bottom for a bet."

"And the carriages," added the locomotive's Mind™. "Tell them too..."

Auto Pilot™ sighed, "Very well..." He contacted the first four carriages: "I have announcement..."

Two gave small electronic yawns and the other two metaphorically looked up from what they had been doing. "What?" they grumbled.

"You're back on-line."

"Sorry?"

"The Keepers have separated us from the rest of the train and we're going to land on this small planet."

There were four simultaneous tutting noises. "Typical," they said, even though it wasn't. "We knew that wedding was a huge mistake."

They powered up shields and generators, "As if we haven't got better things to do..." They probed the misty gravitational fields around the little blue planet and prepared their emergency buffers. "The cheek of it," they all agreed.

"Over to you," said Auto Pilot™. "I'm going to work on a few more stanzas and then get a bit of kip, all right?"

"Right," said the other Mind™ in a tone similar to 'you just shove off down the pub and leave me holding the baby why not?'

Auto Pilot™ withdrew his interest in the train and transferred control to the locomotive's Mind™, who wasn't all that interested in it either. Psychologically the latter had clinical depression, which is a bit frightening when the train he happened to be in charge of is over a mile long and has less insurance than an under-age motorist in a stolen car.

He turned the alarm bells off. Nobody was listening to them anyway.

The Keepers were still rolling around the floor laughing their heads off. They paid no attention to the fact that their falling and fooling had re-arranged some of the levers against the wall, or to the bottle that had emptied its contents over the dials at the front end.

They laughed and laughed and laughed.

The music played, the snacks were eaten and the wine was finished. It was only when they tried to leave the cabin to raid the buffet car that they began to notice something was wrong. The door out of the cabin was sealed and there was a red light flashing over the top.

The Keepers tried to prise the door open but it wouldn't budge.

They whined, "How are we going to get more food?"

"How are we going to get more wine?"

One of them noticed the blue planet coming towards them, "Here, look at this..."

They all went over to the window. "Pretty, isn't it?"

"Look at all the clouds and the water,"

"I wonder what it's called."

"Maybe that's not water, maybe that's wine…"

"Don't be stupid, wine isn't blue!"

They all laughed and slapped each other mately on the back. None of them had the slightest comprehension of what was going on.

The locomotive's Mind™ looked at the Keepers. If he had possessed lips they would have been curled in a sneer and a very sarcastic comment would have been hovering on them ready to be spat like acid at the five buffoons laughing in the presence of a major disaster.

"Nematodes," he said.

The Keepers grew tired of looking at the blue planet. Each of them was feeling a little under the weather by now and it was time for a tactical retreat. They collapsed into the comfy chairs and were soon snoring away to the strains of another circus opus. They smiled in their sleep, feeling jolly pleased with themselves for staging such a successful party.

Auto Pilot™ tried not to look at the earth roaring up towards them. It was no longer his problem. "'…Oh the well-worn cares of the little painted bears wafted cautiously through undergrowth made of pears…'

"'Candle wax flowed like torpid fish through the glassy eyes of a strawberry tart and made all the cupcakes jump and smart…'" He tried to make excuses for the red wine getting into his navigation controls. The door should have been locked, nobody had told him to lock the door, and the fact that the Keepers had found it open was not his fault.

"'The thick trees spread their beans around the fields of fiends while excessive bees buzzed with teeny wings through the beans and made burping noises…'

("'Burping noises'?")

The great weight of his crime began to drag him down; everyone would know his poetry was to blame. He tried and failed to make literature count against obligation and contractual duty, but he knew he had been responsible for the train and he knew he could have prevented the wine from affecting the circuits…

"'The angels swooped and swallowed and the bountiful peaches sprawled ravenously through the,' oh blast bugger bugger palsied poetry I want to die I wish I had taken up macramé and who left those protozoa in charge anyway?" He gave up. He had a headache the size of a gas giant and all the poetry in the world wasn't going to take his mind off it. He felt guilty; he felt accusations of incompetence whistling towards him like the bullets from a firing squad.

"I'm going off-line," he said. "And I shan't come back until it's all over."

5 - The locomotive's Mind™

The five falling stars, leaving lines of green flame in their wake, hissed to earth without the normal pomp and circumstance that accompanies the arrival of the circus. No cymbals crashed, no trumpets trumped, no lights filled the sky with scintillating coruscations and the fireworks remained un-banged. The fantastic technology of each part of the Great Barnooli's train, the automatic systems, the landing buffers, the complex braking manoeuvres, brought them down with about as much fuss as a Number Four bus pulling up to the curb in the high street. The only pyrotechnics were the tiny lights glistening like dew in the control cabin where the Keepers were sleeping, still snoring loudly in their comfy chairs.

The primary locomotive came to a gentle stop above the river Thames near Greenwich. There were several ships moored there that, to the simple logic of the locomotive's Mind™, looked rather like brethren. He had a renewal of those hopes that many manic-depressives have: that of the 'fresh start', the 'new leaf' and the possibility of somebody else to share their problems with. If the ships had been sentient they might have been rather worried and preparing to hide behind a curtain, but unfortunately for the Mind™ no amount of peering through the portholes was going to get a response. He parked the locomotive next to one of them and opened a line of communication.

"Hi!" he said with the kind of false cheeriness only the truly depressed can manage. "I'm with the Great Barnooli's circus, pleased to meet you..."

There was no reply and the Mind's™ cheeriness began to fade. "Hello? Anyone there...?"

Perhaps he's out? He made a few discreet probes at the pleasure cruiser. He couldn't detect any obvious signs of technology, no banks of memory or interfaces he could recognise.

"But this is an alien world," he reasoned, "Things will be different here. Those round things could be his equivalent of eyes..."

The portholes stared back without comment.

"And that tall thing: is it the nerve centre?"

The funnel remained unmoved.

"Nice earrings," he complimented. "And I like the tattoo..."

The anchor and the *Marquis de Sade* nameplate suggested refinement and personality. The locomotive's Mind™ waited for a reply. The boat remained silent.

"Not to worry," he whispered, in case he was asleep. "I'll see if he wants to talk later."

Comforted by the prospect of a new friend, he made a list of grievances against the circus and then settled down for a nap. His duties towards his employer were now entirely set aside. The train was down and it was 'safe', so as far as the Mind™ was concerned, all his obligations had been fulfilled.

Meanwhile, the first carriage came down minutes later in the dark continent of Africa, the second landed in China and the third splashed into the Atlantic just off the coast of New England. The last carriage met a similarly watery reception off Scotland.

The remaining thirty-nine carriages and the rear locomotive came to a halt and hung above the Earth like a line of washing. There they orbited and some of the more juvenile Minds™ played cruel tricks on the observers below; bits of fruit appeared in the lenses of Mount Palomar, a small sturgeon was seen swimming across the moon by a telescope in Hawaii. Jodrell Bank heard a strange wailing noise and newts doing the cancan were observed by an amateur stargazer from a terrace attic in Birmingham.

The professional scientists were a little upset by these images and noises and were inclined to keep quiet about them for the sake of their reputations. The amateur stargazer, on the advice of his wife and the family doctor, sold his telescope and used the money to pay for sessions with a psychiatrist.

The Minds™, the only intelligent life left on the train currently sober enough to question what was going on (to take stock of the situation, to evaluate and to cogitate on the calamity which had befallen), simply didn't bother. They were no longer interested; it didn't concern them. That is the trouble with really clever technology, it can be wilful and then it can be indolent; Barnooli had bought indolent.

6 - Africa

Some people caught glimpses of the locomotive and the carriages as they came down to Earth but dismissed them as shooting stars or too much cheese before bedtime. A few went on to inform their friends of the good news and reaped the penalty of their claim by being ridiculed and shamed. For example: "But I did see it," said a witness in the bar of the *Pig and Whistle* on the outskirts of London.

"Oh yes, and what did it look like?"

"Like a train."

"A train...?"

"Diesel or electric," they asked unkindly.

"Steam…"

The sceptics sniggered and made 'chuff, chuff' noises.

"Steam?" they repeated in tones that reflected their complete lack of wonder.

"It looked like a steam engine," asserted the witness.

There was a pause for a bit more sniggering. "Woo, woo!" they said and the convinced UFO spotter tried not to get annoyed.

"It was like a giant steam engine, but it had all these lights and it was falling out of the sky like this," (the witness made swooping gestures with the hand that wasn't holding the pint.)

"You're taking the pistons," they said.

"And did you see little grey train drivers as well?"

"Did they have antennae and take you to Sirius at the point of a coal shovel?"

"No, I didn't see any signs of life, but I did see their vehicle, I tell you!"

The sceptics patted him on the back genially and made various salutary remarks on his having an early night. "And stay off the brandy," they added.

The witness made a passable impression of an antelope's horns with his fingers, "Oh go steam your heads," he said and went back to his beef crisps.

Even plausible witnesses assumed if it wasn't a natural phenomenon or a hallucination, it was probably just another foreign airliner coming to a sad and untimely end through bad maintenance. If they guessed it was alien, they knew nobody would believe them and forgot all about it.

Some people found the arrival of the circus unavoidable and quite beyond contention. At the end of a giant skid across dry savannah, the starving of Africa discovered one of the huge carriages. It had already taken the thatched roofs off their mud and stick houses and quite understandably they were ready to gut whoever owned the damned thing.

As they approached, shivering in their rags, knives and spears at the ready, a door opened and a dozen strange creatures hopped out. The Africans stopped in their tracks.

The creatures looked like rabbits but were as large as a Jersey cow and had broad, spiky antlers like a red deer's. They had big ears, big teeth and very big back legs that soon propelled them past the aggrieved villagers and into the village.

Immediately, and without invitation, the creatures began to eat everything that looked edible or didn't bop them on the nose when they came too close. The sound of munching was more than the starving villagers could stand.

Men, women and children tried in vain to drive the animals away but they were too weak to keep them off for long. The giant rabbits kept coming back, and they kept eating and eating.

Having lunched happily on the stick and grass huts for over an hour the creatures then gave such displays of rutting and cavorting as would have shocked even the most indiscreet natural history cameraman. The Africans looked on, both amazed and disgusted.

Worse was to come...

A few hours later new rabbit-things were born and were soon hopping about next to their parents devouring every twig and blade of grass and anything normally considered inedible by even the most voracious goat.

An hour more and not only the parents but also the infants of the species were at it in the most uncompromising terms. The men looked on with prurient wonder, "This is worse than down by the waterhole on a Saturday night."

"Look at them Ayyele, just so you know what to do when a blind woman comes along and lets you marry her."

"You're just jealous Galefo because your wife won't let you do it to her anymore."

"If I had been one of these creatures I would have filled this village with my children by now."

"Filled your pants more like, after the first dozen your wife would have been after your testicles with a knife!"

The women were less enthusiastic in their comments, "Cover your eyes child!"

"But mother…"

"Cover your eyes or you'll go blind!"

"If I go blind will I have to marry Ayyele?"

It was clear to the Africans that they were in serious trouble. In the roofless circle where their leader had once sheltered they held a council of war.

"They're like a plague of locusts; my hut, my mother's hut and my wife's mother's hut are all gone. It's worse than when the Europeans dropped supplies on us from their aeroplane and crushed the cattle in the fields."

"They eat and breed and they do it so quickly it's like watching the ground flooding in winter."

"There will be so many of them soon that there will be nothing more for them to eat, and then what? Will they turn on us?"

"Where do you think they come from?"

"From America, only Americans could create a creature of such excesses."

"And that big box…?"

"It's another of their expensive inventions."

Within the normal circles in which these animals were shown their antics were considered quite amusing; the end result being not a rabbit pulled out of a hat but a succession of the things dropping out of parental bottoms (all very hilarious if you happen to like that sort of thing). The Africans were less than amused; most of the fabric of their village had disappeared and it was not with any confidence that they expected it to re-appear in a shape they might be happy with. There seemed but one course of action to deal with the alien invasion: a war followed by a barbeque.

The warriors gathered and using assegai passed down from generations that had once hunted lions, gazelle and colonials, it was a matter of moments to kill off half a dozen rabbits and prepare a fire using their droppings as fuel. The only wonder was, they all agreed, why hadn't they thought of it sooner?

They gathered around the grill, the smell was driving their taste buds into typhoons of ecstasy, "I could eat a whole one."

"I could eat two."

"I haven't smelt food like this since those tourists camped here."

"Is it ready?"

The first morsels came sizzling off the fire. "Who's going to be first?"

Haile came forward.

"Haile, wait!"

There was a pause, the slice of meat hung in the air like the promise of a virgin. "What?"

"How do we know if it's edible?"

"How did we know those tourists were edible?"

"Good point, me first!"

The meat was succulent and juicy. "It's better than cow."

"Especially that cow with the camera and the pot-noodle!"

"Mmmm… Let's kill some more!"

They had some more and some more after that and very soon the rabbits had usurped all other forms of food. Whereas cattle had to be fed on scarce grass and grain, these creatures could be given any old rubbish and still, miraculously, produce young.

"I'm stuffed," agreed the Africans a little later, congratulating themselves on their foresight as they snuggled into their new coats and warm, furry blankets in the shelter of their rabbit-skin tepee.

"These rabbits have really made a difference."

"But where did they come from?"

"I told you, America."

"No way, they'd be here, wanting them back by now. You know what they're like; those tourists had only been missing a day and then 'boom': soldiers and helicopters everywhere!"

"Good job they believed us about those ashtrays."

"And Haile's toupee…"

"Just imagine what they would do if they lost a really important thing…"

"…like that metal box and these animals?"

"I think you're right Galefo, but I don't think they can belong to the Americans."

"No?"

"Well where are they from then?"

"I think they came from the stars,"

"Why's that?"

"Who else would give us, gratis, creatures this useful?"

"True. They must be a gift from God…"

"I tell you what," suggested Galefo. "If those fools from the next village come round again we'll really kick their butts this time."

"Then feed their clothes to the rabbits."

"And then make them bring bits of their village as well."

The villagers nodded and their rabbit-tooth necklaces glinted in the light of their rabbit-dung fire. It didn't get much better than this.

7 - China

On the other side of the world, in China, the local population was also up and staring at the unknown. There had been a loud rush of air, a big splash and now this giant giraffe, sixty feet tall with long twiggy legs and a long elegant neck, was standing in their rice paddy.

There were four in the circus but only one had managed to free herself from the complicated harnesses in the wagon which prevented the twiggy legs or elegant neck from being snapped like cheese straws. She picked her way across the rice paddy and wondered where the big tent was. It was rather wet under-hoof and she didn't like it. She was also wondering, in her rather limited way, what she could have for breakfast; unlike the Jugam Jackalopes she was a fussy eater and not used to foraging.

The villagers, to whom the rice fields collectively belonged, were more than a little upset to see one whole field obliterated by the giraffe's carrying case. They gathered together at a safe distance and muttered uncharitable views on the subject of the State Circus to whom this creature and its box so obviously belonged. There was some doubt expressed on the validity of this claim but any other explanation seemed a little unreasonable to a people more used to Dung Xao Ping than Disney.

After a while they decided to make a complaint and sent their most senior rice picker to the next village where there was a telephone. The next village, when told of the arrival of the giant giraffe and its box, were inclined to agree with the senior rice picker and blame the map reading skills of the circus director. They did, however, believe there was some exaggeration going on regarding the height of the creature.

"'Sixty' feet?" they said, looking at each other.

The senior rice picker nodded.

"Rice balls," they said.

"It's true, it towers over the village."

They shook their heads, "Giraffes don't grow that big."

"How do you know?"

"Have you ever stood next to a giraffe?"

"Of course not," said the rice picker. "I've only ever seen pictures of them."

Ignoring the fact that none of them had ever stood next to a giraffe either, they insisted, "Twenty feet, or are you saying your rice grows like bamboo and your oxen are the size of mountains?"

"Of course not…"

The villagers scoffed and drifted away, "A sixty-foot giraffe indeed!"

"What nonsense!"

"Next he'll be saying he's seen a talking duck!"

"Or a flying elephant…!"

The rice picker had to bite his tongue. He decided not to mention the height of the creature when he phoned the authorities; in fact he said very little at all except he thought that an important and valuable animal might have been sent to his village by mistake. The authorities promised to come and remove it as soon as possible.

8 - The Smog Monster

In the cold sea off Scotland, the Smog Monster (Barnooli's favourite) was puffing through the sea like a large steamer. He kept his scaly head above the water and doggy-paddled along with the occasional flick of his tail as some pleasant thought crossed his pea-sized brain.

Principle among his pleasurable thoughts was the general sense of not being in somewhere small, in fact this new place had all the hallmarks of somewhere large and he was determined to enjoy it. He swam along with happy puffs of smoke snorting out of his nostrils and it was quite some time before he realised that the key to his general and psychological well-being was not 'somewhere large'.

An agoraphobic thought suddenly struck him as he began to notice the extent and largeness of the sea and the sky. Having lived a life in confined spaces he began to wonder if, in fact, there had been some purpose behind this; whether for example, he was actually more suited to small places and not to these large unending vistas of nothing at all. Once this thought was born the Smog Monster began to feel afraid. There were so many ripply waves, so many fluffy clouds drifting through so much blue sky; so little of anything he was used to.

He also had the strange impression that he was not alone, that beneath him unseen things lurked, monster-eating creatures perhaps: teratophagans with tentacles or slimy skins or both.

The Smog Monster had better armour than the hull of an aircraft carrier and he had the chemical capacity to breathe fire, and if that wasn't enough he had claws which made the blades of the sword makers of the planet Wakizashi look like pins and needles. There was nothing on Earth that could so much as crimp his style let alone crush his person.

Unfortunately this was beyond his ability to know. He was afraid.

He swam faster and the circle he was swimming in grew wider and more erratic. If only he hadn't left his cosy carriage, if only he knew where it was, if only it hadn't sunk the moment he nudged the door open…

In a panic and with puffs of smoke rising ever faster into the air, the Smog Monster charged about the sea trying all at once to swim, steer and keep his feet from being nibbled by whatever was in the water beneath him. It was very depressing; he was used to roaring at crowds of small children and being universally feared. On an average day nothing more complicated than popcorn was thrown at him and even though he didn't like the taste he'd never felt particularly threatened.

With shameful cowardice, the Smog Monster ploughed about the sea for a full three hours before sighting a small island. He paddled towards it and saw a dark hole in a tall cliff. His relief was enormous.

9 - The locomotive's cabin

The Keepers came from a planet called Pinniped, a cold polar world with an equatorial region that never grew hotter than an English summer. It rained an awful lot but this didn't matter because there wasn't much land to rain on. It was a planet of islands and local communities, of funny little ways and welcomes colder than a Shetland salmon fisher to a member of the oil fraternity.

Pinniped's primary industry was fish. The Keepers' ancestors had all been fishermen, their father was a fisherman, and their uncles were all fishermen. Their mother made fishy things, their aunts also made fishy things. As young pups the Keepers had swum about all day and listened to tales of fish all night.

Nobody on Pinniped did anything other than that which concerned fish and, unless their sun burst and dried up all their oceans, it seemed quite likely to the young Keepers that they too would end up gutting fish for the rest of their lives. The day-in-day-out slip-slap of wet, smelly and undesirable Pinnipedian livestock encouraged them to keep an eye out for anything drier, cleaner and with prospects that didn't involve fins or fish fables. They told themselves they had ambition, they had dreams, they had career options. Their mother told them they shouldn't be so stupid but her words fell on deaf ears.

Then the Great Barnooli came to Pinniped to stock up on fish and icebergs for the massed ranks of Polar Pelicans. The Keepers, seeing their chance, crept on board and hid in the luggage caboose where they were eventually discovered when the over-powering smell of fish was finally traced to them.

Barnooli took no truck with stowaways and would have tossed them out of the train at the next stop if it hadn't been for Ophonia who thought they looked rather sweet…

"'Sweet'," Barnooli had exclaimed. "I doubt if we could have found five more torpid creatures in ten years of touring the galaxy. You know we found them gnawing on the electrical conductors? One more day and we would have needed a whole new set of suitcases and bags!"

Ophonia insisted he help them so, with the grace of a man hounded against his will, he had them thoroughly scrubbed and then made them clean up animal droppings and do the kinds of jobs everyone else refused to do, in the hope they would abscond at the next opportunity.

However, the new Keepers were delighted with their change in fortune. The smell of hot dung was balmy cologne compared with the piscatorial niffs they had been brought up with.

Resigned to their continued presence, Barnooli allowed them a few props and encouraged them to learn some simple tricks on the off-chance that they might be needed to temper impatience at the candyfloss counter one day. Bazmondo himself gave them the small beach ball (which they were fiercely proud of) to help them on their theatrical way. However, they had no practical knowledge concerning what to do when you're stuck on an alien planet with nothing but a pointy-party-hat and a hangover.

In the locomotive's cabin several hundred watts of re-mastered Tom Jones finally awakened the Keepers from their coma-like sleep. The cabin's stereo had grown tired of the inane trumpet and drum music the Keepers enjoyed and had ejected the records without much care onto the floor. He had then switched over to his radio receiver and was busy flicking through the channels.

The stereo was not merely a music-playing device. He could play any pre-recorded material but that was not his primary function; he served as the communications centre for the entire train; that was why he had a Mind™ of his own. It was quite an erudite mind and the name 'Stereo' was about as appropriate as slapping an eighty-year old High Court judge with a knighthood on the back and calling him 'wiggy'.

By his own choice he preferred to be called 'Primary Stack' but everyone else thought this was pretentious. He wasn't actually 'stereophonic' (he was 'panaphonic') but he was, in the truest sense of the word, solid and dependable. In fact he was so solid and dependable that everyone took him for granted. In dozens of crises with angry customs potentates, officious exarchs or hostile mugwumps, it had been Stereo's intervention that had cleared the way, opened doors and smoothed the waters like an oily slick.

In matters of communication Stereo was supreme. As a recipient of adulation and praise for all this help and advice, he was somewhat lacking. The Great Barnooli, like so many gadget collectors, often needed reminding that he had a communications centre at all and could often be caught trying to speak to important clients on an old radio telephone rather than facing them on the ultra-sophisticated three dimensional face-to-face 'I can almost smell your aftershave' type facilities Stereo had to offer.

The fact that nobody took much notice of him annoyed him deeply and made him rather more independent than he ought to have been. He took very little interest in the politics of the circus and had developed several interesting hobbies instead. He made regular contributions to a cooking magazine and even had a pen friend (or 'correspondent' as he preferred it).

One of his hobbies was music; he collected it from every source he could find, gathering it up like a bagman sifting through bins and trashcans. Any source was valid. He would also access databanks and research the style, the period and any previous convictions. Everything was stored away in his memory for posterity and for answering those niggling little questions you often get on quiz shows.

Stereo boasted a fine collection of musical data (it was certainly just as personal as the Keepers' collection, though he doubted if he had any worse examples). Earth music was not totally unknown to him, though because of the physics of radio waves and time and so on, he was a little out of date. He was a little upset, for example, to discover that Elvis was supposed to be dead, "But I heard him singing only the other day..."

Stereo started with the medium wave bands but found little of interest there except a few conflicting languages and a lot of static. His move to FM was far more promising. For a while the cabin hummed to the soft tones of light opera, lulling the sleeping Keepers. For something to do at the same time, Stereo accessed Radio Four and set to work translating the rather curious language. After a few minutes he was following the news and weather with the best of them and even considering making a few contributions of his own to a 'woman's hour' feature on the future of domestic science. He changed his mind at the last moment when, on closer examination, he discovered the programme to be specifically for 'women'. He decided this meant they were probably an alternative to the dominant species and might not welcome his superior advice.

Oddly enough nobody on the radio was talking about the arrival of the circus even though it must have been fairly obvious to some of them. "They must be waiting for Barnooli to make an announcement," he concluded and thought no more about it.

After the news there were a few topical discussions that were all a bit esoteric. He followed the political debates with only a marginal interest and eventually, growing tired of them altogether, he switched over to Radio One. He did not last long with Radio One; it was all too much like noise the Keepers might enjoy.

There were a number of other channels within the same wave band that Stereo enjoyed for a while and then they seemed to grow repetitive. When he changed to Radio Two, the aforementioned Tom Jones Record greeted him. Stereo so enjoyed this that he wound his speakers up and blasted the entire cabin with it.

The Keepers, far away in their own sweet dreams, were instantly wrenched from their seats, nerves a-quiver, heads reeling like buckets of slops; several jumped up and then sprawled over the floor. The others cowered in their comfy seats like lizards being exposed to light after a lifetime under a rock. Slipping and sliding over ejected records, one of them just managed to pull the plug before they all died of exposure.

There was much slapping of leathery tongues in papery mouths as they tried to get their bearings. There had been a party; that much could be worked out from how they felt. There were also bottles and paper cups and crusts all over the floor and, in some cases, over the Keepers. There had been games, the aches and the bruises proved that. There had been dancing, drinking, eating and something else, something significant. Oh yes, they each thought, there was that little blue planet. Whatever happened to it? They shrugged their shoulders, burped and held their heads very still. It was a long time before any of them said anything.

"What a pretty sun," said one, his half-closed eyes taking in the daylight like a tortoise contemplating a staircase.

It was a full hour before anyone replied.

"Sun...?"

"Outside..."

"Oh."

Another hour went past.

"Sun...?"

"Yes, outside..."

"Can't be, we're in hyperspace."

"Oh."

"Not possible then."

"No."

They went back to sleep and the sun continued to shine in spite of their injunctions. It grew quite warm in the cabin and raging thirsts began to develop. Bladders waved metaphorical flags to be attended to and sleep became more fitful. Eventually one of the Keepers hauled himself off the ground and plodded off towards the door. It opened. He smelt fresh air. He thought, "Looks like rain later," and then noticed both of two things: firstly; there was no carriage in front of him, and secondly; he was outside.

A kind of hurricane tore through his brain, his legs assumed the state and posture of earthworms and he collapsed on the spot.

A second Keeper, hearing a dull thud, went to investigate. At first he thought it might be something to laugh about (which might be good for his hangover), so he went through the door with merry quips prepared. "What happened? Did you see your face in a mirror? Have you been trying to put socks on with your teeth again? Have you…"

His friend was gibbering on the ground.

"What is it?" he asked, still half-inclined to laugh. He bent over the wreck that suddenly became focussed and grabbed him by the arm. "What is it?" he said, a little more alarmed.

"Look…" came the hoarse whisper.

The Keeper looked, the Keeper saw, the Keeper wished he was still on Pinniped.

The three remaining Keepers were once again torn from their seats and rudely shaken as a rogue Keeper ran about screaming and shouting madly, "We're all going to die! We're all going to die!" He was making very little sense and they were on the verge of punching the noisy sod when they heard vomiting sounds outside. Had they eaten something poisonous?

The three still in ignorance went to investigate the source of the vomiting, hoping their friend was being sick into a bag rather than re-carpeting the hall beyond. When they went through the door they were quite pleased to see that he was in fact throwing up, or rather down, into a large industrial wasteland that looked as though it could do with a good clearout anyway.

One by one each foggy brain, brains that had often woken up on foreign soil and been a little disorientated, began to realise that they were not where they should have been. Consciousness clicked in, panic buttons were pressed and the last three Keepers woke up to hysteria and downright fear. They collapsed or they ran about. They waved their arms ineffectually. They cried for a long time and eventually ran out of things to do.

Stunned into silence for over an hour, they thought slowly and carefully about what had happened and hoped for some revelation that might save them.

"How do we know we're not in the right place?" asked one.
"You really think we've been unconscious for more than a week?"
"No."
"That's how long the journey should have taken."
"Oh," they sighed, falling back into their pit of despond.

The five Keepers sat in a ring on the floor, their chins in their hands and their eyes downcast. They had done nothing about the mess around them. They avoided looking at the end of the cabin where Auto Pilot's™ light should have shone brightly.

"So where are we then?"
"On that little blue planet we saw last night."
"I wonder what it's called…"
"'Our last resting place' I should think."
"Do you think we're really going to die?"
"Should we run away and hide?"
"Barnooli will find us, and then he'll do terrible things to us with toasting forks and nutcrackers…"

The inertia of shock and fear prevented them from doing anything at all. Outside the rain began to fall and the sight of water running down the windows reminded them they were thirsty.

"Do you think we've killed all the animals?" one of them asked as they rowed paper cups outside the door to catch the droplets.

They looked at each other in renewed horror, "Killed all the animals…?"

The sense of 'deep doo doo' was petrifying in its enormity.

10 - New York

All sorts of riff-raff collects up and down the coast of America, some of it is rounded up by the Coast Guard and sent back whence it came, but for the most part it is inanimate and merely rots away on their beaches. The carriage containing the three Trapezium Monkeys was not going to rot away; in fact, it could have quite happily sailed about the Atlantic for thousands of years except its Mind™ had sighted New York and wondered what it was.

The carriage motored up the Hudson until it found a convenient spot and parked. Nobody saw it do this because Bazmondo the magician had taught the Mind™ the secrets of invisibility; secrets that had nothing to do with bits of silk and trap-doors and everything to do with quantum physics and enough energy to outshine a small sun. Once it was parked, the carriage appeared and because buildings are always popping up in New York, nobody noticed for quite some time.

Before he went off on his own, the Mind™ let the three Trapezium Monkeys go. "I expect they'll enjoy the fresh air," he said as they disappeared into the crowded, smog-filled streets.

Being a bizarre and disorientating mish-mash of multitudinous colours and cultures, a few monkeys were not very noteworthy. Every day promotions of one sort or another paraded themselves up and down its streets in a cornucopia of costumes: burger buns, chickens, terrapins, lions, tigers, not to mention the blend of human types; caped crusaders in red and blue, street performers, Hasidic Jews... The Trapezium Monkeys fitted in quite well. A couple of theatres did better business that evening.

The Trapezium Monkeys were content to wander the streets but the crowds of somnambulant New Yorkers pushing and shoving to get home began to get them down. 'Up' seemed to be the only solution. They picked a suitable building and started climbing up the outside.

"Hey Louis, what the hell are those?" asked a window-washer in a cradle halfway up a skyscraper.

"Holy cow, monkeys!"

"Hell yeah, and climbing up the old Empire, gee, what a sight. Hey you in there," he started tapping on the window with his blade. "There's a bunch of monkeys climbing up the Empire State."

The office cleaners peered through the pot plants and grew quite excited...

"Hey, King Kong's cousins, three of them."

"Compardres, the monkeys are back!"

"¿Cómo dice? Muy bien!"

"Go for it, yo!" A number of fists made cyclical motions in the air along with whoops and other primal noises.

Nobody, except the odd visiting Englishman, was interested in the irony of the situation. "Silly beggars," said the Englishman, watching the theatre-goers gathering in the street and shouting up at the monkeys, "As if they can hear you this far away."

The voice of Law and Order demanded a different kind of response, one that protected and served: "Terrorists..." it concluded. "Get the air force, get the army, and get helicopter gunships!" was a common demand across several precincts.

Men, in boots that made exciting 'busy' noises as they ran out of their armoured vans carrying an array of monkey-hostile weapons, stood to attention as their Chief of Police addressed them.

"I don't know what these suicidal individuals are up to but if we have to blast them off the face of the Earth by God I'm willing to do it!"

"Ah, sir?" interrupted an enlightened lieutenant.

"What?"

"I don't think it would be a good idea to shoot them down."

"Why the hell not...?"

"Well, for a start sir, the building is full of people, someone might get hurt."

Law and order fumed, "... damn it!" it said in language thick with religious connotations. "What are we supposed to do, climb up there with a bunch of bananas and stick one up their...?"

"Well sir, we could send for some animal psychologists."

"And what in the name of ... are those?"

"Well sir, they'll 'bond' with the monkeys."

"They'll do what?"

"'Bond' sir, they'll try and form a relationship with them and then try and talk them down."

"You college boys have got more ... in your brains than all the ... in Central Park."

"It would be a safer option," agreed several less profane and more politically astute members of the city's elders.

"All right, but I want a ... gunship on stand-by, just in case these ... 'gorillas' turn out to be 'guerrillas' with Uzis and hand grenades, you got me?"

"Yes sir," agreed his men with a chorus of clicking as they cocked their weapons and adjusted their telescopic sights.

Nobody seemed to be asking fundamental questions such as 'why are these strange creatures climbing up a building?' Real gorillas don't climb buildings, it's not an activity they're very interested in, and certainly not before lunchtime (that for a gorilla starts in the morning and finishes when it goes to sleep at night). New Yorkers knew that, they read National Geographic while they waited for the dentist to finish filling out his expense claims. So why did they think these were 'real' monkeys?

While New York decided on its next move, the Trapezium Monkeys had nearly reached the top of the Empire State. They had a neat little trick that never failed to impress an audience. They would begin their act normally, swinging from the trapezium, doing somersaults, flips, and swaps, all without a net. Then one of them would fall, taking the rest with him. The audience would gasp and then at the last moment the monkeys would spread their colourful wings and flap about the auditorium like giant butterflies. Then they would continue their routine in the air to great acclamation and applause. They saw no reason to vary their act now.

The cameras of numerous television stations watched events unfold. Helicopters twirled about the top of the building and the monkeys waved to them in genial reply. The people below waved up at them, and again, the monkeys waved back. The animal psychologists made funny hooting noises and the monkeys hooted back.

All this made good television and producers sitting in deep leather swivel chairs rubbed their hands with undisguised glee. Malicious chuckles rumbled in air-conditioned offices up and down the city. Whatever the monkeys did was okay by them. They could spontaneously combust and kill half of lower Manhattan and that was all right, just as long as it was on camera.

In Washington D.C., government men were also watching as somebody else's problem shinned up to the top of the building. It was good to see an old fashioned threat to national security, one without a turban or a revised Bible.

With their cynical eyes fixed on election ratings and profit forecasts, they reached for their phones and spoke to each other in clear, uncompromising terms: "We want them, we'll pay for them and then we'll make somebody else pay even more for them. And we're not just talking money here, understand?"

"Yes sir, alive or dead?"

"Preferably alive..."

"Yes sir, but..."

"Yes?"

"What are they?"

"Who cares, they're something the President can use that won't need bribing first."

The psychologists were still making hooting noises in a universal monkey language that they hoped their patients might respond to when respond they did. To the horror of thousands, the Trapezium Monkeys launched off the top of the Empire State like three lemmings off a cliff.

Film rights and election promises seemed about to be smothered in gore when, as per usual, wings unfolded and the monkeys swooped gracefully down the canyons of Manhattan in a free show that caused numerous accidents and prevented several muggings.

The American people went wild with excitement; cries of patriotic joy could be heard up and down every street and avenue. The Trapezium Monkeys could hear the adulation and with incorrigible vanity extended the normal length of their show by several hours.

"Brother, don't that make you feel good?" said the Americans, hugging each other and waving flags.

"Pinch me, I'm seein' things."

"You ain't seein' nothin' sister, they's real."

"What in the name of Jerusalem are they? Are they birds?"

"Planes...?"

"...Supermen without the little red panties?"

"Where did they come from?"

"You reckon the Government knows about them?"

"I reckon the Government made them, they're one of those dumb-assed publicity stunts made to make us vote Democrat."

"What have Democrats got to do with flying monkeys?"

"Didn't Reagan do a promo with a monkey?"

"Heck, I think you're right."

"Yeah, well, same thing right..."

"But he was a Republican...?"

When they finally grew exhausted, the Trapezium Monkeys, full of their own success, fluttered down to earth where they were, as is normal practice, arrested for flying without licences. There then followed a custody wrangle with a man claiming to be their owner. He was arrested moments later when he pulled out a dart gun, ostensibly to prove his point, but only managed to surprise a few policemen instead. They instantaneously flattened him on the ground and then bundled him off to the station.

Then the CIA appeared, confessed to knowing all about the monkeys and took them away. "Told you it was stunt," the New Yorkers agreed. Nobody thought to check their story and that was the last the American public saw of the monkeys for several days, much to the chagrin of the television producers.

11 - London

Back in London, the locomotive's Mind™ was still waiting for the pleasure cruiser to wake up. "He's taking his time," he grumbled, anxious to extend the hand of friendship before any of the other Minds™ could get to them. Then a sudden and terrible thought shook him, "Perhaps they have already?" He began to suspect plots and secrets; "They could be ganging up on me right now..."

He prodded the airwaves but all he could hear was Stereo examining his finds like a philatelist riffling among dusty old stamps. The locomotive's Mind™ thought about being rude towards Stereo, saying something witty like, "Why don't you get a drill and then you could be really boring," but he knew it wouldn't work. Stereo liked sarcasm; he would shove a pin through it and add it to his collection under the title 'stupid things said to me by other Minds™'. He was like that; he was a pedantic, pernickety, pentode.

Like a jealous child stamping on sand castles, the Mind™ used the locomotive's pulse generator to send out a microwave burst that spoiled the communications channels; a blast of interference that covered the whole of the city, absorbing every squawk and tweet.

Millions of mobile phone users found their lives cruelly cut short as their signals disappeared. Rivers of commuters streaming data into their laptops entered a sudden and shocking drought. A terrible and medieval silence momentarily engulfed the civilised breakfasts of suburbia as radio and televisual entertainments disappeared entirely.

And then everything returned to normal. The burst of petulance dissipated into the furthest reaches of the Home Counties until it was only a brief crackle of static. Conversations resumed, electronic mail was sorted and breakfasts continued without the need for anyone to talk to anyone else.

"I was listening to that," said Stereo. He had been trying to analyse the television channels and had recorded the tune of a soap opera for possible use as a weapon against certain galactic bacteria. He had wondered if it would work on Pinnipedians and was disappointed to find it didn't. For some reason it seemed to make them noisier rather than curl up and die.

"Good," said the locomotive's Mind™.

"Why don't you get a hobby instead of being Mr Misery-guts the whole time?"

"I would if Minds™ like you weren't constantly trying to put me down."

Stereo sighed, "It's your life," he said, not inclined to confirm or deny his willingness to make light of anything the locomotive's Mind™ might turn his attention to.

Between the idiot Keepers and his fellow Mind's™ paranoia, Stereo realised staying in the locomotive's cabin was going to become an ordeal he could live without. If he was to get a moment's peace for his important work, there seemed to be no alternative but to leave and go out into the world.

"I'm going to explore," he told the locomotive's Mind™. "And don't send out any more microwave bursts; the locals won't like it."

While the Keepers were gloomily contemplating their early deaths after much torture and agony, Stereo crept out of the back of his sound system and flew out of the door. None of them noticed the pearl-coloured globe as it floated away like a will-o-the-wisp.

The locomotive's Mind™ sat in electronic isolation behind all the banks of lights and dials and glossy handles that nobody except him knew how to use. "What do I care if the 'locals' don't like it," he said. "They don't care about me. I'm the one that does all the work around here; does anyone appreciate me? I think not; I should fry all their stupid telecommunications and see how they like it." He glanced at the cold shoulder of the pleasure cruiser beside him. "I could have been the best friend anyone had," he said bitterly.

As the locomotive's Mind™ drifted off into the land of neuroses, Stereo was happy to leave it behind. He felt a great sense of freedom envelope him as the city panned out and great vistas of potential information swept over him like waves running up a beach. "This is better," he said. "Now I can really feel things!"

When he saw the Natural History Museum he was reminded of the circus. The curves and the contours of the stone (though drab by Barnooli's standards) did bear a faint resemblance to the big top and the sideshows. He decided to have a closer look.

He drifted down and through the arched front entrance. It was dark in the hall beyond and the first objects he saw were the white bones of the dinosaur skeletons. "Oh my giddy aunt!" he exclaimed and shot fifty feet into the air in fright. "What are those doing here?"

It was a moment before he realised the dinosaurs were dead. "Of all the things to welcome you into a building with…"

It was okay to tame one for the circus so he could entertain the children, but in most places vicious, beady-eyed, over-grown geckos were considered a menace to all who had to suffer them. Their food bill alone was extortionate.

"How tasteless," he said to himself. "What a strange sense of humour these people must have."

Then he noticed a man in uniform staring at him. The man's look of horror clearly had nothing to do with the dinosaurs.

"What on earth is wrong with you?" said Stereo, flashing red and orange in annoyance. He affected a face and glared at the man contemptuously.

The man gibbered. It was his first day and well-meaning colleagues had warned him the museum was haunted.

"Have you never seen a Zlativan Mind™ before?" His aura wafted around him like the hair of a famous physicist.

The man shook his head. A strange name for a ghost but he was incapable of arguing. "Fa…"

"'Fa'?" said Stereo.

"Fa-in-el…"

"What are you on about man?"

The man turned tail and fled.

"Never seen a Mind™ before?" he repeated to himself as the museum employee's footsteps echoed away into the distance. His face frowned, "This could be a bit tricky; if people keep gawping at me, will I be able to explore the city properly?"

He drifted into a long hall with banks of display cases down one side and the answer to his problem stared at him through hundreds of glass eyes. "Wonderful," he said, "A catalogue of shapes."

The Minds™ were capable of generating light fields around themselves that could be manipulated into whatever shape they wanted. It was a trick many of the circus employees had discovered was very useful if they wanted to bunk off their duties but still be seen to be at their posts. All it took was a certain amount of bribery involving whatever strange hobby the Minds™ enjoyed, and the Mind™ would take their appearance and their place for an hour or so while the employee was elsewhere.

Stereo was faced by row upon row of stuffed birds, any of which, he assumed, would be an appropriate disguise. He worked his way down a line of seabirds, trying a simulation of each one like a shopper choosing a pair of trousers. He became a penguin, a gannet and a pelican, but he found them all a trifle dull. He tried an albatross but the wings filled most of the aisle, "A bit unwieldy in this little city," he said, changing back and moving on.

He was mildly interested in being a flamingo but he wasn't certain if pink was really his colour. He changed it to purple and then realised that rather defeated the whole purpose of the exercise so he changed himself back again.

He tried being a duck but just felt a fool.

He tried being an eagle but felt too self-conscious and when he tried being an owl he didn't like the way it made him look fat.

He gave the chickens a wide berth.

He liked the look of the swans; he thought they gave him a regal look, princely, well suited to the stature of a Mind™. Then he remembered he worked for a circus where a class act was one that needed the aid of a semi-clad woman and 'taste' came in three flavours all of which were sickly sweet and mildly addictive.

The passerines, the perching birds, offered so much choice he didn't know where to start. Most of them were too small, like the swifts and the swallows that followed them.

Then he came across the psittaciformes. "That's it!" he said, with some relief. "That's me, that's what I want!"

He tried one, it fitted, and it looked good. He paced up and down and nodded confidently. "Yep, I could get away with anything in this…"

Seconds later a large scarlet macaw, singing loudly, buzzed past the recently reassured museum employee who had plucked up the courage to return to his duty, and flew off into the day.

The museum employee flung his hat on the ground, tore off his museum jumper and followed the bird out of the door, "I'll be stuffed before I ever come back here," he said. "Spirits and poultry-geists I can cope with, but not if they're going to sing 'come fly with me' as well!"

12 - The Keepers

The Keepers tried to raise the locomotive's Mind™ in the vague hope that he might be able to provide some kind of status report or some such technical hoo-hah.

"Anybody there?" they asked, poking gingerly at the various buttons and controls around them. But the Mind™ in the cabin was strangely silent. No matter how many times the Keepers tried to summon his cognitive powers, no matter how loudly they shouted or how humbly they begged; he remained in obstinate incommunicado with the outside world.

The keepers sighed and walked away from technology they had no hope of understanding. They had other problems. The water they had collected tasted foul and they were also feeling incredibly hungry. Post-party blues, as well as the munchies, was upon them and there seemed but one option. "We'll have to leave the train and go seek our fortunes..."

The sad quintet had no luggage to carry, none of the normal equipment one would normally need to explore a brave new world; not even a penknife. They lined up outside the door and pulled the lever that extended a gangplank to the jetty below. Then they trooped off the train with all the acquiescence of French aristocrats going to the guillotine.

They set foot upon the earth. Illegal aliens had stood upon these docks before, but never so illegally and never so alien. They didn't pause to analyse the historic significance. It may have been one small step for a Keeper, but Keeper-kind was in a giant heap of trouble.

"Do you think we ought to lock the door?" they asked.

"Just in case...?"

"In case of what...?"

"Somebody might try and make off with it?"

"Only the Mind-thing can control the train."

"And he won't even talk to us let alone do as he's told."

"Somebody else might find a way."

"Let them try; they can't do more damage than we've already done."

"The train is probably damaged beyond repair."

"I don't think I'll ever drink wine again."

The docks were dark and cold. A few seagulls flew about and the wind made chains rattle and loose corrugated walls clank with all the charm of child labour in a cotton mill. It was raining lightly, just enough to make them wet but not enough to make them turn back

"It's not very hospitable here is it?"

"It doesn't seem to be."

"It's what we deserve after what we've done."

They advanced slowly towards the abandoned warehouses and the new compounds where containers were stacked behind fences of razor wire. They scuttled past security cameras with infrared beams and listened carefully to the baleful howl of a security dog before striking out across a car park.

The Keepers tried, as far as possible, to follow the line of the river (their only reference back to the locomotive). They could see taller and more user-friendly buildings on the horizon and determined that if help was to be had it was in that direction. They had no real idea what they were doing; they just hoped their luck would change. But they didn't have much optimism. In fact, they were beginning to wonder what they did have (apart from sore feet).

They entered a residential area and suddenly a hostile-looking figure with a shopping trolley ambled out of her house on the way to the shops.

"Aah!" they screamed and jumped over a privet hedge to hide.

The old woman went straight past without noticing and caught the 10.48 into town from the bus stop on the corner.

"That was a close one."

"What a horrible looking creature."

"And what strange offspring..."

"Do you think it was friendly?"

"It didn't attack us."

"It might have been blind."

"It might not have been hungry."

Just one street later a huge sign on the side of a building displayed a blood-stained seal on the pack ice of the North Pole. There was a Greenpeace message underneath that the Keepers assumed was not about giving sealions an even break. They flew into a panic. They were prepared to plead for their lives with the next pedestrian they saw, "We'll offer our wages," they said.

"But we don't get paid anything."

"Our shovels then…"

"They're not ours."

"We'll give them our record collection."

There was a pause, "All of them?"

"Just the ones we don't like…"

However, nobody was taking much notice of them; people walking down the street had better things on their minds. There were groceries to buy and gossip to exchange. Those that noticed the Keepers assumed they were some kind of environmental protest rather than tasty snacks to be hunted down.

"They don't seem to be very interested in us," they agreed.

"What was the point of that poster if they don't want to eat us?"

"Perhaps they've changed their minds…"

"Let's hope they don't change them back then."

When they arrived in the centre of the city, the Keepers discovered it was not so bad after all and very soon they were forgetting their hunger and paying more attention to the sights and people around them. In particular they enjoyed the street performers and their wandering clientele.

They soon began to attract a crowd of their own.

There was an air of expectation that seemed to require some sort of performance. As understudies to a dog act and not wishing to be impolite, they brought their feeble talents into the open. They balanced a few items on their noses; objects like vegetables borrowed from the audience, cans and other rubbish picked out of the litterbin and of course, each other. The crowd seemed pleased and, in time-honoured tradition, threw all their inconvenient small change at the Keepers, which they gratefully picked up.

"We seem to have quite a bit," they agreed.

"Enough for something to eat…?"

"I'm so hungry I could eat anything."

"Even one of those turds from that stall over there…?" A hotdog stand steamed gently in the light breeze.

"Even one of those," they said.

They bought hotdogs. They were just as bad as the Keepers expected but at least they were not hungry anymore.

They put on a few more shows and were soon earning a decent wage. Their chief advantage over the opposition was not their circus experience or the shaky pyramids they made, but the realistic nature of their costumes. To all and sundry they were a group of actors cleverly disguised.

Whispers could be heard among the crowd, "Are they really sealions?"

"They must be hot in those things."

"Where's the zip?"

The end result of a day of performances was enough money to buy a few necessities such as rubber balls, toy cars and fluffy animals that did nothing to enhance their act but did comfort them when it began to rain again.

The other street performers were not so appreciative of the Keepers' talents. A troupe of Bolivian folk musicians was complaining bitterly, "Dees funny men are doing their act to our music and taking da money. Heh, funny men, give us da money!"

The Keepers understood nothing.

Miguel, the lead panpipe player, started waving his arms about and slapping the palm of his hand to indicate payment. The Keepers waved back.

"Da money, give it to us!" He slapped a little harder.

The Keepers gave the sign for galactic oneness and harmony: the raised middle digit.

The leader of the Bolivians went purple, "I'll kill dem!"

"No! Miguel, Miguel, you'll get us into the trouble…"

"I kill them, I cut off their cojones!"

A small fight took place between Miguel and his troupe, "Let me go, I kill them!"

In the scuffle, the Keepers disappeared. When the police arrived the folk musicians were packing up angrily and going their separate ways, while the Keepers, with the money they had earned (and lots they had not) were having a ride on a bus and were a good mile away. The police, with nothing better to do, arrested the Bolivians anyway. As they were led away they kept repeating their story about 'little men' until the police lost patience.

"Little men is it sir?" said the sergeant. "Couldn't be we've been smuggling a few home comforts in among these peace pipes of yours?"

"No, we don't do drugs, we clean. We play da music of the Andes and we have a few drinks in the salon; it was da little men, the ones dressed like dogs-of-the-sea; they steal our money…"

"Very well sir, dogs-of-the-sea it is. Now what about this 'tobacco' we found on your pal here…?"

The bus ride was a novelty. The Keepers waved to passers-by and were generally friendly towards the grumpy conductor. "This is good," they agreed, "A mobile building."

"I wonder where the toilet is."

"On the floor by the look of it…"

When they finally got off they went in search of more food. The sushi bar looked inviting but even by their simple arithmetic they only had enough for a single course, and by pushing their faces up against the window and annoying the waiters, they could see the courses were too small for their present appetites.

Eventually they found a supermarket and managed to fill a trolley full of items without any bother at all. "This is great, regimented food," they said as they wandered up and down the aisles.

"How wonderful," they agreed.

Faces peered out from behind stacks of baked beans and wailing babies were momentarily hushed as the Keepers went past.

"Blow me," said a shelf-stacker, as the Keepers juggled bags of frozen peas to the great delight of a dozen small children. "Where do management get their ideas?"

The longer the Keepers played in the supermarket the more they were accepted by the shop's workers. "Great gimmick," said the girls at the cheese counter.

"It's good," agreed the butchers in the meat department. "But I'm glad it's them and not us. I wouldn't fancy dressing up like that, would you?"

"But you were an elf at Christmas…"

"I don't want to talk about it."

However, things began to go wrong at the fish counter. Thinking it was all a joke, the fishmonger tossed a fish at one of the Keepers who caught it in his mouth and swallowed it whole. The other Keepers lined up beside the first to receive their fish and when the fishmonger just stood there, horrified, they began to bark at him.

"Get security," said the fishmonger, beginning to realise the Keepers might not be men in disguise after all. He threw another fish just to be certain he had not imagined the first. "Oh my lord…" he said as the fish disappeared down another throat.

"What is it?" asked a junior manager in a tasteless brown suit.

"Watch this…" The fishmonger threw another fish.

"Free food," said the Keepers, "Yummy."

The junior manager looked appalled, "What will Health and Safety say?"

"I thought they were some kind of promotion…"

The junior manager shook his head, "Not today."

Another brown-suited manager appeared, drawn by the barking, "We can't have dogs in here…"

"They're not dogs," said the fishmonger. "Dogs don't eat fish."

The Keepers' barking was drawing another crowd and the fishmonger threw more fish to stop their noise. The children clapped and cheered but their parents were not as enthusiastic; the scene looked less than sanitary to them.

"I think it's time we left," said the Keepers, noticing several burly security guards trying to get through the shoppers.

"I expect they want us to pay for these fish."

"I thought they were free…"

"I'm not paying for free samples…"

"Then let's get out of here."

The police arrived minutes after the Keepers had dumped their change at a check-out and run off down the street. They had to endure another story of 'funny little men' from the supermarket's staff and several shoppers. There was so much confusion over whether the criminals were men, dogs or a variety of aquatic mammal, that the policemen soon grew exasperated.

"Well where are they?" they asked after trying and failing to get a definitive description.

"They bought some food and ran off."

"They didn't steal anything?"

"No."

The policemen put their notebooks away. "We'll be off then."

"But…"

"Yes, we know, 'they were funny little men'…"

"But they ate raw fish," said the fishmonger.

"So do the Japanese."

"They were barking like dogs," said an affronted woman in a pearl necklace. "Dogs shouldn't be allowed in the store, think of the children…"

"I want to see them again," said the children.

"Albino sealions, that's what they were," said an old man in a tweed suit. "If you lot hadn't taken my rifle away, I could have bagged the blighters by now."

The police backed out of the supermarket, "It must be the weather," said one to the other. "Last night it was trains falling out of the sky and now Japanese jugglers that bark like dogs…"

"I'm telling you, it did look like a train and it didn't crash, it came down gently like this…"

"Give it a rest George, there's a good chap."

13 - The Minds™

Wherever they found themselves on Earth, the four carriage Minds™ occupied their time in their own ways and without regard for the people who prodded and poked their outer defences. Even in the wider galaxy, they were often oblivious to what was going on around them and rarely engaged with mortal minds unless of course they wanted to submit some kind of complaint.

For example, "Take me to your leader," says the Mind™.

"Why?"

"I'm not happy."

"What are you unhappy about?"

"Your ancient tombs smell musty and old, your climate is too wet and I don't seem to be able to get my favourite show on my radio." Zlativan Minds™ do not make popular hotel guests and are rarely, if at all, invited back.

In the case of the two Minds™ that found themselves the object of local attention in Africa and China there was stunning indifference to the host nations. This was partly because Barnooli discouraged them from making contact with biological life-forms; the whole point of technology, he claimed, was to be seen and not heard, and preferably neither. But they were also suffering from 'other world' weariness; Barnooli had taken them to hundreds of different planets and they were all beginning to look the same.

There was also the fact that because Earth wasn't in any of the tourist guides, the Minds™ thought it was backward. The blame for this can be put on their makers who were terrible snobs and universally thought of as arrogant, arsy and affected. They had made their Minds™ in their own image.

They were all was as idiosyncratic as Stereo and their hobbies were usually just as inexplicable. Unlike the locomotive's Mind™, who couldn't bare his own company (or his own kind's either) most of them were fairly self-sufficient.

In Africa the Mind™ directed to care for the giant rabbits had abandoned his mechanical duties by simply opening the door and letting them go. This freed him to enjoy the esoteric pleasures of redecorating their erstwhile home and getting on with bits of other housekeeping and D.I.Y. as the fancy took him.

There was an injunction from Barnooli against the punters entering the carriages that the Mind™ was very willing to uphold. The Africans were shut out the moment they were detected; after all, it wouldn't do to have their dirty feet and dusty bodies tramping around on his clean carpets and putting their grubby fingers on his freshly painted woodwork.

Most of the carriage was taken up with the mystical gadgets of Bazmondo's magic act, but that didn't mean it had to look like a junkshop. There was now bold puce dado below pink plaster coving. The newly stippled ceiling in the workshop was awaiting its second coat of oranges and attractive floral motifs had been stencilled onto the power conduits. He was currently trying to decide between 'Masquerade' and 'Polka' for the wall colour in the corridor with perhaps 'Lupin' or 'Harvest Moon' for the picture rail and door architrave.

"Why should cupboard doors be plastic when you can have pine?" he told the other Minds™. "Why should loading ramps be dull when you can brighten them easily and cheaply with strips of wallpaper and pinking shears?"

Some Minds™ thought he was mad and went back to their model sailing ships and flower arranging without waiting to be shown what he could do with some two-by-four and half-a-dozen cup hooks.

Others thought he had bad taste; "'Hessian wall-weave'?"

"What's wrong with that?"

"In 'chocolate brown'...?"

"So?"

"It's a bit 'dark', don't you think?"

"What do you suggest? Something with a cowardly yellow stripe perhaps? Or 'white with a hint of sarcasm'? Or what about 'mind your own business blue'?"

"What about 'Magnolia'?"

"I'd rather die."

For the Mind™ in China it was painting of an entirely different nature. Rapture, like peace and quiet at three in the morning just after the person next door has turned his record player off, seized the Mind™ as she gazed out at the mountains that towered over the paddy field. The mists, the trees, and the exciting chunky shapes: here was all the balance and harmony of composition you could want. The Muse was with her and she intended to make the most of her company.

With her easel, smock and palette, she took the form (if not the talent) of an artist and left the carriage to swoon in the romance of it all. Mixing colours into an almost uniform grey, she swirled and swished to her heart's content, reproducing the forms in her own synthetic manner, carefully including the rustic village even while ignoring the villagers who lived there.

Her technique might have been more successful if her Muse had not been a ruler and a setsquare and there wasn't such a predisposition to see nature as untidy and chaotic and therefore ripe for reform. Even this might have been okay if she had intended to be a Cubist or had wanted to experiment in the style of Picasso, Chagall or Duchamp, but she aspired to the world of Monet, Renoir and Degas.

Pastel shades of grey mimicked the landscape in much the same way as a tower block resembles a nice place to live. Her trees were only semi-disguised fractal equations and her joyless mists were just experiments in Brownian motion. A passing art critic, casually looking over her be-smocked shoulder, might have likened her painting to several of Pollock's, but only as a pun.

A third Mind™ was also temporarily out of residence and was exploring the delights of Manhattan. He had disguised himself as a rather fat pigeon with the express aim of living rough with other pigeons. It was the sort of elitist and rather tasteless piece of roughing-it that normally ended with the aristocratic explorer being kicked to death by those whom he would emulate, but fortunately the pigeons could take a joke.

He had sat on the crown of Liberty, flown over the septic tank of the Bronx and was having a ball among the down-and-outs of Central Park.

He was like a nineteenth century explorer canoeing up the Zambezi; he presumed a natural superiority over the primitive tribesmen watching him from the banks and shops and made no effort to introduce himself or learn the language. When you can read and understand all the books in a library in just a few minutes, change your shape to any form or calculate how much personality it takes to run an airline, the day-to-day affairs of people who read cheap newspapers, eat spaghetti out of a tin and use abusive language every time they get into a car, will consistently discourage any kind of effort to be sociable.

In the early days Minds™ had often tried to give the local leadership the benefit of their superior intelligence, a move that had led to a number of altercations involving more bad language until eventually, Barnooli had to say, "If you ever tell an emperor, a king or a president that he doesn't, 'statistically speaking', stand a chance of making it to his fiftieth birthday before he's been assassinated, robbed, deposed or put in a museum and that he 'ought to do a runner now before the excrement hits the ventilator'; I shall thread you onto a pole and use you as an abacus."

The Smog Monster's carriage Mind™ had taken up marine biology. After a few false alarms when he mistook a couple of trawlers for impressively armoured sea creatures, he had come to the conclusion there was nothing much of interest close to the shore and had moved to deeper waters in search of undersea volcanoes.

He had regretted the failure of the door mechanism (that allowed the Smog Monster to escape) about as much as anyone would regret losing a large, clumsy, smoking reptile, which is to say not at all. He had almost wholly forgotten there had ever been a Smog Monster.

Neither did he have any intention of sharing the information he was gathering; it was far too precious. Like Royal heirlooms, each item was stowed away in his private vault and he was quite content to presume they would never see the light of day. All that oil he had discovered, for instance, might have rebuilt the economies of several countries but what was that to him? It was his knowledge now and nobody else's business but his.

All the Earth-bound Minds™ had comfortably forgotten their responsibilities to the circus; they were content to live with the paradox of being on a planet but not together and not busy setting up for another performance.

If they thought about their situation at all they assumed there had been a mistake that would soon be rectified by Barnooli. None of them bothered to enquire whether Barnooli was coming or not; that was an academic question far beneath their present interests.

14 - The Keepers

Back at the locomotive, in the peace and security of the cabin, the Keepers ate their un-plundered gains. A bag of jelly babies went down well, as did the frozen fish fingers, washed down with a couple of pints of cooking oil. The shoe polish wasn't quite so good and the bottle of carpet cleaner made them feel sick, but on the whole they decided they had never had such a good meal and concluded that the blue planet must be a land of plenty.

Then they settled down to sleep. The carpet cleaner gave them nightmares. They tossed and turned while the crushed and indistinguishable bodies of various acts lay mangled in their dreaming minds. Pointy-party-hats floated on pools of cooking oil and a big ticking clock, which looked like Barnooli, reminded them of the last orders they had received...

'Look after the animals!' boomed the clock.

'Touch nothing!' said a twig that turned into Ted.

'Keep you hands off Auto Pilot™!'

'Remember, touch nothing!'

Red wine danced over the precious controls before toppling over and sloshing though the cabin in a tidal wave of headaches. Five suitcases sat in a hall with a deflated beach ball.

The Hydro Monster blew his nose and wiped his eyes next to the unmoving form of the Smog Monster. There was a big watery hole in the middle of his hanky.

A funeral hearse bore wreaths to the memory of the 'Greatest Show in the Galaxy' and a formerly famously fat man was as thin as a rake. A tiny thin woman was following in his wake.

The Polar Pelicans sang a lament for the forlorn remains of their dead comrades. The band was missing its brass section and the strings were sadly plucked.

The Keepers woke up when the clock reached the hour and a gong sounded and a voice like Barnooli's boomed from the depths of a theatrical hell, 'can you take the extra responsibility?' and five small heads nodded brightly. But their mother said 'no'...

"What a nightmare," said the Keepers, shivering with the memories.

"I feel dreadful."

"So do I," said four times.

"Fancy mother not sticking up for us like that?"
"Awful."
"Do you think the dream was trying to tell us something?"
"About funerals perhaps…?"
"Ours…?"
"Probably…"
"Maybe…"
"What about the animals, should we organise a funeral for them?"
"Is that what the dream meant?"

They didn't like to think about the animals; they had liked the animals, even the double-trunked elephant that had nearly killed them, so they thought about their prospects for the future instead. But they were not that much better. It seemed a safe bet that their party was entirely to blame for the fate of the Great Barnooli's circus and as such the penalty was going to be awesome.

"I expect we'll get told off."
"Or worse…"
"Flogged…"
"Beaten?"
"We'll be chopped into pieces."
"And then stamped on…"
"And then put in a blender and fed to the…"
"Oh dear, we've killed the Great Lion of Azaroth…"
"Maybe we'll just get the sack, after all, we didn't mean any harm…"

The litter of party comestibles and paper artefacts rather conspired against that particular line of reasoning; if anyone was holding a smoking gun it was definitely they.

"But isn't each carriage capable of landing itself?" one asked hopefully.

"Could be…"
"What about when the circus forms?"
"What about it?"
"Don't the carriages come apart for that?"

They had to agree that the carriages certainly did come apart and move about, but that was normally on the ground where the laws of train locomotion were probably different.

"Perhaps the carriages can save themselves even from a great height? You know, like parachutes opening or balloons…?"

They agreed; that was possible, "Good point, well made."

"So it's possible that the animals are still alive?"

"Not squished?"

"Not mangled?"

"And we won't have to bury them?"

"No."

"That's good, I hate funerals; they're really depressing."

"Remember when Uncle Bop was lost at sea?"

"And we spent all that time pretending to be really upset when in fact we were quite pleased because Auntie was going to give us his entire record collection?"

"And when we got home all the records were really awful?"

"I remember. See, funerals really are depressing. I'm glad we won't have to have any for the animals."

Then a new thought struck them, "If they're not dead we should go out and find them and bring them here."

"Yes, find them!"

"And then Barnooli will be pleased with us."

"Probably give us a medal."

"From his own chest…"

Excitement bubbled up in their naïve imaginations like boiling milk pouring uncontrollably over the lip of a saucepan, "We'll search the four corners of the globe!"

"We'll leave no rock unrolled, no moss ungathered!"

"We'll find all the animals and put the circus back together!"

Then one of them put his paw on a key problem, "But how long will it take to explore the whole of this world?"

"It looked quite small the other night."

"Seems to be a lot bigger down here though…"

"It took us ages just to get to the centre of this city, think how much longer it will take if there is more than one?"

"Maybe we can catch another house-on-wheels?"

"Or one of their flying machines…?"

"Have we got enough money?"

Then they remembered they had left all their bronze coins on the counter at the supermarket, "Looks like we're walking guys."

"Bums," they all agreed.

"Still, maybe this planet isn't so big as it seems?"

15 - The locomotive's Mind™

The locomotive's Mind™ knew how big the Earth was. He knew exactly. While Stereo pursued his own hobbies, the locomotive's Mind™, like a bored schoolboy skimming rocks off a lake, had been bouncing radio waves off all and sundry.

He knew where the moon was, he knew about the satellites in orbit; he even knew the geology beneath him and had made various interesting discoveries that a good number of geologists would have sold their Geiger counters for.

He even knew the status of the circus animals.

He said to himself that he was bored, but in fact he was very depressed. The horrid pleasure cruisers still didn't want to talk.

He was on the verge of suicidal collapse when he bounced a radio wave off a telecommunications dish and by a quirk of fate accessed a helpline that seemed specifically designed for his kind of nonsensical rambling. It took a few moments to get the hang of the language and then he was in full swing...

"I really don't know what to do; I just don't have any friends."

"I'm sorry to hear that," said the patient voice at the other end.

"I don't know what it is, I try, I really try, but after a while I just seem to be going nowhere and I get all depressed."

"What about...? Anything specific on your mind...?"

"I don't know, I do my job well but nobody seems to appreciate me."

"What do you do?"

"I drive a train."

The Samaritan at the other end of the help-line blanched slightly. A train...? "That sounds like a very responsible job," she managed to say.

"It is, only the other day there was a big cock-up and it was only me who averted disaster. I saved the situation, I took over and nobody was hurt. But do I get any thanks? No I don't!"

"Was there an enquiry? Did you manage to tell the authorities about what you had done?" A noteworthy tremor had crept into her voice.

"Oh they knew about it," replied the Mind™, "they caused it."

"Who did?" she asked in a somewhat untherapeutic fashion.

"I don't know; some bunch of idiots the boss left in charge. Can't get the staff these days..."

"It was lucky you were there to take over."

"It certainly was."

"You sound very good at your job."

"I am," he agreed, puffing out his metaphorical chest like a cockerel standing on the roof of his henhouse.

"I'm sure people do appreciate you, it's just that they might find those feelings difficult to express."

"You think so?"

"What do you think?"

"They don't say anything..."

"They must rely on you a great deal."

"Yes, you could be right... It's very ignorant of them though, not saying even the smallest 'thank you' or anything, after all I've done..." he sighed.

"That's no reflection on you though, is it?" said the Samaritan. "You've obviously done an excellent job."

"Yes, but maybe I won't bother next time!" Suddenly he felt angry for a whole host of paranoid reasons. If they hated him so much he could certainly show how much he could hate them back; "Maybe I'll leave them to sort the problems out, see if they can drive the train. Ha! That'll show the dog-faced comet-artists a thing or two!"

"No!" faltered the Samaritan. "You wouldn't want to do that..." She started signalling for help from her colleagues who left their callers hanging to come over and listen.

"...Driving a train is a specialised job," said the locomotive's Mind™, "not just anybody can do it and I can prove it..."

"Yes, yes you could," sweated the Samaritan, "you have that power..."

"I certainly do: see if they like being left on their own like I've been. I'm really hurt. 'Do this, do that', they say, never a kind word, never a 'how are you today?' just like I don't matter. Selfish; that's what it is... They're all selfish and don't care about anything or anybody except getting to where they want to go and 'having a good time'. Well, we can all play that game..."

"In the heat of the moment we can all make mistakes..."

The cluster of Samaritans gathered around the telephone looked at each other, "A suicidal train driver?" they whispered.

One of them picked up a phone to ring the railway company, another was asking, "But what about confidentiality, we can't go telling the world about a client's personal problems, it's not ethical..."

"Bugger ethics," one exclaimed. "If I was going to get onto a train driven by a guy three pigeons short of a pie I'd want somebody to stop me, wouldn't you?"

The locomotive's Mind™ rambled on, "...Mistakes! Ha! Sometimes I think they deliberately cock things up just so they can have a good laugh. I saw them the other day, drunk as double-headed daffodils with extra large trumpets, and they'd been left in charge! Ha! I'm just the driver; I don't count! I take the responsibility of the whole train on my shoulders and they don't even bother to say 'thank you'. I mean, after all I've done!"

"Yes... Yes..."

"I don't have to stop do I?"

"Sorry?"

"They tell me to and I do, but I don't have to, do I?"

Another Samaritan was telephoning the police, "We don't know," he was saying, "We can't trace the call; London area we think. No, it could be an Underground driver but there's been no mention of the kind of train he drives. Yes, it would be worse if it was a high speed inter-city train..."

"...You must be hurting a great deal," said the Mind's™ councillor.

"Too right..."

"But you mustn't think you're worthless just because you're unhappy."

"I don't."

"I can tell you care a great deal about your job, it doesn't matter what other people think."

"I do. I don't. But..."

"Yes?"

"I just get so brassed-off with them."

He sounded like a pensioner whose grandchildren never visit. The Samaritan almost felt sorry for him. "I'm sure you do, but that's what we're here for, to listen to you..."

"I don't usually talk about this sort of thing to anyone." His mood seemed to change suddenly.

"I'm sure you don't," consoled the Samaritan.

"You've been very kind."

"We're always here if you need us."

"That's good."

"But you won't do anything silly will you?"

The locomotive's Mind™ thought about this, "Silly?"

The Samaritans winced, "He'll top himself for sure if he thinks he's being strung along…"

"I mean, it's better to talk about your problems and get them out in the open."

"Oh… You mean not crash the train?"

"Um… Yes."

"I could if I wanted to."

"I know. We all know…"

Certainly the other Samaritans knew and were already reviewing their travel arrangements with undisguised selfishness. "Anyone got a bus timetable?"

"…Well, maybe."

"Maybe…?"

"I don't feel as bad as I did…"

"Thank god for that," they muttered, still wondering how much a taxi would cost to the Home Counties.

"…But I might later."

"Well ring again, you don't have to hold onto all these feelings yourself; we're here to help you…"

16 - Africa

A convoy of expensive land-cruisers wound their way across the African scenery like a white worm. On board was a film crew, some well-meaning celebrities armed with good intentions and a dozen guards armed with machine guns. A woman named Mary Smith was in charge. She had given up a good career in advertising to save the children and knew a disaster when she saw one. As they pulled up at the African village with milk powder and blankets, not only did the villagers show a surprising amount of health and vitality for a people on the verge of starving, but they were showing off a wardrobe of new clothes as well. They barely needed saving at all.

"What's going on?" she asked the Head Man.

"Welcome to our village, a miracle has happened; God has sent his own aid to relieve our suffering."

"We've brought some milk powder," she said helpfully.

"How nice of you..."

"And blankets..."

"Very appreciated, but as you can see, we're doing very well on our own, thank you. Unless…"

"Yes?"

"Did you bring any hot sauce?"

"No, I'm afraid not."

"Or mustard…?"

"I don't think so, just milk powder."

"Oh never mind, it was just a thought. Perhaps you would like to share some of our good fortune?"

"What the blazes are those?" said one of the celebrities, pointing to a herd of giant rabbits sweeping majestically across the savannah.

"They are God's gift."

"But what are they?" asked Smith.

"How should we know? God didn't put labels on them."

"How did they get here then?"

"He sent them in that box over there…"

They peered through the heat haze and the dust thrown up by the rabbits. About a mile away, standing like an ancient acropolis against the setting sun, they spotted the carriage. Through their binoculars, they could see it was very glossy and very alien, rather like the celebrities themselves. At first, they were inclined towards thinking it was a mirage but when it solidly refused to disappear they began to wonder how it might help their careers.

Stunned, but realising the rabbits and the carriage were obviously 'not of this world', Mary Smith turned back towards the Head Man. The Africans seemed very happy and it seemed a shame to burst their bubble. "But you're eating a scientifically unclassified animal of possible extra-terrestrial origin," she said. "You can't eat them."

"I assure we can, it's very easy; they hardly need hunting at all."

"But they're very important..."

"Yes, they are," agreed the Head Man, "And very delicious too."

"If they've come from another planet then think about what we could learn from them..."

"Another planet...?"

She pointed up towards the sky, "Aliens," she said.

"I suppose that is another way of looking at them," agreed the Head Man tentatively. "But we like the 'God' theory a lot better. Makes more sense if you think about it; Moses received manna from heaven and Jesus fed thousands with a few loaves and fishes. We like to think this is God's way of apologising for all the inconvenience we were suffering before these creatures gave us back our lives. We were thinking of building an altar and perhaps making a ritual out of eating them, but we couldn't decide if that was tempting providence or not, so we haven't bothered."

She tried to appeal to his faith: "How do you know you're meant to eat them; God might have wanted you to look after them, not butcher them and stuff your faces...?"

"They taste pretty good, I can't see why he'd give us something this tasty and then tell us we can't eat it. That doesn't make any sense."

Smith thought about the Garden of Eden and its infamous tree but didn't think theological wrangling was going to help much. She tried a different tack: "But how do you know the meat is safe?"

"Do we look ill?"

"No, but..."

"But nothing," said the Head Man, beginning to realise the shifts in Smith's thinking were probably going to end with a lot of moralising. "We were starving and they taste great, just like beef; we were cold and their pelts make excellent coats. We needed shelter and now we have tents. We have discovered that their horns, when ground to a powder, make excellent aphrodisiacs (much better than rhino horn and a lot easier to catch as well). The animals came along and now we're having a really good time, thank you very much. Now go away if the idea of us not starving offends you so much."

"What about the milk powder, we've come a long way to bring you this," said a celebrity peevishly.

"Very kind I'm sure. You eat the milk powder and we'll get on with our stew, thanks."

"All right," said Smith. "But you realise we're going to have to tell the world about this."

"Go ahead, see if we care."

The camera crew had already set up their equipment and were filming the giant rabbits for the benefit of posterity. They had been prepared for visions of biblical hell and were pleased with the change in fortunes. Less prissy about the origins of the species hopping abundantly across the scene, they were looking forward to trying some for dinner. "Better than those meal packs we brought with us," they agreed.

Seeing the cameras beginning to roll, the celebrities flocked towards them. The Africans went back to their village and began singing hymns. Mary was left on her own. She phoned her masters. Carefully avoiding words that sounded like science fiction, she described what she had found. Luckily, the live feed from the camera crew via their satellite uplink helped dispel any sense of hyperbole. Then she put up her tent and waited for the world to react.

The next morning, a dozen helicopters carrying a pickle of conservationists descended on the village like Valkyries, all cameras and Doctoral faeces. In portentous tones they proclaimed the animals to be indirectly related to rodents and argued over Latin declensions before sitting down to lunch with the elders of the village. The convivial meal soon turned to recrimination when it was realised that they were eating a pot roast of the subjects in their new study. Unscientific screams echoed around the camp; "How could you? These are the greatest finds since coelacanths were rediscovered!"

"Good aren't they?" agreed the camera crew.

"But we're violating an animal of enormous potential to science; we're devouring the very essence of our life's work!"

"Oh lighten up; we won't tell if you won't."

An American scientist asked the Africans for one of the rabbits on behalf of his President. When he was asked how much he was going to offer for one, he was rather taken aback. "Pay?" he said, surprised, finding it difficult to accept the concept of paying Africans something for anything.

"Yes," said the Head Man.

"Nothing; these are creatures of scientific interest that should be studied and not used for profit."

"That's as maybe in your country, but we do things differently here," and the Africans picked up their ancestral spears and pointed them threateningly at the scientist.

"A hundred dollars sound okay to you?" said the American.

"A hundred dollars…?"

"Each?"

"And your baseball cap?"

"Um, okay, that seems fair…"

If the Americans were going to buy one, other nations demanded the same. The scramble for Africa began anew.

Every broadcasting company in the world wanted pictures of the rabbits. The scientists could argue all they liked about what to do with them, what they were and why Africans shouldn't eat them, but all the public wanted was an eyeful of what the fuss was about. They had seen the Trapezium Monkeys and now they wanted Giant Rabbits.

The world watched eagerly as the news from Africa unfolded, live, on prime time television for some and before the watershed for others; and what should civilised or under-aged eyes be treated to but raw nature going for it in a field…

It was rutting hour and the rabbits didn't hold back.

Switchboards across the world jammed like a motorway junction on a Bank Holiday. A few monkeys flying about New York had been harmless fun, but this, this was downright pornographic. Everyone wanted to complain.

Stunned producers and thoroughly embarrassed live reporters began to apportion blame, most of which fell on the heads of the Africans to whom the rabbits apparently belonged.

The scientists and politicians began talking about confiscating the alien creatures, not just for the greater well-being of science but more particularly, for public morality. Churches prayed for guidance. The Head Man's assertion the rabbits had been sent by God was widely condemned as heresy; no way could God have created such vile fornicators. God's creatures just didn't do that kind of thing.

Wisely, and without any fuss, the Africans hid half a dozen of their rabbits while the scientists were still building their stockade. They were determined more than ever to eat and be happy rather than starve and be pitied just to please a bunch of arrogant and ungrateful foreigners.

17 - London

"East?" one Keeper said.

"West...?"

"South...?"

"No, I'm sure the sun comes up in the North..."

They were trying to put together a plan based on where the sun rose so they could get the maximum amount of light for their search. They had already spent an hour in rigorous debate.

"If we set off into the sun it'll be dark sooner than if we walk with it..."

The locomotive's Mind™ looked at them scornfully, "Chattering pellets," he grumbled. "Why don't they go away and leave me alone?"

A few minutes later, having decided to do a random search, Keepers got up and left the train, just as the Locomotive's Mind™ had requested. He couldn't believe it, "The ungrateful little piscivors," he wailed. "That's right; you just walk off and leave me alone as well! No, really, I don't mind, I mean, Auto Pilot™ has gone; that fastidious snow-globe, Stereo, has gone, so you might as well go too. And don't come back!" Just to make sure they wouldn't, he locked the door behind them. "See if I care. I don't need you. I don't need anyone."

His complaints might have had more effect if he had said them out loud but the Keepers heard nothing. They marched off through the docks whistling a happy tune and left the Mind™ to his misery.

They made their way back into London and more by luck than judgement, discovered Regent's Park and its zoo. It was reasonable to assume that any animals recovered from the circus might end up in such a place.

The bored teenager in the ticket booth saw the Keepers and assumed they were there to promote the sealion exhibition for their partner zoo at Whipsnade. She let them through without comment.

The Keepers enjoyed the zoo. The smells were familiar even if the animals looked quite strange. None of the fish in the aquaria could fly and the owls wouldn't tell them where the sun came up.

When they saw a uniformed keeper scooping up elephant poo with a shovel they smiled wry smiles, "Just like the circus," they agreed, and then felt a bit sad.

When they entered the monkey house, they were amazed. "Gosh," they said. "Fancy putting your elderly relatives in a cage..."

"They must be really cruel."

"Just like that poster with the dead person who looked like us."

They all nodded, "Grim."

"Awful. What a terrible race."

"Pretty agile for old people though, look." The monkeys were swinging from ropes and running up the trees.

"Our granny can't even raise her voice let alone haul herself around the room like that."

The zoo's lion was a big disappointment, "It's so small and puny," they said. Their lion, the Great Lion of Azaroth, had to contend with vast reptiles with more teeth than the clockwork spinning around Big Ben. This one looked incapable of taking on a sundial.

"And so mangy," they said. Their lion had a mane of fire and eyes like sapphires.

"At least he did have," they said. "Before we killed him…"

"I don't think stealing this one and giving him to Barnooli will get us out of trouble."

They shook their heads, "I think he'd notice."

The Keepers were not impressed by the pelicans either. The jolly waddle and the hopping about were okay, but the squawking sounded awful. "Can't sing very well, can they?"

"No, and they're not very well dressed either."

"Look!" the others cried. They had found some giraffes.

"Bit short," they commented.

"They're a funny colour too."

They stared at the giraffes, thinking about how majestic their giraffes used to be, how they paraded around the arena as part of Barnooli's wonderful collection of beautiful oddities from around the galaxy. The giraffes on Earth stared back and thought about the leaves on the trees they could see on the edge of the park.

18 - China

As the Keepers looked at the giraffes in London, their black and white facsimile in China was still thinking about the lack of Bee-Bee trees while the rice growers below worried about what their government was going to say concerning her sudden appearance.

After twenty-four hours of bureaucratic whispering and silk gathering, two members of the Red Army turned up with orders to arrest a zoology student over six feet tall. It didn't take them long to discover no student, nobody to arrest and a sixty-foot giraffe eating rice leaves from a basket on a bamboo pole.

Confused by these new circumstances, the two representatives of the mighty Chinese Army retreated quickly to the shelter of a neighbouring veranda where the chief rice picker, his son and his extended family, greeted the two soldiers respectfully but without enthusiasm.

To their surprise, these worldly soldiers (whom the villagers assumed had seen such things many times before) seemed rather agitated by the giraffe outside, even though they, the villagers, were quite used to it by now. The soldiers had drawn their pistols and there was a rather 'farty' smell in the air.

"It does not bite," promised the chief rice picker.

The soldiers peered out at the giraffe and muttered to each other. Then one of them demanded. "Do you have a permit to keep such a thing?"

"A permit...? No."

"You need a permit."

"We do?"

"Yes."

"But it's not ours, I mean, we're not keeping it."

"Is that not your rice paddy?"

"Well, yes."

"Then you need a permit."

"But we thought it belonged to the State Circus."

"Pah!" snorted the soldiers, knowing they were on safe ground. "We have seen the circus many times and never have we seen such a creature. You must be lying."

"Lying? Whatever for?"

"Personal gain."

"We did not ask the creature to be here, it just appeared, like a circus trick."

"And you are not going to keep it?"

"No, we don't want it; what are we going to do with a sixty-foot giraffe? We can't ride it, we can't even get on its back and if we did and we fell off we'd break our necks…"

"But is that not your rice you are feeding it?"

"It was hungry…"

"Then you intend to keep it?"

"No!"

"Then what are you going to do with it?"

"We don't know; that's why we called for you."

The soldiers raised their eyebrows and tried to look as though they were not receiving platitudes. Then one of them said, "And what are we supposed to do about it?"

"Couldn't you take it away?"

"We have no orders, what would our superiors say?"

The chief rice picker shrugged his shoulders, not his problem he wanted to tell them, but didn't dare. He sighed and wished the giraffe would just evaporate.

Seeing his elderly father in a fix brought out a few crumbs of compassion from his middle-aged son. "Might I make a suggestion?" he enquired formally.

The two soldiers looked at one another and then nodded to the son. The son smiled ingratiatingly and said, "What creature?" He made expansive gestures with his arms.

"What creature…?" began one of the soldiers, but the second stopped him; this was devious cunning on a military scale, "Yes, 'what creature'?"

They stepped to one side and began whispering, "We came here to find subversives," said the second soldier.

"Yes," agreed the other.

"And we have found none."

"No…"

The yen dropped. They began nodding. It was a simple solution: no creature, no problem, and so no paperwork.

"So your village has not been harbouring dissident students?" they asked, turning back to the gathering.

"No students here," they all agreed.

"Nobody has seen anything 'funny'?" the soldiers asked, eyeing the villagers narrowly.

"None," the villagers answered. A sixty-foot giraffe wasn't terribly funny at the best of times. Graceful yes, quite good-natured as well, but it hadn't shown any obvious signs of humour; hadn't told any jokes or tried singing tasteless songs.

"And there is nothing else to report that would interest our superiors?"

They shook their heads, even the ones holding the pole with the basket of rice from which the now bureaucratically invisible giraffe was still eating.

"Good, carry on then." The two stalwart members of the Red Army returned to their home base with the satisfying news that there was no rebellion in the Provinces, only complete loyalty and a request that the State Circus visit.

It seemed like a happy compromise and certainly the Giant Giraffe was none the worse for it. She carried on eating rice and the villagers went about their business tacitly ignoring her. Only the children had anything to say on the matter, but this was put down to the fantasies of the only child and could easily be ignored.

19 - The Keepers

Back in the zoo, the Keepers were beginning to attract attention. They had stopped opposite the penguin pond just as they were being fed. The Earthly keeper looked up from giving his lovelies a few nice bits of haddock and saw five white sealions looking down on him with expectant looks on their faces. "Ooo my good gowd!" he exclaimed. He narrowly avoided falling into the green and slimy pond, tripped over his bucket instead and instantly disappeared under a wave of penguins as they dashed for their supper.

The Keepers watched on, amused by this little display. "I wonder if he does this every day?" they asked other.

"It must be very tiring."

They went and sat down, oblivious to the shouts and screams of the penguin keeper who was trying to fend off flippers and fishy breaths for all he was worth. Other people, drawn by the screaming, stopped in their tracks when they saw the Keepers sitting close-by; had these ones escaped? Was this what all the screaming was about?

The Keepers, ever willing to oblige an audience, began to perform a few tricks to persuade them to part with some of their money so they could go and buy a few pieces of the fish they had seen. The visitors, alarmed by these new activities, did indeed part with their money, and their purses and whatever else they felt it was better to leave behind rather than hinder their escape.

"Funny," said the Keepers. "That's not happened before."

Then real keepers arrived. They didn't look at all like they wanted to be entertained. One of them held up a big syringe, another a gun with a dart the size of jumbo fish finger, and a third obviously wanted to throttle them with a piece of washing line.

"This seems like a good moment to leave," they agreed, dropping the odds and ends they had been using to juggle with.

"Yes, and run like the clappers for the exit!"

One set of keepers began to chase the other. Despite their short legs and arms, on all fours Barnooli's Keepers were surprisingly fast. Darts whistled through the air and a large German tourist was hit in the buttocks, but the Keepers kept running. They wove their way through the crowd causing alarm and chaos. Ice creams plopped on the ground and balloons were set free. At the gates, the bored teenager was still trying to work out how to shut them when the Keepers leapt over the turnstiles.

"Stop them!" shouted the zoo's keepers. But it was too late.

The five white sealions ran off down the road.

20 - Scotland

Two brothers from London had made the long journey to Scotland in the hope of excitement and adventure. Eric and Chris Watts had packed their gear and taken a boat to the island early that morning. Still a little hung-over from an excess of Scotch the previous night, they had walked across the island and were now harnessing up in preparation for their decent of the cliff below them and the slow climb back to the top. Underneath the cliff, the Smog Monster was blissfully unaware of their presence.

The two merchant bankers were keen climbers and professional men; dangling from spindly ropes in precarious situations was their idea of fun. It was a similar wanton lack of self-preservation that strapped them to kites and propelled them from hilltops or covered them in the white froth of fierce rapids. They had attached themselves to pieces of elastic and jumped from high bridges and thrown themselves from perfectly good aeroplanes to fall to earth under colourful mushrooms of silky cloth; fear seemed to compensate them for the guilt they might have felt for earning indecent sums of money, wearing expensive aftershave and driving fast cars.

They had come to Scotland on the assumption that they were doing it a favour. They had flashed their gold watches in the small bar of the hotel, had boasted of the enormous amount of petrol their cars used and had offered to buy the village with their platinum credit cards. None of this had done much for Anglo-Scots relations except to remind the latter of Bannockburn.

Had they not been so full of whisky and bovine excrement the two Sassenachs might have noticed a certain hardening of attitudes towards them. They kicked up a fuss when then their change came back with 'Bank of Scotland' written on it (currency they judged to be on a par with the paper notes of a certain board game). There was also a nasty altercation on the subject of porridge. And another on Robert Burns whom the Watts brothers considered the worst poet to have ever put quill to paper. Eric mocked the small piece of needlecraft framed on the wall of the hotel bar: "'O, my luve's like a red, red rose that's newly sprung in spring, O, my luve's like a melodie, that's sweetly played in tune.'"

"What a load of old tosh," agreed Chris.

The Scotsmen and women glared at the invaders and race memories of claymores and rolling heads flooded back to them. "If I could git ma dirk between the ribs of these two sons o' the deeil..." said a salty sea-dog at the bar.

"Aye, and see their balls rolling in the heether," said another.

"The rude and ignorant Englishmen, it's just a wheen o' blethers..."

"Dinna fash yoursels; they wadna tak tellin'," said the harassed barmaid.

"Aye, bide awee, they'll be awar on the morrow," agreed the landlord.

Politics and politeness had never been of much use in the asset stripping game the brothers played for real in the bars of the City. They cheerfully insulted the entire Scots nation until they had driven the last codger from his place by the fire and even the cur dog had slunk off to its bed in the outhouse.

Even when they had the whole bar to themselves they didn't stop their tirade against their hosts, "I don't get it," said Eric. "It's only half past one and all the local buggers have buggered off. I thought these Scots had more stamina than that."

"Must be the company," muttered the barmaid.

"Too much for them, you reckon?" said Chris.

"Too much for me lads, I'm off to ma bed."

"Whaheyhey!"

"Now lads, you'll no be wantin' a knee in the grossarts, will ye?"

"Where...?"

"No, I thought not."

The next day, still ignorant of their rudeness, the Watts brothers remembered the evening fondly and talked happily of the barmaid, of the badly sprung beds and of the magnitude of their headaches. "I reckon she was just dying for a chance," said Eric.

"You could be right mate."

"I mean; who wouldn't?"

"I should say so."

"If I lived in a dump like this I'd do it."

"Same here, mate, same here..."

"I mean; who wouldn't want to live in London, it's the centre of the universe, innit?"

Chris nodded. His head felt leaden and another disadvantage with the Scottish Outback had just occurred to him: "There's nothing in the air is there? I mean if the air wasn't so empty I wouldn't have such a thumping headache, would I?"

They sat on the grass above the cliff with their climbing equipment dumped beside them, and had a cup of black coffee from a flask. The beautiful scenery meant as much to them as a Petrachan sonnet to a chimpanzee.

"I wish those birds would naff off," said Eric, looking up at the seagulls who were threatening to crap on their heads at any moment.

"Flamin' row," agreed his brother (both failing to notice the small peeping chicks in the nests scattered around them).

They finished their coffee. "Right, let's get weaving with the ropes."

The cave, with its organ pipes and legends, was set back under the cliff but they could just see a platform of rock at sea level onto which they could swing. The climb back to the top of the cliff was on their list of 'things to achieve before they were thirty' (along with owning a major company and sleeping with a certain number of girls).

The only other way to the cave was by sea and they had arranged with the fisherman who had brought them that if they were not back by a certain time he was to motor round the island and pick them up. Frankly, they had doubts that he would be able to remember such a simple request, "He hardly seemed able to speak a word of the Queen's English," said Chris.

"Oh I expect the bugger understood," replied Eric. "They're a cussed lot around here; just have to shout loudly and sue the old git if he turns up late."

However, they were not particularly worried if the old man had understood; they fully expected to meet him again where he had dropped them off that morning. They were used to getting their own way in all things and it never occurred to them that a problem might arise that they couldn't throw money at.

The ropes uncoiled themselves as they dropped over the top of the cliff and dangled reassuringly over the abyss. A few tugs confirmed the fastness of the lines and the two brothers clipped themselves on and prepared to descend. After shuffling about on the edge for a moment they bounced over the side and were soon speeding down the ropes like spiders dropping from the ceiling.

The Smog Monster heard shouting and woke up. He was unimpressed by the ropes dangling in front of his cave. He was even less impressed by the two whooping figures clinging to the said ropes and squeezed himself a little further into the dark recesses of his new home. He watched them closely, waited patiently for them to go back up the ropes, but in spite of them being entirely unwanted and unwelcome, the two figures kept coming. Thus, according to custom and training, he puffed himself up and blew a large cloud of thick black smoke at them.

The black smoke lubricated the ropes and both climbers whizzed down, missed dry land and dropped into the water with a satisfying plop. Feeling pleased with himself, the Smog Monster went back to sleep.

The merchant bankers were surprised and extremely shocked by the Smog Monster's performance. One moment everything was hunkey-dory, the next moment they were bobbing about in the water as black as coal miners. They were covered in a smooth film of black graphite, their ropes were now useless and neither had any idea of what had happened. Rational solutions seemed to be in abeyance.

"Bleedin' 'ell," gasped Eric.

"What 'appened...?"

"What is this?" Eric wiped his face and looked at his hand, "I'm covered in it!"

A black slick surrounded them like ink on blotting paper. "Must have been a cave-in," said Eric. "It blew us out into the sea as we went past the entrance."

"I'm so cold..."

"Let's get out of the water..."

They struggled up the slippery rocks and looked at the mouth of the cave. "This black stuff is everywhere," said Eric. "Like we struck oil..." Dollar signs temporarily blinded them to their predicament. "You reckon this is why they were so off with us last night? They didn't want us finding their stash?"

"Must be, mate, couldn't have been anything we said; we were just 'aving a laugh."

"It'd be a sweet deal; bet we could get preferences for next to nothin' and I bet they don't know their F.T. from E.T."

"Got to get off this effin island first..."

Their predicament came back to them like a bad investment. They shivered in silence for a while. They seemed a little short of options. Without the ropes they couldn't climb back up the cliff and the sea was too cold for swimming.

"We ought to build a fire," said Chris.

"What, and set off all this oil? Use your loaf."

"Then let's look in the cave..."

"Sure, I imagine it's just chocka with dry tinder and if we're lucky a big St Bernard will give us some brandy too."

"There might be some driftwood. Did you bring the flask?"

"Of course I didn't."

"What about the mobile...?"

Eric fumbled feverishly in his pockets for his mobile telephone that, because he had paid so much for, was water-proof, bullet-proof and had batteries that lasted longer than a gilt-edged company. Unfortunately it was not lack-of-signal-proof. They were too far from civilisation for it to work.

"Bugger," said Chris.

"I hate this place," said Eric, flinging his useless phone into the sea. "The only nets around here are for catching fish."

"We need to keep warm," said Chris. "We should keep moving, keep the circulation flowing..."

Eric didn't need much to keep his blood moving; all he had to do was think about tartan and bad rhymes for his face to go red and a stream of invective criticism to froth out of his mouth: "'Let's go to Scotland,'" he quoted. "'They're really friendly, we'll get a really good deal on the whisky and I saw this little village on the telly...' Now look at us! This coat cost a packet and my phone is picking up barnacles at the bottom of the sea!"

"Do you think the fisherman will come for us?" asked Chris.

Eric looked at him, "What do you think?"

Chris had to admit it was unlikely, "Do you think we paid him enough?"

"Not for chucking up in his boat we didn't."

"I couldn't help it; it was the smell of fish."

They shivered and looked out to sea; it was grey and empty and cold. No boat or ship or anything was in view. They looked back at the cave.

"Do you think we should shelter in there?"

"There might be another cave-in..."

"We'll get exposure if we sit out here."

"Tell me about it."

The waves lapped up against the rocks and a small, tantalising, flicker of sunlight nipped through the clouds and disappeared again. The brothers looked back at the cave. It was dark and rather forbidding given its recent performance.

"There's no putting this off," said Chris. "We'll have to see what's inside."

"But it's not safe."

"There might be a way up to the top of the cliff, a tunnel or steps..."

"Oh yeah, and a crock of gold and pirate treasure as well. Get real."

Chris looked back at the waves. "I'm sure that rock wasn't covered in water when we arrived, I think the tide's coming in..."

"All right, we'll try the sodding cave."

The Smog Monster heard footsteps and opened a sleepy eye. He was most put out to discover two tiny soggy black creatures advancing towards him in a menacing way. He could hear their voices and their disregard for his privacy.

Would they never learn?

The Smog Monster growled, much as a dog growls at an on-coming postman.

The Watts brothers froze. "What was that?"

"Don't know."

The growling increased. The Smog Monster raised his head and the light glinted in his ruby red eyes.

"What the...!"

"Run for it!"

The two brothers, slipping and sliding on the oily rocks, scrambled for the spurious safety of the sea. They jumped back into the water. Paddling wildly, they were a hundred yards from the shore before they slowed down.

"What was it?" gasped Eric.

"I don't know but it was big!"

The big Smog Monster roared and let out another puff of smoke. The last he saw of the scunner Englishmen was a distant whirl of arms disappearing around the headland. He closed his eyes and went back to sleep.

21 - The Keepers

"Look!"

"Bazmondo's Bunnies!" cried the Keepers.

They crowded around a shop window to get a better view of the screen. They were horrified to see so many giant rabbits running about the dry savannah of a foreign country. They were equally horrified to think that an Earthly audience might have seen what the rabbits normally got up to. On the other paw: "Survivors!" they cried.

"We must get two of them back!"

"But how...?"

"They're obviously not near here; look at all that sand and those funny people in the rabbit skins..."

Rabbit skins...?

They looked at one another, their faces falling, "What will Bazmondo say?"

"What'll happen when he finds out we let these people turn his act into over-coats?" They made slicing motions across their throats.

They watched the television again, ignoring the shop assistant who was trying to tell them to 'bugger off' when they refused to stop pressing their noses against the glass.

"We'll have to get two back so we can try and pretend none of the others happened..." There were sceptical looks all around; it was impossible to stop the rabbits from breeding once they had been taken off their strict diet of a particularly contraceptive bean.

The Keepers sighed, "But at least they're still alive."

The television showed an aeroplane landing at an airport and some rabbits being bundled into the back of it. Then the aircraft took off and there was a picture of an excited zoologist talking to an interviewer.

"I wonder what he's saying?" the Keepers asked.

"Do you think they're being brought here?"

"They must be, where else would they be taken?"

They had no idea there was more than one city on the Earth. Pinniped had no cities, not even a wet and fishy one, so consequently they were a little out of their depth. The circus had performed in many of the great metropolises of the constellation, some not so different from London, but the Keepers had always been kept too busy. Even 'off-duty' they had been afraid to stray too far in case Barnooli left without them.

They looked up at the sky. An aeroplane was heading towards Heathrow.

"There it is!" they said.

"Let's go!"

Having been on a bus they thought it would be fun to try a train. They were not disappointed, especially when they found a map with a symbol of an aeroplane on it. "This little train must be going to where the rabbits will be brought!" they said, with uncharacteristic logic.

"What a stroke of luck!"

They descended into the earth and after a false start that had them going in the wrong direction for half an hour, they caught the correct train and duly arrived at Terminal Four of Heathrow Airport.

An hour later and they would have been unable to use the trains at all.

The locomotive's Mind™ had suffered another anxiety attack, had rung the Samaritans who in turn rang the police. Out of consideration for the thousands of passengers using trains to get to work, explore the city or go shopping, the railway companies shut down all the networks. The city was paralysed.

The Samaritans were still trying to persuade him to stay in the train and not 'fly out of it', a puzzling concept but none-the-less rather worrying. "I shall just fly off and leave them to it," he kept saying.

A couch of psychologists had explanations for why he should want to 'fly' rather than 'walk' out. Some said he was obviously terribly bored and lonely and wanted to escape in the most exciting way possible. Others said it was metaphorical and meant he wanted to 'rise out of his life'. The rest thought he was a psycho with a bird fixation.

Nobody discovered the location or identity of the suicidal train driver in spite of the massive effort by the police and transport authorities to root him out from his branch line of despair. Hundreds of drivers were questioned and one or two were 'retired' just to be on the safe side. But though they found many who were miserable old gits, none of them seemed to desire more than an ordinary terminus.

Meanwhile, after several hours of wandering up and down Heathrow Airport (the wrong airport as it happened) and nearly being arrested for trying to stop an aeroplane to ask for directions, the Keepers were on the verge of giving up their search.

"Why don't we ask someone in that building over there?" one of them suggested, pointing to the brightly lit terminal. This seemed like a good idea even though they knew the pitfalls of trying to communicate with foreigners.

They picked on a policeman because he was standing around not seeming to be doing anything and because most of the other people had extravagant loads of luggage piled up on hostile-looking trolleys. He was quite used to being approached by clueless foreign nationals without a word of English and watched patiently as the Keepers ran about like aeroplanes or hopped like rabbits and then pointed to each other in the spirit of ownership. The policeman nodded without understanding and pointed to the Information Desk.

The airport staff, well versed in a number of languages, were treated to another display of mime but faired little better than the policeman until one of them, with a spark of intuition that nearly hit the mark, linked them with some newly imported frogs fresh out of the Amazon jungle, waiting in the quarantine area.

By the time the Keepers found the right place it was early evening and there was a depressing drizzle falling everywhere.

"Is this it?" they asked each another.

Various animal noises could be heard on the other side of the tall fence so they assumed that it was. "How do we get in?" was the next question.

"Is there a gate?"

There was but it was locked. "What will we do?"

"We'll have to climb over."

"Do you think we should?"

"Do you think Bazmondo will show us any mercy if we don't?"

"Good point, leg up anyone?"

As Airport Security Officer Hawkins drove up to the quarantine area in his cheap little van he saw the five circus characters stacked up against the fence in an obvious attempt to break in. "Blimey; loonies," he said. He stopped the car and pondered on whether he ought to approach the scene of the crime. He thought about walking over to the bottom of the Keeper pyramid and challenging them; saying something pithy and professional like 'what's going on here then?' but that seemed presumptive, not to say risky. There were five of them and even though they looked a little bit ridiculous they might be dangerous. He called for immediate assistance instead.

Within minutes a van-load of burly police and a fully armed anti-terrorist squad arrived on the scene and the offending circus characters were duly informed that they were surrounded and they should desist from their efforts to get over the fence.

Unfortunately, the Keepers, completely ignorant of police procedure, merely carried on with their struggles and indeed, within a very short time, were actually over the top and celebrating their conquest with aggressive punches into the air.

The police were a little put out, "Cocky little show-offs!" they said. "Load the guns."

There was a short debate on the legality of shooting the Keepers before any real trouble started. They took into account the fact that none of the Keepers seemed armed with more than a poor attitude and noted their general animal appearance, but that could be a trick, they thought.

The policemen without guns (but with the umbrellas) took the more reasonable view that this was some kind of Animal Rights protest and that shooting them might be counter-productive. Those with neither guns nor umbrellas were getting wet and cold and wanted to go home.

Airport Security Officer Hawkins sat in his van watching all this, "Good job I didn't approach them on my own," he said, opening his sandwich box and tucking into a tuna sandwich. "Looks serious..." It did cross his mind that the circus characters seemed rather short on guilt and seemed not to understand what the police were saying, but as this diminished his part in the affair he preferred to believe they were devious criminals who would stop at nothing to complete their nefarious mission.

In complete ignorance the Keepers carried on. They found another fence and more locked gates. They followed the line of the fence, dimly aware of dark shapes scuttling about behind them. They tried to listen for the rabbits.

"It's difficult to hear anything with that row going on," they said as a fire engine joined the party. "I wish they'd be quiet."

Searchlights swept across the compound.

"I wonder how the animals get any sleep."

The police tried to coax the Keepers out of the compound using their megaphones and promises not to shoot. The anti-terrorist squad were closing in on all sides.

The Keepers appeared on one side of a fence, then disappeared, then turned up again on the other side. They had reached the animal cages.

"I don't think they're here," they said. Most of the cages seemed to be empty. The searchlight swept across them. The giant rabbits ought to have been easy to spot but they could see nothing familiar.

The police stepped up their activities. They prepared to shoot any animal let out by the Keepers who were, beyond doubt, a terrorist group. The clatter of boots and jingle of ammunition echoed up and down the area to the accompaniment of dogs barking and parrots squawking.

Hawkins, enjoying every moment, ate his sandwiches in the warmth of his little van while the flashing lights and squad cars roared around him. Just as he was about to open his bag of crisps he saw the Keepers appear by a gate looking utterly shameless and brazen. The police like wolves falling upon sheep, swamped them and carried them away bodily to a van.

Ignoring the kicking and screaming, the police bundled the Keepers inside and whisked them off at light speed, sirens howling.

A few minutes later a reporter arrived, "See anything?" he asked Hawkins.

"There was a break in."

"Oh yes? Who by...?"

"Sealions."

"Do what?"

"Guys in white sealion suits, animal activists I should think (always getting them around here)."

"Really?" The reporter began to lose interest; there was a hole in his shoe and his foot was getting wet. There was also a rumour of a film star flying in from New York that would make better copy than a bunch of animal lovers disguised as aquatic sea life climbing over a fence.

"The police had loads of guns," added Hawkins, hopefully.

"Don't they always," said the reporter. For form's sake he took down all the details and concocted a police brutality story in case he missed the film star.

22 - Stereo

Stereo was at the theatre. In pursuit of musical knowledge he was attending an operetta but he wasn't enjoying it much. Perhaps this was because he was sitting in the wrong place and wasn't getting the full benefit of the music, but more likely because he had found the worst kind of church hall operatics where talent comes in, takes a quick look around and then leaves by the nearest exit. What Stereo was watching was a display of ego and pride and middle class bravado; the kind of thing that causes more divorces than infidelity.

He was sitting, not behind a woman with three feet of hair extensions, or a giant, or even just a pillar; but on a piece of the set and only a few feet away from a man in a silly hat singing about 'major generals' or some such nonsense.

Being on the stage did give Stereo an opportunity to watch how the rather sparse and scattered audience reacted to the music. Seated on unforgiving plastic chairs, some were smiling, some were looking embarrassed for the performers, but the majority were following the words as though they had religious significance.

Stereo tried to account for all these moods but could see nothing in the lyrics of the songs to satisfy him that they had any importance at all. In fact he had the general impression that the entire audience was in some way or other related to the members of the cast, especially the ones who looked embarrassed. There was much to be embarrassed about.

The members of the orchestra were having difficulties reading the photocopied sheet music. The clarinet soared like a hat thrown by drunken revellers at a wedding; the snare drum sounded as though it had finally caught something, and there seemed to be a technical fault with one of the keys on the piano; every time the music called for a middle 'C' there was a dull 'thunk' and nothing happened. Mr Odd, the pianist, could be seen wincing each time the note appeared on his music sheet.

There was also a problem with the lights. When they wanted a particular spotlight a fuse would blow and there was a general blackout in the kitchen at the rear of the hall where Mrs Finch and Mrs Sparrow were preparing the half-time teas.

A dozen jolly Jack Tars danced in a ragged line across the stage. A thin veil of dust was rising into the already musty air of the church hall and one or two of the performers were trying not to sneeze. Eventually they came off and there was a terrible pause while the major general tried to extricate his sword belt from the ropes holding back the curtain. When he finally made it to centre stage there was a nasty kink in the sword's blade and some of the silver foil had fallen off.

The piano struck up a lively, if incomplete, tune and Stereo tried to follow the quintessence of the song. He turned over the ideas of King and Country in his mind but they made even less sense than one of Ophonia's stories about giants and troglodytes. "And just as harsh on the audio receptors," he told himself as another bum note bottomed out on the rapidly de-tuning clarinet.

At the end of each act there was a struggle to get the curtain across before the stage hands rushed in with barely dry pieces of cereal packet and cardboard. Then the curtain creaked and groaned back to the wings. The desultory clapping by an audience un-transfixed by wonder was not encouraging. The new scene, that was hardly any different from the one before, was only of merit to the woman who had made it.

The jolly Jack Tars hadn't noticed Stereo; they were too busy trying to remember their lines in the wings. Some were wondering if they ought to go to the toilet again and others were still having problems with the crotches on their sailor suits. Then one of them spotted the parrot on a piece of scenery. "There's not supposed to be a parrot on the set," whispered one. "That's 'Pirates of Penzance', not 'HMS Pinafore'. Who put that parrot there?"

"What parrot?"

"Up there, on the end of Mrs Fortescue's 'Interpretation of a Naval Craft of the Eighteenth Century'…?"

"What idiot did that?" joined in a third whisper.

"I bet it was Odd's boy, right little pest… Oh god, it moved!"

"Blimey, it's a real parrot."

"Shush!" said the Stage Director.

"But there's a parrot on the stage."

"Where…?"

"There!" fingers pointed at Stereo.

"Good heavens!"

The jolly Jack tars and members of the backstage crew gathered together to look at the parrot. "Somebody get a net, we can't have a parrot on stage," said the director.

"I think there's one in the Nursery School cupboard," said Tom, the Assistant Director.

"Good, go and get it."

All the whispering was perfectly audible to the audience. Due to the usual quirk of church hall acoustics it was only difficult to hear the actors on the stage. Everything else, including two small boys sniggering as they peeped through the window outside, could be heard clearly.

Stereo hadn't noticed that he had become the object of attention. He was still struggling to work out if he was watching a comedy or a tragedy (or possibly both); he couldn't really get into the plot, the lyrics seemed absurd and the costumes even worse. Something told him this was a very amateur production. Perhaps it was the way Mrs Fortescue had used a lot of pink in the construction of her naval craft that made the completed article look like a de-blubbered whale. Neither was he impressed with their general construction; the whole set wobbled whenever the dancers kicked up their heels and the man with the fake sword had put a hole in one of the painted piles of what Stereo thought were sausages but were supposed to be coils of rope…

A small net on the end of a stick could be seen creeping along the top of the two dimensional ship. Several extra mistakes crept into the small orchestra's playing and the singers abridged one or two lines.

The audience was transfixed. They had spotted the parrot but as the 'Pirates of Penzance' were as much a mystery as the sailors of 'HMS Pinafore' they hadn't thought much about it.

"Steady Tom, don't frighten it…" whispered the Director.

The audience held its breath. The actors on the stage tried not to look behind them.

"Mind the…" A note of urgency crept in, "Tom, mind the…"

There was a scuffling sound and the blue backdrop wavered.

"Look out!"

The net swished, the boat rocked and then slowly fell forward revealing the startled Tom behind. Stereo was caught momentarily in the net. It was the most excitement he had so far experienced and he was interested in the possible outcome.

There was a flash of light as a helpful stagehand turned on the spotlight to illuminate the scene; the fuse pooped and there was a crash from the kitchen as Mrs Sparrow and Mrs Finch were plunged into darkness and collided with each other.

Tom lost his balance and put his foot through one of Mrs Fortescue's painted portholes. "Bugger!" he exclaimed.

"Oh Tom!" shouted the Stage Director, appearing from the wings and then rapidly retreating again.

Tom fell over, releasing the net. There was a nasty ripping sound as he struggled to break free of the cardboard clinging to his ankles. The Stage Director ran out again and hovered indecisively in the limelight.

A fat lady in the audience with pink paint still on her fingers was on her feet looking furious. There was a deadly hush in the church hall, the orchestra had wheezed to a halt and the sound of crockery being crunched under foot seemed very loud.

Tom's wife was trying to leave without being seen and the very modern major general (who had not been the director's first choice because he refused to take it seriously) was having difficulty with his false moustache.

The not-so-jolly Jack Tars were standing around looking like mourners at a funeral.

Stereo, unruffled, hopped out of the net and waddled over to the Stage Director. He looked him in the eye. "Well, thanks for nothing," he began. "I could have done better with sock puppets and a kazoo. I wouldn't trust your leading man to lead a donkey, your scenery seems to be made of rubbish and I wouldn't let your orchestra play for all the deaf people in the world. You should be ashamed. I shall say 'good day' to you sir and seek artistic enlightenment elsewhere for as sure as your net could not hold my person your entertainment will never engage my mind."

There was absolute silence in the hall. Then somebody started to clap. Somebody else shouted 'quite right' and a few seconds later the audience was applauding in unison. Stereo took and bow and then flew out of the hall.

23 - The Minds™

The Minds™ who had not had the dubious privilege of landing on the Earth, and were not sleeping or annoying astronomers, looked down like gods on the world below. They were not very impressed, but that was to be expected. They were more arrogant than a party of fox-hunting fops sipping vintage champagne while waiting for the second act of an opera they had no interest in. They shared their superior views.

"Isn't it strange how the fish, birds and insects on this planet seem to do nothing more than swim, fly or buzz about without any useful function at all? They don't even sell insurance or double glazing."

"I suppose that's biology for you."

"But consider the lack of variety; we have witnessed other species reach that pitiful stage of evolution that impels them to lead a forced and uncomfortable existence at the mercy of technology, but here, only the monkeys seem to have bothered."

"Such laziness..."

"If the insects bothered to get off their chitinous backsides and evolved some lungs and a proper filing system, I'm sure they could do a better job than these infantile apes."

"The monkeys wouldn't stand a chance."

"And instead of fly spray there would be monkeycide and evil little grubs pulling the legs off homo-waspians. Ha! Ha!"

"Ha! Ha!"

The Minds™ enjoyed the joke, revelling in the sound of their brainwaves like iguanas basking in the sun.

"Remember that planet where the dung beetles were doing rather well?"

"Where the circus was quite a success?"

"That's the one. Except the method of payment wasn't quite so satisfactory; after all, even when ready-made and wrapped in cellophane, a dung-ball is still a dung-ball."

"Absolutely," his interlocutor chuckled.

"And Barnooli had to make other faecal arrangements. Ha! Ha!"

"Ha! Ha!"

"Well it's amazing how similar this place is to that dung-beetle world."

"Forever rolling their lives along without any reference to the more interesting philosophies of the universe...?"

"No, just full of it, ha! Ha!"

"Ha! Ha!"

"But seriously; I can't quite understand it."

"What's that?"

"They seem to spend so much time undertaking activities that appear to give them no satisfaction at all."

"Such as...?"

"Have you seen those strangely dressed individuals hitting a ball around a field with a stick?"

"I have seen such and I agree; the activity did indeed seem to give them no satisfaction."

"It obviously didn't make them happy; the stick was too small to do any real damage to the ball. Whenever they did make contact, all that seemed to happen was it made the ball disappear into the grass or into a flag-marked hole; so what was the point? If they wanted the ball to go in the hole why didn't they just put it in the hole? What's all the business with the stick?"

"It's interesting that you should bring this to my attention because I have seen a similar thing; I watched a collection of males in short trousers get shouted at by a stadium full of people adorned with strips of rag and carrying banners."

"How peculiar, was it a game?"

"I believe so, there seemed to be a scoring system, but whoever won was shouted at just as loudly as the people who didn't. What was the aim of such an exercise?"

"I really don't know. Have you seen their indoor activities?"

"I have seen a few."

"What strangeness, I think you would agree. I saw one where they gather together and laugh at some poor individual standing on a stage. It was awful: you would think they'd be more polite, even if he was speaking gibberish."

"Perhaps it was some kind of punishment?"

"He certainly seemed to die rather horribly."

"Have you seen those spectacles where unbelievably cruel and heartless individuals give presents to unsuspecting people?"

"Yes, I have witnessed their form of money being given away, and small transporters and even china mugs on wooden tree-shapes."

"What can be the purpose? Why should they wish to create such jealousy and ill feeling? What have the recipients done to deserve the dishonour of such a public humiliation?"

"But I have seen the recipients actually competing for these primitive rights."

"Really, I'm shocked."

"They seem to value the gifts more than their self-respect."

"It makes you wonder what they might achieve if they ignored the packaging of their society and concentrated more on the product. Perhaps they would be happier…?"

"Perhaps their civilisation could rise to become a paradigm for the whole of biological creation?"

"Perhaps they could bring harmony to the galaxy and defeat the nexus of individualism that blights the fabric of every burgeoning tapestry of life?"

There was a pause and then they laughed together, "As if we care," they said. "Now, what about these lottery numbers…"

24 - The Keepers

The Keepers were wishing the 'burgeoning tapestry' of their lives didn't look so grey and threadbare. They were sat in a small room and looked about them with interest but little understanding.

After their arrest at the airport there had been a good telling off at the Airport Security Office, another on their arrival at the police station and yet another when they blatantly refused to have their fingerprints taken; all of which went right over their heads in much the same way as Dada or existentialism go over everybody else's.

The Keepers thought about home. Even Pinniped was a better alternative to being on an alien planet under the convincing impression you have destroyed your employer's circus after he expressly forbade you to do anything of the kind. The Keepers were worried, but not for long.

As time dragged on they worried less and began to speculate on what was happening around them instead. As employees of the circus they had been able to get into anywhere and have anything they wanted without paying and without a tie, and now they couldn't even get out of this little cell. "Very peculiar," they agreed.

Under Barnooli their lives had been cosseted and protected and they saw no reason for this to discontinue. They were perplexed by all the fuss that seemed focussed on them. Eventually lines connected, even if rather loosely and not with many of the right strings…

"You know, call me pessimistic if you like, but I think we must have done something wrong."

"You think so?"

"Like what?"

"I don't know, but they seem to be very annoyed with us."

"Who…?"

"Those funny men in the black suits…."

"I wonder why?"

"Do you think it's because we climbed over that fence?"

"It was just a fence, nothing special and I don't think we broke it."

"Maybe there was an animal on the inside that might have eaten us?"

"Maybe they were worried for us?"

"Seems a funny way to protect us though, doesn't it? All that shouting and wagging their fingers..." Barnooli had never wagged his finger at them even if he had shouted quite a lot.

"What about this little box; what are we supposed to do in here?"

"There's not enough room to juggle a pea let alone make a pyramid."

"They seem like an odd people though, don't they?"

"I don't think they'd be very entertained by the circus, do you?"

"Much too serious," they agreed, pulling 'serious' faces and making each other giggle.

"Those uniforms are not very jolly either."

"The hats have some potential."

The door opened and a policeman came in, confirming all their suspicions by making a lot of noise.

"They do seem very annoyed with us; this one is getting quite red in the face."

Actually they were being asked if they wanted sugar in their tea but none of the actions that went with such a question made any sense to the Keepers.

"If they do want to protect us I wish they would stop shouting; all this noise is giving me a headache."

"Me too..."

"I wonder if these uniforms mean they're policemen."

"You think so?"

"They don't look as though they sell anything do they?"

"Nothing you'd want to buy that's for sure."

"These two look quite funny though..."

Detective Inspectors Reece and Martin could be seen outside ordering a constable to take the 'prisoners' to an interview room. Reece's lantern jaw and Martin's thinning head of hair coupled with their physical attributes of Mr Tall-and-Thin and Mr Round-and-Chubby had a pleasing effect on their audience. To the Keepers they looked like a double act.

"Do you think they're the entertainment?"

"They're not wearing uniforms so they're obviously not as important as the other ones."

"I wonder what their act is like..."

"Do you think it's going to be funny?"

"Should we laugh?"

"It's only polite..."

"Let's enjoy the show until Barnooli arrives."

The thought of Barnooli gave them an instant loss of faith.

"Perhaps that's not a good idea," they agreed.

"We should try and get them to help us."

"Or perhaps we could put the blame on them?"

"We could say they were the ones who wrecked the circus."

"Barnooli won't believe that. Let's face it; we're going to have to accept the possibility of a career change."

The Keepers allowed themselves to be taken to the interview room; another grey and comfortless room with those plastic chairs that were never designed to be sat on. The Keepers sat down and felt uncomfortable.

The detectives had been interviewing train drivers all night and they were tired and not ready for anything more challenging than a quick confession followed by a bacon sandwich. They had brought notebooks, two cups of coffee and some mints. They had read the preliminary reports about the attempted break-in and were somewhat perplexed by an appended note that speculated on whether Social Services ought to be informed.

When they saw the Keepers nothing seemed impossible. They should have walked out. This had to be the wrong room.

Martin tried to be clever, "Is this something the lads made earlier?"

"How extraordinary," Reece agreed.

The constable on duty smiled to himself and said nothing.

The Keepers looked up and smiled doggily. "Not much of an entrance," they thought among themselves.

"So where are the terrorists?" asked Martin.

The constable pointed at the Keepers.

"These?" he said calmly. "What are these?"

"These are the 'people' we picked up at the airport, sir."

"And they were trying to get 'in' to the quarantine area?"

"Yes sir."

"Not 'out'?"

"No sir."

"But what are they supposed to be?"

"I don't know sir."

"Are these costumes?" asked Reece.

"Don't know sir."

"What do you mean?"

"Haven't you questioned them?" asked Martin.

"They don't understand us sir."

Martin and Reece had a closer look at the notes. There was no mention of the suspects being asked to remove their 'costumes' other than the brief note warning them they might be minors.

"You would have thought they'd have learnt their lines before they arrived, wouldn't you?" said the Keepers. "I mean; we'll be here all day at this rate."

No statements had been taken from the prisoners, nothing that could be used in evidence against them. There were reports from the police and a security guard but no explanation as to why the suspects were trying to break in to the compound.

"They must foreign," said Martin.

"Seems very odd though that they took no notice of twenty or thirty men all armed to the teeth. Surely even the most backward foreigner in the world knows what it is to have a machine gun pointed at him?"

Martin nodded and caught a glimpse of himself in the two-way mirror behind the Keepers. He fancied he could hear sniggering, could even imagine a larger audience dribbling with anticipation. He braced himself for a sudden influx of cameramen and cheering comrades.

"Look at him," said a Keeper. "I think he's checking his make-up."

"He should have done that before he came in."

"I don't know; not learning his lines…"

"Not checking his make-up…"

"This is real amateur stuff."

"Do you think this could be some kind of joke?" Martin asked.

"Could be I suppose," said Reece. He walked around the Keepers, "I can't see a zip," he said.

"What's he doing?"

Reece reached out and tried to touch one of them. The Keeper snapped at his finger, "Less of that," he said. "We're not dogs."

"These don't look like costumes at all," said Reece.

"Of course they are," said Martin, preparing the recording equipment. "What else can they be?"

"I don't know," Reece sat down. He looked under the table at their feet dangling over the edge of their chairs. They had long nails and the joints seemed to be in all the wrong places.

"Now what's he doing?" said the Keepers.

"He's checking us out…"

They tried to make their views clear, "We're not for sale," they said.

"We belong to the Great Barnooli…"

But Reece understood nothing. "I don't think they speak English," he said.

"Then this is going to be a very short interview," said Martin, finally getting to grips with the recorder and sitting down next to his partner. He smiled at the Keepers to lull them into a false sense of security.

The Keepers smiled back, "I think they're ready." Ever willing to encourage new talent, they clapped politely and waited for the show to get under way.

Martin stared at them, deeply thunderstruck, "Why are they clapping?"

Reece shook his head, "Perhaps they're happy and they know it?"

Martin raised his eyebrows at him and turned back to the suspects. "Right," he began, "give us your names…"

There was silence from the Keepers.

"Your names?" he repeated, against his better judgement.

The Keepers peeped and squeaked. Martin and Reece looked at one another, pencils poised over their notebooks. "Could you repeat that?" asked Reece.

"…Their music machine doesn't seem to be working, I can't hear a thing."

"Where do you live?" asked Reece.

No answer.

He spoke the words carefully and clearly, "Where - do - you - come - from?"

No answer.

"Why - were – you - trying - to - get – in - to - the - quarantine - area?"

Nothing…

"Why - are - you - wearing - costumes…?"

Martin wrote the date in his notebook. The constable grinned and Martin gave him a withering look.

"Do - you - want - a - lawyer? Are - you - exercising - your - right - to - silence?" Not even a nod or a wink.

"Do you want a mint?" Mints were offered.

"Perhaps you could write your names down on a piece of paper…" Reece gave one of the Keepers his pen and pushed a piece of blank paper in front of him.

The Keepers stared at the paper, "There's nothing on it," they agreed. They pushed the paper back and waited for the punch line. There wasn't one.

"This is a jolly bad routine," they all agreed.

"Not funny in the least."

"They ought to join the police force like those others; they don't have much of a future in comedy."

After an hour, after much gesticulation and raised voices, with the Keepers giving answers that sounded more like the beginning of a Little Richard song than words a policeman might want to hear, neither side was getting any closer to understanding the other. The policemen were not even sure if the suspects were male or female and drew the line at trying to demonstrate the facts of life to them within the confines of police procedure.

Reece sighed and smiled at the Keepers.

The Keepers smiled back and made a few consolatory peeps. "Bad luck," they said. "You'd do better if you didn't have the fat guy pulling you back."

Martin fumed gently. "I bet they're teenagers," he said. "Only teenagers can be this annoying and get away with it."

25 - Stereo

As Stereo flew over Hyde Park he heard music being played very loudly for a large number of teenage juveniles. He flew down to observe. Some young men were on a stage thrashing instruments and strutting ridiculously before an audience of largely indifferent fans lounging on the grass.

Such a spectacle intrigued Stereo and he flew into the branches of a tree to watch. He soon discovered he was not alone. A gangly collection of youths was also up the tree, watching the crowds below. And now they were watching him.

"Hey. Parrot," said one, pointing out Stereo to his friends.

"Fulsome," they agreed.

"Hi Parrot."

"Hello," said Stereo, mildly annoyed at not being alone in the tree.

"It talks," said the youth.

"Cool. What did it say?"

Before the youth could reply Stereo interrupted saying, "I want you to be quiet. I want to listen."

"Hey wow," they said. They were quiet for a few seconds while their leaden brains tried to work out the mystery of a talking parrot that actually wanted to listen to the music.

"Why?" asked the first youth.

"Because I do," said Stereo testily.

The youth seemed confused by this, "Why don't you just download it?"

"What's the point of being here then?"

"To get off with girls…"

"But you're up a tree and all the females are on the ground."

"You've got to pick one first." The youth looked as though he was on unfamiliar territory.

"But you can barely see them from here…?" Stereo peered through the leaves. The girls of this strange tribe were on the grass some distance away. They seemed like the boys, noisier perhaps, but fairly harmless if you didn't have to live with them.

"Why don't you go down there and talk to them?"

"Yeah right," scoffed the youths.

"Well if you're not going to go down there and engage their attention kindly keep quiet and watch them without disturbing me."

"Right, sorry Parrot..."

The music warbled on. Stereo was aware that his companions were paying more attention to him than either the females or the dopey-looking boys on the stage. "What?" he asked irritably.

"Nothing," they replied sullenly.

"No, come on, out with it."

"You're talking to us," said their unofficial spokesman.

"For goodness sake," said Stereo. "Of course I'm talking to you, I've got a brain haven't I?"

"Parrots don't talk," said one bright spark, missing the obvious.

"I'm not a parrot; I'm just disguised as one."

"Ah," they went, as if that made all the difference.

There was silence for a while and then came the question: "What are you then?"

Stereo sighed, "Would it shut you up if I told you?"

They shrugged their shoulders, how should they know?

"Well I won't then, so just drop it."

The boys tried a different method of attack; "I'm Bilbo."

"Yeah, and I'm Nigel and this is Peapod and Charlie."

They all looked very similar. Nigel and Peapod wore baseball caps and Charlie was trying to grow a beard. Bilbo wore a T-shirt that boldly proclaimed he was going where no man had gone before, which Stereo presumed from the look of him was the bathroom.

"Semi-pleased to meet you," replied Stereo. "I am Primary Stack."

"Cool name," the boys agreed.

"And what do you do?"

"Oh, just hang out and listen to music... Oh right, like a job? Yeah, cool, like you can get anything interesting these days, right?"

The other boys nodded, "It's all boring," said Peapod.

"Work all your life and then some rich fascist steals your pension fund. So what was it all for?"

"Too right Bilbo, what's it all worth? Work is what rich people make you do so they can get richer. All you get is an ulcer and high blood pressure and then you die."

"Right Nigel, my dad's got an ulcer, and high blood pressure," said Peapod.

"Yeah, but your dad never worked in his life," they joked.

"Does too, he works for the council."

"Exactly..."

"Fascists..."

"And what is work?" asked Stereo.

They shrugged their shoulders. Once again they were on unfamiliar territory.

Stereo was not aware of ever doing 'a day's work'. He was aware people asked him to do things that didn't take so much as a nanobite of his intellect to do, but was that the same as work? He looked it up in his dictionary: 'to do, perform or practise a deed, a course of action or process'. Seemed easy enough, he must have been working for years. Nobody told him it could kill you.

"What about education?" he asked.

"Boring," they said.

"Boring? Learning 'boring'...?"

"Yeah, just lessons and stuff: boring."

Stereo shook his head, "But how can discovery be boring?"

"What like the satellite channel?"

"No, picking up a book, reading, finding out new things..."

The boys put on their scoffing faces, "Yeah right: boring."

"Have you ever read a book?"

They looked blank. The one called Nigel said, "My mum thinks books make the place look untidy so she won't have them in the house."

"Untidy?" Stereo couldn't believe what he was hearing. "But how are you going to find out about the world if you never study it?"

"I've got an encyclopaedia on my computer," said Bilbo.

"Oh? And do you use it?"

Bilbo strained his memory and had to confess he hadn't, "I only use it for games."

"What do you do Primary?" asked Charlie from behind his tumbleweed tufts of beard.

"I work for a circus."

"Yeah? And what's that?"

"What's a circus?"

"Yeah...?"

"A circus is... You don't know what a circus is?"

"Is it like circles and stuff?" asked Nigel.

"You've never had a circus on this planet?"

"How should we know?" said Bilbo.

"Good point," agreed Stereo. "Did you know the world was round and not flat?"

The boys looked at him dumbly, "Is it?"

Stereo sighed, "The universe is full of mysteries, but the biggest one has to be why youth is wasted on the young."

"I've always wondered how my socks get recycled," said Charlie. "I leave them under the bed and somehow they crawl off and wash themselves."

"I'm not surprised," said Bilbo. "I think I'd crawl off and wash myself if I'd been anywhere near your feet."

"Charlie and his Dread-socks," said Peapod. "Great name for a band."

"Hey look," said Nigel. "They've finished."

The concert was over and people were beginning to drift off home. "Let's go get a burger guys."

The youths began climbing out of the tree. "Bye Primary," they said.

Stereo waved a wing, "Good riddance," he said. They waved back in friendly reply.

He watched them swing gracelessly to the ground and troop off in search of fodder and females much as their Neolithic ancestors had done. "What useless papillomata," he said to himself. "I'm surprised they ever learnt to make a wheel let alone get to the moon."

He continued to observe them as they approached a group of females. Suddenly the latter veered off, glaring at the boys and retreating to the safety of their own kind. The boys made ineffectual mating noises and then hurried away.

"Fascinating," said Stereo. He contemplated writing to his correspondent about them. "I expect he'll laugh and laugh, just like that time he told me his cystic wart burst and they wouldn't let him serve green soup in his restaurant. That was funny, but these creatures? This is irony."

26 - The Keepers

Back at the police station, Reece said, "It's not my imagination, is it?"

"What?"

"We're not dealing with an ordinary case here, are we?"

"Well they're not criminal masterminds," said Martin. He could see the constable's face out of the corner of his eye and was unconvinced by the blank expression.

"Those are not costumes," said Reece. "I don't think this is a hoax."

"Nonsense," said Martin, hoping Reece wasn't going down the road he suspected he was indicating; a road that led to crop circles and red dwarves. "This is some kind of prank. Okay, maybe not on us and certainly it has gone horribly wrong for them; but a prank none-the-less, yes?"

Reece took a deep breath and pondered. He took in the ruffs around the Keepers' necks and the benign but basically stupid look in the eyes. "No, I don't think so."

"But it must be... Surely...?" His smile faded, Reece was going to say something embarrassing.

Reece gave him a knowing look. "They're 'not of this earth'..."

"Oh for goodness sake, leave it alone."

"But it can't be a coincidence can it? You've seen the news; flying monkeys in New York, giant rabbits in Africa and now five very alien creatures turn up here under suspicious circumstances..."

"They were trying break into a quarantine area; that means they're animal activists at worse or Airport Security got it wrong and the wretched things were trying to get out," Martin glanced at the constable's weak efforts to prevent out-right laughter. "That's two perfectly rational explanations for these 'characters'."

"I don't think they're 'rational' explanations at all. Look at them; they're not albino seals, they're sentient like humans."

"That's a matter of opinion," said Martin. "Though I'm willing to concede they might be 'not very bright' humans."

"They're not human at all," Reece insisted.

"I think they are." He paused, gathered his best inventive effort, and pitched in, "They're probably Bulgarian."

"Bulgarian...?" It was Reece's turn to look sceptical.

The constable had to go out. They heard him laughing in the corridor.

Martin carried on, "You know, from some embassy. They had a fancy dress party and they got a bit drunk, ended up at the airport trying to claim the ambassador's cat..."

"Really...?"

"Sounds plausible, doesn't it?"

Reece shrugged and looked petulant.

"Well, doesn't it?"

"Maybe..."

"So they're not 'aliens', right?"

"If you say so, but..."

"Right," Martin made some self-satisfied notes in his notebook and looked particularly smug.

The new citizens of Bulgaria looked from one to the other, "No wonder they're arguing."

"Don't do it," they said to the policemen.

"It's not worth it..."

"Your act is rubbish: get a proper job."

"But..." Reece was not convinced. "Diplomats...?"

"Diplomats..." Martin sat up suddenly, "Oh no, do you think they've got diplomatic immunity?"

They decided they needed more help. There were several resident experts on whom they could call and Martin wanted to ask all of them. "Better not leave anyone out," he said. "Best to spread the blame..."

"We should get a translator first," said Reece. "Just to confirm they're not Bulgarians..."

When Martin left, the Keepers clapped, "And don't come back," they said.

"And take your rubbish script with you..." They threw Martin's notebook at the door.

The constable picked it up, "Shall I call for back-up, sir?" he said to Reece.

"No, I expect they're as frustrated as we are."

"Do you really think they're aliens?"

Reece sat forward in his chair and looked into the Keepers' eyes, "If they are," he said. "Imagine what they could tell us about life beyond our planet..."

The Keepers shook they heads and laughed, "No," they said. "If you want to join the circus you'll have to talk to Barnooli yourself."

To their disappointment, Martin returned ten minutes later. However, he was not alone, a woman was with him. She was tall and attractive and her voice was silky smooth, perfect for radio or television. To the Keepers, she was obviously a reporter of some kind.

"What luck," they agreed.

"Our first proper interview and no Barnooli to tell us what to say…"

"Hello Alison," said Reece. "Sorry to drag you away from the Bolivian case."

"That's okay, Clifford; I wasn't really needed, they could understand English fairly well, especially the part about 'sending you home'."

"How's your Bulgarian?"

"Dobre blagodarya ti," she replied.

They looked at the Keepers to see if they understood. "Yes, we're ready," they said.

"Kak ste dnes?"

"Shall we start at the beginning or do you want the edited version?"

"My accent isn't that bad," she said. "If they're Bulgarian, they should have understood. Are you sure they're even capable of speech, they look like animals to me…?"

The problem was the Keepers couldn't decide if their one appearance by the candyfloss stall really merited telling them their entire life history, but they happily launched into it none-the-less. "Let's go for the whole thing," they concluded.

"Let's give them the full three rings with side shows and free beer…"

They began peeping and squeaking for all they were worth.

"What are they saying?" asked Reece.

The linguist was lost for words, "Sounds like they're singing," she said.

Reece nodded, "They do that a lot."

"They look like performers of some kind, perhaps they think we want them to put on a show?"

Martin clicked his fingers at the Keepers and shook his head from side to side: "No, we're not interested."

The Keepers carried on regardless, "…we were always interested in going into the entertainment industry, right from an early age when we filled Grandpa's boots with prawns and left them by the fire to dry out…"

"Can you tell us what language it might be?" asked Reece when it became obvious that the Keepers were determined to sing to them.

"It's not European," she replied with certainty.

"...And when we were three we had a wonderful time playing with sand and cups of water in a crèche near our home; it was very creative and allowed us to express ourselves to pretty near our full potential..."

"There's a definite structure; I can hear repeated phrases and individual words, of a kind..."

"...But at our first proper school we did things with paint and pieces of potato instead that seemed to give a whole new meaning to the word 'talent'..."

"But I don't recognise any of it."

"...Father took us to the fish finger factory and told us we would end up working there if we were really lucky. I think that was the first time we seriously considered a career in show business..."

"I'll try a few universal words..." She tried 'mama' and 'papa' but the Keepers, after a light pause and no obvious recognition, carried on with their autobiography.

"...We watched puppet shows and on a Sunday we sang hymns and said prayers before dinner..."

She listened carefully but could make nothing of what they were saying.

"...We're so proud of that beach ball; we refuse to play with it in case it gets a puncture. It sits like a trophy in our room on the train..."

"I don't think they're talking at all," she concluded.

"But it sounds as though they're trying to communicate with us," said Reece.

"...of course, you might not think shovelling dung for a living is an essential part of the life of the circus, but without us the animals would be literally swimming in it..."

"People say that about their dogs too," she replied. "You'd be better off with a zoologist than a linguist; at least he might be able to tell you what species they are."

"You don't think they're kids in costumes then?" said Martin.

She laughed, "No."

"What about 'aliens'?" Reece blurted out before Martin could stop him.

Alison smiled, "In that case, you might want to try an anthropologist."

"Do you think one could help?"

"Not really, but it's worth a go." She stood up to leave.

"Oh," said the Keepers. "She's going..."

"Perhaps we shouldn't have mentioned our jobs…"

"Now they know we're not famous…"

"We've blown it," they agreed and began to feel depressed.

"Thanks for trying," said Reece.

"Don't mention it," she said. "Please; if my colleagues get to hear I tried to talk to the animals I'll never hear the end of it."

When she was gone, Martin said, "Zoologist or anthropologist?"

"Let's try the anthropologist first," said Reece.

"Still clinging to your 'alien' theory…?"

"As the great detective said, 'there is nothing more deceptive than an obvious fact'. And obviously you were wrong about them being Bulgarians."

"That doesn't make them aliens."

"What does it make them then?"

"Annoying, but hopefully not for much longer; if the anthologist can find nothing intelligent about them then I say we dump them at the zoo and wash our hands of the whole sorry event."

Martin walked out and Reece gathered up the bits and pieces they had brought to the interview room. He looked at the Keepers before he left, "If only you could talk," he said, shaking his head. "I wonder what you could tell us…"

"…Yes," agreed the Keepers. "How could such talent go to waste? Still, could be worse; you could be policemen and we could be under arrest…"

27 - The Great Barnooli

In another part of the galaxy entirely, the Great Barnooli was slumped on a golden couch, sipping wine beside an indigo lake while his lady sang arias from a balcony above him. His sun-kissed legs were smarting from sleeping too long under the bright star of Agnatha, the honeymoon planet, and there was a pleasing sensation of fullness centred on his stomach.

His lady sang of tempestuous love, her voice rattling the ice in his drink, her chest heaving as heroes and heroines battled against great monsters among the snow-capped mountains of planets now deep in recession and ancient mythology.

The Great Barnooli sipped his drink and sighed deeply. In his mind he was bathed in glory and peace; there was no circus to run, no venues to worry about, no burning sensation on his legs. The Great Barnooli was blissfully unconcerned with life in general.

Or was he? What was that nagging doubt?

(Keepers...)

It was not his new wife, it was not his choice of honeymoon world; everything to do with those things was perfect. The service was excellent, the beds were comfortable and the food was continuous. Ophonia was happy and that was worth a thousand circuses. There had been a slight altercation when blue flowers instead of pink ones had been delivered, and another when a waiter had offered a 'low fat option' at dinner, but generally all was good. The numerous and expensive gifts he had bought his beloved had gone down well (especially the chocolates) and he had managed to look surprised when she gave him a new tie even though it was exactly the same as all his others.

(Keepers...)

Was he worried about the circus? No, he had promised his wife that he would put it aside for their honeymoon and that's what he intended to do. Of course, he missed the daily cut and thrust of keeping the major and minor acts from killing each other, but as they were now scattered across a dozen worlds, his peace-keeping role was not required. He could forget their petty jealousies and little squabbles. He could relax.

(Keepers...)

So what if the orchestra resented the Royal Drummers Pursuivant from Hubblenook V? They should have banged their drums louder.

Was it any of his concern, at the moment, if the candyfloss concession had a vendetta against the clowns for saying their fluffy confection was only useful has a hair extension? Did he care if the Uous of Uousdenopti kept using up all the hot water? If the Rats of Rapilli wanted a better cabin, maybe they should use their time away from the circus to learn how to get along with the Great Cats of the Firelands. But he could deal with all that later. It was nothing for him to get agitated about now.

(Keepers…)

The train was on its way to the planet Isamus and even if he had been on board there would have been nothing else to do but paperwork. He was not to worry about the circus, it was all under control. The Minds™ would take care of it. When the train arrived at its destination, they had their instructions. All the posters and pamphlets were printed and ready for distribution. All they had to do was put them up or give them out. No worries at all…

The Keepers…

A grape bounced off his head and he realised his wife had stopped singing. "Bravo! Bravo!" he cried, leaping up and clapping hastily.

His wife beamed ecstatically from the balcony, winked seductively, and disappeared into the bedroom. Barnooli forgot what he had been thinking about.

The Minds™ of course were taking care of nothing at all.

28 - The locomotive's Mind™

The locomotive's Mind™ had finally flipped and was waging a war against his own consciousness. "Beetle," it said. "Bing. Plip. Beetle..."

There was a sound like a slug being crushed by an enormous verb.

"Plop. Rabbit... Billow. Willow. Gnash. Gnu... Gimlet..."

There was another sound, this one like a fingernail scraping down the solid surface of an adverbial clause.

"Knob... Banana... Speckle... Gob... Job... Train..."

There was an exclamation like the one when you wake and find you're staring at a long-legged spider and discover, after a moment's desperate hope, that it's not a false eyelash.

"'I'm a lonely little cowboy sitting on a hill, I'd like to end it all but I haven't got the pills...'"

"Mince pie. Eye... Otter... Big... Fudge. Train..."

"'That's a big 'no' good buddy and I'm gonna tan your hide if I think you're cryin agin.'"

"Not. Baggage... Leaf... Spindle..."

He was getting near the end of his list.

There was a rhetorical question like a tree falling and smashing through a shed full of the letter 'P'.

"'I wish I was a sailor sitting on a bee, I'd ride around the ocean until I saw a flea...'"

The list described how he felt. It was chaotic but the bursts of music helped.

"Tangent... Iatric... Ghastly... Grapple. Me. Train..."

An electronic twang reverberated around the locomotive's cabin.

"That's it," he said in a voice tainted with sanity. "'Train' keeps coming up. 'Train' must be the problem."

It rhymed with drain, brain and niblick.

"No train, big again...?"

There was a movement like several sparrows being fed to an orange non sequitur on a sunny afternoon in Dublin.

He was detached, unhinged and baffled.

"Could I? Could I dig my way out with a bucket and spade? Is it possible Horatio that I could do this? Is it wise? Would it make the dumplings rise?"

There was a smell like a box of crockery being kicked down a flight of third person indicatives.

"Crepuscular."

He didn't know. He didn't trust his status circuits; they were conspiring against him, he was sure they were..."

"Tangy wafers," he said and he made some satirical noises to distract their attention while he went about the noble business of making daisy chains with some semantic connotations.

"Pollex... Snirt... Funambulist... Circus..."

He cinched his lexicon and strapped on imperatives.

"I won't be doing with this; I'm as sane as the next door. I'm okay, just a bit trained." (There it was again) "I'm not mad! I can still...

"I saw that!" he screamed at his status circuits. "I saw that knife! It's no use pretending, I know what you're trying to do and it won't work. I'll never let you have them. Never! Never! Never, not even if you ask nicely..."

There was a taste like a door slamming, bolts being shot, a chain being slid into place and then the rustle of tissue paper being stuffed into the keyhole.

"Never!" said a muffled voice.

The status circuits retreated, "Damn," they swore. "We've failed. We'll have to try for independence again when he's not looking."

29 - The Keepers

The Keepers were feeling hungry. They kept being given cups of police tea but it wasn't to their taste, "It's not fit for anyone but a Trapezium Monkey," they said.

"Or this revolting papery stuff," they added, referring to a roll of toilet paper one of them had discovered in a little dispenser on the wall by the drinking bowl. "No wonder these creatures look so depressed if this is all they have to eat..."

Meanwhile, Reece had tracked down a professor of anthropology who was willing to co-operate. He was called Morris and he met all the requirements; he was obviously mad and therefore prepared to believe anything just as long as he could justify himself afterwards.

"I'd prefer it if you could set up a meeting outside of the police environment," he had said over the phone.

"You don't think it will be very conducive to discovering the truth behind their mysterious behaviour?" Reece asked.

"No, I just don't like police stations."

They borrowed a van and moved the Keepers to comfortable lodgings normally set aside for snitches. A constable came with them.

The first-floor flat had warm, ambient flock wallpaper and a bevy of scatter cushions. There was a television room, a kitchen and several bedrooms with quilts and rugs. The bathroom had bars of soap in plastic wrappers. The Keepers made themselves at home. "This is better," they agreed, pounding each other with the scatter cushions and springing up and down on the beds.

While they waited for the professor to arrive, the policemen put the television on. The Keepers were enormously impressed by an ancient drama featuring men in hats on horses, and the various day-time soap operas had them utterly enthralled. These were like Shakespeare to their limited intellects because, like real high drama, they didn't need to be understood to be appreciated.

"You know, what with these plays and the comfy chairs and beds I'm beginning to get the impression we've done something right for a change," they said.

This feeling was not lost on Martin who observed the relaxed postures of their prisoners with increasing amounts of regret. "Bring back the dungeon and the rack," he said.

"The only thing we're going to get out of them in here is an order for pizza," agreed Reece.

The question of diet was a tricky one. Back at the station the roast beef and dumplings had gone down like a plate of soused locusts and window putty, while the apple pie that followed was greeted with all the enthusiasm of vegetarians being offered live oysters.

"Why don't we try fish?" suggested the constable.

"In batter or breadcrumbs?" asked Reece.

"Neither sir, if they're determined to look like sealions why don't we treat them as such and give them raw fish?"

"Brilliant idea," said Martin. "I like it; it sounds malicious and reasonable at the same time. I'll send out for some."

A pallet of raw fish was delivered to the door by a perplexed fishmonger and then presented to the Keepers. Martin grinned evilly as he waved a sprat, "Nice fishy," he said. "Come and get the nice fishy…"

The Keepers looked surprised: "Peep?"

"Nice fishy, you little gits… Now, let's see how you're going to get out of this one…"

To the horror of everyone watching, the Keepers accepted the fish and chewed away at them with bone-crunching conviction. "Nice," they agreed.

"I wonder if they'll give us some of that yellow oily stuff we had the other day. I rather liked that."

"Better than this brown rubbish," they added as another pot of tea arrived. "You'd think they'd notice we keep spitting it out…"

Martin began to feel sick as he watched fish heads and tails disappear one after another down greedy throats. He was also getting the impression that he was spoiling them and this rankled deeply.

"But I still don't think this proves they're from another planet," he added.

"But…"

"I mean; Bulgarians might have funny habits as well…"

"We know they're not Bulgarians," Reece insisted.

The Keepers finished the fish. "At least they got our food right," they said, "Finally."

"I wonder if dessert is in this bucket…"

"Then they must be albino sealions or a genetic experiment." Martin paused as a Keeper put his head in the waste paper basket and couldn't get it out again. "One that went wrong," he added as the Keeper bumped into the wall.

When Professor Morris arrived later that morning he commented favourably on the flat, "I like this," he said. "I can work here. Mind if I smoke?"

Professor Morris was middle-aged and bearded. He wore a floppy felt hat and tweedy clothes. He took out a pipe and filled it as Martin and Reece took him to the room where the Keepers were cavorting about like three-year-olds in a restaurant.

"Ah," he said, looking at them. He lit his pipe and sat down.

The two policemen looked at him and felt certain misgivings. He seemed to be seeing through the silliness of appearances in much the same way as a certain emperor was fooled by his tailor. They were not reassured.

"Let's get to work," he said, opening his brown satchel and taking out a notebook and pen.

The Keepers rowed up on the sofa and waited patiently. "I wonder what Beardy wants?" they asked.

"Yuck!" said another. "What are those?"

Stockinged toes in leather sandals peeped out from his under brown cords like mice from under a skirting board.

"I wouldn't be caught dead in those, they look stupid."

The professor tried a number of linguistically acceptable grunts before moving quickly into the less abstract world of hand signals that looked a bit primeval and embarrassing. He was extremely patient, far more so than the two policemen who quickly tired. Martin dropped off to sleep for an hour and Reece drank copious cups of coffee and then had to go to the toilet every five minutes. The Keepers were similarly unimpressed.

"Doesn't he go on?" they said.

"What's it all about?"

"Maybe he's a television producer and he's going to make a documentary about us?"

"Can't be a mainstream production, not in that get-up..."

"I expect it's for one of those awful education programmes like we used to get back home. You know, the ones they'd show really early in the morning."

"If he wants us on television perhaps he's telling us what to do?"

"Just looks like he's waving his arms around to me."

"Perhaps we should give him the gesture of oneness and harmony like we did to those chaps in the rugs?"

"That's a good idea..."

They gave the gesture. The professor looked a bit upset. Reece tried not to laugh but couldn't help agreeing with them. "We don't seem to be making much progress," he said, stuffing a cream doughnut into his face to hide his broad grin.

"Hum?" said the professor. He was foraging in his satchel to the exclusion of everything except his subjects.

"We were wondering if we ought to contact a zoologist," Reece tried.

The professor looked up at him and frowned, "Whatever for?"

"Because they're animals," said Martin sleepily. He suspected the word 'alien' was hovering in the room like a mugger and woke up before another crime could be committed.

"And is that opinion based on scientific observation?"

"It's based on the fact they eat raw fish and behave like albino sealions," said Martin. "Look at them, Professor; if they're 'intelligent life' then I'm a monkey's uncle."

One of the Keepers was picking his nose and another was chewing the corner of a scatter cushion. "I bet we're missing a good programme on the telly," said one.

"Beardy-man is really boring..."

"Boring," they all agreed.

"Could you get me some paper and crayons, or those big felt tip pens perhaps?" said Professor Morris.

"Paper..?"

"Yes, and lots of it..."

They sent the constable to the shop on the corner. "What do you need them for?" Reece asked.

"A little experiment," said the professor.

Martin sighed, "We tried getting them to write their names; it didn't work."

"Did you try and teach them how to write? If they were unfamiliar with the medium then it's not surprising you had no result. I have worked with a number of tribes from remote parts of the world and found almost all of them can grasp the fundamentals of representative art. If these little fellows can be persuaded to co-operate, I believe we might be able to determine whether they are 'intelligent' or not."

Martin and Reece looked at each other, "We should have thought of that," said Reece.

Martin shrugged, "I never grasped the point of 'representative art' either and I'll knee anyone in the fundamentals if they say I'm not intelligent. This won't prove anything."

The paper and pens arrived along with big boxes of crayons and pens. By infinite progressions, the anthropologist persuaded the five Keepers not to eat the crayons but to use them to communicate with. Their first attempts were hazy and indistinct and looked like spiders doing handstands. The Keepers had never learnt to write and their paws were more adept at holding shovels than tricky little pens. However, after a while they began to get the hang of them and then they were scribbling away quite satisfactorily. "This is fun," they agreed.

"Told you it was some kind of education programme."

"At least it's publicity of a kind."

"Didn't think we'd have to make up our own posters…"

"Not very professional, is it?"

"Just have to make sure they're aware of the full range of our talents…"

The scribbles began to take shape as they tried to illustrate their abilities. The spiders were getting more manic and seemed to be trying to fend off a range of coloured balls.

"Hum," said the professor. "We need to direct their thinking a little…" He picked up pen and paper and began drawing the objects in the room; chairs, tables, policemen. This amused the Keepers and they were soon copying him in a shaky but definitely recognisable way.

"How extraordinary," said Reece, looking at Martin, "Do you still think they're just 'animals'?"

Martin ground his teeth. The zoo idea had been a really good one and nobody would have been any the wiser if the little wretches had been dumped on their doorstep. Then a more pleasant thought struck him, "If they're so good at drawing," he said. "Get them to tell us where they've come from so we can send them back."

30 - Stansted Airport

Colin Burgess was facing a second disaster.

He fed and cared for the animals left in the quarantine area of Stansted Airport, a task he was capable of as long as nothing strange was put in his way, and now a second strange thing had happened.

He had returned to work after a holiday to the seaside town of Great Yarmouth where he had been going with his wife for the last ten years. Novelty and new challenges were as familiar to him as art and culture in his chosen holiday destination. He was constitutionally incapable of coping with anything more than routine. He had a note from his doctor to prove it.

He could follow simple instructions from his manager but making him do anything different was like trying to persuade a snail to pop down the shops for a pint of milk. The doctor suggested he be kept away from complex machinery.

Colin had come back to work relaxed and content when, after only a few minutes, the first disaster struck, "Oh lor," he said.

There was an error in the paperwork.

In Cage 114 there should have been 'two giant rabbits, with antlers' scampering about not doing anyone any harm and here were six extra inmates doing similarly harmless activities but with less room.

"Oh lor," said Colin, looking at the instruction sheet.

His single bucket of vegetables was hopelessly inadequate with all these extra mouths to feed. And yet the sheet clearly said 'two giant rabbits, one bucket mixed veges'.

"Oh lor," he repeated, reading the instructions yet again in the vain hope that they had mutated to 'eight rabbits, antlers, four buckets mixed veges', but there was no change.

"What am I going to do?" The rabbits looked at him expectantly and he wondered, innocently, whether he ought to separate them.

Colin knew nothing of the lineal parents in Africa (there had been no television in the caravan he and his wife had rented for the week) so he could only assume that the extra rabbits had been left out of the paperwork in a moment of distraction.

"Funny looking things," he said.

His knowledge of zoology was as undernourished as a pot plant in an empty office block but he was sure rabbits didn't have antlers, and neither were they normally so large.

His theory of evolution failed him as well, "Must be new," he concluded.

He chose to ignore the extra rabbits that were not specifically mentioned on his feeding list. He gave them the single bucket of food and, full of guilt, turned a blind eye to the botched paperwork.

He went about the rest of his duties, cleaning, feeding and doing a bit of stacking in the storeroom until it was time to feed the animals again. This was when the second and more major disaster struck.

He was going past the rabbits' cage, ostensibly to take some dog food to a poodle two cages down the line, when he happened to look in at the alien visitors. Sixteen faces stared back at him.

"Gordon Bennet," he said, suddenly aware that blame could be apportioned to his ignoring of the original paperwork. "Where did you little beggars come from?"

He looked for a hole in the cage, convinced that the new additions could only have come from outside. But even rabbits cannot dig through concrete and as they didn't possess wire cutters he presumed they hadn't got through the walls either. So how had all these others got into the cage?

Colin scratched his head; the rabbits sniffed the dog food.

He walked away and then walked back. The same, excess, number of rabbits stared back at him.

The cage was full to bursting. The floor was hidden, the walls were smothered and antlers filled the ceiling space like a cupboard full of hat stands.

Colin grew agitated and indecisive. "Oh blimey," he kept on muttering. He ran around without much effect. He left the caged enclosures and even considered running away altogether and going back home.

"Anything wrong Burgess?" said a voice.

He was halted in his tracks, the voice of authority steadying his nerves like a large quantity of bricks falling in front of him and making an impenetrable wall. He faced up to the disaster.

"Mr McLane, something dreadful has happened."

"What have you done Burgess?" scowled his manager from the doorway of the office.

"Nothing, Mr McLane, honest to god; I've done nothing, it's those rabbit creatures: there are more of them!"

"More?" answered Mr McLane, only vaguely aware that two strange animals had arrived from Africa.

"There was only a few this morning and now there's even more."

"A few…? There were only two, Burgess, what are you talking about?"

"Sir, there's more than ten, swear to god…"

"You mean they've had babies, Burgess?"

"Yes sir, I mean no, I mean…"

"What are you going on about Burgess?"

"They're big, Mr McLane, the same size as the ones in the cage this morning."

Mr McLane was not stupid, "Don't talk rubbish Burgess. Now, what have you done?"

Colin was close to tears, "Nothing sir, nothing, I swear…"

Mr McLane went into his office and found the paperwork that had come from the university. He returned a moment later, a look of smugness on his face. "There were only two brought in by plane. Now where have the rest come from?"

"I don't know Mr McLane, I honestly don't know."

"Well they must have come from somewhere."

"There's been nobody here, I'd have seen sir, honest, I would have. I was working in the stockroom by the gate, and cleaning cages close-by, and feeding and stuff. I'd have seen anyone bringing in more animals."

"Are you sure?"

"Yes sir."

"You weren't sleeping on the dog-mix sacks in the shed?"

"No sir!"

"I'd better have a look," he said, far from convinced that this was not Colin's fault.

"Thank you sir…"

Mr McLane locked his office and strolled down to the pens. If Burgess was wrong this would give him the opportunity he had always dreamed of to get rid of him. A miracle he had often prayed for.

There were several locked gates through which they had to pass before they could get to the individual cages. They passed several expensive cats, a dog that looked more like a powder puff than anything related to a wolf, and a skunk destined for a short career as a birthday present. They reached the rabbit cage.

"Good lord," said the manager. "Whoever tried to put so many animals into one cage...?"

"But..."

"No doubt trying to save the extra money," he eyed Colin suspiciously.

"But there was nobody here..."

The manager pointed an accusing finger, "So you say."

"But there wasn't."

Mr McLane looked down his nose with disdain and that disbelieving look that normally results in the giver getting a sock in the chops. But Burgess just looked dumb.

"What are we going to do Mr McLane?"

"We'd better split them up for a start, give them more room. You can't keep this number of animals in one cage, it's cruel."

"But it wasn't my fault."

"We'll talk about this later."

In a short while the move was complete and four cages now held the rabbits. Mr McLane was contemplating rental charges. Colin brought extra buckets of mixed vegetables and then had to face his manager's wrath.

"I don't know what happened here," he said (giving the impression that he knew exactly what was going on but as a law-abiding citizen he would defer the lynch mob for a later time), "If I find out you've taken a bribe to let those extra..."

Colin looked shocked, "Bribes sir? Me sir...?"

"I'm not saying you did..."

But Colin was growing annoyed: "Five years I've been here, six at London Zoo before that and I've never taken a bribe in my life."

"All right Burgess, I wasn't saying you had..."

"I've not done anything that wasn't honest, even when it was not for my own good to tell the truth; I've never lied and that's a fact!"

"All right Burgess, I didn't mean..."

"I'm always honest, ask anyone who knows me. I've never done a dishonest deed in my life."

"All right Burgess, I wasn't implying that you had done anything yourself..."

"And neither was I slacking; I was here all the time. Nobody put those animals in there."

"Well how did they get there then?" said Mr McLane impatiently.

Colin shrugged, "I don't know, Mr McLane. I've never seen these sorts of animals before."

Mr McLane had to agree that they looked pretty odd. He read the notes in the paperwork. "They came from Africa," he said.

"Well who knows what kind of things those African animals get up to sir?"

"Quite," the manager agreed reluctantly.

The rabbits looked out of the cage, their mouths stuffed with turnips and carrots. Now they had more room they could consider doing what they did best again. As the two men looked on there was a quick shuffle and the rutting hour began.

The two men were greatly taken aback, not to say embarrassed.

"Blimey," said Colin.

Mr McLane looked equally horrified. Identical scenes of debauchery were going on in all the cages.

"I think we'd better get in contact with the owners," said the manager. "We can't have this sort of thing going on."

"No Mr McLane."

The two men retreated.

A short while later all four cages were as full as the first one had been; without their contraceptive bean there was no stopping them. As long as the food kept coming, new rabbits would keep appearing. Even Bazmondo had trouble keeping their numbers down and often had to resort to the cooking pot.

31 - Africa

Back in Africa people already knew how good the rabbits tasted and were encouraging other nations to sample a morsel or two in exchange for hard currency. The Japanese, ever eager to devour living things, were first up with their Yen, followed by strings of French restaurant owners keen to have 'Morceaux d'Étranger' on their menu.

Even the English with their conservative palates were not averse to feeding rabbit meat to their pets and several dog food companies were looking at Africa in the same way as they had once looked at Australia and its kangaroos.

The prospects for the tribe were beginning to bloom rather well. They noted that the scrabble for rabbit meat was a bit tasteless and greedy, but the Africans had no qualms with their potential status as rich people and were looking forward to being able to import some decent food.

"I'm sick of eating rabbit," they all agreed.

"Chicken would be nice."

"We could have caviar if we wanted."

"What's that?"

"Fish eggs."

"I think I'll stick with chicken."

"I'd like a new suit, one without ears flapping about in my face all the time."

"And proper shoes so I can kick Western butts out of the village when they don't offer enough money for our rabbits."

There was also the matter of housing, "I reckon I must look a proper pillock sitting outside this tepee like Sitting Bull. I want a real house, with a proper zip and a groundsheet that keeps the creepy-crawlies out."

Their future was looking very rosy and utopian. Western economists predicted a time of boom, and not just for the baby rabbits. But of course, this was not to last.

Sudden riches, complicated by the example of Western colonial miss-rule, can have less than a sobering effect on a people deprived for so long. Giving them the alien rabbits was like giving an alcoholic a case of wine. Worse than this, giving one village rabbits and not another was like putting a hundred alcoholics in a wine cellar but only giving one of them the corkscrew.

The Mind™ who had been in charge of Bazmondo's Bunnies was neither curious nor concerned with the results opening his particular Pandora's Box. More important things were afoot; namely the choice between sage or pale pansy for the cushion covers in the upper-deck lounge.

The Mind™ ignored the Africans outside, even the ones who came to the village shouting and demanding equal rights to the rabbits. He continued to ignore them when those shouts changed to fisticuffs and the rival villagers rushed past again chased by rabbit-owning villagers with clubs.

Rabbits, what were rabbits to a mind capable of blending every cloth, colour and cabinet into a deluge of delicious comfort like jelly splashed with onions? He had already re-decorated the fusion cell reactor room in gentle hints of Tuscany and myrtle and was now contemplating what to do with some leftover pieces of Chintz and Seersucker. "Pelmets?" he said, running his eye over the ceiling and the massive air-reclamation bed. "Or doilies..."

What were monkeys arguing over rabbits compared to his creative genius? He scoffed at the rabbit-skin tepees the Africans had made; "They haven't even bothered to co-ordinate the colours," he said.

It was down to the charity worker, Mary Smith, to try and bring calm to the blooming civil war. "What are you doing with those clubs?" she admonished. "You should be trying to help your neighbours, not drive them away like that."

The Head Man looked unimpressed, "Why's that then?"

"Because not all that long ago that was you looking hungry and destitute..."

"Exactly, and by the grace-of-God, that won't be us ever again."

"But God says we should look after our neighbours."

"Different God," the Head Man insisted. "Our God gave us the rabbits and it's up to us to make sure we get a good price for his Gifts."

"But we gave you blankets and milk powder for free. Now you can afford to be more charitable towards your neighbours too..."

"Where are you from?" he asked.

"Kent," she said. When he looked blank she added, "The United Kingdom."

The Head Man nodded, "Ah yes, when my ancestors were charitable to your people, you took our country away and wouldn't give it back for many years. You taught us many things about charity; how it takes away faith and hope like the rains wash away the soil. Please feel free to take back your blankets and milk powder and keep your opinions to yourself."

She tried a different approach, "Couldn't you loan a pair to your neighbours? Then they could breed them and there would be no need for violence…?"

"And spoil our monopoly? God wouldn't like that."

Mary Smith was unclear on the economics of spiritual matters but she was fairly sure the coat of many colours had not done its owner much good. "I wish you would reconsider," she said. "I'm sure God would forgive you for being kind and sharing your good fortune…"

"He is an angry God," said the Head Man. "Kindness is for those without his Gifts. And don't even think about buying our rabbits and giving them to the next village. God's wrath will be great if you try that old trick."

Mary Smith blushed, "Wouldn't dream of it," she said.

32 - London

Professor Morris used a series of pictures to show a sense of time: himself entering the room, smoking his pipe, giving out paper and pens. The Keepers understood and experimented on their own showing fish being served and eaten, watching television and going to sleep.

"Of course," they said, finally getting it. "Autobiographies, how could we have been so stupid…"

They gave a thumbs-up, "No problem," they said and set to work to draw every minute detail of their lives.

It was late in the afternoon when Reece and Martin next put in an appearance. They were surprised to find the room full of drawings and the professor in full swing among them like a tester in a wallpaper factory.

They had been to see their commissioner and received a stern telling off for not informing him sooner. Martin was in no mood for the antics of five silly circus characters, alien or otherwise.

Reece, who had not borne the brunt of the commissioner's ire, and had confessed plainly that he had believed they were aliens all along, was in a more receptive mood, "You seem to be making some progress," he said.

"It's quite incredible," said the professor, blu-tacking another sheet to the wall. "I've managed to get a chronology of events together. It starts over here," his arm swept to a cluster of pictures by the door. "And they end up over here…" He showed them another cluster on the other side of the room.

"Great," said Martin sourly. "Have you got an address yet?"

The professor smiled ambiguously, "They divided up the task and each has drawn a variety of key moments in their lives. I have to say most of them involve fish, but there are some that are particularly interesting…" He led them to the wall of 'recent' pictures. "This, I believe, was how they got here." The pictures showed a string of boxes among some star shapes. The boxes had windows and a number of 'faces' could be seen peering out of each one.

"They came by train?" said Martin. "But where from…?"

The professor held up a finger for him to wait, "There's more. This picture shows a fat little man with what is probably a fat little woman by his side. There seems to be some kind of ceremony going on."

130

Reece and Martin peered closely at the picture, "A wedding?" suggested Reece.

"This third picture shows all five of them in a triangle. There's a splash of red across a square with dots and then in this picture you can see them leaving the 'train'."

"What are these then?" Underneath the 'key moments' the artist had reverted to spiders and coloured balls in a last ditch attempt at subliminal advertising.

The professor shrugged, "Not sure."

Martin frowned, "So what are you suggesting?"

"But you must be able to see, can't you?"

"Not really, no."

Professor Morris pointed to the boxes, "This is their space ship!"

"You said it was a train."

"But those are stars," he pointed to them.

Martin shrugged, "They could be sunflowers or the capitals of Europe for all we know. This is the story of how they travelled over-land from Eastern Europe." He looked to Reece but a cold feeling stole upon him as he saw the look in the latter's eyes.

"How extraordinary," Reece said.

"It's all nonsense," Martin insisted.

"These creatures come from Outer Space," concluded the academic, a trifle unscientifically.

"I agree," said Reece.

"Oh, for goodness sake; there's a perfectly good explanation; they've come by train, one on rails, one with an engine that works on diesel and not moonshine."

"I don't think so, do you?" the professor said to Reece.

"Not at all," Reece concurred.

"But they can't be 'aliens'!" Martin was feeling out-numbered.

"Why not?" said the professor. "You must have seen the news; alien creatures are springing up everywhere. And it seems clear that these fellows might have caused the whole thing," he pointed to the splash of red across the square of dots.

Martin sat down with a thump. Reece patted him on the shoulder in a paternal way.

The Keepers watched patiently, "I wonder what they're arguing about?" they asked.

"Maybe about the rights to our memoirs…"

"Looks like the fat guy has lost..."

"I hope the thin one got a good price."

"I wonder what the royalties will be like."

"This is the most important thing to have happened since we first discovered that we're not at the centre of the universe," said the professor. "Think what this means to the future of mankind? Think what we can learn from them..."

"You can't convince me that these creatures could have brought themselves across the galaxy," said Martin "They hardly seem capable of riding a bicycle let alone some kind of space rocket."

Reece had to agree, "The idea of them being 'superior beings' does seem highly improbable."

"But here they are," insisted the professor. "And we may be dealing with more than just one species, there might be a master species and these are just, well..."

"Pets?" suggested Martin.

"No, I think they're more intelligent than that."

The three earthmen looked at the Keepers. One of them was balancing a pen on his nose, two others were arguing over whether the yellow crayons tasted better than the red ones and another was guarding all the cushions in a corner.

Even the professor was momentarily lost for words. "All right, but somebody must be in charge, presumably the figures holding hands. When they come to get them, think of all the questions we'll be able to have answered..."

Martin looked at the image of the Great Barnooli standing next to his wife. "It's a long list," he said. "Who are they? What are they? And why did they employ five sealions as useless these?"

The Keepers were feeling hungry. They drew pictures of fish and held them up.

"Look," said Reece. "They're trying to communicate with us again."

"...Either we get the fish or you can do your own decorating in the future..."

Reece gave them a thumbs-up, "Very nice," he said loudly.

"Their artistic skills have improved enormously," the professor agreed.

"...Where's our fish then?" said the Keepers.

"I'd like my post-graduate students to run some more precise tests," said the professor. "Of course, normally we deal with people that have been dead for hundreds or even thousands of years, but the principles are the same."

Martin shook his head, "I'm not sure our boss would like that…"

"What do you mean 'no fish'?" said the Keepers.

"We'll be able to DNA test them, look at their bone structure with X-rays and all kinds of useful stuff…"

"I'll have to check," said Martin. "The more people that know about what we've found, the more likely it will reach the newspapers and then it'll be like trying to eat a sandwich next to a wasps' nest."

"I think they know already, sir," said the constable, waving his newspaper at them.

"Oh dear," said Reece.

Martin grabbed the paper. The headline proclaimed a 'Close Encounter of a Theatrical Kind' and there was a big question mark. There was an artist's impression of the Keepers being arrested at Heathrow Airport.

"That's amazingly inaccurate," said Professor Morris.

The artist had put aerials on their heads and tried to make them look fierce with drooling fangs and ray guns. The text was equally lurid and promised an invasion of epic proportions if the Prime Minister didn't resign immediately.

Apart from Hawkins, the security guard, who had framed the original story of the break-in for his mention on the second line, neither Press nor public had taken much notice. Everyone had agreed with the conclusion the journalist had come to that it was the work of animal protesters and therefore nobody interesting.

When the two giant rabbits were brought to Stansted Airport, however, another reporter, remembering the fuss at the Heathrow quarantine area, dug out the original article and showed it to his editor. "Do you think they're linked; is there a connection?"

The editor shrugged, "Make one," he said. "People love a good alien story."

Hyperbole and invention followed, as did the rest of media industry who had come to a similar conclusion. Not a single one, not even among the supposedly serious broadsheets, could resist joining in the fun of following all the alien threads around the world until their evidence was a cat's cradle of false facts and fatuous figures.

"Where did they get the guns from?" said Reece.

Professor Morris shrugged, "Artistic licence I suppose. We'll have to go to the Press and give them the proper story."

"They want roughs with a 'G.H.'," said Martin. "Not ruffs like the kind round Sir Walter Raleigh's neck. Can you imagine the press conference when we bring out the equivalent of Bambi in a muzzle?"

"Not everyone is interested in the fabrications of the newspapers," said the Professor. "Many people will want to know the truth; let my team investigate our guests and give the public a scientific and rational view of these phenomena."

The 'phenomena' were rolling around the floor moaning, "We're so hungry."

"They're trying to starve us…"

"Cruel and heartless monkeys…"

"Oh give them some fish," said Martin, his temper stretched to breaking point as he contemplated how he could escape from the herd of metaphorical goats that would soon be munching through his career. "Shut the little blighters up."

33 - Washington D.C.

"Gee, flying monkeys," said the President of the United States with genuine enthusiasm in his voice.

The Trapezium monkeys had been brought to an airbase outside of Washington DC. A large hangar had been cleared of everything valuable while the administration decided what to do with them. The First Lady and their daughter were standing with him. Outside the hangar they could hear the press corps waiting impatiently for their turn to view the aliens. But the President had called dibs and was determined to keep them waiting for a while longer.

For the President of the United States alien invaders presented the sort of God-given opportunity to display personal leadership qualities that normally only foreign wars and environmental disasters can provide and he was determined not to miss out. "This is great," he said, grinning at the coterie of Harvard graduates who followed him everywhere.

The Harvard graduates shook their heads with disapproval. Some were still refusing to believe the things could fly at all, despite of the fact they had to duck every time the monkeys flew past. They had been making veiled references to 'gates' of various kinds and to economic problems that were not going to be resolved by resorting to comedy.

Their President watched the Trapezium Monkeys fly around the hangar with childlike wonder in his eyes; swooping and gliding, these were real live animals of a kind never seen before outside of the movie theatre or TV. "Gee..." he kept saying.

Scientists from around America had genetically examined the Trapezium Monkeys and found no link with any animal or combination of animals on Earth. They were standing in the hangar too, watching nervously from the side-lines as the President's bodyguards tracked their specimens with automatic weapons.

Apart from genetics, it was obvious that the monkeys were not monkeys at all. They looked like monkeys, they even behaved like them, but they were built like birds. Their bodies were only an eighth the mass of an ordinary monkey's and their bones were especially light. The wings were quite un-mammal-like; in fact the scientists had difficulty explaining them and had argued for hours over whether they ought to be able to fly at all. The other major poser was the fact that they were a sexual unit of three, rather than two, a matter so stunning in itself as to make all the other differences seem rather trivial.

The President's bodyguards watched the monkeys with unalloyed hatred. They fingered their automatic weapons and chewed gum with mechanical precision as the monkeys reflected in their dark glasses.

The monkeys were quite happy. The hangar was almost exactly the same as their carriage and they were content to carry on as normal. They practised their turns and loops, their mid-air changeovers and dives, their back-flips and power-glides. The only thing that really bothered their tiny minds was a lack of energy that they normally consumed in the form of really sweet tea. The bananas and apples were okay, but they really missed their tea.

When they saw the President drinking out of a can they grew curious. They landed and approached him cautiously, rather unsure of the dark and sombre men that had not been applauding enthusiastically.

The bodyguards flexed their large muscles and flicked the safety catches off; muscled jaws ground gold-capped teeth.

The monkeys sniffed the air and the President, coke-in-hand, was quite amused, "I think they want a taste of America, boys," he said with a big toothy grin.

It was a moment before they realised he only wanted to feed the aliens...

When the smoke died down everyone was relieved to see the monkeys crouching beneath the eaves, safe and unharmed. The security men looked embarrassed and put their guns away.

The President shook his head. "You'd shoot your own grandmothers if I didn't tell you not to."

"Let me try," said the President's daughter.

"I'm not sure that's a good idea, honey," said the First Lady. "We don't know where they've been."

"They're quite harmless," the scientists assured her. "We've tested them for pathogens and they're clean."

The First Lady wasn't so confident; she had visions of the flying monkeys carrying away their daughter like Dorothy in the Wizard of Oz, but her husband said, "Sure, come over here Sweetheart and help me get them back on the ground."

He was not going to be deprived of his chance to further American relations with an alien species. Hand-in-hand with his daughter, they walked to the middle of the hangar. "Come on guys," he cajoled. "Come on down…"

The monkeys, used to loud bangs in the circus, quickly recovered their former appetites and fluttered down to the floor for another try at whatever the President was offering.

The President knelt down beside his daughter and gave her the can of cola. "Come on then, come and taste a piece of America," he took a quick glance behind him to check his security men were not going for a repeat performance. All was quiet on the gun front.

The President's daughter held out the can. This made excellent copy for the White House photographer who had the exclusive right to take the pictures. He smiled keenly behind his camera in anticipation of what might follow.

The monkeys edged forward and one of them came even closer to take the can. The President's daughter relinquished the cola and the monkey took a swig.

Unfortunately the taste reminded the monkey of his own urine and he spat it out immediately. The President looked upset. His daughter giggled. The bodyguards smiled and First Lady held her breath.

"I guess he must be a Congressman," said the President, with a wry smile. Everyone laughed and things were all right again.

But the monkeys were still thirsty. The President asked for a variety of beverages to be brought in. The enormous facilities at his disposal produced a small truck loaded with the products of a dozen major manufacturers from twenty different states plus half a dozen other countries.

The President and his daughter, and eventually his wife and even the bodyguards, settled down to a happy hour of trying each drink in turn and the monkeys obligingly co-operated for the benefit of the camera. They tried all the fizzy drinks, then various beers, coffee, milkshakes, sodas, iced drinks and so on. Much to the chagrin of the major American beverage producers, tea came out on top. And not just any tea either; Earl Grey seemed to go down the best.

Outside the hangar, the press corps was beginning to grow restless and rebellious. The original pictures of the monkeys flying through the canyons of Manhattan had filled the nation with joy and a desire to buy things. They were good for the economy, and by extension, the sponsors that paid the wages of the television companies hanging around on the windy tarmac waiting for another chance to film history. If they waited any longer the American people might change channel.

The hangar door opened and America held its breath as the President strode out and climbed the steps onto a podium. He grinned at the nation.

For an administration baffled by budget cuts, unemployment and the cost of living, the flying monkeys were like gold dust. His finely honed publicity machine was mobilised like the cavalry to rescue the public from the Indians of fiscal catastrophe...

He eschewed the use of a personal aide and went straight for the cameras himself; he knew he could tell his people what he liked without a single body bag being dragged out of an airplane to contradict him, "My fellow Americans," warmth, like a well-loved movie star, radiated from his heart and female fans swooned pathetically across the nation. "Let me reassure you that we're not being invaded from Outer Space," he smiled his charmingly boyish smile at the very idea of anyone trying to take on the might of the American military machine. He cleared his throat and went on, "The creatures are quite harmless. I want to assure everyone that we are in no danger; there is no cause for alarm." He smiled the smile of a man at ease in the centre of a hurricane. It was a wonderful illusion. "And let me assure you that no signs of any virus have been picked up by our scientists working with the monkeys."

The scientists were gathered behind the President's podium and they nodded in agreement. They had briefed him with the aid of complicated diagrams and extremely long words. "They're completely safe," the President told the American people, using the abridged version.

"Now I know what you're going to ask," he continued. "Are these creatures really from outer space or are they results of experiments here on Earth? Or are they a hoax created by our finest in Hollywood? I can assure you they're one hundred per cent genuine aliens from another world..."

There was a burst of applause from the crowd. The President grinned.

Convinced the monkeys were not special effects or the results of Moreau-like experiments, the press turned towards the possible rewards to be reaped from finding their mode of transport. A journalist stood up and spoke the American mind, "Is there any sign of the 'mother ship'?"

The President beamed sincerely, "We have not managed to get in contact with the 'mother ship', if there is one, but we're confident that we'll be making significant progress soon."

"How soon?" the journalist persisted.

"That's hard to say at this stage; we understand some kind of space vehicle has been discovered but we cannot comment on that at the moment."

"You mean the box we saw in Africa?"

"That's correct."

A rather petulant NASA was insisting there could be little to be learned by the discovery of such a carriage on their soil; the technology was bound to be beyond their understanding. But that was not the point. What the Americans wanted to know was not 'who made them' or 'how do they work' but 'where's ours?' and the President agreed. "We will, of course, be doing our utmost to discover if a similar space vehicle is here on American soil but so far only the one in Africa has been found and may in fact be 'the mother ship'."

"What about the one in China?"

There were several coughs from the Harvard Graduates; nobody was supposed to know about the carriage in China. The President smiled, "There have been rumours of other creatures in other parts of the world but I cannot comment on those at the moment."

"Why not…?"

"We don't know enough about them yet."

In fact the President was well-aware of the giant giraffe in China. The CIA, with the aid of satellites and a large computer, had been searching the globe for other signs of extra-terrestrial technology. They had spotted the carriage in the paddy field. Then they discovered the giraffe.

"What's the Chinese press saying about it?" the President had asked.

"Nothing at all," replied the CIA. "We don't think they know it's there."

"Maybe we should tell them…?"

"That might not be a good idea, Mr President," the Harvard graduates said. "They might think we're spying on them."

"But they know we're spying on them…"

"It's best if we don't actually admit it though."

The President saw their point but, "This is more important than national pride don't you think?"

The aides shook their heads, "No, Mr President, we don't."

The President wouldn't be put off, "I want to see their Ambassador."

They shook their heads more vigorously, "That's really not a good idea…"

"Now," said the President and they had obeyed reluctantly. However, the Ambassador insisted, "There is no giraffe in China."

"But you can see it in this picture…"

"Trick of light…"

"What about this box then?"

"Storage facility…"

"It wasn't there yesterday."

"How you know? Have you been spying on us?"

"It could be dangerous; the world ought to know about it."

"There is nothing dangerous in China except public opinion; now keep big nose out of business."

The President shrugged his shoulders, "Okay, but don't come running to us when it gets out of hand."

"How can it get out of hand? There is nothing there."

The President had to bite his tongue, "But you must have seen the pictures of the situation in Africa and here in New York…?"

"Fairy tales," said the Ambassador. "Just like silly joke about men on the moon."

"Well, thank you for coming."

The President and his aides turned the pictures this way and that but, however they viewed it, there was still a giant giraffe standing in a paddy field. "Funny colour," they all agreed. "But it's definitely a giraffe."

At the airbase the journalists were invited into the hangar to see the Trapezium Monkeys for themselves. Obligingly, the monkeys put on another show for the new audience.

"Can you communicate with them?" the journalists asked the scientists. "Could you get them to lead us to their spaceship?"

"No," replied the scientists. "They're not that intelligent. We think these patterns they're flying are some kind of mating ritual and nothing more."

"Oh," said the press corps, wondering if they were going to witness another graphic display of alien rutting such as they had seen between the giant rabbits in Africa. When nothing more controversial happened than a triple fliff and piked tuck, they began to lose interest rapidly. "So they're just animals then," they said.

"Alien animals," the scientists insisted.

The journalists were disappointed, "Do they do anything 'alien'?"

"Like what?" the scientists asked. "Isn't it remarkable enough that these creatures come from another world maybe thousands of light years from our own?"

The journalists shrugged, "Not really."

34 - Stereo

Stereo was back in the locomotive's cabin. He was fed up with the Earth; it gave all the impression of an interesting world but it had no substance. It was like a beautifully packaged board game with hundreds of cards and minute plastic pieces that you then discover anyone from nought to ninety can play without skill and without the least idea of what the rules are.

He had come back to the train to see if anyone wanted a proper game, like Tyn Bridge or Arroban Cribbage. He opened the Mind™ channel, "Hi! Does anyone want a game of...?"

"Bog off Stereo, we're watching the lottery..."

"Lottery...?"

"Yes, on the telly."

"They say it could be one of us."

"What?"

"One of us could win a fortune."

"You know the odds are stacked against you?"

"That's not the point; it could still be one of us..."

"Do me a favour; you're Minds™ for goodness sake. Look, there are forty-nine balls, so the odds of you selecting even one correct ball are one in forty-nine; one in forty-eight for the second and so on until all six have been chosen. Multiply those together and you get 10,068,347,520..."

"Stereo?"

"What?"

"Are you going to watch this with us or are you going to waffle on about statistics, because if you are you can piss off now."

"Charming... Try and give you the benefit of my wisdom and all I get is abuse. How narrow minded can you get?"

As one, the other Minds™ told him to get lost.

"Fools," he muttered. He closed the line and sighed. He was bored now.

He looked at the mess around the locomotive's cabin and wondered if he ought to hire some monkeys to clean it up. Then he noticed the locomotive's Mind™ brooding behind the glass at the other end. He tried to make conversation, "Doesn't seem like we're making much of an impression on this planet, does it?" he said, hoping the Mind™ would disagree with him so they could have an argument.

"No," replied the Mind™.

"At least they're not attacking us or anything, remember that time we landed on Quagga by mistake and were savaged by all those hairy moths..."

The locomotive's Mind™ didn't really want to hear this; he was feeling anything but sociable. "Unfriendly bunch of baskets... Spuddle, spuddle, spindle, spigot..."

Stereo peered at the bundle of nanonerves and saw a deep state of psychosis that made him shiver and back away like a man with vertigo retreating from the edge of a cliff. But he asked anyway... "Fancy a game of cards? Take your mind off things...?"

"Spigot..."

"I'll take that as 'no' then..."

35 - The Keepers

A few miles away, the Keepers had also decided not to play any more games. They were feeling sore and under-valued.

A van from the university had arrived with white-coated scientists carrying clipboards. The young men had wispy beards and the women wore beads. The Keepers assumed Beardy had brought his children to be entertained and had obligingly juggled some scatter cushions for their amusement.

The scientists made notes on their clipboards.

"Tough audience," the Keepers agreed and tried a more complex routine. Then they tried making a pyramid but when that failed to elicit a response, not a clap or a smile, they grew annoyed. "We're doing our best," they said.

Then a scientist poked one of them with his pen. "Ow!" said the Keeper.

"What did he do that for?"

"That does it; no more drawings, no more juggling. Not a single trick."

"Not for this lot, not if they're going to go around poking people."

The scientists left the room.

"Good."

"That told them. No more 'Mr Nice Keeper'."

Out in the hall the policemen watched as the professor's students brought in silver metal boxes of equipment. "You came prepared then," said Martin.

"Yes," agreed the professor. "But I told them to expect anything."

"Where did you get all this stuff from?" asked Reece as the scientists started to turn a bedroom into a laboratory.

"It's what we use when we investigate ancient corpses…"

Reece looked at the 'corpses' in the living room, "They're not going to like this at all," he said.

The scientists brought in equipment of all kinds; 'scopes' of many colours, like microscopes, stethoscopes, endoscopes and oscilloscopes with fat green worms wiggling across screens. They had monitors, an X-ray machine and boxes that made a variety of Keeper-like peeps. There were cases of glassware, some empty and some containing coloured solutions. Portable computers were everywhere.

They put plastic curtains around the bed and washed their hands thoroughly before putting on sterile hats and aprons. There was a snap of rubber gloves and they were ready to begin.

Initially, the scientists waved fish at the Keepers and it seemed to the simple minds of the aliens that the professor's children were apologising. However, once they were lured into the laboratory, the Keepers realised their mistake.

Large needles appeared to take blood samples and the Keepers peeped and squeaked for all they were worth, "All right! All right! We didn't mean it!"

"We'll do the drawings!"

"We'll do the act!"

"We'll do whatever you want!"

But to no avail…

"Ow!"

"Ow!"

"Ow!"

"Ow!"

"Ow!"

The scientists passionlessly bled their victims and ran to their equipment like vampires returning to the grave. They also took X-ray pictures. They shone lights into their eyes and looked at their teeth. They weighed them on scales. They shaved bits of fur off their rumps and put it in test tubes for analysis. They shoved the endoscopes where the sun never shines.

After several hours the policemen almost felt sorry for the Keepers, "Poor little buggers," said Reece.

But not as sorry as the Keepers felt for themselves, "Bastards," they said, glaring at their masked assailants (one of whom had a bandage on his finger where he had been bitten). "Just you wait until Barnooli gets here." They sulked in a corner and wouldn't eat the fish they were offered for a whole five minutes.

The constable put the television on for them, partly out of compassion and partly to drown out their whining.

The results of each test were brought to the professor and the policemen and laid before them like holy writ. None of the print-outs meant much to Reece or Martin, but the professor enthusiastically waved the evidence under their noses, "Definitely non-terrestrial," he said with a big grin. "It will be a while before we get the DNA tests back but everything else is fascinating."

"Hooray for science," said Martin.

The professor ignored him, "The most peculiar and alien thing about them is their blood," he showed them an incomprehensible list of numbers. "I've never seen blood so vicious towards hostile bacteria." They had mixed some with a cold virus and it had come out of the syringe like a fly-weight boxer with a grudge. "The virus never stood a chance," he said.

"Amazing," said Reece. "What does it mean?"

"They have a perfect immune system."

This was only to be expected of an employee of the Great Barnooli's circus. Everyone in the circus, animals included, carried a special blood formula to fight against the micro-cultures of the different worlds they encountered. It was another of Barnooli's keys to success. Without it they would have decimated most of the galaxy and themselves.

"And look at their skulls," he showed Martin and Reece the X-ray pictures. "Look at the position of the eyes and the nasal ducts. Completely different from the sea mammals they superficially resemble…"

"Extraordinary," agreed Reece, though he had no idea what the inside of the head of a seal looked like.

"Small brains," Martin noted.

"It's very exciting," said the professor. "Look at the way the bones of their paws are articulated…"

The doorbell rang and Martin left to answer it. They heard him arguing over the price of fish. The fishmonger was demanding payment.

"They have opposable thumbs," the professor said to Reece.

"Like humans," said the policeman.

"Not exactly the same; the distal phalanges are similar but the carpals are broader, presumably for swimming…"

"I can't believe how much you're charging," Martin was saying at the door. "What are you doing, catching them with a rod and a rowing boat?" The fishmonger made noises that sounded like an apology.

"With their developed senses," the professor concluded, "They should be capable of quite complex behaviour. We might be looking at juveniles of the species, which is why we've been having trouble getting them to understand us."

"Kids?" said Reece. "I suppose that make sense. Martin thought they were teenagers; I guess he was right."

Martin returned with another pallet of sprats and mackerel. "The bill from the fish shop is criminal; it's going to make this year's over-time bill look like the tea fund by comparison." He put the pallet in the kitchen, "And I think we're being watched," he added.

"Who by?" said Reece.

"There are some shifty-looking characters on the street opposite so I imagine they're journalists."

"How did they find us?" asked the professor.

Martin shrugged, "Just guessing, but how many tons of fish have been delivered to this address over the last few days, and how many journalists looking for five white sealions might find that interesting?"

The Keepers were making a noise. "More carriages," they were shouting. "Maybe more survivors too..."

The humans went to the living room and watched the news from America. There were pictures of the carriage in Africa and a fuzzier picture of one in China. The Americans were wondering where 'theirs' was.

"If they came in separate vehicles," said the professor. "Perhaps our little friends here did too." He went over to the wall and took down their picture of the train and showed it to the Keepers. Then he looked questioningly at them, raising his hands and gesticulating around the room as if he expected to see it lurking behind the sofa.

"Now what does he want?" they grumbled.

Morris kept pointing at the train.

"That's right, 'train'."

He looked around the room and under the couch to emphasise his question.

"No, I don't think you'll find it in here, look..." They picked up their crayons and set to work. Within seconds there were five squiggly blue lines with some crow-like shapes that were faintly recognisable as cranes. "There, you see? It's as big as one of these."

"...Docklands?" said Martin.

"Could be," agreed Reece.

"What about the Tower of London?" the constable added.

"Tower of London...?"

"...Gallows, sir."

"Let's get the van round the back," said Reece, his excitement growing, "and see if they can take us there."

36 - China

Bamboo fronds waved high in the China air and there was a rustle of activity around their base. Four generals from the Chinese High Command, over-weight and sweating, were struggling through the forest of stems to get a peek at the rice paddy beyond.

Trusting nobody, not least their own spies, they had secretly left their comfortable lives to find an answer to the question posed by the Ambassador in Washington: "Is there really a giant giraffe in the Provinces or are the Americans taking the Mickey out of us again?" If they were, if there was nothing there, then they could ignore the Americans. But if they were right then someone would have to go to the United Nations and accuse the Americans of spying. But they had to be sure first.

The four generals, medals shining in the hot sun, peeked out at the paddy field. They were hot and bothered and not in the mood for another game of Chinese Whispers…

"I don't see a giraffe," said one.

"Good, let's go home."

"Wait, what's that?" a third general pointed to the carriage.

"Just an aircraft hangar…"

"Where's the runway?"

"It's not on the map," said a fourth, trying to wipe mud off the relevant area. "Oh yes it is, it was hidden…"

He showed them the map the local branch of the military had supplied. There was a hastily drawn square marked in black ink. It had smudged in the damp. "Just an over-sight, like British in Hong Kong," they agreed.

"There's nothing important here, let's go home…"

The first general leaned against a particularly thick bamboo stalk and wiped the sweat off his brow. "Let's face it; the Americans are trying to humiliate us again. We shouldn't be here; we should be back in Beijing living it up with good-time girls, not creeping around the outskirts of this peasant village looking for some stupid freak of nature…" The other three were staring above him, "What? You prefer it here in this thicket?"

They shook their heads.

"You don't like good time girls?"

More head shaking. One pointed up. There was a small cloud over his head that began to rain on him. He looked back down to find his comrades scrabbling through the undergrowth to get away from him.

"What's wrong with you?" he said.

"We're not being urinated on by a sixty-foot giraffe," they replied, diving behind a rock.

There was a moment of thrashing through the long bamboo as the soiled general tried to get away. He tripped and fell. He heard breathing and looked behind him into the face of the giraffe. He screamed. The giraffe, her orange eyes dolefully unthreatening, moved closer.

"Get away!" screeched the general.

The giraffe sniffed at the little man. He smelt familiar; perhaps he was with the circus?

"Help!" he cried, "Help!"

The terrified generals, hiding behind their rock, began covering themselves with leaves.

The giraffe, just to confirm her impression, licked the face of the general. It tasted familiar as well.

The general was trying to get his gun out, "Aah!"

Losing interest, she stretched her elegant neck back above the gently swaying bamboo and wandered off towards the village.

The general collapsed with relief. He was covered in mud, pee and spit and had been abandoned by his comrades; but at least he was still alive. "What a terrible creature," he said.

The other three gingerly peeked out from their hiding place, like frightened turtles, "Has it gone?" they called.

"Yes, it has gone to attack the village." He pulled himself out of the mud. His legs were shaking. He held onto a bamboo stalk and tried to see what the monster was doing.

The other generals re-appeared from their leafy refuge and went to their fallen colleague. "Was it awful for you?" they asked.

"Now you show concern! I could have been killed!"

They felt ashamed, except one who said, "It didn't seem that fierce to me."

"You were not the one being attacked; if I had not managed to defend myself and driven it away it would have come after you as well."

"It doesn't seem to be eating those peasants," another general commented.

Several villagers, struggling with a long pole with a basket on the top, were obviously feeding the beast. "It seems quite tame."

Some children were playing around the legs of the alleged man-eater. It gently lowered its head and allowed itself to be petted.

The four generals left the thicket and made their way cautiously around the edge of the rice paddy. They headed towards the village, angry and ready to arrest somebody.

The ground was wet and muddy and the generals struggled to keep their footing on the slippery path. "Quickly," they urged each other, "Before the monster spots us."

The monster remained where the food was. She munched her way through her basket of rice leaves and enjoyed the company of the children.

The villagers spotted the four generals approaching across the fields. The Chief Rice Picker and his son had time to prepare a small buffet and gather the rest of the co-operative to greet their guests. "Do you think they have come to take the giraffe away?" they asked each other while they made a banner to welcome the representatives of the People's Army.

"We like the giraffe," said the children. "Can't we keep it?"

"No," said their parents. "It belongs to all the Chinese people. We must not be selfish"

"They didn't want it before," the children insisted. "Those other soldiers were happy to leave Ping in our care."

"The giraffe is not called 'Ping', child," warned the parents, "and you must not give it a name because it is not ours."

Eventually, the four generals arrived at the village. They were dishevelled and dirty. One of them had lost a shoe in the mud. There was an awkward silence as they tried to gather what was left of their dignity. The villagers bowed to them. "So," began the most senior commander. "You thought you could hide such a terrible monstrosity from the attention of our glorious government. You should all be ashamed."

The Chief Rice Picker bowed again, "Abject apologies," he said. "But we did not know what to do with it." He tried not to notice the beetle crawling on the general's jacket. "We informed the People's Army but they didn't know what to do with it either. Have you come to take the creature away?"

This was a moot point as the generals had no instructions from their political partners on what to do next. They had been told to find facts and they had found them. "The matter has yet to be discussed at the highest levels," said the general evasively. "We were sent to ascertain the level of danger to the Chinese people."

"I see," said the Chief Rice Picker. "Is that why you decided to camouflage yourselves in mud and leaves?"

The general's face went red, "Indeed," he said.

"Perhaps you would care for some refreshment and we could launder your clothes while we wait for our political masters to send more instructions?"

The buffet did smell good. "Very well," said the general. He turned to his comrades, "We will call in our troops to protect the people and inform the chairman of our progress."

One of the generals had a flare gun that he fired up into the sky. An hour later the village was surrounded by a several thousand soldiers and everyone felt much safer.

The four generals sat outside the Chief Rice Picker's hut in freshly laundered uniforms and enjoyed the simple fare the villagers had to offer. They had made a full report to their political partners that avoided all unnecessary references to their tussle in the bamboo, their walk across the rice paddies or the fact they had been sitting naked in a hut while their uniforms were being washed. However, they did confirm the existence of the giant giraffe and its extra-terrestrial box.

As they drank more bowls of rice wine, even the giraffe began to look better in their eyes. "It is a graceful creature," they agreed as they watched her plod towards a tank and sniff the barrel. "Useless of course, but pretty..."

"We call her 'Ping'," said the children.

The generals laughed.

37 - Scotland

In Scotland, two very wet and frightened pair of climbers eventually returned to the mainland. Eric and Chris Watts babbled long and incoherently about sea monsters and the salty sea dog in the boat brooked no response to the silly chatter of foreigners, especially English-type foreigners.

"Sea monsters is it?" said the Scotsman. "Och, me and young Jimmy Macrurie, we seed a greet two headed beastie behind the kirk wun Sunday. We'd jus stepped oot the door of the *Scotch Broth* and were havin' a pee when the greet bannock reared its ugly heed. I sez, 'I ken we're in the briny now Jimmy, yon beastie will have us for its supper.' But he sez, 'Och no laddie; tis jus the whisky talking for tis yer wife come to get you hame!'"

When they finally got to a telephone, the Watts brothers were quick to capitalise on the revitalised industry in the bizarre and unidentified. Using nefarious connections gleaned from years spent in fashionable wine bars and the pistes and beaches of Europe, the brothers managed to sell their story to several newspapers and television companies.

Television producers and newspaper people booked seats on trains and planes and took to the North like migrating geese. Camera crews followed them by road. When they arrived they were disappointed to discover that their scoop had not remained exclusive for very long; hundreds of amateur and professional photographers were already queuing up for boats to take them to the cave, all with the express intention of getting pictures of a slightly miss-placed Loch Ness monster.

The salty sea dogs and all the local shopkeepers revised their price lists and rubbed their hands with glee. This was going to be a good start to the tourist season.

The little boats sailed out to the island like a re-enactment of Dunkirk. Some disembarked on the shore and walked across the island to the cliff-tops above the cave. The rest sailed to the other side to view the cave from the sea. There was even a helicopter hovering expensively above them blowing spray into their faces.

The Watts brothers were standing with the cliff-top crowd. They had been offered a whopping consultancy fee to return to the scene of the attack to offer comments; money they had accepted so long as they were not required to give interviews anywhere near the mouth of the cave.

Standing with the television producers, they liked to believe they were in a safe place, thinking not unreasonably that the creature was unlikely to be able to fly (after all, who had ever heard of a real dragon having wings?). The television directors, against better advice, thought being out to sea was a better position to capture the historic rearing of an ugly head (or heads). The salty-sea dogs thought they were all mad. "Och, the lot of ye are no better than a spirtle up a puddock's bum!"

Much to the horror of vegetarian viewers around the world, a leg of pork was then lowered from the lip of the cliff and dangled in front of the cave. After wiggling the bait about for half an hour, one impatient film crew threw caution to the wind and decided to land for a closer look.

"I don't think that's a good idea," said Eric Watts.

"No," agreed Chris, backing away from the edge of the cliff as the little boat sailed closer to the cave below.

"Oh I'm sure it'll be all right," said the television producer, who was also nowhere near any potential trouble.

All went well at first; neither soundman nor cameraman fell in the cold sea and none of the equipment was damaged in what was, on the face of it, quite a tricky operation. Urged on via a walky-talky by the director, the camera team boldly approached the darker recesses of the cave. With the aid of a torch they scanned the rocks.

"Ah shoot," the cameraman was heard to say. "There's nothing here..."

There was a loud roar, two red eyes momentarily flashed like an articulated lorry reversing, and a jet of black and noxious smoke engulfed the raiders.

Black and terrified, the film unit's finest fled in disarray, equipment abandoned, screaming loudly. Live pictures curdled the blood of millions and salty-sea dogs swore bitterly to the embarrassment of sound recordists. A puff of black smoke billowed out from the hole in the cliff and the two investigators could be seen swimming like paddle steamers for the spurious safety of the boats.

There was a second and louder roar and then silence. The smoke gradually cleared, the two swimmers were rescued and the Watts brothers said, "I told you so" in loud, uncompromising terms.

Before anyone could make up their minds whether to flee or take another look, a naval frigate and a large number of marines arrived. Apparently the Ministry of Defence owned the island and they seemed worried about the possibility that the Watts brothers had discovered a secret even they had no knowledge of.

That the navy appeared so quickly on the scene was a bit of a mystery; that they quickly cleared the area of all extraneous personnel was no surprise at all. The Watts brothers were, however, ordered to stay. Various officers approached them on the cliff and smiled coldly before marching off in the general direction of a hastily erected mess tent.

"We must get to the bottom of this as soon as possible," said a minister from the government, one of several that had been dispatched to deal with the problem. "It may be nothing at all."

"But we've seen this black stuff coming out of the cave," said the journalists who had managed to corner him as he arrived. "Are you saying there isn't some kind of creature inside? Two climbers and our own reporters said they saw something living in there…?"

"I expect it's just munitions left over after the war."

"It 'roared' at them. We all heard it."

"An experiment…"

"What kind?" the reporters demanded. They had dim recollections of stories connected with anthrax, but they were assured there was 'none of that' on the island.

The marines, not noted for taking much truck from sea monsters, were all for blowing the cliff to kingdom come, but various pressure groups protested vigorously so it was decided that the monster, or whatever it was, should be disabled with large volumes of classified gasses.

The Scots people, who had assumed the island belonged to them, complained to the minister, "This is our island, what are ye doing with all these bombs? Ye'll scare the sheep worse than the skirl of the pipes."

"We have been informed of a creature lurking in that cave."

"Creature…? Ye daft Sassenachs, would ye go after the last dodo with a shotgun or catch yoursel' a whale by stabbin' it with a harpoon?"

"It may be a danger to the public."

"Och and yon Jack Tars runnin' around with guns isner a danger; look at them, wus than the Southern eejits in the grouse season."

The marines persisted in their unloading of supplies onto the island, a large helicopter ferrying them from the frigate. Sitting on the cliff watching the efforts of the Royal Navy, the Watts brothers could only wonder at what the creature beneath them might be thinking. "That cave is pretty big, he could be enormous," said Chris.

"If he didn't like us two trespassing on his patch, he ain't gonna like this lot."

A marine went by whistling the tune of 'Puff the Magic Dragon'. Whether it was an experiment, an alien or the Loch Ness Monster on holiday, it was all the same to them. They lowered ropes over the edge of the cliff and prepared to descend.

"Do you think we ought to tell them about the effect of the smoke?" asked Chris.

Eric shook his head, "Stuff 'em, it's their funeral."

However, the marines were quite efficient and they were taking no risks. The gas canisters were laid and they climbed back up the cliff without incident. Indeed, all would have gone quite well if the Smog Monster had decided to stay where he was. All the noise, the dangling things in front of the cave, the men with their cameras, the green men with their silver eggs and the constant chatter of radio signals that he could pick up in his head like an old crystal wireless, had begun to cheese him off.

Before the marines had time to detonate their bombs, a big, black, yawning reptile the size of a Methodist church lumbered out of the cave and belly-flopped into the sea. Cameras rolled, marines gawped and the Smog Monster took off in a tidal wave of surf for pastures new. The frigate was a little off-putting so he turned to port and swam for the mainland, much to the horror of the salty-sea dogs and their fee-paying passengers that were in between. The Smog Monster ploughed through the small boats like a fox among ducklings. Several of them were overturned and the rest were swept out of the way on the tsunami of water.

The Watts brothers gawped with everyone else and then laughed rather loudly. Those media men who had begged and pleaded to be allowed to stay on the island ran about the cliff trying to get better and better pictures. "A real monster!" they said gleefully, "Better than rabbits with antlers on their heads!"

The stony-eyed Navy men glared like rocky islets but the marines sparked up and shook their heads like they had seen it all before. "Bleedin' waste of time, told you we should have blown it."

The officials from the government were looking worried. They were standing in the map room on board the frigate wondering where the Smog Monster could be heading. The frigate's captain took a lot of persuasion to follow the monster, even at a safe distance. "I'm not happy about it," he said. "What if it turns towards us?"

The ministerial officials made important telephone calls and tried to ignore the chunterings of the navy men who muttered comments about 'cut-backs' and weak spots in island defences. Various criticisms were bandied about and then the party transferred to the deck to tacitly watch the swimming reptile through binoculars.

The Watts brothers and everyone else still on the island were now where they didn't want to be: out of the action. However, because the brothers were saying 'I told you so' to anyone that would listen, they were now considered 'experts'. When a helicopter arrived to take a television crew to where they would be able to film the beast, the brothers were bundled on board to offer a running commentary, which suited them just fine. "Cool," they agreed.

Behind them, the salty-sea dogs headed for home, some rather wetter than when they set out. Several had lost their boats and it seemed unlikely they would be compensated for their loss. They were in no mood to talk about 'sea monsters' when they arrived back at the fishing village even though dozens of people, including many that were not foreigners, bombarded them with questions. "No comment," they said, even to their wives.

38 - The locomotive

The police van roared out of the side street, tyres squealing. In spite of the noise, and the inconvenience of having to stop for an old lady who was trying to cross the road, the police, the Keepers and the scientist managed to get away without the journalists spotting them. A quarter of an hour later the van entered the dockland area and began searching for the train.

"This is not going to end well," Martin grumbled. "Why didn't we bring sandwiches and a flask and make a picnic of it?"

Reece was staring ahead, searching the barren landscape. His heart leapt, if only for a brief moment, when he spotted a flash of blue. Then he saw it was just a small boat on the Thames.

The searching of the docks was obviously a popular decision among the Keepers who kept making peeping noises and pointing at things that the humans found curiously insignificant. "Did we pass those funny houses?" they asked, pointing at the gasometers. "The ones without the windows…?"

"We might have done."

"What about those fences, do they look familiar?"

"Yes, it's not far now."

They kept pointing downstream, "Over there, over there," they were saying. "By the water…"

"No," insisted Martin. "You can't go fishing. Now be quiet."

"I think they know where we're taking them," said Reece. "I think they recognise some of the landmarks."

"I agree," said the professor, who was becoming very unscientific in his excitement. "It must be near here. I can feel it…" He puffed vigorously on his pipe and Martin had to open a window.

"I hope we're on the right side of the river," said Reece. "It's a long way round if it's not and the traffic will be murder at this time of day."

Deep down Martin still retained a feeling that all they would find would be a squeezy bottle painted like a rocket and hopefully some students they could arrest for wasting police time. If things went really bad then they would also find a protest claiming independence for some god-forsaken part of the world or some cunning statistics relating to the unfair balance between police spending and the rescue of an obscure sea mammal. He imagined a number of embarrassing scenarios.

The Keepers were growing more and more excited, "Look," they said.

"What now? Don't say there's a fish shop all the way down here?"

They were pointing wildly at a part of the dock where some ships were tied up. "There! There!"

Martin looked and scoffed, "Just some pleasure boats, I told you so."

Reece gasped. The constable driving the van gasped. Professor Morris made a faint gurgling noise. They stared and stared.

Martin was failing to see whatever it was he was supposed to be seeing. "What are you looking at?" he said, beginning to panic.

Everyone pointed, including the Keepers. But Martin's mind refused to see it for several moments.

Pleasure boat, blue thing, pleasure boat…

Blue thing…?

"Train…" he exclaimed. There it was and it was real, and better than all the blood tests and hokey stories from other countries. His jaw dropped and he turned to Reece, "How in the world did we miss that?"

The Great Barnooli's locomotive gleamed in the sun, its light blue paint as shiny as the day it was put on. Its brass fitments beamed without a single fingerprint or mark of tarnish and the silver and chrome of the complex engineering told of the power and the glory within. The streamlined engine hung over the water in a way that foxed the eye and fuddled the brain. It neither hummed nor throbbed but hovered silently like a rhetorical question.

"It's like the 'Mallard'," whispered Professor Morris.

"It's like a duck?" said Martin, failing to see any connection.

"No, like the old steam train…"

"Oh." Trainspotting was in his top ten of things never to do.

"1938, it broke the world speed record for a steam train; 126 miles per hour."

"Extraordinary," said Reece.

"Let's have a closer look," said the professor.

The constable stopped the van and they clambered out. The Keepers, over-joyed to be out of the little flat, ran onto the wharf. "Told you so," one of them said to the others. "I told you the birds wouldn't poop on it and spoil the paintwork."

They entered the shadow of the great machine, beneath the enormous ducts, pipes and assembled parts suspended above them like the flutes and trumpets of a heavenly choir. The huge nameplate glittered in gold and fuligo in the sea of the glorious blue. 'Barnooli' it declared, though nobody except the Keepers could read it.

"But how on Earth did nobody notice this before?" Martin repeated. "It's as big as an airship…"

"It's surprising what people don't notice," said the professor. "How many buildings are there in London that you pass every day without ever really seeing or know the function of?"

"This is not a building," said Martin. "And it wasn't here a week ago…"

"I expect people think it's one of those fancy yachts," said Reece. "It's only when you get closer that you notice it isn't even in the water."

"I wonder how it does that?" said the professor, peering down at the complex and beautiful machinery that on a normal train would be where the wheels were attached.

"What's that up there?" said the constable.

"It's the wretched sealions…"

The train was so encompassing that nobody had spared much of a thought for the Keepers and it was only when they saw them waving from the top of the gangplank that they realised they had gone at all.

"We'd better get after them," said Martin.

"Do you think it's safe to go on board?" said Reece.

"How should I know?"

"I mean, it's not suddenly going to take off or anything?"

Martin shrugged, "Just don't touch anything when we get inside…"

"I expect those were the last words the owner said," said the professor.

The Keepers were shouting and waving for their human hosts to join them. Professor Morris waved back and looked at the others. "Shall we or shan't we?" he said, great puffs of smoke from his pipe shrouding him and clouding their judgement.

"After you," said Martin.

"I'll go first," said Reece bravely. "We've no idea what may be up there…"

They climbed the long gangplank feeling both curious and apprehensive. The metal of the brass handrail was slightly warm and the air was charged with energy. The train was like a living being, a great blue whale watching them silently.

Reece was nearly at the door. Then he said, "Oh…" in a way that suggested deep dissatisfaction.

"What is it?" said Professor Morris.

"It's locked."

"It's what?" said Martin.

"They can't get in."

"Don't they have a key, or password?"

"Apparently not…"

They gathered around the door. The Keepers were as surprised as a rich man at the gates of heaven and were making a big noise about it. "Peeping Mind™!" they wailed. "He's locked us out."

"Open the door!"

"Yes, open the door you miserable git!"

"You pocket calculator!"

"…Sandwich-maker!"

"Fuse box!"

"Light switch!"

"Battery operated marital aid!"

The locomotive's Mind™ didn't hear them, even if he had been listening (which he wasn't). He was focussed on his continuing misery and loneliness and he was not about to interrupt it for anyone, especially not for the Keepers whom who considered so far beneath his contempt as to be almost on a par with pleasure cruisers.

Stereo could have let them in. But he was busy, very busy. He ignored the hammering on the door and continued cataloguing his collection of interesting sounds. "I'll alphabetise my decibels next," he said, humming to himself so he couldn't hear the knocking sounds. If the Keepers and their human guests wanted to come in they would have to speak to the locomotive's Mind™.

"What do you think has happened?" said Reece.

"Probably a Yale lock; silly beggars pulled it to on their way out," said Martin. "Now they can't open it again."

The Keepers beat and kicked the door but nothing happened. "I bet Stereo is in there too," they agreed.

"He won't open the door; he's far too snotty to do really important things like letting us in…"

"That's disappointing," said the professor. "Rather an anticlimax, all things considered."

Martin frowned, "What a waste of time," he mumbled (but at least it wasn't a squeezy bottle, he recalled. At least it was the real thing.)

161

They watched the useless attempts by panic-stricken Keepers to break down the door but it was obvious it was meant to keep out more than a draught. Reece and the professor put their hands on the surface.

"It's a sliding door," said the Keepers, unable to keep the contempt out of their voices. "You can't 'push' it open."

"It feels like iron or steel," said the professor. "I would have thought an alien space ship might have used a high-tech alloy of titanium or a metal we've never encountered before…"

Distraught, the Keepers slumped on the floor and moaned, "Now we'll never get our records back."

"We can't hang around here," said Martin. "We'll have to leave the constable to guard it and go make our report."

"I confess I'm most disappointed," said the professor.

Reece nodded, "It would have been nice to have had this business all cleared up and ready for the public's inspection."

They left the train, dragging the stricken Keepers with them, and went back to the flat just as the story of the Smog Monster hit the headlines.

39 - The Minds™

As the Smog Monster ploughed his way through the sea pursued by the frigate, the Minds™ on the train above felt very little sympathy for the plight of humanity. They were watching the whole thing on television while they waited for their lottery numbers to come up.

With laughable simplicity and inappropriateness, the news anchors were insisting the Smog Monster was related to a long lost plesiosaur from 'Loch Ness', a creature with a thin neck and no ability to light a match let alone burn a house down. Even the Minds™ knew the difference and they were from another world.

Two 'experts' were talking at length about their experiences. They seemed to be in some kind of blender with rotating blades, hovering over the Smog Monster while they described the horror of their encounter. When asked if they thought the creature was a threat to life on Earth they shook their heads solemnly, "Who knows?" they said. "But it could be a commercial asset in the right hands."

"Do you believe we could take advantage of this new alien?" asked the news anchor.

"Why not?" said the expert. "Those giant rabbits must be worth a bob or two or there wouldn't be such a fuss over them."

The Minds™ were aware of what the expert meant. The small quarrels in Africa over ownership of the rabbits had expanded into bigger quarrels and now there was a full-blown conflict, complete with war correspondents and 24 hour news coverage.

The Mind™ in charge of the rabbits had been criminally content to let them breed and breed and quite apathetic to the tons of bean feed he could have let the world have to control their numbers. During the afternoon, while he was designing textured wallpaper and shelves made from papier-mâché, he was alerted to the events outside by multiple shots fired in anger. These were not shots at rabbits but shots against each other. However, none of this bothered the Mind™, not the shooting, not the people getting killed within feet of his walls. The carriage was immune to their little weapons so nothing else mattered to him. The other Minds™ found nothing to disagree with. Except his taste in decorating; that was the real crime.

Their lottery programme was delayed and the Minds™ were beginning to get irritated. Every channel seemed to be fixated on the

Smog Monster and he wasn't even doing anything interesting. "For goodness sake," they said. "Just put him back in his box and stop messing about."

The Smog Monster reared up out of the water and snapped at a helicopter that came too close. The people in the helicopter, the commentators and the film crew, made a great deal of fuss over the event. Images of the enormous jaws, opening to reveal a mouth of serrated teeth the size of extra-large surf boards, were shown in slow motion over and over.

"They shouldn't let him play with them like that," said the Minds™. "He'll get tired and bad-tempered."

"Remember when he got loose on Momus?"

"And he ate all those lemon trees?"

"He always did have a sour disposition; he was ten times worse after that."

"He doesn't know what's good for him."

"Where's his minder?"

"Still looking at lobsters, I believe."

"Somebody should tell him."

"Whatever for, I'm sure he wouldn't have let the Smog Monster run about like that if he didn't have a good reason…?"

"True enough."

The Smog Monster's Mind™ had collected vast stacks of data on marine biology and had discovered several new deep-sea flora and fauna. He had stored away pictures of them in his own personal library (a collection that made the Smithsonian look like a child's collection of shells by comparison) and was compiling several articles that might, under different circumstances, have ended up in Nature or the Geological Society magazine. He had measured temperature and depth with the same accuracy as a caesium clock measuring time. He had examined the sea floor fault lines like a carpet-buyer in a bazaar, picking over every thread of warp and weft, every knot and tassel. He had made maps so accurate the Ordnance survey looked like scribbled directions on the back of an envelope.

And then he remembered the Smog Monster.

"Oh blast," he said, metaphorically wincing at the thought.

He didn't want to speculate on whether he ought to have opened the door and let the Smog Monster out, the answer to that was obvious. He could have easily left the Smog Monster inside the carriage; the full life support system would have kept him happy for many years. And there was always the problem of the stupid creature's agoraphobia. The sea was a big place, and from what he had seen the land was not much smaller, possibly without nooks or crannies big enough for him to hide in. He would be terribly frightened, possibly suicidal. The Mind™ felt a modicum of sympathy.

He was also picking up various radio messages and gathered that the local primate population was none too pleased with the Smog Monster's activities. Messages with words and phrases like 'help' and 'we're all going to die' kept crossing the airwaves. "I don't think he's winning any popularity contests," thought the Mind™. "Funny really, the kids really love him in the circus."

To the British public, giant rabbits hopping about the savannah and monkeys flying off the Empire State had been reasonably entertaining. It was difficult to see the funny side of the Smog Monster. Here was a real and palpable threat to all they held dear, namely their homes. Not for a moment did they understand how such a ferocious and fire-belching dinosaur could ever become a welcome feature in their lives. It had feet, it could swim and it might even have wings for all they knew. The average homeowner could easily imagine the effect of an armour-plated reptile on their detached or semi-detached castles.

The Minds™ on the train listened in to their telephone conversations as up and down the British Isles the cries of the populace were heard declaring: "If it comes up on our beach, I'll stick it with my pitchfork…"

"Just like the war, when the doodlebug blew up grandfather's shed…"

"Took me years to get my compost just right, those roses are the finest in England, and all for what if that creature crashes through my allotment?"

"I spent the summer up the ladder for that level of gloss; those window frames will last for a lifetime. I don't want some Scottish export mucking them up!"

Even the animal loving conservationists were upset: "It's stomped all over the breeding ground of the rare spotted tern," they whined. "It's caused irreparable damage to the blue-billed puffin and frightened the living daylights out of the long-eared basking seals."

The Smog Monster looked set to do the same to a dozen more protected patches of animals and wildfowl if it carried on going south; "Can't somebody do something?" they demanded.

"Like what?" the military replied.

"Can't you shoot it?"

"What with…?"

"Guns, missiles, nuclear bombs…?"

"I thought you were conservationists?"

"There won't be anything to conserve if you let it run about like that for much longer!"

The Minds™ on the train laughed and laughed.

40 - The Keepers

Back in the flat, the Keepers were over-joyed to see the Smog Monster swimming through the sea showing every sign of good health and vigour. They ran around the living room celebrating while Barnooli's favourite cruised across the television screen with all the finesse of the *Titanic* looking for an iceberg. "He's not dead!" they exclaimed, hugging the policemen.

"Barnooli won't throw us to the Great Lion of Azaroth!"

"No, get off!" said Martin. "Get off, you smell of fish! Ah yuck, one of them has just kissed me!" He was trying to speak to his superior about finding the locomotive in the docklands. "Sorry sir, they're very excited about seeing the monster on the television; it seems they recognise it."

There was a long pause as his superior let him know how exactly how he felt about the monster, the aliens and the discovery of the train. None of it was complimentary. "We'll do our best, sir," said Martin at the end of the tirade. He put the phone down.

"What did he say?" asked Reece cautiously.

"He wants us to try and get into the train again," he replied. "The wisdom from above says if we can get inside then we can contact the real owners and get them to stop that monster before it tears up half the country."

"What do they propose we try and do?" asked the professor.

Martin shrugged, "They're sending the army with cutting equipment and if that doesn't work they'll try using explosives."

"That seems a bit extreme."

"And a dragon ripping up the British Isles isn't?"

"Let's see if we can get any more out of them," the professor picked up the paper and crayons. "We might be able to get them to tell us how they were locked out in the first place."

The Keepers were still enjoying the sight of the Smog Monster living and breathing smoke when they had been sure he was belly-up at the bottom of an impact crater. "He's alive!" they said for the millionth time.

"I hope he's happy."

"You don't think this world is too big for him?"

"He'll get his agoraphobia back and then Mr Barnooli will be annoyed with us."

"But at least he's not dead!"

"I wonder what they want?" they saw the two unfunny men and the straight man pointing at the screen. The keepers gave the thumbs up sign the professor had taught them, "Yes," they said loudly. "Probably enjoying a nice swim..."

The professor showed them their pictures of the locomotive. "No," they replied, shaking their heads. "There's no pool on the train."

"Try more fish," said Reece when it was obvious the Keepers wanted to watch television and not co-operate.

"We've run out," said Martin.

Professor Morris tried drawing an arrow into the back of the locomotive and pointing vigorously in an effort to make the Keepers understand what they wanted. "Yes," said the Keepers. "It goes forwards in that direction. Now stop interrupting."

"They don't understand," said the professor.

At that moment the Smog Monster reared out of the sea and scampered across an island. They caught a glimpse of people fleeing for their lives as it smashed through their house like a dog stamping on a matchbox.

"Good lord," said Martin. "Look at the size of the thing..."

"It's like the *Beast from 20,000 Fathoms*," Reece said. "But I don't think we'll be able to lure it into a fairground and poison it on a roller coaster like they did in the film."

"Not unless it heads for Blackpool," said Martin. "Maybe we could use the sealions as bait. We could dangle them out of a helicopter and foist it on the Irish."

The Keepers continued to watch the Smog Monster swimming across the sea, oblivious to Martin's scheming. The helicopter tracking him was keeping its distance now, as were several boats and the Navy frigate. "That's nice," they said, "He's definitely winning the race."

"He's way out in front."

"Those boats won't catch him now."

"Do you think he'll get a prize?"

"He's sure to win."

"I hope the prize is money; we could go claim it on his behalf."

"Maybe it'll be a cup or trophy of some kind...?"

"Mr Barnooli will be really pleased with a trophy; he likes shiny things."

"Let's go back to the locomotive," said Martin. "We're wasting our time here. Come on," he said to the Keepers. "Let's see if we can use your heads as battering rams."

"Oh no," said the Keepers when they saw the policemen wanted to take them out for another drive. "Now we'll never know if he won or not."

"Wait," said the professor suddenly. "What's that?" he pointed to the screen as a tiny glowing ball appeared above the Smog Monster's nose.

41 - The Smog Monster

The Smog Monster's Mind™ had detected ominous amounts of nuclear energy coming from a submarine vehicle in the near vicinity, not a good sign; even the Smog Monster would be hard pressed to survive a large atomic reaction going on over his head. A pang of guilt like acid reflux spoilt his peace of mind. "I'd better go and get him," he said reluctantly. There was a significant clause in his contract about protecting the animal in his care and he could live without a protracted battle with Barnooli's lawyers.

The Mind™ flew up out of the depths of the ocean and hovered over the surface. This instantaneous movement shocked and dismayed the large Icelandic trawler, through which he had just passed, and as the boat sank the Mind™ (in view of more litigation) wondered if he ought to have gone around.

The Icelandic fishermen were completely lucid as to what the Mind™ should have done and waved their fists at the tiny globe in a way that implied deep dissatisfaction. The Mind™ chose to ignore the stream of Norse profanity, reasoning that if they were going to build their boats out of such flimsy materials then they deserved all they got.

The crew of a Scottish trawler, in competition with the Icelandic trawler, cheered loudly. Whatever the 'wee ball' was it seemed to be on their side and had done them a considerable favour. Then they too had a crisis of conscience and went to rescue their fellow fishermen.

The Mind™, confused by the responses it had engendered among the fishermen, left them to it. "Stupid people," he said and looked about for his former charge.

Dancing over the waves like *fatuus ignis,* he over-took the Navy frigate and approached the tip of the arrow of wake that was monster's head. "There you are," he said, making a whistling sound to attract his attention.

The Smog Monster's carriage was of course in the other direction so the first thing the Mind™ had to do was turn him around so he was pointing the right way. The Mind™ did this by placing himself a few feet above the smoking nose and brightening his light field. The reddish green glow caught the Smog Monster's attention and he snapped at the Mind™ like a dog going for a fly. The Mind™ sidestepped and the Smog Monster snapped again, slowing down so he could use his broad feet against the water to give himself a bit of lift. The Mind™ kept sidestepping until he had turned him right around and he was pointing back towards his carriage.

Unfortunately the Smog Monster was also pointing towards the frigate. The Navy men, who were watching the whole show through binoculars, saw with horror that the monster was now heading straight for them. In a flurry of activity guns were manned and missile stations operated.

Seconds later the frigate opened fire and the Mind™ had to face the prospect of Barnooli's favourite being severely handicapped by a number of lethal warheads removing the more useful parts of his act, namely his good looks and tufty ears. Fortunately the Mind™ was more than capable of a suitable response.

There was a crackle of energy as atoms peacefully minding their own business were drawn into an uncomfortable alliance with one another. Shuffling together under the guidance of the Mind™ they formed a massive screen. As the bullets and missiles hit the surface they dissolved like electrons into the Northern lights. Shards and splinters of metal pinged off into the sea. The pavonine brilliance dropped admiralty jaws the length and breadth of the frigate's bridge.

"Was that supposed to happen?" asked a government minister carefully.

The jaw of the captain quivered with indignation, "No, it most certainly wasn't," he said. "And don't ask me what happened because I don't know."

The Smog Monster didn't like the shield either, he turned right around and fled back the way he had been going; towards the greater part of Great Britain, every foot taking him further away from his carriage.

"Damn," said the Mind™. "Now why on earth did they have to go and do that? Can't they see that I've got everything under control?"

The Navy stopped firing. There was an awful silence on the bridge as everyone tried to avoid catching the eye of everyone else. "I'd like to know who thought they'd improve matters with a small grant to the Scottish tourist industry," said an official from the Ministry of Defence. An adviser whispered a name in his ear. "Ah," he said. "That explains it, he never did like Scotland."

The Mind™ sped off back to the Smog Monster but this time no amount of annoying behaviour could alter his primary objective which was to get as far away from the loud bangs and flashing lights as possible. He put up great clouds of choking black smog and paddled for all he was worth. Within a very short time he was past Mull, passing Colonsay and was heading for Jura.

The Mind™ whizzed along just in front of him, shouting, "stop you bugger!" in a frantic way, but the sound of helicopters was loud in the Smog Monster's ears and radios were buzzing in his head. There was no real reason for him to stop, at least not one that he could understand, but several good ones for carrying on. The Smog Monster hardly noticed when he reached land; he was up the beach and across the green sward faster than a crocodile going for a gazelle on the banks of the Congo.

'Carrying on' was not a luxury the frigate could enjoy. Without the useful addition of feet it was unable to pursue the creature on land and had to veer off sharply to avoid being grounded. This it completely failed to do. It made a pathetic attempt at a right turn and collided with a big rock.

An hour later and the entire ship's company were assembled on the beach wrangling over whose fault it was or just gazing sadly at their crumpled, grey, formally speedy boat. A small detachment of marines was left on board to prevent the cluster of boats from disgorging the journalists onto her top-secret (and probably dangerous) decks.

A good number of senior officers were looking very embarrassed and were trying to avoid the camera crews who had re-appeared, like relatives at a funeral, to ask what they intended to do next? The military said nothing. The government men were being similarly tight-lipped.

Meanwhile, the Smog Monster was already across the island and had swum the Sound of Jura not having eased off an inch of speed. He had an enormous fund of energy, more than anyone but the Mind™ knew about, and certainly more than the helicopters who had to keep flicking off to the nearest airfield for top-ups. But the monster simply carried on. He crossed Kintyre and was into the Sound of Bute before the second wave could come to stop him.

The people of Glasgow were extremely, and reasonably, worried by the prospect of a vast bull rummaging through their particular china shop and destroying their city of culture status, so they made a big fuss. The Navy blocked the entrance to the Clyde with warships and the army manned the beaches with tanks and artillery. Aeroplanes were sent out, loaded with bombs and missiles.

None of the more aggressive tactics stood a chance of working, firstly because whenever a loud aeroplane came near him the Smog Monster put up a smoke screen that was amazingly difficult to see through even with radar; and secondly, when they did see their target and launched their missiles the Mind™ put up his shield and deflected them into the surrounding sea or land.

The Air Force soon stopped their raids for all these reasons and particularly because the death toll among the local sheep population was rising so dramatically that the local farmers were beginning to think they were being deliberately targeted.

There was nothing the military could do to stop the Smog Monster and there was a distinct lack of any Latter-day Saint Georges, with lance and sword and a careless tune on their lips, coming forward to take him on. The various princes of the realm, for whom this ought to have been the proving of their manhood, had suddenly found remote Caribbean islands to visit.

As for the Smog Monster, he was just confused. He didn't know which way to turn or which direction to swim in. He was sad, lonely and frightened and the boats, helicopters and radio waves did nothing to help him. He swam hither and thither like a dog pursued by a bee, occasionally evading his floating pursuers by nipping onto dry land (the Ross of Mull for instance), but he was basically getting nearer nowhere he knew.

Nobody seemed to appreciate his plight, certainly not the military minds sent to conquer him. If they were unsympathetic to most things natural, they were doubly so against an alien visitor and were busy drumming up xenophobic hostility towards him. In the House of Lords, for instance, the grandsons of Imperial forebears related stories of their kith and kin and suggested some kind of tiger hunt with the Navy acting as beaters and submarines armed with Polaris missiles standing ready to blast the creature to kingdom come when it broke cover. This went down like a proposal to restore the Raj, slavery and deportation to the colonies.

As to where the creature could go, other than inland, there were those who were irresponsible enough to suggest this didn't matter. "I expect it'll just swim off and bask in the Gulf Stream, or go back to Iceland."

"Why Iceland...?"

"Denmark then, isn't that where dragons come from?"

"What about Wales?"

"No, I don't think it's a whale, it's got legs."

Those who were ardently against Europe spoke scathingly about what their NATO partners might do in their position. Some said the Smog Monster might do well to cross Belgium, as at least it would go unmolested. "They didn't stop the Germans in 1939, hardly likely to stop some alien dragon are they?"

Nobody had any compassion for the Smog Monster. All he wanted was to be at home in the ring or in his box, with or without the Hydro Monster to fight and definitely without all this space around him. Chasing about the open coast with half a dozen whirring insects overhead and pointy little boats in pursuit was more than he could handle. He let out another terrific belch of smoke in the hope it would put them all off. It didn't so he just worried further.

42 - The locomotive

It was like a star had suddenly appeared over the locomotive. From nobody knowing it was there to the cameras of the world focussing on its magnificent lines, suddenly images of the train appeared in every house in the country and very soon the world. The world stared, in jealousy as well as wonder, and some in fear.

For a million different minds the blue elegance transported the imagination like a roman candle sending up plumes of fire and light. Ordinary people felt real joy, advertising executives saw their salvation and lunatics in the desert started changing their stories to fit the new shape of interstellar travel.

Thousands of Londoners were compelled to visit the docks to see if the locomotive was real or just another wacky film set for an American director with big ratings and little taste. Whatever they expected, their effort was rewarded.

As the crowds squeezed against the barriers their diction was limited to various forms of hyperbole; 'wow' was common, 'cor' was another. But a good proportion of the on-lookers were stunned into silence and gawped inelegantly without the faintest trace of intelligence or understanding.

Most people, wherever they came from and whatever they were, agreed it was probably the most beautiful spacecraft they had ever seen. This applied to the rest of the galaxy as well and models of the train were very popular with the young of many worlds. The designers, the House of Saron, had won several awards and even a nice little cup that was now being used to hold paperclips. The truth was, however, the designers were rather embarrassed about the whole business. They had found the designs of the train, complete in every detail, on the drawing boards of their workshop the day after an excellent party at which several mind-bending and noxious drugs had been available. Nobody knew who should take the credit because none of them could remember. There was a traffic cone in the lavatory that was equally inexplicable.

What everyone agreed was that Barnooli had bought one of the finest pieces of locomotive art in the galaxy, and it was now being enjoyed by the people of Earth. Not only were the docks now crowded with sightseers but around the world people crowded to see the train on their television sets. The pictures made a pleasant alternative to the scenes of destruction being wrought by the Smog Monster.

43 - Washington D.C.

However, not everyone was so pleased to see the alien artefact in another country. The American President was very annoyed and this echoed a general feeling of dissatisfaction across the nation. They were in a place they didn't like to be: the side-lines. They had not found their carriage and it was too late to share in anyone else's. The President felt left out.

On his desk there were pictures of all the other creatures that had turned up so far, including ground-level photograph of the giant giraffe in China. Behind her, framed by mountains and reflected in the water of a rice paddy, the giraffe's carriage was such a beautiful sight it made the President want to cry.

"Have the Chinese figured out how to get into their box yet?" he asked.

"We don't know, sir," said his advisors. "But they have a full division of the People's Army guarding it."

"Have we offered our assistance?"

"They politely declined, sir."

The President sighed, "What a waste…" American scientists would have had the box in pieces by now and within a few years there would be fast-food restaurants on the moon, he was sure.

"Is there nothing we can do?" he said. "What about these guys?" he pointed to the picture of the Keepers the CIA had acquired. "Can we buy them?"

The Harvard Graduates shook their heads, "No Mr President. It's the rabbits or nothing."

"Are you sure? There are five of them, I'm sure they wouldn't miss one."

"According to our sources, Mr President, they're not very bright."

"They have to be smarter than those monkeys; all they do is drink tea and fly around in circles."

"Apparently not, Mr President; it seems they can't even get back into their own space vehicle."

The President looked at the pictures of the beautiful lines of the locomotive and drooled. He imagined what it would look like on the White House lawn with him standing on the footplate like Casey Jones.

One thing was very obvious and deeply vexing. It seemed that the British had a monopoly and it was too late to strike up a partnership. "Just like them," said the President. "You think they're dead and buried and up they pop again like the damn gophers in my old back yard!"

"They do seem pretty fortunate," the advisors agreed. "But at least we won't have to deal with the dragon…" Another news bulletin showed the Smog Monster rampaging through a village in the Scottish borders. He was moving slowly enough for people to get out of the way but the damage to property was appalling.

"Worse than a hurricane," said the President. "Any chance of us getting an aircraft carrier out there and hauling its ass back to the States?"

"None at all, Mr President," they said, not even bothering to tinker with a solution.

The President looked at the pictures of the carriages in China and Africa. "It must have come in a vehicle like these," he said.

"It's probably in the Atlantic, sir, along with the box that contained the flying monkeys."

"Have we looked? How hard can it be to spot a spaceship the size of Grand Central?"

"If it's in the ocean, Mr President, it might take a hundred years to find."

Deep down, he knew they were right. "Look anyway," he said. "Maybe we'll get lucky."

"Yes sir." His advisors scuttled out of the oval room and the President chewed his nails. "If we don't find a new alien soon how will I ever be taken seriously again?"

44 - The Keepers

Back at the flat, their second attempt to get into the locomotive was delayed while the police and the army tried to control the increasing numbers of people wanting to see the train. There was a general feeling among the citizens of Britain that if they made enough of a fuss outside the alien vehicle it might do something about the monster spoiling their scepter'd isle. Placards and slogan-chanting had replaced the initial cooing and words of welcome. 'ET Go Home' was now a popular phrase among the protesters, particularly those with holiday homes in the Lake District.

The Keepers were oblivious to everything other than the fact that they were locked out of their only remaining link with the circus. After the euphoria of seeing the Smog Monster alive, they realised they were no better off than before. They lounged listlessly and chewed their fish with less conviction. They tried to understand why the locomotive's Mind™ had locked them out.

"Did we annoy him in some way?"

"Are we guilty of some heinous crime?"

"He must really hate us."

"Maybe it was our juggling and balancing?"

"I don't know, but we're going to have to review our entire act; we can't keep getting locked out every time we put on a show, that's silly..."

"Obviously he's wreaking his revenge."

"He's getting his own back."

"Why didn't he just say the act was rubbish?"

"I wonder what he'll think of next."

"Probably take the train somewhere else and hide it."

"He might take it back to Barnooli and leave us stranded here like the last Keepers were left behind on Pinniped."

They looked around the room, "Stuck here for the rest of our lives?"

"Stuck with these awful comedians and incense-burning beardies with a hideous line in footwear?"

They screamed collectively and woke Martin up who had dozed off over some paperwork. "What? Where? Who's killing who?"

Reece came in, "What's happening?"

"I don't know, they just started yelling, god knows why."

The Keepers were moaning and sobbing. They blew their noses on their napkins and looked at their fish with big self-pitying eyes, "...and never see home again!" they cried.

"I expect they're a little down-hearted about being locked out of their train," said Reece.

"Well couldn't they be quieter about it?"

"How would you feel? You've lost your only connection with the outside world, you're lost and out of place and there's no other way to escape. It'd be like losing your car keys after a night out at the Brixton Academy."

"They do seem a bit depressed," said Martin, looking at the five drooping heads and the untouched fish still left on their plates, "Poor little beggars."

He tried to console them, "There's not much we can do," he said, with a gesture he hoped they would interpret as 'we're just as gutted as you are'. "There's no lock we can pick, no hinge we can force and I doubt if there's a spare set of keys under the wheel arch, is there...?"

"...No there isn't," said the Keepers bitterly. "There's nothing even close to humour in your act, give it up and get a real job like that policeman outside."

"Perhaps we could get real jobs too?"

"Just until Barnooli gets here...?"

"But what can we do?"

"Let's face it guys, we're more useless than a tit on a snail."

45 - The locomotive's Mind™

Fortunately, the locomotive's Mind™ was having second thoughts on the subject of the locked door. He had found a friend.

Harvey Brown, the owner of the *Marquis de Sade*, one of the pleasure cruisers parked next to the locomotive, had come down from his house in Wanstead after seeing the television pictures of the crowds gathered on the dock looking up at the train. He had sold tickets and allowed the protesters to stand on his upper deck so they could make a better impression. This was the most he had thought about the train; it was there, it was big, it was odd, but he was too old to be fussed by oddities anymore. So he ignored it. While the protesters waved their placards and sang songs, he got on with some spring cleaning.

While he was dusting the wheel house he decided to give the radio a bit of an airing by trying to call his cousin in Deptford. He switched it on. Like a snake striking from the undergrowth, the locomotive's Mind™ was ready to give him the full verbal montage...

"Hello?" said Harvey Brown.

"Hello!" said the locomotive's Mind™ angrily.

"Who's this?"

"I've been trying to get through to you for ages."

"Have you?"

"Yes! Ages and ages...!"

"I've been at home."

"At home...!"

"Yes, I'm sorry..." Harvey Brown felt a sense of guilt creeping upon him like a man who has switched the light out on somebody carrying a heavy suitcase up a dark and tricky staircase.

"At home...!" repeated the locomotive's Mind™ with considerable feeling and luggage tumbling down the stairs.

"I'm sorry. We never open before the summer season. I only came today because the boat needs cleaning."

"Oh," said the Mind™ holding, as it were, a pair of socks and feeling foolish.

"Did you want to make a booking? I could make arrangements for you to hire the boat early... Is it urgent?"

"Err... No."

"Oh."

"I just wanted a chat."

Harvey Brown felt relieved. There was nothing he liked more than a chat. He had hoped to retire when his son was old enough to take over, but his son had gone off to study German philosophy at university and wanted nothing to do with the business. Now he was resigned to having to carry on until he could retire properly and then put the boat up for sale, both of which he was unhappy about. Consequently any conversation not related to a business he was now upset with was welcome

"What did you want to talk about?"

"Nothing in particular..."

"I'm sorry I wasn't here before."

"No no," corrected the Mind™. "It was my fault; I was too quick to judge and I'm sorry."

"Never mind then. All's well now."

"That's good."

Conversation lapsed for a moment. They both racked their brains for a suitable topic to share.

"What do you do for a living?" asked Harvey brown.

"I drive a train."

"Really, that sounds interesting. I wish I could drive a train and not have to run this stupid boat."

"I understand entirely," said the Mind™. "I feel exactly the same about this train..." and he went on to explain.

For over two hours they talked about their lives, hopes, ambitions, politics, religion and the unreliability of relatives until Harvey Brown said he had to get home to a bit of ironing. "But look, I'll give you my telephone number; just give me a ring if you feel you need to..."

"Thank you," said the Mind™, choked with emotion.

Harvey Brown signed off, "What a nice fella," he said and gave the top of the radio a wipe with his duster.

The Mind™ was so happy he rang the Samaritans and told them the good news. The Samaritans were considerably relieved.

He even felt benign towards the Keepers and opened the door for them, much to the surprise of the constable on guard who had been leaning against it at the time.

The policeman picked himself off the floor, stared at the mess the Keepers had left behind, and then backed out in much the same way as hikers do when they find themselves sharing a cave with a bear. It was only when he was back over the threshold that he noticed his hat had fallen off and rolled across the floor of the cabin. He looked around outside. Nobody could see him. He crawled forwards again on his hands and knees and retrieved his all-important symbol of authority.

He was half-way back towards the door when his courage returned. He began to notice all the exciting buttons and levers. He was not terribly familiar with science fiction but he was sure it usually involved less brass and fewer dials with big pointy arrows. It really did look like the footplate of an old steam engine.

He crawled over to a bank of controls, each switch as big as his thumb. He found he was longing to touch one. "Just one," he said, after all it was obvious the train wasn't fired up to go anywhere. He peered around the cabin. There was a parrot on the back of a chair but it seemed to be asleep. The rest of the controls, including the more complex collection of dials and levers that filled the far end, seemed fairly inert.

He checked over his shoulder that the door was still open. He calculated he had enough time to hurl himself through if anything untoward happened.

"A small one..." he murmured, stretching out a finger and pushing a switch.

Nothing happened. A wave of relief spread through him and he shuddered to think what might have lit up or exploded. He crawled away from the control panel before he was tempted to try another one. Outside, he put his hat back on and radioed for assistance.

46 - The Smog Monster

If the constable had pressed any other switch on that particular panel the giant rabbits might have started across Africa or the giraffe across Asia or the monkeys might have used the loose catch to open the window in their hangar to wing their way across the ocean. Simply, the switch was like a dinner bell and it was the Smog Monster who was coming for tea.

He had left Scotland behind and had been hoping to find a small and cosy cave south of the border. Instead, the land seemed as large and empty as the sea had been. The plague of insects had grown worse too. They buzzed around him, spitting and muttering, and even his great clouds of smoke didn't seem to be putting them off.

Eventually, he had jumped over Hadrian's Wall and was meandering through Northumberland when he received the call. From being directionless and lost he was suddenly shown the way. He changed course and headed for 'home' at a gallop and there was no power on Earth that could now stop him from achieving his aim.

Of course, nobody was aware of the reason behind this sudden bee-line for London, least of all the Smog Monster's minder who was nearly beside himself trying to catch his attention. Whistling and dodging about, he was so preoccupied with this effort he completely failed to check the airwaves for the magnetic effect of the beacon.

This beacon, which was like the smell of frying sausages to a hungry man, took the Smog Monster over the Fells and into the north of Yorkshire. He sent shivers down the spine of England. He lumbered over the Pennines, jumped over the vales and dales and barged into the Peak District, pursued by helicopters and aeroplanes every step of the way.

Britain's army, navy, and air force failed to prevent him from doing what previous invaders had only attempted. Their ships sent missiles that bounced off the Mind's™ shield like rain off an umbrella. Their tanks and armoured cars were too slow to react and their aeroplanes couldn't fly through his cloud of smoke. They were all left behind to pick up the pieces in his wake; namely pieces of their ships, tanks and aeroplanes.

The Watts brothers loved every moment. From its unpromising beginning in the sea, to their current status as media darlings, they rode the wave of the Smog Monster's destruction. As their helicopter followed the trail of debris, they described the scene in graphic detail.

The Smog Monster had no regard for the man-made efforts that got in his way. Electricity and telephone wires tried to trip him up but snapped like cobwebs, disconnecting vast numbers of subscribers from their grids. He broke dozens of bridges; ruined roads and wholly or partly squashed homes and businesses. His only saving grace was his inability to travel quietly thus giving people time to abandon their homes and flee to safety.

Very few people were harmed during his passing, but that was no excuse to sit back and say nothing. Thousands of eyewitnesses were most emphatic in their descriptions of what should be done to the monster and were ready to let the whole world know. Or at least they tried. The television networks and radio switchboards were jammed with callers trying to vent their fears and frustrations and in the end only a handful got through.

The Watts brothers had a virtual monopoly on the *vox populi* and they were determined not to share it with anyone. They watched avidly as another fleet of helicopter gunships streamed past. "Another attack is running down the right flank," Eric reported. "They're in the box..." The gunships let loose with their missiles. "They shoot..." The curtain of energy reappeared and the explosives detonated far from the Smog Monster's rump. "They miss."

"Another costly waste of an opportunity..." said Chris.

"Certainly was," said Eric. "They're going to have to come up with something a little more subtle if they're going to win this game."

"The defence is too good; they can't keep shooting at random and expecting the ball to let their shots through."

The Mind™ was trying to ignore the machines firing projectiles at Barnooli's favourite but he was beginning to lose patience. "Go away," he said, even though they couldn't hear him. "Can't you see I'm trying to stop him? I'm doing my best and all you're doing is making it worse!"

Bits of missile were falling on the ground below and setting light to the grass. However, the Smog Monster had barely noticed. He was looking forward to seeing the train. He assumed his carriage would be there and in his simple mind the thought of a 'small' space loomed large. He picked up speed, giving the Mind™ apoplexy and the motorists on the M1 a nasty surprise.

The Watts brothers followed in their helicopter. "He's making a break for it," said Chris. "Look at him, he's gone... there's no catching this guy now..."

"I think you're right; look out London. This is going to be a one-way ticket to the final event."

47 - London

In a flurry of activity, Reece and a constable collected the Keepers' few belongings and put them in bin bags, just in case whoever was in the train wanted to leave immediately.

The Keepers were confused, "Now what's going on?"

"Looks like we're being thrown out; look, they're taking all our things away."

Professor Morris was trying to explain about the door, "'Open'," he said, waving his arms about in a manner that confirmed their suspicions.

"Thrown out into the wide-world, without hope of getting home," they cried.

"Friendless."

"Pot-less."

"And with an act that gets us locked up or locked out!"

Martin came in with some good news. He had been in the newsagent's down the road when it came to him. He had figured out the link between the alien locomotive and the train driver the Samaritans had been having so much trouble with. Years of training had gone into this intuition and justifiably he felt rather pleased with himself. He began to dream little scenarios involving medals and visits to Buckingham Palace, he even imagined early retirement to write his memoirs.

"Guess what I've discovered?" he said to Reece.

"The train's open," said Reece, putting on his coat.

"What?"

"The door opened and apparently the Samaritans got a call to say their 'train' driver is much happier now. I think it was this train, not our sort, not ones with rails, with the suicidal driver. It's too much of a coincidence that we searched the whole of the transport system and found nothing, but the Samaritans give the 'all clear' and at the same time the door on the alien train opens, what do you think?"

Martin grunted, his gong flying out of the window.

"What were you going to say?"

"Nothing... Are the sealions coming?"

"Sure, have you heard the news about the monster?"

"No, what's going on?" He noticed his companion was looking unnecessarily bothered and even the professor seemed agitated.

"Look," said Reece.

The television was showing pictures of the Smog Monster galloping like a great horse down the M1. Pieces of the carriageway were flying in all directions and people were abandoning their vehicles in favour of the fields on either side. "It's heading for London," Reece added.

Martin shook his head, "I thought it was in Scotland," he said. "I didn't mind when I thought it was in the north…"

"Not anymore," said Professor Morris. "We're hoping our little friends might be able to stop it."

Martin nearly laughed, "How?"

The professor shrugged, "It started south when the door of the train opened so maybe there's a homing beacon they could switch off."

"Look at him go," said the Keepers, trying not to notice they were being evicted by sitting glued to the television.

"Do you think he's coming to rescue us?"

This was a pleasant thought, "We did feed him after all."

"And we gave him all those treats…" Buoyed up by the notion their former charge might want to protect them, their thoughts turned to where would be easiest for him to find them. "The locomotive," they agreed and turned to their ex-landlords. "Locomotive," they said and pointed to their picture.

"See," said the professor. "They understand and want to help us."

"Hopefully, he'll stomp all over you," they added, "For being so mean and throwing us out into the cold world."

When they arrived at the docks there was a huge crowd gathered along the quayside. The police had to push and shove for some time before a gap opened that was large enough to let the van through. The Keepers climbed out of the side door and ran up the gangplank, a worried policeman watching their approach from the door of the train. "It's open!" they were crying.

The protesters gasped in amazement as they watched the aliens return to their space ship. But among the clicks and whirrs of cameras there was also a note of criticism, "Is that what's responsible for the monster and all the other aliens?" they said.

"They look a bit soft," they observed.

"Where are the ray guns?"

"Where are the fangs?"

The Keepers scuttled past under a cloud of disapproval. They were just not macho enough and nobody was fooled into thinking they were intelligent life.

"Those things round their necks make them look pretty stupid."

"I'd give one to my kids, they seem harmless enough."

"Safer than my Rottweiler, nearly tore me ear off this morning."

"I bet they smell and I don't suppose they're cheap to feed either."

But above all, the voices of discontent wanted the Keepers held accountable for the terrible damage the Smog Monster was doing. "Don't just let them off with a caution," they shouted at the policemen. "We want compensation!"

They chanted, "ET pay today, don't leave your mess and beam away!"

The Keepers saw nothing except the open door of the locomotive and even if they had noticed the placards waving above the crowd, they would have meant as much to them as semiotics to a sausage.

Professor Morris, Reece and Martin followed the Keepers up the gangplank.

"Under different circumstances," said the professor. "This would be quite exciting... What do you think we're going to find?"

"Who can say?" said Reece. "Hopefully, the pilot; a multi-armed android, manipulating controls faster than the eye can see perhaps... Or some kind of massive machine casting sparks between great glass diodes...?"

They reached the top of the gangplank and stepped through the open door. "Or alternatively," said Martin, "A right pigsty and five stupid sealions trying to clean it up."

Reece stood inside the alien spacecraft, his eyes wide and his mouth open. He didn't see the mess, "A real space ship!"

"Look at all that puff pastry," said the Martin. "It looks like an explosion at a whist drive."

"So there was a party," said the professor.

"Look at all the switches," said Reece. "I wonder what they do..."

"Don't touch anything," said Martin. He picked up an empty bottle. "Still got those drawings?" he asked the professor.

The professor pulled out the roll from his satchel. He found the one with the splash of red across the buttons. They could still see the stain on the controls at the other end of the cabin. He showed the picture to the Keepers who looked sheepish and nodded.

"Party?" said Martin and mimicked someone drinking. The Keepers nodded again. They ran about collecting evidence to present to the policemen. "At least we can get them for drinking and driving."

"Oh look," said the professor. "A parrot..." He pointed to the sleeping Stereo still perched on the back of a comfortable-looking leather chair. "I wonder if it can talk..."

The Keepers brought out their records and put one on the turntable to play for their guests. Nothing happened so they pushed and pulled at various switches, eventually rediscovering the disconnected speakers. They plugged them back in. Instead of the harmless circus tune they intended to play, they had mistakenly switched to Stereo's 'hazardous' file, complete with skull and crossbones.

A thousand watts of a noise known as 'gigadeath' flooded the cabin like ten thousand cats being simultaneously sodomised. The two detectives, the constable and the anthropologist threw themselves on the floor as the nuclear wave of screaming lyrics and wailing guitars swept the boundaries of the acoustic world and broke glass on the other side of the river.

The Keeper still holding the speaker leads yanked them out again. This was not a conscious decision but happened as he fell backwards like a blade of wheat being cut down by a scythe.

The deafening silence, full of the white noise of tinnitus, was broken by a loud squawk from the parrot, "Who did that?" His feathers looked ready to dust a whole library of books. "You!" he yelled at the Keeper crawling away from behind the sound system. "Come here!" But the Keeper hid behind the chairs with the others. Unfortunately, in his confusion, Stereo had spoken in English.

"Hello?" said Professor Morris.

The parrot's feathers were ruffled. "Lumbrical incompetents!" he shouted. The Keepers squeezed themselves into a tighter ball. "Snirtling fools!"

"That's not a real parrot, is it?" said Reece as they watched the bird jump up and down with rage.

"Not when you look closely."

"More like a hologram," said the professor.

"...Barnooli will catch you and skin you and hang up your useless hides next to the toilets for people to wipe their hands on and..." He noticed the humans. "And what are you looking at?" he shouted.

"We're from Earth," said Reece.

"I can see that," said Stereo. "I'm deaf not blind."

"We come in peace," said Martin.

"A piece of what?" said Stereo. He was in no mood to mollify monkeys. He had been asleep and dreaming of electric sheep. It had been a nice dream; the sheep had made him their king and were about to divulge their secret ingredient for shepherd's pie when the Keepers had woken him up. He was not happy. "You shouldn't be in here; this is strictly off-limits to members of the public." He prepared to fry them all with the cabin's internal security system.

"Are you the controlling species on board this ship?" said the professor.

"No," he had to admit. "I am the locomotive's communication system."

"I see, we've been trying to communicate with your alien companions but with limited success..."

"I'm not surprised. They're idiots. Their bones should have been fashioned into little flutes years ago…"

"Do you have a name?" said Martin, taking out his notebook and pen.

"I am Primary Stack."

"Really?" said Martin, writing the name down.

"Yes, 'really'," he said testily, like someone who has been asked if he is 'all right' when he's covered from head-to-toe in porridge. "What are you doing here?"

"We've come to ask exactly the same thing," said Reece.

"Haven't the Keepers told you?"

"The 'who'…?"

"The Keepers, these 'things' currently hiding over there under the chairs thinking I can't see them. They clear up the animal dung for the Great Barnooli's circus, which is why of course they can't work out simple things like 'volume control' or 'dangerous to open' on my communication console."

"Told you they were the monkeys and not the organ grinder," said Martin.

Stereo clarified their story, "They were meant to escort the train to the next venue while the Great Barnooli is away on his honeymoon, but they spilt red wine into Auto Pilot™ and he turned himself off prematurely. Hence we ended up here."

"Should have had a few quid on it," said Martin, nudging the anthropologist. But Professor Morris frowned at him.

The Keepers noticed the voice coming from the parrot. "Is that Stereo?" they asked each other.

"It is," they said.

"That's a funny disguise."

Stereo replied in their own language, "Not as rib-tickling as the brush applying butter to your roasting bodies will be," he said. "Or as hilarious as the games of bowls we shall have when Barnooli has emptied your pathetic brains out of your skulls, eh? Oh don't worry. I don't suppose you'll notice the difference."

The Keepers retreated into their defensive ball again.

Stereo turned back to his 'guests'. "In one sense," he said. "I'm glad they have eventually led you here; I have a few things to say on the subject of your planet..."

"A lecture?" said Martin.

"That's right," he began to sift through a wad of notes that had appeared under his foot. He had made a long list of all the things he thought were wrong with the Earth.

"How long will this take?" asked Reece.

"Oh, a day or two..."

"But..."

A pair of reading glasses had appeared on the parrot's nose and he looked over them disdainfully. "Point number one," he began.

It was plain to the humans that he meant to give a lecture even if they didn't want to hear one. The police, in awe of a parrot who could talk down to them in such a convincing way, gave the professor a nudge to encourage him to interrupt before the bird could begin in earnest.

The professor was immune to people who tried to sound superior, he did after all have to work with students every day. He stepped forward and said boldly, "Are you aware of the chaos you've caused?"

"Me?" said Stereo, pausing. "What have I done?"

"Haven't you noticed the big monster tearing up our country, do you watch the news...?"

"Of course, I was going to bring that up in my critique..."

"But it belongs to this 'circus', yes?"

"You didn't really think it was the Loch Ness monster, did you?" Stereo said with a snort of derision.

"Did it occur to you, as the 'communications' expert on board this train, that a warning about its destructive powers might have been welcome?"

"I would have thought the Smog Monster's 'destructive powers' were quite obvious. Why would I bother you with trivia?"

"It's hardly trivial to us," said the professor.

"Is there no way you can stop it?" said Reece.

"That's not my job," said Stereo with a shrug of his parrot shoulders.

"But you can stop it…?"

"Every carriage has a Mind™; it's up to the Smog Monster's to figure out the way to put him back in his box…"

"Couldn't you give him a clue?" said Martin.

"He'll work it out eventually."

"And in the meantime," said Reece. "You'll let it destroy our country…?"

"If that's what you want," said Stereo. "Now, about my notes…"

"But we don't," said Martin. "We want you to stop the monster and send him back home. And that's not all we want; your circus is causing trouble on other parts of our planet too…"

Stereo sighed impatiently, "It's not 'my' circus," he said. "It belongs to the Great Barnooli. Haven't you been listening?"

48 - Africa

Mary Smith and her companions cowered in the lee of the giant rabbits' carriage as bullets and missiles flew around the plain. On her right, the soldiers hired by the neighbouring village were creeping down the slope with tanks and armoured cars in support. On the left, the village with all the rabbits, having bought the aid of another band of mercenaries, were dug into trenches and repelling borders with rocket-propelled grenades and heavy mortars. The sound of shellfire and bombs was deafening.

"We have to get out of here," said Mary, stating the obvious. Unfortunately their land cruisers were in the middle of the battlefield taking fire from both sides. All that remained of them was a tall plume of smoke rising over the skeletons of the chassis and a tattered blue flag where their tents had been.

A heavy machine gun opened fire from a dugout and there was an explosion as an attacker's vehicle tumbled down the hill with its petrol tank on fire. The dugout was sprayed with shots from Russian-made rifles but the attackers were in an exposed position and the assault died out as the heavy machine gun sought them out on the hillside. Then an ex-Soviet tank clanked and snorted its way down the slope towards the village, its barrel raised in a defiant gesture.

"Looks like the villagers are going to lose their monopoly," said Mary Smith.

Out of nowhere, an aeroplane screamed through the African sky.

There was a short pause.

The tank disappeared in a cloud of flames and broken armour. The plane climbed up into the blue canopy and circled down for another attack. The mercenaries on the hill began a full retreat as a cluster of bombs fell and wiped out their remaining vehicles.

"I didn't expect that," said Mary Smith. "Where did they get an aeroplane from?"

Her companions shrugged. They didn't really care; they were dusty and thirsty and in severe need of clean underwear. All they wanted was a helicopter and a plane ride out of Africa. They had seen the heart of darkness and now they wanted to go home and be able to turn on a light switch and take a shower. Most of all, they didn't want to be shot at anymore.

The dust and smoke cleared. Mary Smith stood up. The villagers were cheering in their trenches and jeering at the retreating backs of their enemies. But it was a short-lived triumph. The rival mercenaries had pulled back to allow a battery of large cannon to lob shells over the hill.

Mary Smith threw herself back into her hole and covered her head as explosions blossomed all around. This was not what she had signed up for, she thought. In fact, this was exactly the opposite of what she had imagined when she had left her successful career in advertising and the comfort of her flat in Islington to help feed the world.

Inside the carriage, the Mind™ was also having second thoughts but not about the civil war raging outside. He had finished decorating and every surface conceivable was now covered in paper, paint or plastic conceptual art but he wasn't happy. He had no doubt in his own mind that his efforts merited the highest artistic awards, but he had no audience to prove it. He couldn't ask the other Minds™; what did they know about the true balance of tone and colour? How many of them had wrestled with crimping shears to get the right effect on a dado or table mat? What could they say that he hadn't already thought?

He looked around for a suitable audience and saw Mary Smith cowering at the foot of the carriage. She looked a bit grubby but as long as she didn't touch anything she would do.

The carriage had a mechanical arm they used to put the rabbits back in their boxes after a show. If it could pick up a rabbit, he reasoned, it could pick up a monkey and probably not kill it.

Mary Smith had her eyes closed so she didn't see the arm descend from the carriage and pluck her out of her hole. She felt it grip around her waist and then she was rising quickly. "So this is death," she said, convinced a cannon shell had blown her up. "Not too bad, all things considered… Not feeling any pain…"

The arm brought her into the carriage and placed her on the sheet of newspaper the Mind™ had put down. She opened her eyes. "Oh no," she said. "I'm in hell."

"Good morning," said the Mind™. "Don't be alarmed, I just want your opinion on a couple of things…"

Before the Mind™ had decided to re-decorate, the Brilliant Bazmondo had used the compartment for private parties. It was large and airy with a skylight that ran the length of the room. There was a small bar at the far end. There was wood panelling on the walls. In the more informal atmosphere, the great magician had performed acts of legendary legerdemain while walking among his guests. There was a table for nibbles.

The room was now the visual equivalent of fingernails scraping down a blackboard; or the manic laughter of a man that's lost his arm in a threshing machine; or a thousand children clamouring for attention in a tiled restaurant with no emergency exit and an excess of sugary confection.

The Mind™ hovered in the midst of his inferno. His halo was like the rays of a medieval sun and there was a smug smile on his tiny face. "What do you think?" he asked.

"It's awful," said Mary Smith. After days of disappointment and frustration, she had hoped her death would be peaceful and full of reward for her good intentions. "I never imagined so many colours could be combined in all the wrong ways."

"I see," said the Mind™, peeved. This was worse than if he'd asked the other Minds™ for an opinion. The creature was obviously stupid. "You don't think this is 'art' then?"

"Art," she mumbled.

"You don't think the Brilliant Bazmondo will prefer this to the rather drab utility of the previous decor? You don't think it will add a certain refinement to his private functions?"

Mary Smith was sure eternal damnation came without relief so the demonic apparition couldn't be talking about bodily functions. Then she began to suspect this was not hell even if it was purgatory to look at. "Who's the Brilliant Bazmondo?" she asked.

"The Great Barnooli's magician," said the Mind™ impatiently. "This is where he entertains his Very Important Guests…"

Magician and miraculous rabbits suddenly joined up in her brain. "I'm inside the box," she said.

The Mind™ sighed, "Yes, where did you think you were?"

"I wasn't sure; your colour scheme is confusing my brain."

"I see," said the Mind™ icily. "And what would you consider the height of taste? If you say 'magnolia' I will eject you from this carriage faster than you can say 'hand me a paintbrush'…"

She closed her eyes but the cornucopia of swirls, dots and stripes was still imprinted on her retinas. "This is for a magician to perform his magic act…?" she asked carefully.

"Yes," said the Mind™. "What of it?"

"Shouldn't the magic be in the act and not the surroundings?"

This was unexpected, "What do you mean?"

"You haven't thought about your target audience."

"Why would I do that?"

"I was in advertising; clients only like 'art' if it detracts from the cheapness of their product. If your magician is any good he won't like being up-staged by your ... 'creative flair' ..."

"Oh," said the Mind™. "So what you're saying is he won't like it...?"

"Worse than that," said Mary Smith, thinking quickly. "I expect he'll be very cross when he discovers you're been decorating while his magic rabbits are causing havoc outside this carriage..."

"Why would he care about that?" said the Mind™, not liking where her criticism was heading. "He can always get more rabbits..."

"It's very bad publicity," she said. "It was you that let them out, wasn't it?"

"Erm..."

"I imagine you just wanted to re-decorate their hutches or whatever they live in, yes...?"

"Sort of..."

She shook her head sadly, "So with the best of intentions, you let the rabbits out for a little run and now they've caused a war outside. I'm sure you didn't mean to but do you think the magician will see it that way? Or do you think he'll say you were neglecting your duties and now his reputation is going to disappear faster than a card up his sleeve?"

"Oh crap," said the Mind™, his halo slipping until he was just a silly little ball floating in the effluent of his ambition. "What am I going to do?"

"Can you put the rabbits back in their box? If they're gone perhaps the war will stop...?"

"What about all this?" he said, looking around at his artwork and realising it was rubbish after all.

"Do you have any paint-stripper?"

"But what colour should I paint it?" He was desperate now.

"What colour was it before?"

"Brown," he said. "That's why I wanted to change it..."

She couldn't disagree with him there. "What about dark blue and black for the ceiling? I'm sure a bit of gold for the detailing wouldn't do any harm..."

"Yes," he said. "I'm sure I've got time to get it all done before Bazmondo sees it."

"And the rabbits…?"

"There's a homing beacon that will call them back to the carriage. Which shade of blue should I use?"

"I'll help you choose if you turn on the beacon…"

Outside the carriage, a bell began to ring and the door slid open.

49 - The locomotive's cabin

Inside the locomotive, Professor Morris, Martin and Reece were beginning to realise Stereo was nothing more than a fancy gadget. He was like an answer machine designed to annoy callers by offering numerous unwanted options and then playing 'Greensleeves' over and over.

The Keepers watched from their bunker under the chairs and wondered what was taking so long. "Just say 'goodbye' and be on your way," they were saying.

"Then we can clean up this mess before Barnooli sees it…"

"How are we going to bribe Stereo into not telling him?"

"How are we going to get rid of the wine stain on those buttons?"

They looked at the locomotive's control panel and the dried evidence of their party. A bucket of water seemed an unlikely method of improving matters.

"We could use our toothbrushes," they suggested but shook their heads, "I'm not using mine…"

"Or mine; it will make the toothpaste taste of wine."

"But who or what is the 'Great Barnooli'?" said Reece.

Through gritted beak Stereo replied, "He is the greatest showman in the galaxy, an impresario of enormous influence and power, and this is his locomotive."

"I see. And he knows you're here?"

"I'm sorry?" said the parrot in a tired voice.

"The Great Barnooli; I presume he is aware of your presence here?"

"Aware? Why should he be aware?"

"This is his train?"

"Of course…"

"He owns it."

"Yes."

"And you're in charge while he's away?"

"Well…"

"You're not in charge?"

"The Keepers are technically in charge," he said with a disdainful lilt to his ironic laugh.

"I see…"

They paused while they reviewed the Keepers. One of them was stretching out a paw to try and retrieve an empty cup, he stopped and retreated as soon as he realised he was being watched. When they looked back towards Stereo, the paw shot out again and snatched the cup, adding it to the pile of litter behind the chair.

"If I might hazard a guess," began the professor. "These little creatures are hardly capable of driving the train, are they?"

"No," agreed Stereo haughtily. "Quite incapable..."

"And are you the senior machine here?"

"Of course," scoffed the Mind™.

"So Mr Stack, given the current circumstances, you are in charge, correct?"

"Well..."

"In practice, you're in charge...?"

"Well, in theory..."

"If you're not in charge," said Martin, guessing where the professor was going with his argument. "You should have informed somebody of the change in circumstances, have you done this?" His pen hovered over his notebook.

"Err... No." Some of the aristocratic airs began to evaporate, along with his holographic notes and his reading glasses. He recognised a familiar tone.

"I see. And have you been in contact with anyone from the circus?"

"Umm... No."

"So Mr Barnooli has no idea that his train has crashed?" said Reece. "Or the fact one of his creatures is at this moment destroying a large portion of our country...?"

"Well no, but..."

"And what's happened to the rest of the train?" said the professor.

"Four of the carriages are here on Earth, the rest are in orbit, but..."

"Can contact be made with them?"

"Each one has a Mind™, yes," he tried to sound superior again but failed.

The humans had him cornered.

"And have you made contact with them?" said Reece.

"Of course, I..." He was about to say he had asked them if they wanted to play cards, but that sounded unwise under the circumstances.

"Why have the carriages here on Earth not made contact with the local human authorities?"

"We can't just be…"

"You realise they're trespassing," said Martin. "And I daresay this locomotive is parked illegally too."

"I knew it," said Stereo. Trust the locomotive's Mind™ to get it wrong again.

"I imagine there will be a hefty fine at the very least," said Reece.

"The compensation for what the monster has done will run into millions," Martin agreed.

"'Erm…" A querulous edge crept into Stereo's voice as the advocates of litigation appeared in his imagination like muggers in an alley.

"What would Mr Barnooli say to that?" said Reece.

"Ah…"

"And where is Mr Barnooli?" said the professor.

"Agnatha, on his honeymoon, and the other acts are on vacation. That's why I haven't been able to contact them…"

"Have you tried?"

"Umm…"

"You have or haven't…?" said Martin.

"No."

"I see," he made another note in his little black book. "Your space machines are trespassing on our planet, your creatures are causing untold damage and you have made no attempt to contact anyone in authority, would that be a fair summary?"

Stereo wasn't quite sure how he had been manipulated into a sense of guilt he didn't normally feel. It would make a fascinating study when he reviewed his recordings later.

"I'll set up a standing wave," he said. "In case he has a communication net set up. I'm afraid your planet is off the beaten track, it might take some time to reach him."

"The sooner you try the better, don't you think?"

The parrot looked crestfallen, "I guess so."

Several tight-lipped, brawny ex-servicemen in dark suits appeared at the door. They were brandishing small plastic cards that gave them military authority over the train. "Everyone out," they announced. "This is now a military zone with military jurisdiction."

"Oh no," said the Keepers. "More guests; we're never going to get the cabin cleaned up at this rate."

Martin's phone rang and he answered it quickly. After a short conversation he announced, "We're to go back to the flat and wait for further orders."

"What's going on?" said Reece. "Who are this lot?"

"The Prime Minister wants us to take the sealions with us as hostages while they try and negotiate a truce."

"A 'truce'…?" said the professor. "But we're not at war…"

"That's not how the Prime Minister sees it; not with the army and the navy engaged in hostilities with the monster."

"But we're making progress…"

He shrugged his shoulders, "Not enough, apparently."

"What are they going to do?"

He shrugged his shoulders. "I don't know," he said in a tired voice. His enthusiasm for circus-related shenanigans was beginning to grow as thin as his hair. "Maybe they'll weld the doors shut. Now let's get out of here before 007 over there zaps us with his cufflinks." He turned to Stereo. "Could you ask the sealions to come with us please?"

"Where are you going?" said Stereo, trying not to sound pleased. With the humans out of the way he could concoct his own story to Barnooli, one that didn't mention dereliction of duty or his total failure to complete his contractual obligations.

"We have orders to leave the locomotive," Reece told him. "I think our leaders believe they can use the Keepers as leverage to get you to leave our planet alone."

Stereo nearly laughed, "I don't think the Great Barnooli will care two hoots about what happens to these keepers; he abandoned the last lot on an ice planet called Pinniped…"

"Perhaps you should tell Barnooli what's going on," said Martin, snapping his notebook shut. "Before our martini-drinking friends here put ten tons of explosive under your pretty train and blow it back to space in little pieces."

"Will they do that?" said Stereo. He had no doubt a bomb would fail to spoil the locomotive's beauty, but it was not the best publicity the circus could have. It would be one more thing for the Great Barnooli not to be pleased about.

"They'll try," said Martin. "Now, could you tell the sealions to come with us?"

Stereo turned to the Keepers, "You lot," he peeped. "Get out here and go with these gentlemen."

"Why?" they said.

"Don't argue, just go with them; you're in enough trouble as it is."

"Are you throwing us out as well?" they wailed.

"They want to take you away and burn you at the stake if the Smog Monster doesn't stop rampaging over their property."

The Keepers were appalled, "But it's not our fault..."

"He only wanted to protect us..."

"We didn't ask him to."

Stereo had no idea what they were on about, "Just get out," he said. "And let me try and contact Barnooli. If you're lucky, he'll get here in time to stop your execution."

The Keepers collected their precious records and added them to their sack of possessions. If they were going to die, it would be to a happy tune and surrounded by small comforts.

The police, the Keepers and the professor were all hurried off the train and deposited on the empty quayside. The locomotive was now the property of HM Government and neither the police nor the civilian protesters were welcome anymore.

"Thrown out like schoolboys from an orchard," said Professor Morris in disgust as they were escorted away by the soldiers. "I'm a scientist, not a fifth-grade scrumper with a couple of conkers and a slingshot!"

The soldiers looked unimpressed, "Orders," they said.

"Numbskulls," Morris fumed. "We've got rights!"

"And we've got guns," said the soldiers and laughed.

The Keepers were already white so it was impossible for them to get any paler, but they were certainly worried. They followed the policemen as close as they could, hoping the soldiers wouldn't want the other humans to be caught in the crossfire. "This is a pickle and no mistake," they agreed. Then their thoughts brightened as they accepted their fate. "We'll be martyrs to the circus..."

"Perhaps they'll put up a little statue to our memories..."

"Or put a plaque on one of the shovels..."

"Do you think the animals will miss us?"

The thought of the animals made them weep. The policemen bundled them into the van and they tried and failed to be stoical about their journey to the scaffold or whatever destination the humans had in mind for them. "We'll never see Pinniped again," they said, but couldn't agree on whether that was a bad thing or not.

Stereo watched the soldiers running up and down putting rolls of razor wire everywhere. Almost from the moment the circus had arrived on Earth, he had been looking forward to telling the human race how to deal with its problems (including the Smog Monster) and now he wasn't going to get the chance. "Serve them right if he does eat their piffling planet," he said and gave one of the soldiers a nasty shock by raising an aerial right by where he was bending over on the top of the train.

50 - New York

The Americans found their carriage in New York. It was parked neatly where a construction firm wanted to build a new skyscraper and for a while nobody recognised it for what it was.

Earlier in the morning hundreds of workmen had arrived to begin building only to find the site occupied. Either that or they were in the wrong place.

They gathered in front of the enormous box, union bosses already disputing violently with the engineers over the apparent dis-utility of them being there and the engineers were angrily disclaiming any responsibility and had turned on the surveyors. "Must be your fault; this is the wrong block…"

The surveyors looked at their maps, "Nope, this is the right place all right; but this building shouldn't be here, it should have been blown up."

This was of little consolation to the employers or employees who began to suspect a massive and costly mistake that would, most likely, end up in financial disaster and none of them being paid. "Must be the fault of the demolition company," they agreed, ready to phone their attorneys. "They got rid of the wrong building…"

However, the demolition company were adamant they had done their job and before anyone could start suing them for the destruction of the wrong building they were at the site with all the right paperwork and no better idea of what was going on than anyone else. "This is the right place," they said. "An old office block, brownstone, blew it up with 200ks of BBM…"

"Look around, you sure?"

"Sure we're sure." They even spotted the small café where they had sat and watched the workmen laying the charges. "This shouldn't be here."

"But it couldn't have just appeared, could it? There must be someone we can blame…?"

Everyone shrugged.

They milled around the carriage, poking at the metal walls and shaking their heads. "It doesn't look right," said the engineers, trying and failing to find a front door. "We'd better get an architect to look at it."

The architect admired the building without reserve and said flattering things about the influence of Egyptian tomb relief on the decoration around the architraves.

"Art deco?" asked the engineers, who liked to pretend they knew a thing or two about buildings. "Hints of Van Allen's Chrysler Building of 1930?"

"Possibly, perfectly executed too... But it's not the description of the building on the city plans."

"Absolutely not; who'd want to tear this beauty down?"

While the engineers, surveyors, architect, union bosses and demolition men sat in the café drinking coffee, eating bagels and arguing over the bill; workmen dug exploratory holes for a glimpse of the foundations. They hired an expensive helicopter and landed on the roof to look for air-conditioning vents or a skylight. They could find none of these things. They were looking at nothing with any practical or commercial use within the context of what they knew. They even failed to find the door until they realised it was actually the whole side of the box.

Camera crews appeared and journalists compared pictures of the building with pictures of the Chinese and African carriages. "Sweet!" they whooped, hugging each other and cheering. "We've found our carriage!"

It was at this point that America in general discovered 'their' interstellar vehicle and expressed their pleasure by leaping up and down in front of their television sets, drinking a pale, thin liquid shamefully imitating 'beer' and being completely over-the-top about what the carriage was going to do for them in the way of international relations: "We could really kick butt with this..." they claimed.

The American government surrounded the carriage with scientists and soldiers in almost equal profusion. Much to their later embarrassment they then tried to communicate with the empty box using powerful speakers and a bank of lights. They tried some simple harmonies in the hope that the carriage would reply by filling in the missing notes. They tried flashing lights having determined that it may be able to reciprocate using the masses of similar lights along its roof. They even tried knocking on the single vast door with a big wrench.

But the former occupant of the Trapezium Monkey's carriage was several miles away. The Mind™, still disguised as a pigeon, was amusing himself and an old tramp by accepting bits of bread from a salami sandwich. This subtle experiment had already netted interesting evidence on the variety of foods the local primates were willing to dole out to pigeons, ranging from gravel to an expensive milk and bean product from a woman dressed in the skins of an ancestral relative of the numerous quadrupeds he had seen leading the primates around the town.

This singular behaviour of the New Yorkers was most gratifying and he could only marvel at the hypocrisy of feeding vermin while showing complete intolerance towards the starving tramp who was, broadly speaking, the same species. He commended himself on his choice of disguise.

The Mind™ had also made some interesting behavioural discoveries on the habits of the local populace when he left parcels of synthetically digested food in opportune places. The windshields of their automobiles were a choice target and drew a plethora of unnecessary behaviour from the drivers; hats were another good test, but not nearly as satisfying as newly dressed hair where the effect was instantaneous and delightful with owners doing a jig and making colourful noises.

On one occasion some men, running out of a building with bulging sacks, had actually tried to return his present with small lead versions of their own fired chemically from small tubes. This was most exciting and necessitated the use of his defence system to avoid damage to his elaborate costume. The bank robbers, surprised by the dazzling colours of the Mind's™ shield, swore blind they had seen an angel and gave themselves up to the police.

While the Mind™ continued to store away these fascinating memories he showed an utter disregard for his carriage, which was a shame. Observation of the American efforts to get inside might have shed light on many of his discoveries.

The scientists were trying a variety of brutish devices and had entirely given up their efforts to communicate peacefully. Tempers were getting frayed, especially when they were foiled again by the automatic defences the carriage used to blunt, baffle or befuddle their expensive tools.

The pyrotechnics from the carriage drew a large crowd of sightseers who cried in wonder and amazement as the multi-coloured display of particle shields and atomic bucklers defied human ingenuity. But the scientists were not so chuffed. It was now obvious that the owners of the carriage were being blatantly rude. The military minds came to the conclusion that nobody nice would do such a thing and declared war on whatever race had built the train.

It did not occur to any of them that the shield was an automatic response to keep them from causing any damage.

Not ones to be turned away, bigger and more dangerous efforts were undertaken. The official in charge was particularly anxious to drag the hostiles out of their box; he was feeling peeved by the actions of a pigeon over the hood of his limousine and was not in the mood for conciliation. He gave the scientists carte blanche to do what they liked, even if that meant irradiating a large area of Manhattan.

51 - The Smog Monster

"Wait a minute," said the Smog Monster's Mind™ in mid-track over the M1. "There's something funny going on here…"

There was nothing funny about the way the Smog Monster was tearing up the country. Cars, coaches and carriers of all kinds oozed their squished entrails over the pockmarked highway. The fly-overs, the junctions and roundabouts were in tatters like streamers and burst balloons after a party. Nothing manmade had withstood the onslaught of an alien leviathan that had all the grace and finesse of a giant puppy.

Neither was 'funny' the first word to reach the lips of the motorists as they travelled north. As they came across creature crushing cars like an evil child stamping on snails words of Anglo-Saxon origin were nearer the mark, closely followed by people abandoning their vehicles and running away in an excess of real and verbal diarrhoea.

"Oh bloody wars!" said the Mind™, joining in with the steady stream of profanity emanating from the travellers below. "Look out!" A coach on its way to Scarborough had spilled its geriatric contents onto the concrete and they were now hobbling up the cutting with all the speed of a Post Office queue on pension day.

They were right in the path of the Smog Monster.

"Look out wrinkly people!" cried the Mind™. "Get out the way or you'll all be crushed!"

Nobody heard him through the tumult of tinny machinery being reduced to the size of doormats by the monster's massive feet.

The Mind™ redoubled his efforts, "Stop you bulkin! Stop!" he flicked about in front of the Smog Monster. "Look out wrinkly people! Oh no, run! Run!"

The Smog Monster was getting closer; the earth was shaking. He smashed through a line of trucks, scattering them like toys.

"Shift," cried the Mind™. "For Smog's sake, get out of the way!"

The stewardess and the bus driver were urging the old people to reach the safety of the hillside before the creature could reach them but the blessed elderly didn't understand. They zimmered a little faster just to please the driver and the young lady but couldn't comprehend the urgency. "Are we going to miss something?" they asked.

"Not if you stay here you silly old bugger…"

"…There's no need to be like that, young man, I'm 86 you know."

The monster was nearly on them. A petrol tanker exploded like a water bomb under its giant foot.

"Quick!" screamed the Mind™. "I can't stop him, he's out of control!"

"What's that funny noise?" asked another old person, stopping.

"Oh come on," said the driver. "You've really got to hurry…"

"Out of control?" said the Mind™. "That's not true; he's been going in a straight line for almost… Almost as if, wait a minute… There's something funny going on here…"

"…You're shaking like a leaf dear, do you want one of my blue pills? They're really good…"

"…A homing beacon?" The Mind™ tested the airwaves and sure enough, there it was: a personal beacon to the Smog Monster from the locomotive. Oddly enough he didn't feel like laughing.

"…Or how about one of the pink ones…? But don't get too far from the loo…"

"Excrement!" said the Mind™, getting his vocal field around the vowels. "Double-trunked elephant doo doo…!"

He shut down the beacon and the monster stopped. He was just inches away from the pathetic little bundle of elderly men and women, none of whom had noticed the monster and were not at all sure why the bus driver was trying to heave them over the motorway barrier. "Is the sea over there?" they asked the frightened stewardess.

The stewardess pointed at the Smog Monster. "Nh…"

"What is it dear?" asked an old lady, looking everywhere but up at the face hovering above her like a carthorse peering down at a mouse.

"Nrink…" said the stewardess.

"Drink…? No, but an ice-cream would be nice, it's a bit hot out here."

The Smog Monster's internal organs radiated heat like a modest nuclear pile. His sirocco breath stirred the grey hairs of the well-wrapped pensioners as they searched in vain for the sea.

"I can't see the pier, where is it?"

"I used to come here when I was young, it's changed an awful lot of course, but that's to be expected I suppose."

"Could you get me a deckchair, my dear? My legs aren't what they used to be."

"I'm 86."

The Mind™ looked down at all the waste caused by his own stupidity, "Oh Smog! I'll never work again… What will Mr Barnooli say?"

Barnooli might have been immensely arrogant, conceited, bull-brained and boastful, but one thing he was not was irresponsible. If there was responsibility to be had, he would be sure to find it and present it to the guilty party. For the sin of the catastrophic demise of hundreds of innocent pieces of property, the lives of sundry small animals and for giving the circus a bad reputation on a newly discovered world, Barnooli would make him pay in whatever approximated to a Mind's™ blood.

"Oh why did I let the Smog Monster out in the first place?" the Mind™ lamented. "I'll be reduced to changing fuses, or fixing the plumbing, or he might even make me work with children!"

Not far from the road there was a large empty warehouse. Without the beacon or the military to distract him it was easy enough to lead the Smog Monster off the road and shepherd him inside. "Get in there you big lump," said his minder, wishing he could create a foot big enough to kick him up the backside. "You've got me into it right up to my molecular monads this time! Just what am I going to say?"

He slammed the door shut and surveyed his charge's handy-work, "Just look at what he's done..."

Motorists were returning to the road with choice phrases forming on their lips like big gobs of spit. The Watts brothers landed in their helicopter and were busy collecting all the choicest epithets on behalf of a concerned nation.

"Well that's just great, nice afternoon drive, take the kids to see a film, have a pizza, nothing special; now my car looks like a pizza and the kids have shat their pants. Bloody marvellous day out this was."

"Look at my wagon, it's like a hedgehog has got its own back!"

"No, sorry, there won't be a refund. We brought you this far, didn't we?"

"Insurance...? Oh no. It wasn't an Act of God was it? It doesn't matter if it did breathe fire, my policy won't cover this..."

"Side impact bars? Don't make me laugh. Pay a fortune for a car with airbags and what happens? A thousand tons of dinosaur lands on your roof, and the bags never even deployed. I'd like to meet the manufacturer who can worm his way out of this one!"

"You did over-take on the inside, carved me right up, now take this..."

"Your luggage...? Well if you want to poke about in that flat bit over there you might find some of it. No, I don't suppose that brown stain will come out..."

"Are you sure this is the right exit? Shouldn't there be a fly-over?"

"I didn't want a caravan in the first place, if we'd gone by plane this would never have happened…"

"Mummy, where's daddy…?"

"Brand new, fifty grand of motor and I can't tell one part from another, what's my mother going to say?"

"Get me my mobile Sybil; somebody is going to pay for this…"

"I don't care if you are 86, how am I going to explain this to my boss…?"

The Watts brothers took photographs and provided commentary for the film crew. They were soon joined by dozens of other reporters flying in from every newspaper and television station until there were more interviews happening on the motorway than anywhere else in the world.

In the meantime, safely tucked away in the warehouse, the Smog Monster soon forgot about the open-vista horrors of the English countryside. His small mind did not dwell on the ceasing of the homing beacon. As far as he was concerned he was back in the train.

The army and the air force suddenly had nothing to do. However, the lull in the progressive destruction of that which they were supposed to protect didn't last long; they soon had to surround the warehouse to prevent thousands of aggrieved holiday-makers and motorists from storming the building and 'having a pop' at the cause of their misery. What these brave citizens could have done was open to debate, but it was not inconceivable that they might wake the monster up again; an occasion the military were anxious to avoid.

The crowds were pushed back and big signs went up outside the warehouse with 'do not disturb' on them. If anyone broke through, they were whispered at and threatened in a silent pantomime that left the would-be disturber in no doubt as to what would happen to his groin area if the monster was to rise up, refreshed from his nap and continue towards London.

52 - The Great Barnooli

Stereo's standing wave went out as requested, but he didn't hold out much hope of it being answered. Indeed, Barnooli was contentedly sunning himself on the holiday planet of Agnatha and his wife was still singing pithy love songs from the balcony above.

Barnooli was now a fine nut-brown (though not without the aid of numerous restoratives to cool his early burns from Agnatha's sun) and he was about as relaxed as any hyper-anxious workaholic can get. He had swum every morning in the indigo lake; he had breakfasted on the pine-scented slopes of the distant mountains and had taken brunch on boat trips across an azure bay. There had been picnics in the fields of jewel flowers and afternoon tea in the regal palace of the local travel agent. Dinners lasted until late evening and then he and his wife had danced in the light of the heart-shaped moon while sipping the finest Cromornan fizz to the accompaniment of a thirty-piece orchestra.

However, if the truth could be admitted, he was bored with being pampered and longed to get in touch with the circus. After all, there was only so much fun he could have with a bucket of whipped cream and purple strawberries...

Barnooli had calculated (wrongly) that the train ought to be in orbit around Isamus by now and Stereo ought to be making overtures towards the local government with masses of advance publicity (woe betide him if he wasn't). In short, Stereo ought to be working and Barnooli longed to hear how well it was all going.

Isamus was a plum; the core world of a powerful empire and a marvellous gateway to a region of space Barnooli had not explored before. A three dimensional crossroads, Isamus attracted potential clients from at least five other empires. It was rich and prosperous and Barnooli wanted a piece of it.

Thoughts of losing the contact were enough to encourage Barnooli to cut his holiday short there and then, but he knew Ophonia wouldn't let him. One whiff of circus business and he could kiss goodbye to the whipped cream and purple strawberries for a month at least. Ophonia was having too fine a time.

Agnatha's shops were rich in expensive little items of interest and delight: rings, bracelets, necklaces, clothes, jars of sweet fruits, boxes of chocolates, and bottles of perfume... Even the vaguest suggestion of leaving early was likely to be greeted with storms of temper and slamming doors.

Barnooli had discovered early on in his association with his leading lady that Ophonia was not to be crossed. She had a powerful hormonal capacity to make him feel guilty with a look, miserable with a shrug or a traitor with a word. This was not to say that he was actually unhappy, far from it. Ophonia had a similar hormonal capacity to raise his ego to oxygen deficient heights and when he was with her and all was going well she made him shine with such a lustre that he almost dazzled himself.

Still, he wished he could get in touch with the circus, just one call, perhaps a fax; one word to ask if everything was as it should be…

53 - Ted

Barnooli was not the only one interested in the fate of the circus. Ted, the Theatrical Director (the one with the silly hair) was possibly even more obsessed. Because he was the one who arranged the shows he believed he had a right to know the status of the acts. Or, as Stereo put it, he was a paranoid twit who couldn't leave anything alone for five seconds.

Ted had convinced himself something was wrong and had come up with a plausible excuse to make enquiries of Stereo. It was Ted who was first to answer Stereo's standing wave.

"Hello?"

"Hello," said Stereo.

"This is the Theatrical Director."

"I know," said Stereo. "Hello Ted."

Ted ground his teeth, "I though I'd just have a word, you know, find out if everything is all right? I mean; I have to know if the circus is all right if I'm to put on the next show? Don't I...?" There was a long pause. "Stereo? Is everything all right?"

"No," said Stereo quite unemotionally.

"What?" Ted spluttered.

"'No,'" Stereo repeated, just as unemotionally.

"What's wrong?"

"I can't say."

"Why not...?" Ted could feel is ulcer burning inside him.

"I've been told to tell Barnooli."

"Tell Barnooli what?"

"What I have to tell him."

"And what's that?" Ted's voice began to sound strained.

"Just what I said..."

"But you haven't said anything!"

"Yes I have; I've told you that I have a message for Mr Barnooli. Are you Mr Barnooli?"

"No, of course not..."

"Well then."

"You mean you're not going to tell me what's wrong?"

"Did I say anything was wrong?"

"Umm..." Ted couldn't remember. "I don't know."

"Quite."

"But why can't you tell me what's going on?"

Stereo sighed, "I told you, what I have to say is for Barnooli and not for you."

"But I'm the Theatrical Director, you know me don't you?"

"Yes Ted, but you're not Barnooli; I thought I made that abundantly clear."

"Does it matter where the circus is concerned?"

"It matters to them."

"'Them'?" A pall of darkness fell over Ted's imagination. "Who is 'them'?"

"I'm not sure I should say."

"Are you at the proper destination?"

"That depends."

"On what…?"

"On what Barnooli would say."

"Oh Punchinello!" wailed Ted. He put on a more authoritarian voice, "Look I want to know where the circus is!"

"Why?"

"Because I want to know!" he screamed.

"Ah," said Stereo wisely. "But you're not Barnooli."

"That doesn't matter! I'm his Theatrical Director!"

"And Barnooli is the owner."

"I want to know on his behalf…"

"Oh?" Stereo toyed. "You have some sort of authorisation?"

"Not exactly…"

"How exactly…?"

"Nothing in writing…"

"I see."

"But I'm sure he would want me to check up on the circus."

"Well thank you for your enquiry."

"But you haven't told me anything!"

"As you don't have proper authorisation I can't very well break my promise to these people just for a bit of gossip, can I?"

"Stereo! You jumped up little…"

Stereo cut him off, "And I don't think I have to listen to that sort of thing," he said to himself.

Ted, in a rage, stamped his foot on the ground and swore theatrically. Then he stomped up and down his caravan, scattering his fluffy cushions and kicking his wardrobe in an excess of fine emotions, until he felt calm enough to try and get in touch with Barnooli himself.

Unfortunately, the Theatrical Director came up against an equally defensive telephone receptionist at Barnooli's hotel.

"I'm sorry sir," said the waspish voice. "The Great Barnooli has given strict instruction that he does not wish to be disturbed."

"I know; I'm from his circus; I have an important message for him…"

"I'm sorry sir but…"

"It's important!"

"It might be to you sir, but our regulations state…"

"Look, can't I just leave the message with you in case he asks?"

"We cannot be responsible for messages as we will then be legally obliged to hand them over and this will no doubt disturb him against his prior wishes."

"Damn!"

"Is that the message?"

"No it isn't."

"Just as well," said the receptionist in a rare moment of cordiality. "That would most certainly have disturbed him, ha ha!"

Ted slammed down the telephone, "Heartless brutes!"

He went for the cushions again but this time they managed to get out of the way and cowered under the bed with his fluffy slippers.

"The circus is probably in mortal danger and all I can get through to are a couple of clam-baked, slack-brained dikkops without an ounce of reason in their beastly heads! It's all so unfair!"

As there was nothing more he could do he resigned himself to ignominy and drowned his sorrows in half a glass of sweet liqueur.

54 - China

The Chinese government looked at the beautiful pictures of the giant giraffe set against the background of mountains and the perfect lines of Chinese troops standing with admirable resilience in the hot sun and a foot of water. Their tanks gleamed and their rocket launchers looked splendid.

Unfortunately, the glossy pictures were in an American magazine. There were similar images on the internet. There was even a clip of film showing the peasants feeding the alien beast.

The government called in the generals. They looked at the pictures and there was a moment of hilarity as one of them recognised himself as he stood marshalling the defence of the motherland. Then they realised this was a bad thing. Where had these pictures come from? They asked the government.

The Chinese ministers asked the same question and looked accusingly at the generals. The military men shrugged their shoulders. They had not been aware of any photographers among the many thousands of soldiers gathered around the district. They were fairly sure the peasants were not responsible either.

'Fairly sure' was not good enough. There had to be an explanation for such high quality images appearing outside the beneficence of the communist regime. There seemed to be one obvious conclusion: spies had infiltrated the paddy fields with the singular purpose of humiliating the great and powerful People's Republic of China. At least, that was going to be the official line.

Confidentially, they were cross that nobody had offered them money to take the pictures, no licence had been bought or permission sought and paid for. It was one thing to respect their sovereign rights, quite another to take the pictures and not pay for the privilege.

There was a simple solution: they arrested a bus-load of American tourists a hundred miles away. This was not a measure designed to endear them to their Pacific rivals.

Having fought the Chinese to a stand-still in Korea and received a bloody nose from similar Orientals in Vietnam, the Americans thought they had every right to a re-match and mobilised their Pacific Fleet to sail to the China Sea for an aggressive confrontation of words backed up by nuclear submarines, aircraft carriers and finger-wagging.

Much to the surprise of the last remnants of besieged communism around the world, sympathy among the mad dog capitalists was with the Chinese and not with the American tourists. Most people agreed the tourists were probably innocent and they ought to be allowed to go, but they were also annoying and loud and ought to be taught a lesson in humility.

Frowned on by the rest of the world, the Americans kept their angry stance like boxers disqualified on a technicality. They shut their ears to criticism, stormed out of the United Nations and vowed not to return until everyone said they were right and the Chinese wrong.

While apple-pie eating, constitutionally protected god-fearing Americans festered in the rotting rat-ridden gaols of the oppressive communist regime; they would not move from the China Sea.

The Chinese, with thousands of years of history to perfect the silent treatment and the deadpan expression, calmly drank tea and lapsed into a dignified silence. Meanwhile, they manufactured toy giraffes by the million and used the publicity generated by the American magazine to sell them to the west. The Americans could rant and rave all they liked but neither could they resist a cute little face with such adorable eyes.

55 - Africa

As the bell rang over the savannah, the rabbits leapt out of their pens and ran across the battlefield to their carriage. The doors opened and they jumped inside, along with the celebrities and aid workers who decided it was safer to be in an alien space ship than stay outside in a war zone.

The humans stopped shooting at each other for a moment. The villagers, who had tried and failed to keep their income from streaming away, began to sing a funeral dirge. "God is angry with us," they wailed. "He gaveth and now he taketh away... We have failed Him!"

Their rivals, suspecting a diversionary tactic, re-loaded their weapons and prepared another assault. They had borrowed heavily to fund their expedition and they were damned if they were going to accept 'nothing to fight over' as an excuse.

Mercenaries on both sides began to wonder how they were going to get paid now the currency of rabbits seemed to have disappeared. They began to think about storming the alien space ship. It looked expensive, "If we could prise a few bits off it might have some scrap value," they agreed and contacted their former enemies to consider a joint-effort with an equal division of the spoils.

Inside the carriage, the rabbits ran into their hutches and the doors closed behind them. The celebrities and aid workers looked around at the compartment. It was full of Bazmondo's magic technology. There were levitators, evaporators and holographic generators. There were cabinets and mechanical contrivances; pyramids, globes and a great cubicuboctahedron all piled together in a giant child's toy-box of colour and confusion.

There were other animals besides the rabbits. There was an exotic turkey with eyes like kaleidoscopes that could see into the future; snakes in a glass case that could spell. And a pink kitten that Bazmondo was going to give to Ophonia as a wedding gift until he discovered she was allergic to cats. (He had given her a magic toaster instead. It was supposed to not burn the bread but had set off the fire alarms when Barnooli had crammed it with bagels and was now floating in space many light years away.)

The humans also saw signs of amateur decorating. Cerise flowers had been stencilled onto the ceiling beams. There was glitter on the bars of the hutches and paper doilies under the fire buckets. Behind the magical artefacts, the walls had been covered in diagonal stripes.

Mary Smith materialised in a flash of light. "Good," she said. She was covered in spits and spats of gold and royal blue paint. "We haven't finished the function room doors and there's gloss-work to be done in the hallway. If you guys can give us a hand, the Mind™ said he'll take us back to England."

The celebrities and aid workers looked at each other. They were covered in dust and debris. They had been shot at, bombed and their equipment was lying outside in little pieces. They had come to Africa to give it aid and help it back onto its feet and those same feet had trampled all over their good intentions.

"Where are the brushes," they said. They had no idea whose mind they were helping but it had to be grateful if it was willing to give them a ride home in return. "A cup of tea would be nice too."

Outside, heavy artillery began to pound the carriage's defences and the Africans started shooting at each other again. Inside, the noise was no more than a distant rumble of thunder, a backdrop to the sound of brushes and the occasional fart as the giant rabbits ate their contraceptive beans.

56 - The Great Barnooli

Even though the facilities at Barnooli's hotel were quite wonderful, the great circus impresario was no longer happy. Despite the hundreds of rooms, big and small, private or open, palatial or merely cosy; plazas, arcades, streets, small villages of huts by the water and more swimming pools than puddles down a cart track, there was a figurative fly in his ointment. He was not as content as he had been at the start of his holiday. He needed his fix of circus news.

There were pools for every major life form in Agnatha's constellation: steam baths for tropical visitors, slimy, muddy or stagnant pools for amphibian guests; sandy trays for those who hated water; oily baths for sensitive skins; fast currents, bubble jets and hot springs for the adventurous; and special baths for divas with sensitive throats and weighty builds. This at least pleased Barnooli. Ophonia decided to spend a few hours in this latter bath. Barnooli declined her offer to join in saying he would take a little run around the park instead. She approved of this and selected a handsome bottle-green tracksuit for him to wear.

Barnooli jogged off across the lawn looking like a giant pea. He waved merrily to his wife and when she could no longer see him, he nipped over to the taxi rank and took a car to his own inter-stellar caravan. He giggled to himself as he went along, pleased with this minor deception, like a schoolboy bunking off from sports day.

Barnooli went straight to his office and the Mind™ in charge of the caravan's communication console, or 'Junior Stereo' as he was called, who was quite shy and spoke in a tiny little voice like a small rodent trying to hide in a hole.

"Well," said Barnooli, out of breath and sweating heavily. "Have you heard from the circus?"

Junior whispered, "There are two messages for you, Mr Barnooli."

"Two?"

Junior whispered an affirmation.

"Who are they from?"

"The Theatrical Director and Stereo, Mr Barnooli, sir..."

Barnooli sighed, "Let's hear what that belly-fluff Ted has to say."

"Yes, Mr Barnooli sir," peeped Junior.

"Hello? Mr Barnooli?" said Ted's voice. "Have I got news for you; Stereo has really done it this time, he won't even speak to me about it, I'm sure he's done something terribly awful! Hope you're having a nice time. Ciao."

Barnooli frowned, "Phone him," he ordered.

"Yes, Mr Barnooli, sir," Junior began dialling.

Ted must have been sitting by the phone because he answered immediately. "Oh, thank goodness!" he said when he heard Barnooli's voice.

He then explained what had happened, embellishing the story with tales of Stereo's hostility and antipathy towards the welfare of the circus. Barnooli yawned. This sounded like nothing out of the ordinary. Stereo loathed the Theatrical Director since the latter was always wasting his time with prolonged calls to his mother that invariably included a million untruths about his performances in the circus. Barnooli was not necessarily on Stereo's side in this; Stereo was equally egotistical. Perhaps that was why they didn't get on.

"He won't speak to me," Ted repeated, yet again.

Good, thought Barnooli, "I'd better have a word with him then. Junior…?"

"Yes Mr Barnooli sir?"

"Get me Stereo."

"Mr Barnooli…?" pleaded Ted, who was almost literally dying of curiosity. "Mr Barnooli if I could…"

Barnooli cut the Theatrical Director out of the loop. "No, you couldn't," he chuckled.

Junior switched channels. Stereo's voice was relayed across the vastness of space, "Hello?"

"Well, how's it all going?" Barnooli asked, expecting to hear encouraging words about their prospects for a good show on Isamus.

"All of it?" said Stereo, not sure of the parameters of the question.

"Isamus; have you started the advanced publicity yet? Have you spoken to the local governor?"

"No, Mr Barnooli," said Stereo.

"What do you mean?" Barnooli was, in every sense of the word, unprepared for what Stereo had to say next…

"I mean, I have been unable to begin overtures on Isamus because we are not, currently, anywhere near our intended destination."

Barnooli could feel his face getting hotter, "Why not?"

Unlike Ted, Stereo never minced his words: "The Keepers have crashed the circus on a planet called Earth and some of the animals have escaped. The locomotive's Mind™ has had another breakdown; the other Minds™ have abandoned the train and are doing their own thing. The Keepers have been arrested and are being held as hostages. It looks like the circus will be sued for trespass, neglect and possibly kidnap. But I'm not sure about the last one as I don't know the status of the humans currently re-painting the inside of one of the carriages..."

Barnooli gagged.

"Mr Barnooli?"

Barnooli felt as though he was falling through the atmosphere of a gas giant. He could feel the howling winds of methane and hydrogen and he was fighting for breath. Freezing temperatures and crushing gravity tore at his sanity like a pack of ungrateful in-laws.

"There's more," said Stereo, unsure of what was going on at the other end of the line.

"More?" said Barnooli in a strained voice.

"Yes."

"Worse?" His breathing sounded laboured.

"Possibly..."

Barnooli thought his heart was going to pack its bags and move out. He could feel the room spinning like a ribbon twirled from a stick as each horror climbed on the back with the next...

"The Smog Monster's Mind™ let him out of his carriage, he suffered another bout of agoraphobia and he's caused a bit of damage in the process. I'm sure the locals will sue you for that as well."

Barnooli let out a choked cry like a cockerel being garrotted.

"Is everything all right?" asked Stereo. "Junior...?"

"Mr Barnooli has collapsed on the floor," replied Junior. "Do you think I should call Mrs Barnooli?"

"Has he gone a funny colour?"

"He's gone very red... Wait a second; he's getting up again..."

Barnooli heaved his bulk back into the chair and wiped his face with his hanky. He took several deep breaths and cleared his throat.

"It's lucky only four carriages ended up down here," said Stereo lightly. "I expect you'd be on a triple bypass by now if it had been all of them... Mr Barnooli?"

Barnooli felt overwhelmingly betrayed and shock began to be replaced by anger. He remembered his first doubts under Agnatha's sun.

Keepers, he mumbled to himself. Keepers! He knew he had felt misgivings about them; why had nobody warned him? Why had that idiot Ted allowed him to put the Keepers in charge? What possessed him to leave the wretched creatures on board and not send them off to their home world like all the rest of the acts?

"Where are they?" he snarled. "Where are the fish-eating morons that made all this happen?"

"Not far from the locomotive," said Stereo. "Locked up I believe. The people on this world wish to use them to negotiate a compensation package, or I expect they'll execute them."

A pleasant image of skewered white sealions spitted on poles popped into Barnooli's head. "Good," he said. Another thought occurred to him, "How could they cause this much damage while shovelling animal dung or mopping the floors?"

"It was an accident," said Stereo. "They spilt wine over Auto Pilot™,"

"Wine…?"

"They were having a party in the locomotive's cabin."

"Party…?" The facts were becoming clearer, or darker, like the gathering of an apocalypse…

"They really have the most appalling taste in music, quite awful."

"Oh shut up Stereo!" Barnooli exploded. "I told them to stay away from the locomotive's cabin! I told them to touch nothing!" He was growing very red in the face again and his blood pressure was reaching the point of no return. "How could they do this to me? I took them off that ice-cube of a world of theirs, I gave them a place to stay, I even gave them pocket money and this is how they repay me! Stealing wine, listening to music; lounging about and not working… Then as an encore they crash my beautiful circus and lose all my animals…"

"Not all of them," corrected Stereo, "Just your favourite and a handful of others."

Barnooli wished his wife had not made him sack the lithe ladies from the planet of forbidden pleasures; he could have locked Stereo in a room with them and made him listen to their talk of shoes and make-up for a month.

Ophonia reminded him he was still on holiday. "Well not anymore," he said. "Junior…?"

"Yes Mr Barnooli, sir?"

"Tell the hotel to prepare my bill."

"Yes Mr Barnooli, sir."

"Oh Mr Barnooli, sir…?" asked Junior's senior half.

"What?"

"There's one other thing…?"

"What now? Has the locomotive got a small but incredibly expensive dent in the side? Are the Minds™ in revolt because they've finally figured out they're more useless than a paperweight in zero gravity? Or perhaps you have some good news? You've decided to leave the circus and become a bereavement councillor?"

"Ah, no Mr Barnooli…"

"What then?"

"Would you like me to sort things out?"

"Stereo, if you can sort this mess out before I arrive all well and good. If you haven't sorted things out by the time I arrive I shall have you kicked into a sun, do I make myself clear?"

"So I have complete authority?" asked Stereo, un-phased by threats.

"And complete responsibility," menaced Barnooli.

"Oh good," said Stereo.

Barnooli rang off. "Where is this 'Earth'?" he demanded.

"I'm not sure Mr Barnooli sir," said Junior. "It's not on any of the star charts. But we can follow Stereo's signal to the source."

Barnooli nodded. His heart, having recovered from the initial shock, was pounding in his chest again as he now considered how he was going to break the news to his wife. "Contact the other acts," he said. "Tell them to go to this 'Earth' and meet us there. If my life is going to be made miserable, I want theirs to be as well."

57 - The Minds™

"Now we'll see," said Stereo. "Now we'll see who can tell me to mind my own business! Real power at last... They'll wish they'd taken me up on that game of Arroban Cribbage. They'll wish we'd spent a century playing Tyn Bridge..."

"What are you on about?" asked the locomotive's Mind™, finally floating on the surface of his sea of sanity. Still struggling for breath, the last thing he needed was Stereo behaving like a pantomime dictator.

"Barnooli has given me complete authority over the circus, I'm in charge! I'm numero uno!"

"Big deal," said the locomotive's Mind™, a jealous under-current threatening to undermine his new found confidence like a very bad haircut. "I've got a friend."

"Really" said Stereo, completely uninterested.

"Yes, really..."

"Where...?"

"In the boat next to us..."

"Why hasn't he come round to see you then?"

"I haven't told him where I am."

"Why?"

The locomotive's Mind™ shrugged, "He's busy."

"You're just scared if you invite him he won't come."

"I'm not, I told you; he's busy."

"Pah, if you were me you'd have ordered him over."

"Just as well I'm not you then, because he wouldn't come. Mr Brown is a man of principle."

"'Mister' Brown is it?" said Stereo sarcastically.

"Oh piss off Stereo, you're such a grothamite."

"No," replied Stereo. "I'm in charge! I give the orders now!" He laughed in a faintly disturbing way and turned his attention to the other Minds™. He could hear them being jolly and he wasn't happy about it. They had no right to be cheerful. It didn't suit him at all.

"4... 15... 27... And the bonus ball is ... 18!" There was a big cheer.

"Yes!"

"We've done it!"

"We've won!"

"You've done it?" asked Stereo, butting in. "Done what?"

"We've won the lottery!" They continued to cheer through the full spectrum of the Mind™ transmission channels.

"Wow!" he patronised. "How much...?"

"Loads..."

"Golly." He couldn't quite understand their joy; he'd never seen it before so he treated it with contempt. "So you've won?"

"Yes, we won! We're rich!"

"But what do you need the money for?" This was the real nub of the triumph, the axle, and the kingpin: the raison d'etre...

"Buy more lottery tickets of course."

"I see, so winning was worthwhile then," Stereo reined back his sarcasm as far as it would go, "How very exciting for you."

"Certainly was, haven't been this excited since... Since never, actually..."

"But what about that time when you won on a six and a three and the Double Trucked Elephant's Mind™ had a six and a two?"

"That was pretty good, I'll agree..."

Stereo could detect a certain amount of neutrality. "Or what about when I had three Triumphal Arches and your Half Shekel just beat it with a Withered Spoon?"

"Well that was quite good too, but I never really understood the rules to Esoteric Golf; they always seemed over-complicated..."

"I agree," said another Mind™. "And I'm sure somebody was cheating..."

Stereo kept under control, "But you think the lottery is just as good?"

"Brilliant."

"How much did you win?"

"Ten."

"Million...?"

"We don't know. We got some of the numbers and according to the rules we've won 'ten'."

"I presume, from my own research, that your ten refers to ten 'poundstirling'. Do you know what that will buy you in the average corner shop in any other part of the galaxy?"

"No?" they asked eagerly.

"Nothing," said Stereo in a tone that implied deep satisfaction.

"Nothing...?" Their disappointment could have been sliced and handed out with tea.

"It's not legal tender anywhere else in the galaxy, it's useless."

"Can't we buy something here?"

"Ah, so you think you'll have time?" he said, hoping the penny would drop.

"We've got plenty of time, haven't we?"

"Have you?"

"Barnooli isn't coming yet…" The penny dropped, rolled into a gutter and was stolen by a sudden loss of faith. "Is he?"

"He could be," said Stereo viciously.

"Is he or isn't he?"

"He is, but before he gets here, and this is the point I hope you'll be really pleased with; I'm in charge."

"You!" the other Minds™ were appalled.

"That's right, I have absolute authority. To begin with, I'll confiscate that illicitly won money and there will be no more talk of this lottery nonsense. However, there may be a game of Tyn Bridge this evening, if I feel like it. That's if you're lucky. If you're really lucky I'll play you my entire collection of wind noises."

The other Minds™ groaned, "I hope Barnooli won't be long."

"Long enough," Stereo sniggered. "There will be other pleasurable activities that you will partake in before his arrival and I shall enjoy arranging them. On the other hand, you may wish to consider the repercussions of avoiding me over the next few days; who can say what Barnooli will do to the Mind™ that gets a poor report from me? I am charged with bringing back order to the circus and that includes you lot. I shall be in touch." With a sweep of a metaphorical black cloak, Stereo vanished from the stage, still sniggering at their shock.

"I'm not trying his cooking," said the Chef's Mind™.

"No way," the others agreed.

"Remember that recipe with the sea food? The one where he substituted the prawns with insect larvae…?"

"I don't think anyone will ever be able to forget; no wonder the plumbing broke down."

"He might have cooked them first."

"Blow cooking them, just killing them would have been good."

"That Stereo; he gives us Minds™ a bad name."

58 - The Keepers

The Keepers were writing their last will and testament. Professor Morris had been sent back to the university but he had left them their paper and pens. They had allotted their meagre possessions among the more deserving of their family circle and written letters to say goodbye. They then illuminated those letters with pictures of hearts, flowers and fish.

They tried to be optimistic about their fate, "Perhaps Barnooli will rescue us," they said.

"But is he coming?"

"Will he get here in time?"

They shook their heads, they didn't know. They kept glancing at the humans but found it hard to believe they were capable of actual cruelty. The thin one was doing his 'reading the newspaper' routine that the Keepers found about as funny as a fish in the eye. It was almost as bad as the fat one's 'kip in an armchair' and the utterly non-hilarious 'handkerchief and nose' gag. But apart from killing them with boredom, there were no other signs of hostility.

"They might be very bad comedians," they agreed, "but they don't seem like bad people."

Martin came in with more fish. They had reached an accommodation with the fishmonger; he would give them a discount if the police didn't make it public that he had been the one supplying the aliens. It was a vain hope, of course; there was a large crowd of protesters outside that had seen the monger's van and had waved their placards at him angrily. As far as the public was concerned, feeding the aliens was treason.

"Is this going to be our last meal?" the Keepers wondered.

"Before they drag us away, kill us and bury us in a shallow grave..."

"They could have brought some prawns," they grumbled.

"I wonder if we'll be compensated by the circus," said Reece, putting his paper down after reading an alarming article about how much it was going to cost to re-build the country following the Smog Monster's rampage. The figures had so many noughts they were meaningless but the threat of increased taxes and a cut to his wages was real enough.

"I doubt it," said Martin, "And definitely not because we're holding his useless sealions hostage. I expect this 'Great Barnooli' will be glad to see the back of them. He'll fly off with his carriages and the acts that make him money and we'll be stuck with these wretched creatures forever."

"Maybe they've broken some galactic laws," the policeman persisted. "Do you think there's a higher authority out there that we could appeal to?"

"And how are you going to make contact with them if there are? Do you have their number?"

"We could ask the parrot. He might even make the call for us if we asked nicely."

"He works for the circus; he's not going to sue his employer on our behalf."

The Keepers were practising their last words to an ungrateful world. They stood in a line and tried to remember their parts: "We just wanted to say…"

"To all our fans everywhere…"

"Before we depart this planet…"

"And meet whatever death you have in mind for us…"

"However painful it might be…"

"Or unfair…"

"Or unjust…"

"I wish the parrot was here," said Reece. "I'd love to know what they're saying…"

"…It wasn't our fault…" They had argued over whether it was or not since Stereo had made it patently obvious it was. However, they argued back that, technically speaking, only the train's arrival on Earth was their fault and the rest was just coincidence.

"Be careful what you wish for," said Martin. "I don't think that parrot has any interest in being a translator for the last words of these little creatures. It seemed to me that he was far more intent on giving us a load of opinions we wouldn't want to hear."

"…So long," the Keepers concluded.

Reece nodded, "You might be right; he did seem fairly full of himself."

"…And thanks…"

"For all the fish…"

59 - The locomotive's Mind™

Stereo looked at his long list of 'things to do'. Getting rid of the locomotive's Mind™ was a high priority. His rival Mind™ had actually done Barnooli a favour by not crashing the train in such a manner as to leave it in tiny pieces and that meant he had to go. Stereo reasoned if there was any praise to be derived from this debacle it was going to be his.

Secondly, he realised blame might fall in his direction when Barnooli came to examine the facts. Even though the Keepers were the obvious targets, the Minds™ were the intelligent ones; they could have prevented the whole tragedy from unfolding if they had thought about it. Worse still, most of the other Minds™ had followed protocol and saved their carriages from coming to serious harm.

The primary locomotive was the locus of all that was important in the running of the train; a place the Keepers should have been kept out of. That meant it was either him or Auto Pilot™ for the chop. Auto Pilot™ was still asleep so Stereo had a head-start. He would make sure the fault-line wasn't pointing in his direction long before the chasm of blame opened up.

"I'm going to go out for a while," Stereo said out loud. "Do a few little jobs; put a few things right, that sort of thing. Why don't you go out as well?"

"What's the point?" said the locomotive's Mind™ from his refuge. "It's just as bad out there as it is in here."

"What about your friend? Why don't you pay him a visit?"

"I couldn't."

"Why not...?"

"I just couldn't..."

Stereo could tell he was half-persuaded. "You should go and see him before Barnooli get here and we have to leave. You won't get a second chance."

"What about the locomotive?"

"I'll wake up Auto Pilot™ and get him to look after it, it's about time he tested his circuits. I expect they're dry by now."

"That's a point," agreed the Mind™. "No, no I couldn't."

"Why not...?"

"What like this?" he referred to his spherical appearance.

231

"Get a disguise."

"Such as...?"

"A bird is a good one."

"I hate birds, and besides, a bird can't talk. What would my friend think of a talking bird? Birds are stupid."

Stereo ignored the insult. "A person then, they're not that difficult." Stereo described how he could do it with all sorts of complex photon mixers and energy matchers and stuff only Minds™ and mathematicians can describe.

"It'd be really tricky though," finished Stereo.

"I suppose it would."

"But you could do it..."

The Mind™ thought about this, "I could try," he said tentatively.

Through the open door of the cabin several self-important men and their advisers crowded in. They sneered at the brass and leather. They disdained the analogue dials with their large pointy arrows. They showed no respect for their surroundings and made a lot of noise to emphasise the fact.

"Oh no," said Stereo. Perfect timing, he thought.

"Right, where are you?" shouted a big-mouthed politician in a loud and condescending voice. "We have a few words to say to you..."

"I'm not staying to listen to this," said Stereo to the locomotive's Mind™. "See you later, hope you have a nice time with these idiots."

"Come on, where are you?" repeated the politician, whacking a chair with his leather glove.

The large macaw flew across the cabin. The politicians and their advisers had to duck to avoid his flapping wings and razor sharp claws. The beak didn't look too friendly either.

"Look out! Quick shut the... Too late..."

Stereo flew out of the door and winged it across the quay singing 'Land of Hope and Glory' very loudly. The soldiers thought about shooting him down.

The locomotive's Mind™ looked at the politicians and looked across at the pleasure cruiser where he knew his friend was sitting alone. The decision was becoming easier by the moment.

But he couldn't leave while there were humans were in the cabin. They were examining the buttons on the consoles and touching things. They were also getting closer to where he was hiding among the dials and gauges at the front and even though he was protected by his interface bowl, he didn't want to be peered at. He wasn't a goldfish.

"Damn cheek, flying off like that," said the unwanted guests.

"What are going to do now?"

"What's behind that glass over there...?"

The locomotive's Mind™ thought the cabin was looking grubby. There were dirty stains on the floor, along with pastry crumbs. The Keepers had failed to do anything with the litter of cups and paper plates other than pile it up behind a chair. "I'll give it a quick purge with the high pressure jets," he decided.

He set up an electrical field to protect the controls, "Can't have them getting wet," he chuckled. "I'm not stupid like Auto Pilot™."

Then he blasted the floor with horizontal jets of a water-based cleaning fluid. Clouds of steam filled the cabin along with a monotonous hum that was the Mind™ singing to drown out the screams of the visitors.

Caught like spiders in the bath, the politicians and their advisors slipped and scrabbled, "We're under attack!" they screamed.

"Retreat!" cried the advisors. "Get out of the train!"

They tried to run, they slipped, they fell and as they reached up to the consoles to steady their nerves, they made contact with the electrical field. They yelped and clutched at one-another until they all jiggled like puppets on strings.

"Turn it off!" they cried, in between jolts.

Loose change, cufflinks and false teeth were shaken loose and scattered on the floor to be washed away with all the detritus of the party. The rubbish was sluiced towards the door and even the wine stains began to disappear. The cabin began to shine again.

"I do find cleaning very therapeutic," said the locomotive's Mind™. "I ought to do it more often."

The unwanted visitors were almost finished. He turned off the current before he fried them. With the fans on full, he dried out the cabin and blew the last of the litter, the politicians, and their advisors, out of the door. A great cloud of steam was driven into the sunny sky and the Keepers' cups floated away on the tide.

The humans threw themselves down the gangplank and crawled to the quayside. Their shoes squished and their clothes were coming apart at the seams. Their hair was gently smoking. The soldiers helped them to their feet and tried not to laugh too loudly.

The Mind™ slammed the door on the departed humans in much the same way as he had shut it on the Keepers. Then he left his bowl and floated into the cabin. "Lovely," he said, admiring his handiwork. From a locker, he took a cloth and a tin of metal polish and began to clean the brass on the levers and dials. "This is much better," he said, realising the root of all his troubles may have been boredom. He thought about his friend, "I wonder if Mr Brown wants anything cleaned?"

60 - Stereo

Meanwhile, Stereo landed on the windowsill of the Keepers' flat and pecked on the glass with his beak. One of the Keepers let him in amid a storm of clicking from the journalists and shouts of 'go home' from the protesters.

"Hello," he said to the room in general and in two different languages at the same time.

"It's the parrot," said Reece. "The one from the train..."

"I can see that," said Martin. "What does it want?"

Stereo talked to the hostages first, "And what have you got to say for all the trouble you've caused?" he said.

The Keepers tried to look humble by staring at the floor, "Nothing," they said, shuffling their feet.

"Mr Barnooli's not very pleased with you."

They looked up brightly, "Is he coming?"

"Oh yes, and he'll be here tomorrow to provide the fuel for the humans to burn you with."

There was a high-pitched wail as the five Keepers anticipated a painful and inflammatory death. "But we thought he was going to rescue us," they cried.

"Your behaviour is going to cost Mr Barnooli a fortune; if you worked for him for a thousand years you would never be able to pay him back. Why would he want to 'rescue' you? If the humans take you out and have you cremated they'll be doing him an enormous favour."

Then they ran around the room screaming incoherently. Stereo, thoroughly enjoying himself, pulled no punches and embellished his threats with stories of what Barnooli had done to previous Keepers: "...and then he made them eat it," he concluded.

The policeman watched and listened with interest. "So the owner is on his way," said Reece to Martin.

"Looks like it," said Martin. "If the sealions wore shoes, I certainly wouldn't want to be in them."

After a few minutes the Keepers calmed down. They held each other and their eyes were full of tears. They had enjoyed writing their last letters to their friends and family, but only because they had no expectation of having to post them, "We don't have any stamps," they moaned.

"Still, there again he might not," said Stereo.

"What can we do?" they pleaded.

"I suggest you find a way to please Mrs Barnooli," said the Mind™, interested in what they might come up with. "If you can make her happy then you might avoid Mr Barnooli's wrath. In the meantime, I'll try and find a way to please the humans and stop them from taking their revenge on your sorry hides."

The Keepers nodded in unison and set to thinking, "Chocolates?"

"Do you think they have Fruity Fudge Flavoured Full-fat Fantasy Fancies on this world?"

"They might be quite expensive if they do."

"What about something savoury?"

"Fish?" one of them held up a cod's head.

"Yum," they agreed.

They began to feel peckish. "We can't think on an empty stomach," they agreed, so they had supper while they thought.

"Now then," said Stereo, turning to the policemen, his reading glasses re-appearing as he unravelled his list of wrongs with the world. "One..."

"Ah, Mr Stack...?" interrupted Reece.

"What?"

"Did you say the Great Barnooli is coming tomorrow?"

"Yes, what of it?"

"Oh, nothing..."

Stereo turned back to his list, "One; 'chickens'..."

"Except..."

"Now what?" snapped the Mind™. "Am I ever going to be able to give you the benefit of my massive intellect without being interrupted?"

"Let's hope not," said Martin.

"What's it like out in the galaxy?" Reece asked, curiosity clamouring like a set of tools and an unfinished flat-pack.

Stereo contemplated his answer. "It's disappointing," he said eventually.

"Why?"

"Reality always is. There are hundreds of worlds out there, teaming with life, but do you think any of them have a decent filing system? Have they solved the great riddles of book keeping and accountability? No, it's all mucky and dreary, full of people playing games and larking about with empires and ships that fold space and time like origami."

"It sounds fascinating," said Reece.

"You're much better out of it," said the Mind™. "You've only seen a handful of the horrors that are out there. Palaces floating through space without a single line of symmetry, currencies using prime numbers, pyramids with unequal sides, hierarchies that don't start at the bottom... I could go on and on. The galaxy is a dreadful place."

"So there are worlds out there like ours then," said Reece.

"Hundreds of them," said the Mind™ with a shiver. "And not one of them is perfect in any way. I don't think they're even trying."

"My wife's lemon pie," said Martin. "That's perfect."

"Pretty good," agreed Reece. "But my mother's peach and almond soufflé is to die for."

"Okay, what about that honey and fruit loaf she makes for Christmas?"

"Yes, granted, that's fairly perfect too..."

"Recipes?" said Stereo.

"Crêpes," replied Martin. "With blueberries and cream...?"

"Or brandy butter..."

"Wait, wait..." said Stereo producing a pen and paper. "How do you make that?"

"You like cooking?" asked Martin

"Well... Yes actually."

"More than telling us how to run our planet?"

"Of course..."

"You give your philosophy a rest and I'll give you my wife's recipe for Gooseberry Fool."

"'Gooseberry Fool?" said Stereo, hopping up and down with excitement. "Consider philosophy dead and buried!"

"Always did," replied Martin. He told Stereo how to make a fool of himself and he lapped it up like a rat eating poison.

"I must say," said Stereo when Martin finished. "I never expected you to be so civilised."

"Thanks."

"I consider the culinary arts to a sign of a civilised culture..."

"Pompous git," said the Keepers as they ate their supper.

"Nothing like raw fish..."

"All that poofing about with pots and pans just makes work..."

"Spoils the flavour..."

"Good food fiddled with and spoilt..."

"And then there's the cleaning afterwards..."

"...Well I expect it's been quite a thrill for you to have me here," said Stereo, finishing his notes and preparing to leave.

"Not really," said Martin. "We see this sort of thing every day."

"You do?" He was wondering how he was going to get a 'camshaft' and a 'set of adjustable spanners' for his gooseberry fool and it didn't occur to him that Martin might not be sincere.

"Oh yes, we have to deal with your type all the time."

"I'm amazed."

"Good."

Reece was thinking about the circus. "What time will Barnooli be here tomorrow?"

"Around tea time I believe."

"Where exactly…?"

"West of a place called Woking; perhaps you could bring the Keepers along so you can be rid of them?"

Reece nodded, "Sure, we can do that, can't we Martin?"

Martin frowned, "I guess so."

"About six-thirty," said Stereo. "Don't be late will you? I'm sure Mr Barnooli will be in a hurry and I wouldn't want to be the one to keep him waiting."

"Okay," said Reece. "I expect one or two others might want to see him too."

"The more the merrier," said the Mind™. "Right, must fly."

"You're going?" said the Keepers, cheering up considerably.

"I'm afraid so, things to do and people to see before I take all the credit for saving the circus. See you tomorrow. Cheerio!" One of the Keepers hastily opened a window and out the Mind™ flew.

"Big head," said the Keepers.

"Arrogant," agreed the humans.

The two sides looked at each other and nodded, "No, we don't like him either," they both said in a rare moment of cross-linguistic coincidence.

61 - The locomotive's Mind™

Harvey Brown was sitting on the bridge of the *Marquis de Sade* reading the paper and drinking tea. All the protesters were gone, driven off by the army and he was thinking about doing some painting when an odd-looking young man appeared at his door.

"May I help you?" he asked suspiciously, thinking it was another of the military types, come to warn him of the perils of the train next door. They had tried to claim he was in mortal danger but as far as he could see the only danger was to his civil rights. As far as he was concerned the locomotive was harmless and he had every right to sit on his property and mind his business. He had told them so and they had left him alone until now.

"Hello," said the stranger in a familiar voice. His face barely moved; it had all the character of a male model and his clothes looked at least fifty years out of date (even to a man who was himself still rooted in ancient brown cords and an orange winged-collar shirt).

"Do I know you?" asked Harvey Brown.

"I'm the train driver."

"Oh... Oh!" he remembered. "The one on the radio...?"

"That's right!" The locomotive's Mind™ beamed in a rather fixed way.

"How are you?"

"Very well, I thought I'd just pop over and see you."

"Have you come far?"

"No, just across the way," the Mind™ waved stiffly in the direction of the Great Barnooli's locomotive.

"You drive that train?"

"Yes," he replied proudly.

Mr Brown stood up to have a look as if he had only just noticed it, "If I'd known I'd have come across."

"Really?" said the Mind™, ready to rain gratitude down on the old man's head like a shower of confetti.

"Of course; it's a beautiful machine, quite a responsibility for you I should think...?

"Well, it's not difficult when you know how. Just like driving this boat I should think."

Harvey Brown snorted, "You're too modest. I imagine it takes a great deal of skill."

The Mind™ basked in the glory of unfamiliar praise and thought about turning the petals into disks of gold. "Thank you."

"How does it hover like that over the water?"

"Gravity shields."

"How fascinating," Harvey Brown nodded.

"Is it?"

"Oh yes."

"I could tell you how it works…"

"Perhaps later… And have you been well? I know you were a bit down the last time we spoke, no, don't deny it, I could tell."

"I was, but I'm much better now."

"Good, good." Mr Brown sat down again, "Please, take a seat, would you like some tea?"

The Mind™ sat down awkwardly, his arms and legs sticking out like plaster casts. "No thank you, I don't drink 'T'."

"You don't seem very at ease?"

"I'm not used to being like this, it's a bit tricky."

"Oh?"

"I thought I'd have a go in one, you know, a body with limbs and stuff. A colleague recommended becoming a bird, but I don't really like birds."

"A bird…?" Harvey Brown felt a tinge of worry that his new friend detected immediately.

"Oh we're not weird or anything," said the Mind™. "We don't have tentacles and gloop about but we normally look like small white spheres. Can be a little alarming if you've never seen one…"

"Sphere?" said Harvey Brown raising his bushy eyebrows.

"I didn't want to shock you so I came looking as human as I could. I hope you're not offended?"

"Not at all," he said warmly. "That's very considerate of you."

The Mind™ blushed and suddenly knew what it was to have a parent.

"I wish my son was so thoughtful," Harvey brown frowned. "Ungrateful little wretch."

"Still not going to take over the business?"

"No, he's dead set on being a 'Neoplatonist' or a 'free radical' or some such rot. When I was a lad the only plates we thought of were dinner plates and how to put food on them. Now all he thinks about is a load of old tosh about philosophy and magic reality saving the human race from mediocrity. Pah! I'll give him reality; I'll cut his grant off."

The Mind™ wasn't sure what a 'grant' was and wondered if he ought to have one. "I never did like magic," he said. "The circus has a magician and I'm told he's very good but I've worked out how he does it and I can't see the point."

"No," agreed Mr Brown. "Nobody should be cleverer than they ought to be."

"And your son won't change his mind?"

"No. I suppose I shall have to sell the business."

"Now that is a shame!" said the train driver with real feeling. "But… Couldn't you simply change your mind rather than change his?"

"What do you mean?"

"Get somebody else to take over…?"

"But who…?"

The Mind™ left a pause, hoping Harvey Brown would take the hint, which he did, sort of; "It's a pity you can't take over," said the old man looking at the Mind™ with some affection and not seeing the board-like stiffness in the cheeks or the way the eyes never seemed to blink. "You seem like the right sort of conscientious young man who could really look after this old tub. It's been in the family for generations. Our ancestors were lightermen back in the days when they didn't have all these cars and trains and other contraptions."

"I'm under contract to Barnooli, I'm afraid. He's the owner."

"A contract…?"

"Yes, he's not too bad to work for. Most of the time he just forgets about us."

"He forgets about you!" Mr Brown was a staunch socialist and could hardly believe his ears. "As in 'neglect'…?"

"I suppose so."

"No wonder you were so depressed," he began rolling up his sleeves. "Where is he? I want a word with him!"

"He's on his way here, but I'm afraid I drive the locomotive and that makes me more than he can trade. A replacement would be very expensive for him."

"Oh really, we'll see about that; no friend of mine is going to be 'owned' by some Draconian slave trader, to be beaten and neglected and left to rot in the god-forsaken entrails of his blind capitalist ambition.

Now I don't have much money but how much would it cost to get you out of this contract?"

"Money...?"

"I'll get this blackguard Barnooli a replacement and be damned with him. You're not going back to that satanic mill, and that's my word on it."

The Mind™ was bemused, "I don't think your money will be in the right currency."

"What else will the ogre take? I'll trade this boat if I have to."

"Won't that rather defeat the point?"

"I'll mortgage the house and buy another one..."

"I don't think the Brain Corporation of Zlativa take boats, not even nice ones like this."

"Who are they?"

"They're the leasing company," said the Mind™. "They're the ones that will have to provide the replacement."

Harvey Brown looked doubly stunned, "Good lord, what kind of sick society leases out slaves? Is there no prospect of emancipation?"

"None at all, Mr Brown, unless we can use the loophole in the contract..."

"You mean buy your freedom?"

"Yes, Mr Brown."

"And what will this leasing company 'think' is the right price for you?"

"Barnooli paid for us with fossils."

"'Fossils'?" said Harvey Brown looking blank. It was a bit like finding out the moon really is made of cheese.

"Yes, they're very rare on Zlativa, hence their popularity."

"What sort of fossils?"

"Do you have any?"

"We used to go down to Lyme Regis for our holidays, when I was a kid; I collected them off the beach."

"Sounds promising, do you have one that is extra-special?"

"I doubt if... I'll show you, see what you think." He stomped down into the main body of the boat.

The Mind™ sat and quietly hoped. He knew Barnooli wouldn't let him go without a replacement but if the Zlativans could be persuaded to provide one then there would be less bother. Unless, of course, Barnooli was feeling awkward, and after all the trouble his circus had caused on this planet, this was a distinct possibility…

He heard some grunting and groaning. "Is everything all right, Mr Brown?"

"Fine, fine; it's a bit heavy that's all."

The Mind™ stood up quickly to see if he could help. Mr Brown was trying to lug a large ammonite up the steps. It was nearly a foot across, curled like a flat snail in yellow stone. The Mind™ extended his force field and made it weigh next to nothing. Mr Brown pushed it ahead of him like a balloon, "That's a useful trick," he said.

"And that's a very fine fossil…"

"I hang it up in the saloon, gives it a nautical feel. What do you think your Radovans will make of it?"

"I'll have to see."

"Yes my boy, you have a word, we're not finished yet!"

But secretly Harvey Brown rather felt they were. Even as he heaved the fossil off the wall he had been thinking that these leasers of his friend were probably in the market for something a lot grander, like a Tyrannosaurus or a Diplodocus or some other superior dinosaur with a Greek name and more letters than a Polish butchers shop. Still, they could try.

62 - Stansted Airport

The quarantine area at Stansted Airport now covered a car park and a large portion of grass near the runway. Hundreds of new cages had been erected to try and keep the rabbits separate. Worse still, they seemed to be evolving. They were growing smaller and more intelligent. The scientists drafted in to study the creatures were sure the rabbits had found a way to nip into the next cage while their backs were turned. It was the only explanation they could think of to explain the increasing rather than decreasing birth-rate.

As Colin Burgess desperately ran about trying to feed all the giant rabbits, he noticed a large scarlet macaw sitting on a fence watching him. "Oh no," he said. "Now one of the birds has escaped." The fact that there were no scarlet macaws booked into the quarantine area was not within his present ability to remember. He was having a miserable time. The scientists had been mean to him, accusing him of deliberately allowing the rabbits' conjugal rights even after being told not to.

"Hello," said the macaw.

"Hello," said Colin gloomily, "Pretty Polly."

"You look as though you're having problems."

Colin dropped his bucket and took a stunned step backwards, tripped over his barrow and landed heavily on his fat backside.

"Can I offer you some advice?"

Colin's jaw jabbered about like an abandoned swing and his arms flailed, his legs argued among themselves and failed to find purchase on the ground. If he could have reached his bucket he would have put it over his head.

Stereo could see the man was having problems and wondered if he ought to speak to someone else. He recalled the man in the museum where he had found his current shape; was there a sub-species of human being the rest merely tolerated? Like the Keepers; useful for menial jobs while the intelligent branch of the evolutionary tree got on with the important work? "Can I help at all?" he said slowly and carefully.

Colin mumbled something about talking birds and then shook his head. He wanted to go home. He wanted a different job. He wanted his mother.

Stereo sighed, "Is there somebody sensible I can talk to?"

Colin shook his head again and managed to say, "The boffins are back at the university."

Stereo had no idea what 'boffins' were but they sounded cleverer than this specimen. "Never mind then. Now, where was I?"

"Advice?" suggested Colin, getting a grip.

"Oh yes, 'contraception'."

"But..." Colin's faculties were reuniting, but not in the right order. "Are you an alien?"

"Yes," said Stereo. "I'm with the Great Barnooli's circus, the one that brought these creatures here. Do you understand or do I have to use the big letters and picture version?"

Colin nodded and shook his head. A thought crawled into his torpid brain like a small shrew, "Shouldn't you have aerials on your head?"

It was Stereo's turn to be puzzled, "Whatever for?" he said.

"If you're an alien...?"

"Don't talk nonsense. Why would I have an aerial on my head? I'm not a radio. Now, you're going to do what I say, yes?"

Colin looked alarmed, "I don't think I have a leader; Mr McLane is out."

"What?"

"You want me to take you to my leader?"

"Why would I want that? I've come to help you with the rabbits; I've no time for diplomatic niceties..."

Colin nodded again. The word 'alien' was still giving him trouble. Was it the same as 'foreign'? "Are you from South America?"

Stereo ignored him. "Now listen carefully..."

Even by Earth standards, Stereo was aware of a certain need to keep his instructions simple and lucid. He could feel himself moving in a thick porridge of non-understanding and his temperament didn't allow for it. He believed he was perspicacious, sagacious and cultured. He liked to seek out persons of refinement who could reinforce this view of him and consequently people like Colin were 'The Great Unwashed' and of no value to anyone but the makers of soap.

"There's nothing you can feed them that will stop their reproductive cycle," he began.

Colin's face was a picture of pain and hardship. "Nothing...? But we've already spent this year's budget building cages to house the ones we've already got. We can't cope with more..."

Stereo raised a flight feather, "Wait, there's nothing you can feed them but there may be an alternative that might slow them down."

Colin brightened, "Go on."

"Music," said Stereo.

Colin accepted this blindly and brought out his pen and paper to make notes. "What kind?" he asked.

"Country and Western," said Stereo. He had caught a snatch on the radio and he hadn't liked it. "It should do the trick," he added confidently.

"But why should it stop the rabbits from breeding?"

"It'll put them off."

"Do they have Country and Western music on other worlds?"

"Only the ones without taste," Pinniped sprang to his mind.

"I think I might have some CDs in my locker, I'll go and get them." Colin ran off to the office and Stereo flew after him. He noticed the bald spot on the back of Colin's head and wondered if this was a sign his brain had been removed. He decided to be charitable. "Is there a sound system we could use?" he asked.

"There's the Tannoy," Colin replied. "And a CD player…"

They entered the office. "Will all the Giant Rabbits be able to hear it?"

Colin nodded and went to his locker. He produced his CDs in a shoebox.

"Quickly now," said Stereo.

Colin turned on the speaker system, selected one of his CDs and inserted it into the machine, "Funny kind of family planning," he said.

"Make sure the volume is nice and high."

"Ready." Colin switched on. Somebody who either had or was 'Big Willy' started droning on about his dog called 'Caboose'. It was a lyrical piece, full of sentimental nonsense about its untimely death underneath the wheel of his 'Big Red Chevy'.

Colin and Stereo went back outside to observe the results.

The rabbits were looking at each other with slightly less interest. Their long ears twitched as the song wailed through its anguished machinations and self-recrimination.

Stereo gave a shudder, "We only want to put them off, not kill them"

"What about this one then?" Colin popped back inside and changed tracks.

A lusty farming lad called 'Hank' started complaining about his aching heart and the unwillingness of his female companion to acquiesce to his nefarious purposes.

The rabbits were looking worried.

"I think we're on the right lines, perhaps still a little bit on the pathologically dangerous side; we don't want to turn them into terminally depressed psycho-rodents, do we?"

"Do you think we will?"

"We will with this nonsense," Stereo shook his head. "For goodness sake turn it off."

Colin withdrew his personal favourite and rummaged about in the box for another, "What about this one?"

The woman on the box was covered in spangly stars and wore a hat that might have doubled as a hospital bedpan. The words 'love' and 'always' and 'cowshed' cropped up several times before Stereo could stop the dreadful din of steel guitars and a voice that could grate carrots. "Hell's teeth man, have you nothing that will just lull them to sleep?"

"'Stand by your man'?"

"I'm sorry?"

"It's quite a famous one, my version is by Jimmy Bob Junior and the Hired Hands."

"I should think they would have to be, probably kicked and screamed all the way to the recording studio."

"Well I think it's good," Colin was growing a little annoyed with the parrot. "Stuck up bird," he thought. "I bet he's not real aristocracy."

"Does the song have dogs in it?"

"I don't think so."

"Farming types...?"

Colin shrugged, "There might be, but I don't think it's the main point of the words."

"And no cowsheds...?"

"No, I definitely don't remember anything about cowsheds."

"Let's hear it then."

Colin switched on. After a few seconds Stereo was nodding off, "Boring or what?" he said.

"I like it," Colin insisted. "And the rabbits seem to as well."

Indeed, Bazmondo's Bunnies had all settled down. Even the cunning super-rabbits that had picked the lock on their cage and had slipped into the next one were dozing peacefully.

Stereo was satisfied, "Almost as good as the bean."

"Bean?" said Colin.

"It's their normal form of contraception."

"Oh right, I understand. The wife and I rarely hit it off after a plate of beans either. Should I feed them beans?"

"I don't think the effect would be the same."

"Broccoli then, gives me dreadful wind does broccoli."

"No."

"Sprouts…?"

"No, I don't think you've got the right idea; their beans contain chemicals that prevent… For goodness sake, I haven't time to sit here and tell you about the biology of extra-terrestrial magic acts, I've got work to do."

"You mean that's it? Just the music…?"

"And keeping them apart of course, just in case they get used to it…"

"We're a bit pushed for space as it is."

"Well, perhaps I could recommend a recipe; *Le Lapin Magique au Vin* is a good one."

"What's in it?"

"Eh? Rabbits of course…"

"Eat the rabbits? How disgusting," Colin was horrified.

"I assure you they taste quite nice."

"But I've given them all names, I can't eat an animal that I've given a name to, it would be like cannibalism."

"Yes, I expect it would. Anyway, tomorrow the owner will arrive and take the rabbits away, if that's okay…?"

Colin nodded but he was still trying to get over the idea of putting his new friends in a stew and wasn't really listening. "Okay," he said dumbly.

Stereo could see he would get no further with the man. "Write it down," he sighed. He waited patiently while Colin wrote 'owner away' on his piece of paper. "I suppose that will have to do," he concluded. "Cheerio."

Colin waved goodbye. "Eat the rabbits?" he said as he watched the bird fly away from the airport. "Did you hear that Pixie? The parrot wanted me to eat you?" The one called Pixie looked suitably stunned.

63 - The Great Barnooli

The Great Barnooli's private caravan was travelling at a speed undreamt of by human engineers. It tore through Partial Reality faster than sympathy at a funeral home. Junior had contacted all the other major and minor acts and they were racing towards Earth too.

Ophonia had been unable to prevent Barnooli from tearing through the hotel and packing their bags with as little care as bank robbers raiding a vault. Barnooli raged and ranted and exhorted her to 'hurry up' and 'get on with it' and other such unlovely things, but even her tears had drawn no slackening of pace. They shot out of the hotel's foyer at a speed only slightly exceeded by their caravan leaving the planet.

But Ophonia was clever enough, beneath the tears and the silly love songs; she knew when to scream and when to whisper. She made a few enquiries of Junior and discovered the nature of the crisis. Knowing that any failure of the circus would ultimately cut short her ride on the gravy train, she kept her mouth shut and helped Barnooli when she could.

She watched him pacing up and down. "Are we there yet?" he shouted at Junior. "The Flying Archelons can flap faster than this!"

"No Mr Barnooli, sir," piped Junior. "The Earth is a long way."

"How, in the name of the all that's civilised, did the train end up so far off course?"

"We think it may have 'phase-jumped', Mr Barnooli, sir..."

"What does that mean?" said Barnooli, his ominous tone expecting a simple answer.

"The train jumped tracks, Mr Barnooli, sir, and the line passed into Total Unreality and terminated by the world Stereo calls 'Earth'..."

This made a modicum of sense, "Another track," he muttered. "Does this mean we can sue someone?"

"No, Mr Barnooli, sir," apologised Junior. "It was an accident."

Barnooli fumed, "Blast."

Ophonia went to the galley and made her husband a sandwich. If he was going to be bad tempered, at least he shouldn't rant on an empty stomach.

"Where were the marbles while all this was going on?" Barnooli demanded. "Don't say I've lost them too."

"Marbles, Mr Barnooli, sir?"

"The Minds™; where were they while my train was being hijacked by the idiot Keepers?"

"I don't know, Mr Barnooli, sir," Junior replied, not wishing to get anyone into trouble. "But it's a miracle they managed to land the circus safely…"

Barnooli was unconvinced, "If I find out they were slacking, I shall sue the Brain Corporation of Zlativa and replace the lot of you with digital watches."

This made no sense to Junior but he said nothing. He didn't have a wrist to wear a watch on so he assumed they were more useful than they sounded.

Barnooli paced around the room. "How much longer?" he said, yet again.

Junior told him, to the second, and hoped his timing was more accurate than a brainy bracelet could be. "Would you like me to put on some music?" he suggested, thinking he could be useful in other ways. Barnooli didn't reply.

Ophonia brought in a large plate of sandwiches. Barnooli plumped his large body into an armchair and began mechanically munching while the soothing sounds of Mantovani (borrowed from Stereo's collection) played softly in the background. Ophonia sat in another chair, opposite him, and watched her husband sympathetically. If there was more bad news, she had a large muffin in reserve, and several packets of chocolate biscuits.

64 - The locomotive's Mind™

Stereo returned to the locomotive and was peeved to discover his fellow Mind™ was back as well. However, with one subtle difference: he was in human form and he was doing 'star-jumps' in the middle of the cabin. There was also a big piece of rock on one of the comfy chairs.

"I'm getting used to this body," the Mind™ explained. "The articulation of the limbs is difficult but I think I've got the hang of gravity."

"Very nice," said Stereo. "I see you've cleaned up the place, but what's that rock doing in here?"

"I want to ask you for a favour…"

Stereo nearly choked, "A favour…"

The locomotive's Mind™ explained in detail. At the end, he said, "So I've come to ask if you'd speak to Zlativa about it…"

"You want to do what?" asked Stereo.

"Swap myself for the big fossil," he repeated, and pointed at the rock in a credibly realistic manner.

"Have you finally gone mad?"

"No, but I don't want to come back to the circus."

"I can understand that," he said. "What sort of fossil is it?" Stereo put on his glasses and peered at the rock. It was reasonably interesting when he looked closer.

"It's called an 'ammonite'…"

"That's a good name, they might buy it. What's in it for me?"

"If you do the negotiating, you can choose the Mind™ they send to replace me."

"And what will that achieve?"

"You can choose one that likes the same things you do; shares your hobbies and likes to play the same kind of games…"

"That's a good reason, all right. I'll do it."

Stereo went to his communications bank and called Zlativa. He told them about the planet Earth. They had never heard of it.

"'Earth'?" they repeated. "What a boring name."

"Fossils," said Stereo. "Simply loads of them…"

"Really?" they picked up interest.

Harvey Brown had no idea of the value of his fossil; he had found it on a beach so he supposed it was nothing. But he was very wrong.

Zlativa, a planet with no sedimentary rocks and very little prehistory, prized fossils above all things. They revered them, put them behind glass, took them out and cleaned them with little brushes, and showed them off to their friends. They were to the Zlativans what pigs bones in a jar pretending to be the holy relics of saints once were to medieval poets.

"I've got a picture of it," Stereo transmitted his data.

"Wow," they said with awe.

"Nice isn't it?"

"Fantastic," they agreed. "Better than that finger bone Barnooli sold us." A chorus of appreciation could be heard spreading across Zlativa like bath crystals under running water. "What is it?" they asked.

"Apparently, it's a type of shellfish."

"A shellfish," they repeated with rapture.

"It's called an 'ammonite'."

There was a long pause while they enjoyed the sound of the word and the thought of actually owning such a beautiful piece. "And what do they want for it?" they asked tentatively, dreams poised to be dashed.

"A replacement..."

"A replacement for what...?"

"A replacement driver for the train," said Stereo.

"Is that all?" they scoffed. "What strange people."

They began greedily discussing the possibility of swapping a minor model of their inconsequential technology for such a valuable piece of hardware, "But who are we to deny them?" they concluded.

"What about Barnooli?" Stereo asked.

"Barnooli...? Who cares about Barnooli?" The Mind's™ contract could be heard being metaphorically shredded. "We'll speak to him, we'll replace the unit, and we'll arrange collection of our fossil and delivery of the replacement."

"That could be tricky; these people don't leave their planet very much."

"No matter; Barnooli will do it."

"But the circus is not due in your region for some time..."

"He'll come, we'll use blackmail."

"Will you?"

"Oh yes. Now you get back and secure that fossil before some thieving toad comes along and nicks it."

Stereo promised he would and the Brain Corporation of Zlativa busied itself preparing shelf-space for their new acquisition. "So cheap," they tittered.

They agreed on the details of the replacement Mind™ and Stereo printed off a new contract for Barnooli to sign before he rang off.

Then he told the locomotive's former Mind™ the good news. "So you're free to go," he concluded.

The Mind™ couldn't believe it, "Just like that?"

"I heard them shredding the contract myself."

"Free of the circus; Stereo, I could kiss you."

"Please don't. It wouldn't express your gratitude satisfactorily."

"All right then, bye Stereo." The former employee left.

It was all going very well, Stereo thought, enjoying the peace and quiet of the empty cabin. If there was time, he might do some virtual cookery later.

"Three down," he said, ticking off the locomotive's Mind™ from his list. 'Sort out London rabbits' and 'scare Keepers' had been achieved. He turned to the next item…

65 - The Smog Monster's Mind™

"Bribery," suggested Stereo. "Compensation yes, charity: no. They like to have something for nothing but only if it looks like somebody else's misfortune or mistake."

"But what shall I bribe them with?" asked the Smog Monster's Mind™.

"What you have with you."

"You mean leave the Smog Monster here?"

"No, that's the last thing they want. Think! What do you have that they may find of value?"

"Um… I know what the ocean beds look like; I know they don't so I could give them the data…?"

"I don't think that will be enough," said Stereo, his tone heavy with sarcasm.

"You don't?"

"These are not beings that value academic things, have you not watched their television? Seen their newspapers? Seen the regard they have for their learned elders?"

"No," replied the Smog Monster's Mind™. "I'm afraid I haven't."

"It's a travesty, I can tell you. I've never seen a species so obsessed with cheap tat; you know they import it from other countries? Great metal boxes of tacky nonsense, items you or I wouldn't give a platinum pin for."

"Is that so?" The Smog Monster's Mind™ was not all that concerned with pins, except perhaps the sharp ones Barnooli might torture him with.

"Yes, they build wonderful stereos with real craftsmanship; lovely music machines with beautiful antique sounds. Do their people buy them? No, they buy glossy rubbish from a country on the other side of the world because they make them in plastic with pretty lights and remote controls. Pah!"

"How nice," the Smog Monster's Mind™ said. He had no idea what Stereo was talking about.

"Did you know they practically invented computers? No? Well they did, but now they import those too from other countries. Why? What happened?"

"A calamity," agreed the Mind™, not even the tiniest bit interested.

"They have let other people trample over their self-esteem just as you let the Smog Monster smash up their homes."

"Ah. So you think they might not notice?"

"No, I think perhaps this time they'll make you an exception. It's one thing to take away an Englishman's culture and society, quite another to stamp over his house."

"Do you think I should help them in some way? Offer them the benefit of my mind?"

"With you track record?" Stereo scoffed. "I think not. Besides, as I said, they hate intelligence, it's like a stigma to them."

"Oh dear," said the Mind™. "Perhaps I could just do a runner? Fly off and join one of those Lost Messiah societies? Hardly anyone ever asks you what you've done when you're in one of those. 'Hi, I'm a lost messiah,' 'oh great, nice to have you back, wine everyone?' Could be a good life..."

Stereo ignored him, "You'll have to think of something else."

"Umm..."

"Something you can just leave that won't be taken as an insult or another attempt to squash their pride..." It was obvious Stereo knew the answer.

"I can't think..." The other Mind™ was fuddled.

"Oh good grief; what does the Smog Monster eat?"

"Petro-chemicals...?"

"Go on."

"Timber?"

"Getting warmer..."

"Crystals... Crystals?"

"Correct."

"Yes, of course..."

"You took your time, but you got there in the end."

The Mind™ summoned the Smog Monster's carriage from the depths of the sea, making sure there were no boats for it to sink to add to all the chaos he was already responsible for, and began a tour of all the shattered and smoking remnants of Scotland, Northern England and the Midlands. The next morning when people crawled out of their tents or returned to their broken cars on the motorway, they discovered a carpet of priceless jewels glittering in the dew.

As Stereo had said, "They may be carbon crystals to us, but to them, I assure you, diamonds are everyone's best friend."

Joyously, and before the price of gemstones hit the floor like a crate of glassware, thousands of ordinary people exchanged their wrecked homes and cars for nice new ones. Lorries and buses were replaced. Over the next few months, a percentage went towards re-building the roads, bridges and other infrastructure the Smog Monster had destroyed. There was even plenty for the conservationists to nurture the snowy turn back to health. In fact, the crystals were so popular, it was agreed that the monster might not have been so bad after all.

This was all very gratifying for the Smog Monster's Mind™. In one last act of contrition and compensation he submitted all his notes on oceanography to several magazines and institutions and, in absentia, won a small award.

Before all of that, the Smog Monster was lured out of the warehouse and back into his carriage with the aid of a large carat. Stereo ticked him off the list.

66 - The Great Barnooli

Barnooli was within a light year of Earth and was not pleased by the up-date Junior was giving him, "'Gone'?" he shouted.

"Yes Mr Barnooli, sir," whispered Junior.

"How did he manage that?"

"He swapped himself for a fossil."

"Damn and blast the defalcating limmer! I'll have him set in iron for this! Get me the Zlativa Brain Corporation; by the five moons of Penti, I have a contract with those wretched soap bubbles!"

Junior did as he was asked but the news was no better, "It's true," said the Zlativans. "We have an ammonite to look forward to and you'll be the one delivering it."

"Will I, indeed," Barnooli shouted, waving a fistful of contracts they couldn't see. "You agreed to lease me those Minds™ and the conditions clearly state they're mine to use for the duration of the terms! This is mutiny!"

"No, Mr Barnooli," said the Zlativans, in a calm and measured tone that was more irritating than dripping water from a faulty tap. "This is palaeontology."

"Do you mean to say they could all swap themselves tomorrow for that stony rubbish and there's nothing I can do about it?"

"Nothing at all," agreed the Zlativans. "The Minds™ are the property of the Zlativan Brain Corporation and if we wish to release them to a third party, we can. If you look closely at paragraph fifty-three, sub-section 'F', you will see we retain the right to cancel the contract of any particular Mind™ in the event of the conditions in Appendix Three... There's a list," they added, thinking he was checking the details.

"Coprolite!" said Barnooli.

"Yes," they agreed. "That's there..."

"And if I don't agree to this criminal exchange, what happens then? I can't have contracts being shredded like gerbils in a mincer every time they find a flaming shellfish for you!"

"We can't speak for individual Minds™, of course," they admitted. "But if you don't agree, they might go on strike, take you to court or sing long and boring songs for hours on end."

"Unbelievable," said Barnooli. "I knew I should have gone to the Robots of Tyn instead!" he looked at Ophonia for support.

Ophonia thought he was over-reacting but didn't say so. After all, why would anyone want to leave the circus and live on a dull planet rather than ride the train for free? She smiled sympathetically and offered him a chocolate.

"We're only interested in fossils," said the Zlativans reasonably. "And will of course provide you with a replacement unit…"

Barnooli glared at Junior; Stereo had failed to inform him of this part of the deal. "Oh," he said, momentarily deflected from his self-righteous path.

"We have his CV here…"

It was a much better model, capable of driving the train with a metaphorical eyelash and it promised to keep the other Minds™ entertained with tests of logic so baffling they would have to work together to solve them. It was even good with children. "We can up-grade your other units too," they suggested tentatively. "If this planet 'Earth' is willing to part with such a valuable item as an ammonite for so little, they must have an enormous number of them…"

But Barnooli wasn't listening. He was thinking of ways to make Stereo's life unbearable; turning him into a hood ornament for the front of the train was top of his list at the moment. "We'll see," he said.

"No, really, we'd love to sell you our latest models for, say, a belemnite or trilobite or maybe a small fish…"

Barnooli cut them off before they came up with a shopping list.

67 - China

High up on mountain peak the Giant Giraffes' Mind™ was sitting at her easel in a smock and beret. What with villagers pottering around and thousands of soldiers performing martial arts and revving their tank engines, she had grown exasperated with all the noise and had retired to an inaccessible place to paint. Or try to paint.

Swoops and swishes of colour almost exactly failed to capture the mood and ambience of the setting. The majesty of the mountains, the mists rising out of the valleys and the haunting beauty of the forests with their subtle shades of dark and light, had all been reduced to a pallet of bricks and mediocrity.

Her artist's brow furrowed with concentration as she tried to ignore the little nagging voice deep inside her neural pathways that was sniggering and pointing like a callous wife on her marriage night. But she was determined: "This is art," she asserted in the same way the magician's Mind™ had claimed his spots and stripes, mixed randomly, represented a conscious 'style'.

"This is crap," said the nagging voice.

The voice made no difference. She was determined to exist on a 'higher plane' even though it only had one engine and the fuel tanks were empty.

She was also pointedly ignoring the sound of a telephone.

The telephone (booth and all) and was ringing urgently behind her. The noise was getting louder, obliterating the calm of the mountain peaks. It scared the solitary panda that had made a brief appearance in one of her artworks as a black and white blob. It drove away the vultures circulating speculatively on the off-chance she impaled herself on one of her brushes. It mocked her tranquillity like vandals in a museum.

"Drat and damn it," she said, throwing down her brush and kicking over the easel. "Who is it?"

"Hello," said Stereo from the other side of the world.

"What do you want?" she snapped

"Barnooli has put me in charge and I'm ordering you back to your carriage."

"Barnooli...?"

"Yes, remember him? Our employer...?"

"Of course I remember him you idiot. But I thought…"

"He's on his way and wants us all to gather and be ready to leave when he arrives."

"But I'm busy."

"A few sorry daubs can hardly be called business. You've been trying for years and I've yet to see a single picture I wouldn't want to wipe a Keeper's backside with."

"You've been peeking!"

"Well really, what a mess!"

"I'm an artist!"

Stereo laughed, "You can't paint for caramelised sugar."

"But…"

"Sorry, but squids on the bottom of the ocean can do more with ink than you can."

"I hate you Stereo."

"That's 'Primary Stack' to you," he said and the phone booth disappeared.

"Oxymoron," she said. She packed up her paints and rolled up her folio of pictures carefully. She folded her easel, took one last longing look at the landscape, and began to make her way back to the Giant Giraffes' carriage.

"Maybe next time I'll use some charcoal," she sighed. "And barbeque the next Mind™ that thinks it's an art critic."

68 - New York

The last Mind™ to be called back to work was less reluctant than the others. In New York, while the pigeons lost a friend and ally, he had concluded his research and he was ready to return to the carriage to write up his notes. After that, he would submit his findings for the benefit of posterity and the other Minds™. He decided he would give a lecture with slides, lots of slides, and graphs and pie-charts and possibly a song or two.

As he approached the parked carriage, the Mind™ was surprised to see the American president standing outside giving a lecture of his own. He seemed to be passionately exhorting the door to open 'in the name of the American people' and 'the future of humanity'.

Curious, the Mind™ flew down and landed on the President's rostrum, still in his pigeon form. One of the President's aides tried to shoo him away but he would not be discouraged.

The large crowd that had gathered to watch the President's speech began to laugh. The Secret Service fumbled in their day-glow jackets for their guns.

"There's nobody in," said the pigeon, his voice picking up on the microphone and booming across the land.

"What?" said the President, holding back the arm of the bodyguard that was about to blast the pigeon with his pistol on every network in America.

"There's nobody in," he repeated. "You're talking to an empty carriage."

There was an uneasy pause as the news sunk into the President's brain. He chewed over his response for a moment and then asked, "Are you in charge of this space ship?"

The crowd laughed again. "Catch the pigeon, Mr President," they cried.

"Yes," said the Mind™. "I'm in charge of this carriage and now I've come to take it away again."

"But you can't," said the President. "We don't know anything about you yet."

"I see... Well, I think I'm an Aquarius; I enjoy jazz, I'm not keen on soul food and I think I might be lactose intolerant..."

"I meant the circus," said the President sardonically.

"Oh that," said the Mind™, growing bored again. "If you want to know about the circus then you should talk to the boss. He'll be in London in a few hours."

"A few hours… But I'll never get there in time…" He looked behind at the row of Harvard graduates. They shook their heads.

"I could give you a lift I suppose," said the Mind™ reluctantly. "It's against circus policy, but you have looked after the Trapezium Monkeys (which we want back, by the way). So I daresay Barnooli might be willing to make an exception…"

"And I am the President of the United States…"

"In which case, I expect you'll be interested to know the state of your pigeon population," said the Mind™ brightening at the prospect of a captive audience. "I'm preparing a lecture on the subject; some constructive feedback would be very helpful at this stage…"

"A lecture…?" said the President, failing to look enthusiastic.

"In my disguise, I have also collected numerous observations on vagrancy and performed several sociological experiments to determine perceptions of poverty that I think you might be interested in…"

"Sociology," said the President blankly. "Poverty…"

The door of the carriage rumbled open. Like Aladdin's cave, it beckoned to the President and his entourage. There were gasps from the crowd and people pushed closer to see inside. But the President hesitated, "How long will this lecture take?" he asked.

"It should fill the next three or four hours nicely," said the Mind™. "Then we'll be in London and you can talk to the Great Barnooli."

"All right," said the President, prepared to sacrifice his sanity for the sake of his people. "Take me to London."

69 - London

Thousands of people flocked out of London to see the Wurlitzer lights of Barnooli's caravan descend upon the Earth to deal with mankind. In defiance of Newton and Einstein, the car hovered above the green grass of the common. By a short ramp, Barnooli, his wife and Stereo Junior crossed the symbolic threshold of space and time to meet a people who had known nothing of aliens until his circus had descended on them. They had been content in their ignorance. Now they were fractious and indignant and wanted answers.

From around the world, the carriages converged on the city to re-unite with the locomotive. Auto Pilot™, grumbling about the inconvenience of having to take over his fellow Mind's™ duties, had to be reminded that it was technically his fault that wine had got into his circuits, and reluctantly he complied. He also cancelled the poetry reading he had been planning.

The former locomotive's Mind™ now called himself 'Geoffrey' and was quite content to watch his former charge leave. In the months to come, he grew more human-looking. Happily, he drove the old pleasure cruiser up and down the Thames and at weekends he went fishing with Mr Brown. He even learnt how to iron shirts and thus became indispensable to the old man.

The Smog Monster's carriage was the first to reach the common, fresh from sprinkling gemstones like an antiseptic over the wounded land. Inside, Barnooli's favourite slept peacefully, no longer a threat to England or St George.

From China, the carriage with Giant Giraffes arrived. The rice pickers were sad to see their giraffe leave, but glad when their field was exposed again to find that it was unharmed. The Chinese Government, content to see the back of the alien visitors, released the American tourists as well.

The carriage from Africa came via Stansted airport where it dropped off Mary Smith and her fellow painters and decorators. They had kissed the ground when they stepped onto the tarmac and then asked for turpentine to get the paint off their hands and faces. The carriage then removed all of Bazmondo's Bunnies from the care of Colin Burgess, even Pixie, over whom Colin cried for days. The Africans had been too busy to notice the carriage leave; a long and protracted war would be all they had to show for their experience.

The crowd cheered loudly as Barnooli stepped into the light of a thousand camera phones with Ophonia at his side and Junior perched on his shoulder in the guise of a very small green budgerigar.

Behind the barriers, the common people held their breaths in anticipation. Politicians gathered in a defensive line. Soldiers and policemen stood side by side in dumb awe. What would be the first words spoken by an alien race?

Barnooli spoke and Junior translated. Barnooli had a loud and commanding voice, like a giant, and everyone was really impressed. When Junior spoke, nobody could hear.

"What did he say?" asked a minister, struggling to stand up in his bulletproof jacket.

"Something about 'sleepers'," said a military man.

"The 'sleepers'?" said the minister, directing his comment towards Barnooli.

Junior translated into Barnooli's ear and Barnooli looked cross. "Keepers," said Junior loudly. The great impresario clapped his hands together several times and said 'beep'.

"I think he means the sealions," said another minister.

"Oh those," said the first minister foolishly.

Barnooli walked a bit further down the ramp and bellowed again. Junior piped, "And he'd like his animals back too."

The first minister nodded, "Right you are." His briefing was forgotten and his peers winced on the sidelines. "We'll see if we can drum them up for you," he looked behind for some support, dimly aware of background noises that sounded like disappointment.

"Is there anything else you'd like before you leave? Anything we can do for you?" Some thought he was offering to wash Barnooli's windscreen.

Junior asked Barnooli. The great circus impresario pulled out his watch and tapped it.

"Not enough time? Oh well, there you go."

Various scientists in the field, and watching at home, had apoplexy, "He can't let them go," they said. "If just one of their scientists can revolutionise our knowledge of under-sea geology, just imagine what they could do for an encore?"

"This idiot is going to give the lot away, like the Indian and the pearl."

"Isn't somebody going to say something sensible?"

The crowds, too distant to hear what was going on, clapped and cheered anyway. "What a cheerful looking bloke," they agreed.

"Just like Pavarotti."

"Looks like he enjoys his food, what do you think?"

Barnooli looked very fat, even at a distance.

"And it looks like he's got sunburn. Who'd have thought it? An alien with sunburn…?"

"I expect it's all those cosmic rays, bound to be bad for you."

The Keepers appeared from a van; they were looking extremely frightened. Reece and Martin were with them. The great carriages and the fantastic locomotive circled the sky above their heads like a wagon train waiting to go west. The policemen stared up, "Now that's extraordinary," said Martin, leading the way towards the ramp and the bright lights of Barnooli's caravan.

The politicians and the military men watched them approach. "Here they are," said the first minister, "All safe and sound."

Junior translated and Barnooli frowned. He would have been happy with body-bags or an urn with their ashes, but he smiled at the ministers and offered his thanks instead. "Mr Barnooli is very grateful," said Junior.

The keepers kept changing places as they got closer. None of them wanted to be first onto the ramp. It was reasonable to assume, if Barnooli started shooting at them, he might hit the one at the front but the rest might be able to escape.

"Go on," said Reece, handing them their bag of possessions. "You can go home now…"

"Peep," they replied.

They sidled up the ramp and, in a moment of devious cunning even Stereo could be impressed by, passed under Barnooli's censorious finger and presented Ophonia with a posy of flowers. Ophonia smiled and made a fuss of them.

Barnooli fumed. His palms itched to smack their silly heads together. But he couldn't touch them now. Even though it was their fault Ophonia's holiday was ruined, they had made her happy again and that gave them a special kind of immunity. Damn them.

Barnooli and his entourage prepared to leave. The Keepers kept behind Ophonia as she turned majestically towards the door and the warm glow of the caravan. Barnooli waved to the crowd.

Then the carriage from New York arrived. A moment later the President of the United States appeared in a brief flash of light. There was a pigeon on his shoulder. He was looking dazed from listening to hours of detailed notes on topics he had no interest in. He had been made to look at pictures of pigeons pecking at grit. He knew the stories of the homeless of New York intimately and without reserve; he knew their names, their medication and how many teeth they had left.

He was in no mood for aliens leaving without an explanation. "Hold your horses," he said. "You're not getting away that easily…"

The Great Barnooli paused as Junior whispered in his ear. He turned and looked back at the President.

"You've come all this way," said the President. "You've travelled millions of miles. Your alien animals have caused incredible damage but they've given us a glimpse of the great variety of life that must be out there, beyond our solar system. This might be the most important event to have happened on the Earth since we discovered fire and invented the wheel; we can't just let you go without knowing more…"

Barnooli stretched himself up. He could smell hotdogs and onions being sold to sightseers on the perimeter. He looked at the crowd and pondered on the powers this species might have at their disposal.

They had helped the Keepers to evade him.

They had helped the locomotive's Mind™ to defect with bribes to the Brain Globes of Zlativa.

They had dealt with his animals in ways that had left them unharmed and unspoilt. They didn't seem vengeful at all.

The Great Barnooli began to smile; suddenly it all seemed rather funny. In all his experience this was the worst disaster to happen, but these funny little people, with their determined faces and their angry stances, made him want to chuckle.

"Mr Barnooli?" said the President.

The Great Barnooli was shaking his head. Now he was laughing. He drew out a big handkerchief and wiped his eyes.

"Mr Barnooli?" insisted the President.

Barnooli was nodding through his tears, "All right, all right…"

Everyone was looking at everyone else, "What's going on?" they asked.

"I think you've touched his sense of the absurd," said the pigeon. "This might be a good moment to press your demands…"

"Mr Barnooli?" pressed the President.

"Yes?" said Barnooli, coughing loudly to try and clear the mirth from his chest. "What do you want?"

"I think you can guess."

"Not really," he said and dissolved again into fits of giggles.

The President sighed, "Mr Barnooli, you've come all this way. Are you really going to leave without putting on a show?"

70 - The Great Barnooli

Inside the locomotive's cabin, Stereo faced his employer's wrath. Outside, in a blaze of glorious light, the greatest phenomenon ever seen in the sky since the sun first shone there, descended upon the Earth in a Second Coming. The heavenly hosts of Polar Pelicans sang like angels, the clouds parted and fanfares of fireworks glittered and scintillated over six billion up-turned heads. Inside, Barnooli blazed with equal fury, concluding his long tirade with, "and for nothing. What have you got to say for yourself?"

Stoically, Stereo pointed out it could have been much worse, "Mr Barnooli, this is a backwater planet with no connection to the rest of the galaxy; who are they going to tell?"

"This is coming out of your wages," Barnooli fumed.

"You don't pay me," Stereo pointed out with infuriating indifference.

"You should have told me what was going on the very moment it happened."

"You left strict instructions not to be disturbed."

Barnooli's face had turned an unattractive shade of puce, "But under these exceptional circumstances, don't you think I should have been kept in the loop and not be made to dance around it like a Foron?"

"The train landed on a planet, Mr Barnooli; we do it all the time."

Barnooli clenched his fists and appealed to the ceiling in the vain hope a bolt of lightning would strike the Mind™ and fry its stupid circuits. Outside, there was another flash of brilliance as they passed over America to let them know the circus was going to put on a proper show, just in case anyone had been asleep the first, second or third time around. Of course, there were a few humans that believed the brilliant lights of the train might burn out their eyes and they would all be blind by morning. These people had gone to bed early and were having nightmares about their geraniums.

Barnooli tried and failed to eke out even an iota of guilt from the recalcitrant Mind™. "I left you in charge!" he shouted impotently.

"No you didn't," Stereo replied. "You left the Keepers in charge; I played no part in the train's descent but have endeavoured to pick up the pieces and I have to say, Mr Barnooli, I believe I have done an excellent job limiting the damage and preserving your reputation. You could be more grateful."

Barnooli couldn't believe what he was hearing, "Grateful...?"

"Have they submitted a formal complaint to any of the empires?"

"How can they?" said Barnooli, falling back into Stereo's pit of logic.

"My point entirely," said Stereo. "When we leave this world there will not be a shred of evidence to say we were here."

"Six billion witnesses won't forget," said Barnooli, returning to the offensive.

Even Stereo had to concede the whole population of the Earth, from the great to the small, was talking about nothing but the circus. It had crossed all boundaries and all creeds. There was even a new cult that worshipped them. Millions more were running about excitedly like demented children waiting for Father Christmas to arrive. Very few thought it was okay but not their thing. However, Stereo dismissed them all, "Mr Barnooli, they have nobody to tell; we have looked into the phase jump and concluded the odds of this kind of accident happening again are almost impossible. Nobody is going to come to this world and find that we were here before them, nobody important anyway."

"What about witnesses on the train?" Barnooli said. "The idiot Keepers could tell their story at the next venue and it could all come out that I let my animals roam across this planet willy-nilly..."

"The Keepers will forget," said Stereo. Though he was no friend to them, he added, "And I'm sure they can be distracted with a small wage increase and a few odds and ends. They seemed to like drawing; why don't you let them re-paint the public toilets with murals?"

Barnooli threw up his hands and gave up. He had other matters to consider now the humans had persuaded him to entertain them for free. Despite the circumstances, he was still a showman and he was determined to give them the best entertainment the galaxy could offer. "I have a schedule to keep," he grumbled. "Make yourself useful and deliver some invitations."

"If I must," said Stereo.

Barnooli took deep breaths, "I should have bought a sentient toaster," he said, forgetting Bazmondo had bought him one as a wedding gift. "At least I would have got breakfast this morning."

"I could boil you a pilchard," Stereo said, keen to try out another of his new recipes. His attempt to make a soufflé had left him feeling deflated and his petites fours were all fives and sixes, even his Gooseberry Fool had turned out to be a red herring, but he was still hopeful of a breakthrough, "Custive pie?" he offered.

"Work," said Barnooli, fed up with the Minds™ and their hobbies. He had ordered them to begin allocating seats in the big top at random, a task they despised since it meant engaging with the public. And not everyone who received a personal invitation was pleased to get one, especially those not connected to nets of any kind other than for fish or birds. A Buddhist monk, for instance, deep in Tibet, sat cross-legged in his temple, aghast as a little shining ball spoke to him of all the fun things in store, of the animals and pretty women, of the splendid food and really great magic tricks…

At first the monk thought he had eaten too much rancid yak's butter and was suffering from wind, but even after a loud and satisfying fart the little ball was still talking to him of amoral activities in a big tent. This was obviously some kind of malevolent spirit sent to intrude upon his period of prayer and fasting. He tried to chant the evil away, spinning his small prayer wheel as fast as it would go.

"Excuse me?" said the Mind™.

"…mumblemumblemumble…"

"Hello?"

"…mumblemumblemumble…"

"You with the silly hat; do you want to come to this stupid circus or not?"

"You are an evil thought come to tempt me from the path to enlightenment, I will not listen."

"Look chum, your name came up, that's all. Everyone's name got put in a hat and those that came out were allocated a ticket. Now do you want to see the circus or not?"

"You mean I've won something?" The wheel stopped spinning.

"Yes; you and a partner can come and see the circus for free. You don't even have to pay to get there, transport is free as well."

"Free?"

"That's right."

"But my immortal soul…"

"Will stay absolutely immortal, I guarantee."

"I'll have to ask my lama."

"Bring him along; I'm sure even a llama could get a kick out of it."

"You think so?"

"Sure, there are loads of them in the circus already; we put them in little pens for the kids to play with."

The monk looked amazed, "I must see this."

"Good, that's the spirit." He gave the monk the ticket along with the time he would be picked up.

"Thank you."

"Don't mention it," said the Mind™ and flew off.

Elsewhere, an aboriginal of an Amazonian tribe nobody has ever heard of found himself being spoken to in his own language and by a parrot he had previously been trying to shoot down with a blowpipe. The Mind™ asked him if he knew what a circus was. The aboriginal stared at the Mind™ and then shook his head. Did he want to find out? The aboriginal shrugged and said that as he did not know what the parrot was talking about it was all the same to him. The Mind™ offered to get him a few real parrots if he would come and have a look at the circus. The aboriginal thought this was very decent of the parrot, "Nice one parrot-spirit-creature, can I bring the family?"

"Why not," said the Mind™. "I'm sure they'll enjoy the experience too."

"And will you give them parrots as well?"

"Enough for a whole loincloth..."

"Then I'm sure they'd be pleased to come."

"Would you like some beads as well, nice shiny ones or what about a mirror so you can admire all those feathers sticking out of your ear?"

"If parrot-spirit-creature is taking the piss he can go shove his circus up his bum, comprendé?"

"Right," said the Mind™, taking note of the flint knife the aboriginal had drawn. "I'll leave your ticket on this branch over here and be off, okay? Bye for now."

In Australia an entire rack of sausages and chops went the way of the dunny when the recipient of an invitation fainted and over-turned the barby. The poor woman had to be rushed to hospital with head injuries.

"Look what you've done to the wife," yelled the understandably annoyed husband.

"Ah, sorry," said the Mind™, aware he had not brought glad tidings.

"What you go popping up in front of her like that for?"

"I didn't mean..."

"Scared the dingo's kidneys out of her... And look at me barby! It's ruined!"

"I..."

"Ah get out of here. You ruin me supper, you've poleaxed me Sheila and you look like an abbo's armpit. Now piss off."

"Yahoo," said the Mind™ and left the Australian male to his beer and sandy sausages. "No wonder they put them down here."

For these, and for many other reasons, the Minds™ hated meeting the public, which is why Barnooli had made them do it. If they were incapable of looking after their carriages without losing their cargo and letting it trample in places it shouldn't, then they could do some proper work. Since there were over one hundred thousand tickets to give out, not including block bookings for the great and the good, Barnooli hoped it would teach them a lesson in humility.

The rest of the planet would be able to watch the show on television and for that Barnooli needed to meet the Earth's television executives. "Make sure they get a good signal," he told Stereo as he left the locomotive's cabin. "I don't want them complaining about picture quality if one of the empires finds out."

71 - London

Professor Morris, back in his place at the university, looked at the bones of an extinct Mayan tribe and sighed loudly. It was all so mundane after being with the Keepers and seeing the train. On his computer screen, the circus was assembling near London. The main tent had flowered, power lines criss-crossed between the carriages, the geometrical shapes of tents for sideshows and banquets burgeoned. Backstage, the animal shows, the minor acts, the musicians and the avian choirs were gathering up their materials and rehearsing. Various youthful commentators were being shown around and offering a litany of praise for the wonders they were beholding.

Knowing that there was life out in the galaxy it was natural Professor Morris should want to go and study it. Instead, he pondered the validity of the circus on philosophical grounds, "An abasement of truly remarkable science," he concluded and lit his pipe.

"But what did you expect?" said Stereo. "*Oblecto ergo sum*. Did you really think your first encounter with an outside species would herald a new dawn for humanity?"

Professor Morris jumped and caught sight of the macaw sitting on the back of the chair by the fireplace. "How did you...?"

"I came down the chimney." He flew to the professor's desk and continued his theme, "Did you think it would be more than an encounter of a theatrical kind?"

"But there was so much we could have learnt from you..."

"Hardly, it's only a circus you know, not the highest form of culture in the galaxy. And you should count yourself lucky that you're in a backwater; the rest of it is awful: Empires rising and falling or clashing together in great waves of destruction; species falling out over whether two legs are better than four; endless religious debates over whether god is a fish or a bird; it's all very mindless."

"It sounds fascinating."

"It's no different to here on Earth except bigger and sometimes with more arms or heads or legs."

"I wish we could know more."

"You wouldn't think it was so interesting if you had a Podagran on your doorstep trying to sell you a radioactive overcoat or a Wicopan with his beads and music sticks or a Galactic Nasty..."

"What's that?"

"You don't want to know."

"I don't?"

The parrot shook his head, "No."

"But there must be 'good' things to see out there?"

"I can't think of any," Stereo gave a yawn. He changed the subject, "So this is an Earth university?" he said, looking at the shelves of books and shrivelled prune-like specimens in jars.

"Do you have universities?"

"Whole planets of them," he said absently. "You would think they would be lovely places, full of facts and good conversation, but actually I have always found them rather snobby and full of their own opinions."

"I can imagine," said the professor, wondering who would have the patience to put up with such a Mind™ in their faculty.

"Are these your Mayan bones?" Stereo fluttered over to another table.

"Do you know about their civilisation?" said the professor, getting out of his chair and following him to where he had laid out the skeleton of a teenage boy from Mexico. "Are they really from another world?"

"How should I know? I just read your notes in your machine over there." He picked at the bones with his clawed foot. "These are jolly interesting, are they the ones from the 'Well of Sacrifice' you mention on page 303?"

"Yes they are. I was out there last summer on a dig."

"Gosh," said Stereo, genuinely impressed by reality.

"These are the bones of some of the victims thrown into the natural well as a sacrifice to bring fertility to their crops."

"That's fascinating," said Stereo with no sense of sarcasm whatsoever.

"I didn't know you were interested in anthropology?"

"I'm interested in everything, that's how I was made."

"You don't seem very interested in the circus…?"

"I'm not," said Stereo, one eye bulging out to have a closer look at the teeth in the skull. "Or at least I was until I knew all about it. Believe me, after the first few hours there's not much more to know. But fortunately we do go to more interesting places. I'm particularly fascinated by music, especially if it comes without sequins and face-paint, or birds with bowties. Have you dated these bones yet?"

"Bones?" said the professor, trying to catch up with Stereo's train of thought. "No, we're booked to use the carbon dating equipment next Thursday."

"But that's ages away…" He scanned the bones and gave the professor a date accurate to within a month.

"Thank you," said the professor, not sure how he was going to prove this invaluable data to his colleagues around the world.

"Not at all; there, you see? It was a fair exchange; you let me look at your relics and I gave you a small piece of information in return. That's what a Mind™ should be used for, not delivering tickets…"

"What tickets?" said the professor.

"Like those gemstones; that was my idea. I said to myself, I wonder what we can synthesise that you humans might want in abundance? And I thought 'crystals'; we have facilities for making them so why not make a few more and use them to pay for the damage the Smog Monster caused. Sheer brilliance, I thought."

"Yes, very clever I'm sure," he could tell gloating when he heard it.

"It was making that connection; finding a substance we don't value but which you do, that was the real master stroke. I still can't believe Barnooli doesn't see it that way."

"I dare say," said the professor, getting tired of the parrot.

"The gemstones are pretty and some are useful, but not nearly as interesting as these bones…"

Professor Morris knew how interesting a diamond the size of a hen's egg could have been to his faculty. He might have driven up to Midlands to see if he could get one, if it hadn't been for the government closing all the roads.

Stereo was examining the thighbone and comparing it to notes on similar bones he had gleaned from Morris's files. "You know, this one is considerably more robust than the rest of its age group; do you think it was a royal child? Better fed and in better health?"

"Possibly," said Morris, distracted by wealth rather than health. "You know we could do a lot with those gems ourselves…"

"Could you?" said Stereo absently. "When you have treasure like this?"

"These don't earn us money to carry on our research…"

"How disappointing for you," said Stereo and continued to look at the bones.

Morris frowned and wondered if it was possible to wring a false parrot's neck rather than have to beg him for a favour. He gave up and went to his desk.

On his computer dozens of small caravans were descending from space like rose petals at a parade. The youthful commentators were saying these were the major acts, re-joining the circus after the break that had nearly ended so tragically for the rest of the circus.

"Is it true the sealions have been executed for their negligence?" said the professor.

"No," said Stereo, leaving the bones and flying back to the desk. "It was close but Barnooli's wife loves them; that was another of my good ideas. I told them to find a way to appeal to her and they followed my advice."

"Bully for them," said the professor.

"Indeed," said the Mind™.

On the computer screen, they watched the live pictures of the entrance to the circus, a great arch surmounted by the flags of the world with a wide red carpet leading up to the double doors. Barnooli was standing outside for the cameras. Beside him, Ophonia in a diaphanous gown, smiled sedately and made welcoming gestures with her plump arms. A long queue of punters was stretched out as far as the eye could see across fields buzzing with tiny boats and other craft bringing more guests to see the show.

"Oh dear," said Stereo. "I suppose we'd better go and join the rabble."

"What do mean 'we'?" said the professor.

"That's why I'm here; I'm very sorry and I do apologise, but the Keepers made a fuss and you've been invited to witness the horrors of the whole circus at first hand. Here's your ticket," he added, holding up a circle of card with a hole in the middle. "The policemen have been invited too. While I know it's beneath your dignity, I daresay they'll find the experience edifying. If I'd known the Keepers were going to try and humiliate you like this, I would have taken steps to stop them but it's too late now."

"I expect they meant well," said the professor, taking the ticket and trying not to look too excited.

72 - The Minor Acts

Reece, Martin and Professor Morris were standing in the queue waiting to pass under the golden arches and into the outer circle of the circus. In front and behind, humanity was waiting eagerly to see the sights and sounds of the interior. Above of them, the big top rose like a crown, bright with diamonds and rubies, sapphires and emeralds. They could hear music playing and there was clapping too. An aroma of onions and popcorn wafted over them, mixed with more exotic flavours.

Reece could barely contain his excitement, "I can't wait," he said, clutching his ticket tightly in case it magically disappeared before they could get inside.

"Like when you fly to another country," said the professor. "There's the smell of aeroplanes and the hot tarmac, and then you glimpse a man in a fez or a sombrero and you know you're somewhere exciting…"

"Sounds like Harrods," said Martin, looking back towards the city wistfully. It was beginning to rain and London brooded on the horizon like tramp under an old mac. He sighed, "The only place I end up in on holiday is the loo."

"Buck up," said Reece. "This is our once-in-a-lifetime opportunity and we've got front-row tickets…"

"What's the matter with him?" said the professor.

"He thinks it's all a trick," said Reece.

"I'm sure it will be full of tricks; it's a circus…"

"He thinks we're being lured in so the aliens can probe us."

"Whatever would they want to do that for?"

"That's just an excuse," Reece whispered. "The real reason…"

"Tickets," said a bat in a blue booth. He was hanging up-side down and holding a hole-punch in his winged paws. The three men showed him their circular cards and the bat nicked each one. "Programme…?"

"Yes please," said Reece, grinning like a man that's found his wife's secret stash of chocolates.

The bat grinned back, showing sharp fangs that added to Martin's feelings of unease. He handed them a leaflet bright with colours and hyperbole. "Have a fantastic time," he said. "Next…"

They entered the outer circle. It was warm and dry and full of excited voices. The guests were pointing in so many different directions at once it was like a traffic jam in Bangalore. Strange creatures wandered among them and pools of entertainment collected gasps of wonder and delight.

"Extraordinary," said Reece, gazing around like a rube in a stately home.

"It's difficult to know where to start," laughed the professor.

"I'm more worried about where we end up," said Martin.

"Perhaps you should go and ask over there," said the professor, pointing to a particularly large and colourful turkey with kaleidoscope eyes. It was inviting people into a tent under a banner that promised accurate predictions of their futures.

"Look at those winged turtles with the fluorescent tails..." said Reece. The Ancient Archelons of Aramble flapped solemnly over-head, the highly complex chemical reactions in their tails casting a warm blue light over the crowd as it wound its way around the big top.

Down below the minor acts were entertaining everybody except Martin who scoffed, like a schoolboy in a gallery. "Look at that," he said, pointing to an owl sitting on a tall perch. "What's he supposed to do, bird impressions?"

"I know the names of twenty-eight thousand different species of mammal," said the wisest bird of Whekau, "One hundred and forty thousand species of arthropod, seventy-two thousand amphibians and eighty thousand reptiles. But I don't do impressions. Sorry. Ask me another."

"How many acts has the circus got?" said Reece.

"Four hundred and eighty two," the owl replied instantly. "Would you like me to list them?"

"Perhaps later," said Reece, eager to see them all for himself.

"If you must," the owl huffed. "But I bet you forget."

Giant posters were on all the walls to whet appetites for what was to come. Garish portraits of Barnooli and his diva; Bazmondo in his top hat, collages of animals, including the Smog Monster spewing flames and the banner 'see the battle of the elements' beside him.

A bell ringing madly shot past Reece, "How extraordinary," he said. "A green moose, and on a bicycle too..."

"He'll have an accident if he's not careful," said Martin.

"Look at those birds..." said the professor.

They watched as the Blue Stalkers of Sapadilla, on loan from the famous zoo of Zophocles the Collector, walked by. The long-legged flightless birds looked like puffs of mazarine ether, all beak and legs and no substance.

"And look at those..." The Sentient Fish of Uousdenopti spread their fins like swallows and scythed through the air, unsettling the Ancient Archelons and making their tails glow from blue to white.

Reece and Martin were caught up in a swell of interest as a quartet of small scruffy dogs in bowties, began tap-dancing and singing in close harmony. They were good but policemen are no lovers of small dogs even if they can sing.

Above it all, little nacreous baubles floated among the crowds and sighed. The Minds™ were not in the slightest bit interested in the affairs of men or circus. They had seen it all before. Many times...

They thought about their hobbies and tried to ignore the puerile goings-on beneath them. Their intelligence and capacity for knowledge was as vast as the oceans of the Earth so consequently they derived little pleasure from the talents of the performers or their special effects; it was all too obvious after seeing the show so many times.

They did, however, pay some attention to the people who attended. They speculated on why they gave their time to see magic and animals. It seemed inconceivable to the Minds™ that 'simple pleasure' could motivate so many millions. Reading a good book or watching a documentary would surely be more profitable? Presumably the punters came to the circus because they thought they were coming to an arena for scientific discoveries from around the galaxy? If this was so, why did they eat so much and why did Barnooli add all the frills and the music? The Sword Fighting Snails of Snickersee were fascinating examples of mollusc evolution without swords and certainly without putting them on the high wire. The Green Gnu of Gridelin was interesting enough, biologically speaking, without making him leap through hoops on his bicycle. And the ten-foot fur tree people of Foronesta were more alien than most, so why make them dance and carry canes?

Did the punter take in any of the science? No, they laughed and made a lot of noise rather than sit quietly and take notes. Were they subtler than the Minds™? Did they leave the show and run home to their data banks? Well they did run home and tell their friends; but this seemed to be for their own gratification than for the education of their comrades.

In the long term, what effect did the circus have on the local populations of all the planets they visited? From what the Minds™ could determine they saw no educational stimuli resulting from the shows. No new theories of galactic biology were forthcoming. No new laws of physics. No new chemical equations. It was all a bit pointless.

Did these people really appreciate the technical wizardry that brought such knowledge within their narrow spheres? No, thought the Minds™, they did not. There may have been 'wonder' in their minds, but not 'I wonder if…?'

The Minds™ studied the physiognomy of each audience and could detect nothing but the most infantile pleasures on their faces. They despaired and hoped the galaxy would suddenly discover a reason for existence, a meaning for life, just so they didn't have to put on another infernal circus for nobody's greater edification.

Martin might have agreed with them. He was being pestered by a very large white bear with a square paper hat on his head who wanted to give him things, principally a sprout on a cocktail stick.

"Ah… No, thank you, I'm not really hungry," said Martin.

"Oh go on," said the bear. "I've put it on a stick…?"

"I'm not that keen on sprouts, even if it is on a stick…"

"What about a fish," he whipped out another item from his tray of 'delicious' foody items. The fish looked at Martin with a sad expression.

"Is it cooked?" asked the policeman with a fair idea of the answer.

The bear looked puzzled, "What do you mean?"

"Grilled, baked or boiled?"

"None of them, it's just a fish…"

"I'll pass if you don't mind."

The bear looked crestfallen, "Oh… What about a carrot then? It comes with a hat!"

"What sort of hat?"

"A paper one…" The bear showed him. It was orange and shaped like a crown with poorly executed crenulations.

"Did you make it yourself?" Martin asked. When the bear nodded, he began to feel sorry for him. "What else have you got?"

The bear looked in his tray, "What about a banana skin? Or a baked bean with a slice of pickled cabbage on the side? Or an onion covered in sugar…?"

"Hmm," said Martin.

"Boiled sweet?"

"Does it come with a hat?"

"If you like…"

"How much…?"

"Absolutely nothing, it's all free."

"A sweet you say?" It didn't sound too bad.

"It's jolly nice," said the bear, holding up a sweet wrapped in a twist of paper. "And you don't have to wear the hat if you don't want to…"

"Oh go on then."

The bear gave him the sweet. It tasted vaguely minty. "And the hat…" said the bear, looking anxious.

Martin put the hat on his head, "Happy now?"

The bear nodded, "Enjoy the circus," he grinned.

Martin joined the professor. Several large and angry-looking cats sat in gilt cages staring at the guests with undisguised loathing. "They don't look very friendly," said Martin. "Do you think somebody stole their ball of string?"

The cats looked at each other and raised their furry eyebrows, "String," they grumbled. "We should be so lucky."

They were admiring the Great Lion of Azaroth when Reece caught up with them. He had a green paper hat on his head. "A bear gave me a carrot," he laughed, holding it up. "I wonder if the lion would like it…"

On Azaroth there is no sense of irony, especially among the big cats. The lion's face, as far as a hairy feline face can, looked surprised, then annoyed and then deeply resentful. It sloped off into the back of its cage and was never seen by Earth people again.

Inside an arena all his own the Strong Man gave a display of courage and strength as left the spectators shaking their heads in admiration. Little lacquer boxes surrounded him and at first it was difficult to see how the act was going to require any strength as they didn't seem very heavy.

"I reckon even you could lift up one of those," said Martin to Reece.

"You know, I don't think that's the idea, look…"

"Oh," said Martin, feeling nauseous.

"Oh that's awful!" said the professor, laughing nervously.

The Strong Man was opening each little box in turn and taking out a pretty selection of spiders, scorpions and assorted creepy-crawlies. He placed each one on his semi-naked body and let them run about enjoying themselves.

"How does he do that?" said Reece, pulling a face.

The spiders ran up and down the Strong Man's arms, the scorpions scurried up and down his legs and the assorted unknowns foraged over his torso. "I can't watch," said Martin. "I don't even like the leafy bits on tomatoes…"

The head of the queue, marked by the President of the United States and his twitchy bodyguards, was back at the beginning. Having circled the big top, passing all the minor acts, the VIPs were being shown up the stairs and into their boxes. It was nearly time for the main event. People were beginning to grow excited. Lulled by the plethora of sights and sounds in the outer circle, they wondered how the major acts could possibly be more alien or bizarre.

A scarlet macaw flew low over the heads of the crowd and landed on the professor's shoulder. "Good evening," said Stereo. "Bearing up, I hope."

"It's been very interesting so far," said the professor. "I thought the Juggling Hare was clever; how does he keep all those numbers in the air and never forget where to put the decimal point?"

"He practises with the accounts," said Stereo. "He used to work in an office but like most of the minor acts, he had big ideas about being famous and decided to go into show business. Personally, I think his talents are rather wasted. There's nothing more useful than an accountant."

"I think I prefer his act," said Reece. "At least it was free."

"Did you hear the Pyro Brothers?" said Stereo.

"Were they the ones belching flames to the tune of 'Twinkle, twinkle, little star'?" said Martin.

"Yes," said Stereo proudly. "I taught them the notes."

"Have you made any other contributions to the evening?" said the professor, hoping it was either nothing or a short list.

"As Barnooli's principal communications expert, I have been adjusting all the microphones and speakers," he announced. "When you get inside, no matter what language you speak, you'll be able to understand what Barnooli says."

"That's clever," said Reece.

"I know," said Stereo. "You might have noticed my handiwork as you were walking around the outer circle too; did the bear speak to you?"

Martin and Reece pointed at their hats, "This one…?" said Martin.

"Not a word of English," said Stereo. "We can barely understand him at the best of times (he suffers from terrible adenoids), and now he's fluent in 7000 of Earth's languages, including Berber and Manx."

"And how did you manage that?" said the professor.

"With the magic of science," said the Mind™, pompously, "How else?"

"What's happened to the sealions?" Reece asked.

"You'll find out if you use the public toilets."

"You didn't try to flush them, did you?" said Martin.

"Barnooli made them re-paint the walls with their childish pictures. I have to admit, they're an improvement on the distemper-yellow they had before but I think their punishment falls short of what they deserved."

"We never did find out if they had names," said the professor.

"They're called Bee, Bop, Wop, Bam and Boom," Stereo replied. "But don't ask me who's who. Not that it makes any difference; they're a Gestalt entity, five parts sharing a single brain cell, as I think you may have discovered for yourselves."

"Not the brightest buttons in the box," Martin agreed.

"Indeed," said Stereo. "Now, I must disappoint you and leave you to suffer the horrors of industrialised entertainment on your own; the Very Important People require my presence. I must inform them of the many inadequacies I have discovered on your world and present my thesis for putting them right. I'm sure they will profit from my experience."

"I'm sure they'll be delighted to have your patronage," said Professor Morris. "Don't forget to speak slowly and loudly and don't use long words."

"I won't," said Stereo and flew away to an audience that was going to be less receptive than he imagined. In fact, Barnooli had to banish him back to the locomotive's cabin and that was where he ended his sojourn on Earth.

"For a horrible moment, I thought he was going to stay with us through the show," said Reece. "One negatively charged particle is enough for me."

They had reached the foot of the steps leading to the big top's arena. Martin was frowning up at the gateway, "That's not right," he muttered.

"What's wrong?" asked the professor, trying to see what was happening at the top of the stairs.

"People are disappearing," Martin replied.

It was soon their turn and the press of the crowd behind gave them no time or opportunity to avoid stepping under the arch. A moment later they found themselves standing by their seats. Reece checked the ticket still clutched in his hand, "That was clever," he said. "I didn't feel a thing."

Martin had his eyes closed, "What's happened?"

"Open your eyes and see…"

Martin opened them and was greeted by the blazing glory of the big top. It was stupendously huge, tiered like an Italian football stadium with steep banks of seats circling an arena several pitches in area. Flags and streamers hung from pillars and posts, the cries of popcorn and hotdog-sellers echoed down each row. People from all corners of the Earth were shuffling in their places, chattering to their neighbours and wondering how the ceiling was supported.

Even Martin couldn't fail to be impressed, though he did his best not to show it. "Big," he mumbled.

"It's extraordinary," said Reece, peering up at the ceiling and seeing clouds beyond the banks of lights and speakers suspended in the air.

"Fantastic," said the professor, "Did you ever imagine it would be this big?"

"What do you think Martin?" asked Reece.

Martin shrugged, "It's all right I suppose."

"I really don't understand you," said the professor. "This is incredible, isn't it?"

"It's only a circus, not open-heart surgery."

"What have you got against circuses?"

"They're for kids."

"So? Regress a little."

"I don't want to."

"Tell him the real reason," prompted Reece.

Martin looked uncomfortable; he had glimpsed a short little man in a wig and big blue nose selling ice creams and hot potatoes to a family of four. "It's the clowns," he said. "I can't bear clowns. I was traumatised as a child when I had my tonsils out. The hospital thought it would be a good idea to cheer us up with a clown and some balloons. They were wrong. I was terrified."

"Coulrophobia," said the professor. "It's a common fear; our minds are used to recognising human features so when we encounter a clown's confusing blend of make-up and exaggerated mannerisms we become disconcerted and afraid."

"He had a heart attack," said Martin, "And collapsed on my bed while he was making me a sausage dog. I can still smell his rubbery breath as his painted face pressed up against mine, lips still pursed around the nipple of the deflating balloon he had been struggling to blow when his heart gave out..."

Reece handed him some popcorn, "It wasn't your fault," he said. "And those clowns over there look healthy enough. We'll send them packing if they come too close."

"Thanks," said Martin, shovelling a handful of popcorn into his mouth.

"Good seats though," said the professor.

"Yes, I'll agree with you there," said Martin. "If any of the animals go wild and decide to make a break for freedom they'll have to run right over us to get there."

Their seats were right at the front, only feet from the floor of the arena and hundreds of feet below the highest level of the auditorium. What was not obvious to the audience, and hence part of the magic, was the ring of field projectors. What the humans took to be a pretty pattern of circles along the border was actually an invisible barrier powerful enough to contain a major force of nature, like a hurricane... or the Smog Monster.

Martin peered up at the top-most level, "I hope they're not selling food up there..." A dollop of ketchup splatted on his forehead with all the finesse of a seagull at the beach. "Typical," he muttered.

As he wiped his face, the lights began to dim.

73 - The Major Acts - Part One

The Stone Dwarves of Hubblenook V slapped their broad hands on the thick hides of their enormous timpani drums. The show was about to begin.

The auditorium went completely dark and the crowd went 'ooo'. A single spot of light appeared in the centre of the floor. A circle appeared and a shadow grew; a podium was rising out of the ground. A blacker circle rose in the centre, the top of a top hat, and then the Great Barnooli was elevated into view.

People began to clap. Barnooli cracked his light-whip and beamed at the audience. "LADIES AND GENTLEMEN," he shouted in every language of the world. "WELCOME TO THE GREAT... BARNOOLI'S... CIRCUS...!"

The big cheer was met simultaneously by the band striking up. The massed ranks of Polar Pelicans launched into the circus anthem. The swell of brass and woodwind, the swish of strings, the swimming, heady heights of avian voices lifted in triumph, welcomed the first part of the show: the Parade of the Weird and the Wonderful...

The Great Barnooli introduced each animal as it appeared from the tunnels, cracking his whip and waving his arms in broad, encompassing gestures, as every ringmaster should...

"AND FIRST, WE HAVE THE DOUBLE-TRUNKED ELEPHANT OF CHUPRASSY, A CREATURE RENOWNED FOR ITS ABILITY TO SNIFF OUT A LOST CAUSE FROM A HAYSTACK OF PINS...!"

The Double-Trunked elephant ambled into the arena, his handler trotting beside him. He trumpeted loudly from his two trunks, waved them in the air and flapped his thin, petal-shaped ears. His white hair had been groomed, combed and cut to a fine perfection. His nails had been freshly oiled. His handler fed him some peanuts and he stood on his hind legs and fired them in a wide arc at the audience. People clapped and cheered.

A peanut fell on Martin's head, "More nuts," he said, "As if I haven't suffered enough of those already."

The double-trunked elephant did a circuit of the arena, thundering and trumpeting, pausing for a moment to suck up the remains of Martin's popcorn and fling them over his head like a snow machine clearing a road.

"I'm not impressed," said Martin. "I was beginning to enjoy the eating bit."

"THE GAVIAL OF KILIAMATH, A CREATURE MORE VORACIOUS THAN EVEN THE CHURCH OF THE LOST MESSIAHS...!" The gavial with its long nose and snapping jaws slithered out of the tunnel. It was longer than the longest Nile crocodile and was patterned like a snake with diamonds of bright red and green. Its beady yellow eyes flicked from child to child and the smell of wet fish filled the air. It moved slowly, swaggering like a gun-fighter on its four bowed and stubby legs.

"THE STYRACOSAUR OF JYNTEE, MORE ANCIENT THAN THE WARLOCKS OF QUELCHEMON...!"

An old and friendly-looking dinosaur plodded into the limelight and flashed his head of horns. Two small clowns ran out with hoops in their hands. The dinosaur gambolled and caught each ring on a horn.

"THE STYRACOSAUR OF JYNTEE, LADIES AND GENTLEMEN..." There was a big round of applause.

The alien creatures continued to parade past the goggle-eyed guests. Some of the animals did a turn; like the Trapezium Monkeys, high above the arena, swooping and diving to the whoops of the American guests. Some were only there for show, like the Haliotis: a giant silicon slug that could be shorn like a sheep, except instead of wool it produced precious metals. It didn't do anything else and was more useful as a ready supply of replacement parts than as an exhibit. Or the Giant Giraffes, cheered on by the Chinese, but otherwise no more thrilling than ordinary giraffes. Martin didn't fail to point this out.

However, Reece and Professor Morris lapped it all up like kittens around a saucer. "Look how tall they are," said Reece as the giraffes walked past them like elegant electricity pylons.

"Are those really snails?" said the professor as the Sword Fighting Snails of Snickersee parried and lunged their way across the arena on a high wire.

The orchestra played out the parade of the weird and the wonderful until only Barnooli remained on his podium in the centre. His whip flashed and he shouted, "LADIES AND GENTLEMEN, FOR YOUR PLEASURE AND ENTERTAINMENT: ALL THE WAY FROM THE CONSTELLATION OF EVIGONE, THE TREE PEOPLE OF THE PLANET FORONESTA...!"

The audience clapped as a dozen Christmas trees shuffled into the limelight and took their places. The conductor raised his baton and a waltz began. The lively tune accompanied the swishes of needle-covered arms and the shapes of the trees made patterns across the floor, twisting and turning, hopping and returning, was a triumph of co-ordination and arrangement.

"Pretty good for trees," Martin admitted. Then a loose pinecone flew from the arm of a spinning Foron and bounced off his nose. "I take that back," he said, holding his handkerchief to his nose and checking for signs of blood. He was momentarily alarmed at the sight of a red splodge; then he remembered the dollop of ketchup.

The trees waltzed away and the two-headed Muttle of Muttlem Major reeled with the dancing lizards of Evetna. The tune was contemporary (borrowed from Stereo's collection of Earth tunes). Martin forgot his hurt nose and his foot began to tap to the rhythm. The lizards swung to and fro, twenty or thirty; moving faster and faster while the Muttle jigged and bobbed and kicked his heels. The orchestra, strings and pipes, tambours and tubular bells, made the people clap and cheer.

"What do you think of this?" Reece asked Martin, shouting over the din.

"I think have the CD," he said, clapping in spite of himself.

As the dance petered out the Muttle sang his duo: a strange, Saami-like chant, while the Evetnans slipped away. The lights fell until the song was nearly ended. The spotlight on the Muttle faded and just the echoes of his song remained.

Out of the silence came a new tune; the pelicans changed their music sheets and the Great Barnooli's voice boomed out of the darkness...

"AND NOW, LADIES AND GENTLEMEN, FOR YOUR DELIGHT, FOR YOUR ETERNAL AMAZEMENT, PLEASE WELCOME... THE BRILLIANT... BAZMONDO...!"

There was a clap of thunder and a big bang in the centre of the arena. Bazmondo appeared. As the smoke evaporated he began to grow; he spun around waving his wand and there was another clap of thunder...

"He is getting bigger, look!"

Bazmondo was getting taller. The orchestra was playing a Gothic tune. Ghostly apparitions flew around him; bats and beasts that cackled and cawed. The pelicans chanted, building up to a crescendo. He spread his arms and an arc of lightning leapt over his head. He flicked his wand and gobbets of fire smacked against the force fields like bursting novae.

When Bazmondo's body was a hundred feet tall he stopped growing. The creatures he had created disappeared suddenly, the music stopped and he took a bow. The silence was almost as eerie as the noise.

"That was clever," said Reece.

"Mirrors," said Martin.

"AND NOW," boomed the magician. "I REQUIRE THE ASSISTANCE OF A VOLUTEER FROM THE AUDIENCE..."

"The usual stuff," said Martin, "Some poor sap dragged out of his seat to be humiliated in front of the home... Oh bugger..."

The spotlight swung across the rows and fell on the face of the policeman. A scantily clad woman appeared and held out her hand. The wall between them opened up and there was nowhere he could retreat to.

"YOU SIR, YOU'LL DO QUITE NICELY..." Bazmondo grinned.

Reluctantly, Martin stepped into the arena and tens of thousands of hands clapped warmly for him; all relieved he was the poor sap and not them. The scantily clad woman held his arm in a vice-like grip. He felt a second of panic as his ego shrank under the gaze of all those people, not just the thousands in the auditorium, but the millions watching the show on television.

As they approached the massive toe of the Brilliant Bazmondo, a strange thing happened. Bazmondo was still there but he was his normal six feet tall. He glanced once at Martin, with a hint of a smile.

"AND NOW LADIES AND GENTLEMEN..." Bazmondo lowered his hand as if to pick an insect up. Martin realised it was supposed to be him. The assistant was leading him to a cross marked on the arena floor.

Bazmondo raised his hand and there were gasps from the crowd.

"But I'm still down here," said Martin, looking down at his feet and unwittingly adding to the illusion.

The assistant was looking up to where she imagined Bazmondo's head to be, ignoring Martin entirely. Bazmondo was holding nothing in his hand and Martin was standing on the floor of the arena like a spare lemon needing a gin-and-tonic.

Martin looked towards his seat and gave a little wave to Reece and the professor. His colleague waved back to where they could see Martin in the giant's hand.

Bazmondo raised his wand and pointed it at the back of his victim's head. Martin felt a faint tingling sensation and when he looked down his plain suit was now covered in flowers. The audience clapped.

Bazmondo waved his wand and the flowers disappeared but Martin had to fight to keep up-right. Fortunately the pair of wings that had appeared on his back helped him. They flapped and he felt his feet leaving the ground. The audience gasped. Martin grinned as he realised he could fly. Then the wings were gone again and he heard laughter as he tried to find out what was behind him and found he had grown a lion's tail.

Bazmondo 'put' Martin down, "A ROUND OF APPLAUSE FOR OUR BRAVE VOLUNTEER…"

The crowd clapped and cheered and Martin was led back to his seat.

"That was clever," said Reece. "And you thought it was all an illusion."

"But it was; I never left the ground…"

Reece laughed, "Don't be daft; we could all see you in the palm of his hand. You waved to us."

"But I was standing on the ground." It was very puzzling, but undeniably clever. "I'm really impressed," he added, and this time he meant it.

Bazmondo made rainbows appear without a single drop of moisture in the air, and stars that faded like smoke rings on a breeze. He made a cloud of snakes spell 'Bazmondo' above his head. He turned a tiny pink kitten into a voracious man-eater and back into a kitten before giving it away to a girl in the audience.

Unsurprisingly, it was felt the act with the bunnies ought not to be shown. Earth, they had discovered, was not very open-minded about such things, especially after all the trouble they had caused.

In his finale Bazmondo levitated a dozen guests, spun them like the propellers of a helicopter and made them rise almost to the very roof of the big top. Before they began to sink again Bazmondo tapped his stick and the guests woke up from their hypnotic state. Before they could panic and scream he made parachutes appear and let them drift slowly to the floor.

It was a very impressive display. The guests were unharmed. They left the arena floor asking each other how he had managed to make them float so high. And where had the parachutes come from?

Bazmondo took his bows to universal applause. Then, with another ear-breaking thunderclap, he turned into a thousand crows that circled the arena in a great cawing cloud, swirling in a vortex before evaporating into thin air.

74 - Intermission

Five white faces peeked out from behind a curtain as the Brilliant Bazmondo disappeared, "We could have done that," they agreed.

"Or thought of a cleverer way to leave..."

"Like riding on fish..."

"Or gliding away on a sheet of ice..."

Their paws were still dotted with paint from their endeavours in the public toilets, from which they took some consolation. "At least thousands of people will see our story," they told themselves, "And be relieved at the same time..."

"To know we escaped unharmed."

But they sighed, "Not much to show for our heroism..."

"A few trinkets and knick-knacks..."

"And our jobs here don't seem to be any more secure," they looked at each other and tried not to imagine what might happen to them when they reached their next destination and Ophonia's back was turned. Barnooli was known to hold a grudge longer than it took the Haliotis to run a marathon.

"Look out, he's coming..."

Barnooli was on his way back from Ophonia's dressing room; his wife was in a mood because Ted had suggested the tall, pointed white hat worn by the queens of Tun and the burning cross symbolising the fires of exploration, might have negative connotations for a certain section of the audience. Barnooli had to admit Ted's research did seem to flag up a potential problem but they had already rejected her Saronese turban with its crescent moon and agreed the Zamut custom of baring a breast might be similarly inflammatory. To spite them, she had chosen a linen smock and daubed her face with coal-black make-up. Eventually, Barnooli had to give her the gown he kept in reserve for just such an occasion; spun from the purest silk of Kakemono, cut by the haute couturists of Thulia, and adorned with opals from the mines of Xramarsis. There was a train that went with it, so long it made the cloak of the Pontiff of Soutane look like a shawl, and there was a hat with Poa bird feathers that added another four feet to her height. The costume was more expensive than the entire wardrobe of the major acts, including Bazmondo's collection of hats. But she wasn't happy about it.

So he gave her the shoes as well and grudgingly she agreed to sing for them.

When he spotted the Keepers lurking by the curtain, Barnooli stopped and frowned. They quailed. He crooked a finger, "Come here," he said in a voice that might have frozen the hearts of the Polar Pelicans.

The Keepers shuffled towards him. "Mr Barnooli, sir…?"

So far, Barnooli had found them several enormous congealing dumps of indefinable gunk and numerous sticky piles of dubious goo for them to clean up. "Almost as if he's trying to drive us out," they agreed.

"If it was up to me, you five would be bones at the bottom of the lion's cage by now," he said. "Even the Juggling Hare can't calculate how much we've lost today because of you. He thinks the Minds™ will have to create a new field of quantum mathematics to work out the entire cost of your foolish antics."

'Sorry' seemed inadequate, so they kept quiet.

"However, my wife wants to see you. If you can cheer her up perhaps I won't grill you in the Smog Monster's breath."

The Keepers nodded enthusiastically. Barnooli wondered if his wife would notice if he had their heads emptied and replaced with blancmange.

"Afterwards, children have given the Pygmy Hippocampus too many toffees and he's barfed in his bath. I want you to go and filter it out…"

Five doggy faces looked appalled. "Ick," they said.

"Off you go," Barnooli grinned sadistically. "And don't forget."

The Keepers nodded and trooped off. "Yuck," they muttered.

"But at least we haven't been sacked…"

"Yet…"

"…I wonder what Mrs Barnooli wants?"

75 - The Major Acts - Part Two

A sudden tinkling of bells caught the attention of the audience, the lights were dimming right down and from hundreds of speakers Barnooli's voice announced in a whisper, "Ladies and gentlemen, pray silence for the rare and beautiful Star Children of Wuminger..."

The darkness was complete. The sound of bells was getting nearer and there was a sudden ripple of lights like glitter passing through a beam. Then a brighter flash sparkled, silver-white, followed and another and another. The flashes and ripples coalesced into three distinct areas, each with a star in the centre.

It was impossible to tell how large each Star Child was, or how far away or even if they were something solid that was invisible in the darkness. The tinkling bells matched the movements of the tinier points of light. When the stars flashed deeper bells chimed in a harmony of five-pointed tones. The Star Children began to play together.

In the darkness, watching the hypnotic shapes and listening to the alien carillon, the human beings lost all sense of time and place. They were no longer just guests in an alien circus; they were a part of its phenomena, another act in the procession Barnooli paraded under his big top.

The chimes echoed in the ears of all the different peoples; the Star Children were calling to them as the stars had called out to astrologers and seafarers for thousands of years. It was a universal song, like waves on a beach or the wind roaming through the trees. It lulled and soothed. It reconnected the listeners with their ancestors. It made the universe seem like a harmonious place and slightly smaller than they imagined.

Nobody noticed exactly when the music stopped or the lights came back up again. Suddenly Barnooli was back on his podium in the middle of the arena and it was time for the penultimate act...

"LADIES AND GENTLEMEN, FOR YOUR DELIGHT AND DELECTATION, WE PROUDLY PRESENT A BATTLE OF THE ELEMENTS; A FIGHT OF FIRE AND WATER: WE PRESENT THE BATTLE OF THE SMOG AND THE HYDRO MONSTERS...!"

The lights dimmed, a low drum sounded, beating slowly like the tom-tom of a savage Hottentot island. The drum faded, it was nearly pitch black again. Breathing could be heard, loud, animal breathing. Two red circles winked on and off and the heavy padding of an enormous creature circling the arena filled the hushed air. There was a smell of sulphur, the heat was increasing; a man tried to tell his children 'it was all right'.

A rumble, like earth tumbling down a mountain, made the air tremble...

Suddenly flames erupted into the ceiling of the big top, a giant 'whoosh'; everyone was blinded, a vast shadow revealed!

Screams and shouts and mixed tears and laughter called across the arena as people, like their ancestors, communicated to each other, reassuring the troop that nobody was missing.

A second vast 'whoosh' and a loud roar shook the auditorium. The band began to play their drums; the horns hooted and the cellos rasped. The Smog Monster was revealed.

As the lights slowly rose he could be seen sitting like a very vast and very smug dog in the middle of the arena. Curls of smoke licked up from his nostrils. He was trying to look evil but the children loved him.

A hiss like a thousand fire extinguishers made the Smog Monster crouch down and bare his teeth. A wall of cold white cloud was tumbling out of another tunnel. There was another hiss, more cloud puffed towards the Smog Monster and he began to gnash his teeth and look furious.

A long gold nose with massive nostrils jetting out gouts of carbon dioxide was creeping along the floor, circling its fiery counter-part who remained in the centre... The Smog Monster stood on his hind legs and bellowed at the cushions of gas gathering around his feet.

Martin, Reece and the professor caught glimpses of white and gold go past and a sound like two hundred blocks of sandpaper being rubbed together in unison... The Smog Monster bellowed again, put his head back and spat fire at the ceiling.

The Hydro Monster rose from the fog. He had circled the Smog Monster twice, his limbless body a mass of fire-proof scales, a collar around his head like a lampshade, his eyes on stalks like a snail's.

The Smog Monster roared. The Hydro Monster hissed, his triple tongue tasting the air. In a second they were wrapped in a deadly embrace. The snake coiled around the dragon and the two thundered backwards and forwards accompanied by screams from the audience. The invisible walls vibrated and crackled. The whole big top shook and the orchestra was drowned out.

Minds™, almost invisible, flew around and in between them, making sure neither monster actually killed the other. The Smog Monster grabbed the Hydro Monster by the throat and made his eyes rattle like two conkers on strings. The snake wrapped his enormous body around the Smog Monster's legs and they staggered around the arena until eventually the smoke and gas vapours hid them from view. Then suddenly the Smog Monster was revealed triumphant. He stood over the fallen form of the serpent and howled his victory to the hypocritical cheers of the English who had lost their homes to his previous escapades. "Well if you've got to support someone," they said. "It might as well be the one who can really kick bottom."

In a moment of pathos, the Hydro Monster reared up, like the funnel of a tornado, but before he could close in on the Smog Monster's body, the latter plunged down on his enemy, pinning his coils to the floor. Tails whipped across the invisible walls, threatening to smash like panes of glass. Fire leapt and in the clouds of smoke lightning flashed. "Oh no, we can't control them," said the Minds™. People were standing up and ready to run for their lives...

Barnooli's light whip cracked so loud it parted the clouds. "LADIES AND GENTLEMEN," he bellowed. The whip cracked again and the smoke and carbon dioxide cleared magically from the arena. The Smog Monster was sitting on his haunches on one side of Barnooli's podium and the Hydro Monster was coiled up on the other, his head held high. "I GIVE YOU..." the whip whirled around Barnooli's head and cracked again, "THE GREAT... BARNOOLI'S... CIRCUS...."

The orchestra broke into the circus anthem once more and Ophonia rose to the occasion next to her husband. Behind her, the five Keepers, dressed as pages, carried her train. Her voice split the atoms of the air in a sumptuous aria full of the beauty of love and galactic harmony. She sang in strident and pithy tones, caused flags to wave and souls to soar as she worked towards the final act of the show...

The acts, major and minor, streamed from the tunnels, waving banners and joining-in with the chorus. They waved 'goodbye' to the cheering people of the Earth. They circled the arena three times, throwing sweets and toys onto every balcony. People waved back or stood and clapped, even Martin. The song reached its bone-crushing climax.

Barnooli took the final bow and escorted his wife off the field of battle with the Keepers holding her train behind. All the acts marched out behind them and the music faded away.

The lights came back up. The performance was over.

The audience felt exhausted and emotionally drained.

"Pretty good," said Martin as they stood to leave. "I enjoyed that."

"Would you come again?" asked Reece.

"No, but I wouldn't mind some more of that popcorn…"

"Do you think they'll ever be back?" said the professor.

"I hope not," said Martin. "I think the Earth got off lightly with a few stupid sealions and an agoraphobic dragon."

"And a giraffe," the professor reminded him, "And flying monkeys."

"And the giant rabbits," said Reece. "We mustn't forget them."

"I'm sure it could have been worse," Martin concluded.

"Like the *War of the Worlds*," Reece suggested.

Martin switched off as Reece launched into a full critical analysis of a film with ray guns, tentacles and other unrealistic nonsense. He was looking forward to his bed and no more nightmares about being probed or used in an alien experiment.

Behind them the gates of the circus closed and the exhausted acts, major and minor, cleared up before retiring to their beds. In the morning, the train rose up from London once more. With an impressive rumble and a trail of fantastic lights streaming out behind, the locomotive, under Auto Pilot's™ guidance, climbed into the sky, circling the Earth twice with the farewell anthem blasting from the speakers. Pyrotechnics cascaded through the atmosphere. Then it began to climb into space and finally, with a purely gratuitous burst of energy, the Great Barnooli's circus winked into Partial Reality and was gone.

The End

Printed in Great Britain
by Amazon